Mooring [illegible] hames

Lauren Westwood

Books by Lauren Westwood

The House of Second Chances

The House of Hidden Secrets

The House of Love and Dreams

Moonlight on the Thames

My Mother's Silence

The Daughter She Lost

My Secret Sister

First Edition published by Aria (Head of Zeus)

Second Edition "Moonlight on the Thames"

Cover design by Emma Graves

Moonlight on the Thames

Lauren Westwood

For Eve, Rose & Grace, with love

- i -

'Snow fell in the garden of the Tsar, turning everything to a pure, pristine white. Would she come again? Young Ivan pulled his fur coat over his mouth, masking the telltale cloud of his breath as he hid behind the fountain, its waters frozen in a brittle cascade of ice. He'd been waiting for hours, and now, the cold lay heavy on his eyelids and sleep stretched out her arms to draw him near.

But just then, the soothing howls of the north wind drew silent. One second, two, and then he heard another sound, faint in the distance and yet drawing nearer. A beating of wings.

The Firebird swooped down over the wall, making for the one tree that still bore fruit. Her flaming feathers singed his brow, but he couldn't look away. She grabbed the golden apple hanging from the branch and hurtled herself skyward, her wings flapping desperately against the bitter chill that threatened to bind her to earth.

And as she disappeared into the sky, from above him, a single golden feather danced playfully to the ground. Ivan gazed upon it, transfixed. It sizzled and flared as it settled on the snow. He reached out to touch it, but already it had faded to a black cinder.'

'The Firebird', *The Anthology of Russian Tales*

Chapter One

1st December, Waterloo Station, London

She wasn't meant to be here. That was the worst thing.

She should be sitting in a plush velvet seat at the bar, sipping a champagne cocktail, feeling a growing frisson as the minutes ticked by. Enjoying that little spark of tension not knowing exactly when he would arrive...

Nicola winced as she stepped on to the escalator, her shin colliding with a fold-up bike. Though rush hour was over, the escalator from the underground to the main station was packed solid on both sides. A crush of bodies, swinging ruck-sacks, surreptitious jostling and pushing. At the top of the escalator there was a pile-up and the tip of her stiletto heel almost got caught in the moving metal. With an almighty lurch into the man in front of her, she came on to stable ground.

Her phone buzzed in the pocket of her coat with an incoming text. She retrieved it, hope rekindling inside her. Maybe he'd changed his mind – he was texting to say that he was on his way to the little hotel on Charlotte Street that was *their place*. She pictured him: walking in, wearing his smart suit and black cashmere overcoat, his hair combed, his face clean-shaven, a hint of cologne. Polished and perfect, ready for her to dishevel, deconstruct. Teasing her, pretending to look at other women, but in the end, his eyes locking only on her...

Damn Ollie.

As she drifted along with the other commuters towards her usual platform, Nicola opened her messages. The new one was from Chrissie, her PA, reminding the department that Friday was 'Christmas jumper day!' She deleted it and opened the texts from Ollie in case she'd missed one. There were work texts, flirty texts, downright shocking texts. Texts that had once made her fizz with the anticipation of seeing him again. And the last text:

Sorry Nic, duty calls. Can't make it tonight. Ox

Nicola put away her phone. It was fine – *really* – it would have to be. She made a plan. On the fast train, she'd be home in thirty minutes. Turn off her phone, kick off her shoes, have a long soak in the bathtub, a glass of wine. Or two—

'I am sorry to announce that the nineteen twenty South-western Railway Service to Reading via Richmond is cancelled...'

The announcement droned on.

Nicola stopped moving and looked up at the boards. The words blurred as her eyes filled with tears. Every train delayed, cancelled. This was just... so... wrong—

Angels we have heard on high
Sweetly singing o'er the plains
And the mountains in reply
Echoing their joyous strains

She turned as the chorus of voices rose up over the background noise. The crowd of commuters closed in around her. She was almost at the middle of the station opposite the WHSmith, where, over the weekend, a giant Christmas tree had been put up. Its branches were sprayed white, and it was trimmed with red and gold baubles and white lights. Above, the station clock was trimmed with a big red bow and sprigs of plastic mistletoe, like the stage set for a bad production of *Brief Encounter*.

In front of the tree, standing on risers, was a choir.

Glor oo oo oo oo oo oo oo oo oo oo oo oo oo oo oo ria.

In excelsis Deo!

Nicola looked at the earnest faces, the 'O' shaped mouths. The choir was made of up men and women of a range of ages – about twenty members in all – wearing red or green jumpers and black skirts or trousers. Some of the women had glitter hairbands of holly or reindeer antlers, and a few of the men were wearing Santa Claus hats. Along the sides of the risers, two women and a man were carrying around trays, passing out mince pies and iced gingerbread stars.

In front of the choir, his back to her, was the conductor. He was a tall man with thick dark hair that came down to the edge of his collar. He was wearing a black suit and knitted fingerless gloves in a bright Christmas pattern. She watched his hands: his right hand rose and fell vigorously in time with the music, while his left hand cued the various voices in the choir. He shifted on his feet, almost like a dance, conducting his band of train station carollers as if they were a famous choir singing at the Royal Albert Hall.

The jostling and nudging started up again as people in the crowd edged closer to get a better view. A few hardened-looking commuters dropped shoulder bags and rucksacks to their feet, and, after the next verse, began bellowing out the chorus:

Glor oo oo oo oo oo oo oo oo oo oo oo oo oo oo oo ria.

In excelsis Deo!

Nicola tried to move away – she was in no mood for festive cheer – but she was hemmed in on all sides. If she could get through the crowd, she could pop in to M&S Food and buy a bottle of red wine. But, just then, a platform was announced (not her train) and a river of bodies flowed towards the ticket barriers. She gave up swimming against the tide, the M&S Food shop receding like a mythical island swallowed by mist. She managed to extricate herself near one of the old ladies with the trays of sweets.

'Smile, dear,' the old lady said cheerfully. 'You look like you need a mince pie.'

'No, I do not,' Nicola said through her teeth, holding up her hand. She *needed* to get away. She squared her shoulders, ready to push her way out of the wake of the choir.

But as she did so, the song ended. Applause erupted around her.

The conductor turned to face the crowd. Along with the ridiculous gloves, he was wearing a candy-cane striped tie over his starched white shirt. Nicola felt an irrational surge of anger as he bowed low with a flourish, his hair falling over his eyes. He rose from his bow and addressed the crowd.

'Thank you for listening,' he said. He had a strong accent – Italian? Eastern European? 'We are the Choir of St Anne's Church. My assistants will be handing out song sheets.' He gestured with a flourish to two women in choir garb who were holding baskets and passing out papers. 'Please feel free to come and join us, even if it is only for a few minutes while you wait for your train.'

The women with the song sheets were swamped by commuters eager to join in. While the song sheets were being passed out, the conductor launched the choir into an up-tempo version of 'Deck the Halls'. The noise seemed practically to take over the station:

Deck the hall with boughs of holly,
Fa la la la la la la la la!
'Tis the season to be jolly,
Fa la la la la la la la la!

'Excuse me.' A bald man in Lycra wielding a rucksack like

an offensive weapon sidled past Nicola and caught her off balance. For a hair-raising second, she teetered on her heels, barely managing to stay on her feet. The man drifted into the space that had been cleared in front of the risers, and was subsumed into the musical spectacle. Setting down his rucksack, he sang off-key at the top of his lungs:

Don we now our gay apparel
Fa la la la la la la la la!
Troll the ancient Christmas carol
Fa la la la la la la la la!

'Oh for God's sake,' Nicola muttered under her breath.

The conductor stepped back to make more room for commuters joining the choir, until he was only a few feet away from her.

Nicola gave up trying to get away. She stood there watching the scene the way people stop to look at a car crash. The song seemed to go on and on.

With a sigh, she looked back over her shoulder at the board (still no time shown for her train). When she turned back to the choir, three men and a woman wearing navy uniforms, orange vests and name badges had joined in the wretched singing: Southwestern Railways staff. Annoyance turned to something bordering on fury. The rational part of her knew that they had no control over the delays. But, surely, they should be trying to look like they were in control, or at least show some concern over the cancelled trains. Make some kind of effort at customer service. Instead of *enjoying themselves*.

The song ended. The crowd applauded again. A hand – someone put a hand on her arm. Nicola whirled around. It was a young woman with large dark eyes and black hair tied neatly back in a French twist. She set down the basket she was holding and held out a song sheet to Nicola.

'Would you like to join in?' the woman asked her with a cheerful smile.

Nicola stared at the woman – maybe for a second, maybe longer – it was like time had stood still. 'No. I. Would. Not,' she said with a hiss. 'And frankly, I wish you people would just shut up!'

The conductor turned around. He had a handsome face: high cheekbones, full lips, a sharp, aristocratic nose. His eyes were dark brown, and they narrowed as they met hers.

'I mean, don't you people have jobs? Things to do? Places to go?' Nicola's voice rose in volume, as she turned away from the woman and began venting her rage directly at the conductor. 'I've had a bad day. I don't want to listen to carols or think about Christmas. I just want to get my train, go home. But no, I can't, because, in case you hadn't noticed, every damn train is delayed or cancelled. I'm trapped here. And they…' she gestured in the direction of the train staff, 'don't seem to care one bit. I mean, this is a bloody outrage.' Without even meaning to or realising what she was doing, Nicola kicked at the basket and it tipped over. Song sheets went everywhere. The dark-haired woman looked at Nicola, her mouth opening in shock.

The crowd started to murmur, and a few people turned to look up at the boards. It was as if her making a scene had jarred some of the people, at least, back to the reality of being stranded in a freezing station.

The conductor moved forward until he was right in front of her. Nicola felt the world narrowing to a bubble around the two of them, with people outside watching tensely to see what would happen next. Nicola shivered, uncertain whether he would shout at her, swear back at her, or say nothing. He opened his mouth.

'I am sorry that you feel that way,' he said. 'I hope things get better. Happy Christmas.' And then his face broke into a smile that lit up his face, the amber flecks in his eyes shining like sparks. He turned back to the choir, now doubled from its original number, breaking the moment. 'Next we will do number six on your song sheet. "Joy to the World".'

Nicola didn't hear the loudspeaker announcement or notice that a slow train to Richmond was now boarding from platform 17. She stood there unable to move, as the song began. The dark-haired woman and a few people from the crowd knelt down to pick up the scattered song sheets. She watched the conductor, mesmerised by the energy flowing between him, the singers, and the audience. The song echoed through the station, growing in volume, gathering strength:

Repeat the sounding joy
Repeat the sounding joy
Repeat, repeat, the sounding joy.

It was only as the crowd surged towards the platform that Nicola once again came to her senses, went through the ticket barrier, and boarded the train.

Chapter Two

Nicola walked across the cobbled yard towards the three mews houses along the River Thames. The one on the right had a wreath of evergreen and holly on the door and tasteful white lights around the windows. The one on the left had a wreath of silver tinsel and plastic baubles and flashing coloured lights around the door. The house in the middle was dark.

Her house.

Nicola shivered as she unlocked the door and went inside. The heating was off – she spent so much time at work that she didn't even bother with the timer any more. She adjusted the thermostat and took off her coat. A hot bath, a glass of wine (she hadn't managed to buy a bottle of red at the station, so she'd have to settle for white) try to forget about the evening with Ollie that hadn't happened, and the embarrassing 'incident' with the choir that had.

God, had she really done that! Kicked over that basket, made a scene? Everyone must have thought she was a complete nutter! The choir director – he'd been laughing at her, she realised, with that bright 'Happy Christmas'. No doubt he was off home to his family: a wife, a couple of kids. Though it was barely even December, they'd have their tree up already, with shiny presents underneath. Stockings hung by the fire, music, laughter... Things that she might have wanted once – or not. She really didn't know any more.

Nicola took off her coat and hung it on the rack next to the gilt-framed mirror. She looked at herself in the glass. Smart suit that accentuated her figure, and underneath she was wearing some of Ollie's numerous 'gifts', of the satin and lace sort. Most people – men in particular – saw the image she projected: confident and sexy, in control of every aspect of her life. Tonight had proved that nothing could be further from the truth.

She closed her eyes for a second, imaging the evening that should have been: lying in bed next to Ollie in their hotel room, her hair splayed out on the pillow, drinking chilled champagne. Sometimes she'd have him only for an hour, occasionally, the whole night. Sometimes he would talk about going away together – to Paris, or New York – and starting again. The words would wash over her like a warm tide. Having a life together, a family even...

Nicola opened her eyes as the fantasy fizzled away to nothing. Ollie already had those things. His wife was called Chloe. Nicola had never met her, tried not to imagine her. Or his children, a girl and a boy, aged five and nine.

She took off her high-heeled shoes and rubbed absently at a blister that was forming on her toe. For months now, she'd felt a gnawing urge to end it. To let go of the guilt that she felt, even if he didn't. And yet, up to now, she hadn't done so—

Her phone rang, jarring her from her thoughts. She fumbled for it in the pocket of her coat. If it was Ollie, she'd silence the call. Tonight's effort had been a last-ditch attempt to save something that never should have been in the first place. It was over and acknowledging it would be a relief. If only it wasn't December, the long run-up to Christmas... What she'd had with Ollie had been very little – but it was better than being alone.

Nicola pulled out the phone. 'Jules' came up on the screen. By force of habit, she answered with a cheery 'hello?'

'Nic – you OK?' Her sister sounded hassled and out of breath. Jules had what many people would consider the perfect life: a perfect husband, a perfect house and three perfect children – and therefore took it upon herself to appear busy and stressed at all times.

'Yeah,' Nicola said, 'I just got home from work.'

'Really? That's early for you.'

Nicola went up the stairs. The house had three floors: two bedrooms on the ground floor, a sitting room and kitchen on the first floor, and the master suite taking up the entire top floor. She made a beeline for the kitchen – she needed that glass of wine. 'Yes, well, I had a client do but it got cancelled.' The lie came out so easily.

'You didn't answer my email about when you're coming over,' Jules said. 'Is it Christmas Day, or Boxing Day? Mum, Teddy and Ben are coming on Christmas Day. So that's probably best. And are you bringing Ollie? I need to finalise numbers.'

Nicola cringed inwardly. For the last two years she'd made up a story for Ollie's sudden and unavoidable absence at the family festivities. It wasn't vanity that made her lie – not *just* vanity, anyway. It was the fact that all their lives, Nicola had done her best to shield Jules from the ugly truths about life. Not that it had worked, but she still felt it was her duty to try.

'Sorry,' Nicola said. 'I just need to confirm, OK?' Putting the phone on speaker, she checked the bottle rack underneath the worktop. No red, as she'd suspected, but there was a bottle of champagne from a closing that she'd forgotten about. Perfect.

'Sure,' Jules said. 'I mean, assuming you even want to come at all. That you're not jetting off somewhere exotic.' Jules sighed. 'God, I envy you. With your career, your glamourous life. Tickets to Paris Fashion Week, business trips to Milan, dinners at—'

'That's just work,' Nicola said, cutting off the litany of so-called enviable things. In the beginning, when she'd joined Privé Capital, it had been glamourous. The private equity firm specialised in raising finance for fashion and luxury goods companies. She'd risen through the ranks quickly and become one of the youngest partners. Not to mention the only female one. Jules might see the glamour in it, but she didn't know about the sacrifices it had taken to get to the top and stay there.

'Whatever,' Jules said. 'But if you and Ollie are coming, I need to figure out where I'm putting everyone.'

'OK, sure. I understand.' Nicola opened the fridge and closed it again. With the hours she'd been working lately, she hadn't bothered with a grocery delivery. It was looking like dinner would be champagne and Weetabix.

Jules continued to rattle on about menus, Christmas puddings, quantities of alcohol. In a way, it was comforting to know that these were the biggest stresses her sister was likely to be facing. Nicola pictured Jules in her enormous kitchen, making lists and seating plans. Jules had always been methodical. Every year as a child, she'd written a detailed letter to Father Christmas about what she wanted for Christmas, managing to post it to the North Pole before the start of December. Jules always wanted a puppy, a pony, or a kitten. Up until age eleven, she never got one. Still, despite Jules' inevitable disappointment on Christmas morning, those years had been happy ones.

Nicola twisted the wire from the top of the bottle and popped the cork into a tea towel. She fizzed the liquid into a glass and went into the sitting room. The room was tastefully furnished in shades of cream, beige and green, with a wall of books, and French doors that went out to a balcony overlooking the river. There were no Christmas decorations or cards, no photos. The only thing in the room that jarred was the old piano from their childhood home that was next to the balcony doors. She had never played, but she remembered that piano from holidays long ago. Her mum had trimmed it with an advent wreath of fir branches, a red bow and four tall red candles. Her dad had played at family Christmases – lively nights of carolling and board games.

She sat down on the sofa, staring at the piano. Maybe it had been the choir at the station – their overwhelming enthusiasm and festive cheer – but for some reason, Nicola felt an unusual pang of nostalgia.

'Do you remember when we were kids?' she said to Jules, the memories taking shape. 'When Grandma came round just before Christmas and we made a gingerbread house?'

'What?' Jules stopped mid-flow, sounding surprised. They rarely talked about those days – those Christmases *before*. Before their mum moved out, divorced their dad and married her boss, Teddy. Nicola had been fourteen; Jules, eleven. 'I guess so,' Jules said. 'We made iced biscuits too, didn't we? And got sprinkles all over the kitchen trying to decorate them.'

'Yes, we did.' Nicola smiled, thinking of their mum's face as the sprinkles crunched underfoot, ground into the lino.

'And the tree had pink and purple baubles,' Jules said.

'Yes,' Nicola said. 'And all those awful decorations we made at school.' They both laughed – for a second.

'God, whatever happened to all that stuff?' Jules sounded wistful.

Nicola took a long sip of champagne, the good memories fading away. 'In my attic, I guess, along with the rest of Dad's stuff.'

This time, the pause from Jules was much longer. Nicola wished she hadn't brought it up in the first place.

That first Christmas in the new regime, Teddy had bought Jules the puppy she'd always wanted, along with horse riding lessons. Her loyalty and affection thus sorted, Jules went to live with them. Nicola had stayed with their dad – someone had to. Wracked by depression, his decline had been swift and total. She'd tried to take care of him: cook his meals, get his newspaper, return his books to the library. But despite her efforts, it was like the dad she loved – the one who was kind, and funny, and full of life – wasn't there any more. The next four or five Christmases were spent shuttling back and forth between her mum's new family (by then, the family had an addition: Nicola's stepbrother, Ben) and the flat she shared with her dad in Isleworth. Nicola had tried to brighten the place up with a tree decorated with a string of cheap lights and the pink and purple baubles that their mum no longer wanted. She'd got a cookbook and tried to cook turkey with all the trimmings and make mince pies – her dad's favourite. Her cooking efforts never turned out quite right, but it didn't matter. In the end, she was powerless to stop the rot. Turning down a place at Durham, she went to uni in London so she could continue to look in on him. Which she'd done almost every day, even on that last morning – when her dad was run over by a woman in a Range Rover doing the school run. The woman swore he'd stepped in front of her. No one, not even Nicola, had tried to argue.

'Yeah,' Jules said, slowly. 'Your attic – that makes sense. Do you think maybe—?'

But Nicola wasn't listening any more. The memories continued, unstoppable, careering towards the place in her mind that she kept locked away. *Christmastime, a holiday party...* The breath seized up in her chest; the hand holding the glass started to tremble. *Breathe...* this was silly. *Christmas...* She'd never told Jules, or anyone else, the real reason why she hated this time of year. *Ice on the pavement... footsteps behind her... that smile...* Jules was her little sister – she had a duty to protect her. There were some things that she didn't need to know—

'Nicola, are you still there?'

'What?' She gasped out the word. It was fine. Everything was fine. As quickly as it came, the panic subsided. She was home. She was safe. How ridiculous.

'I said, can you come over early and help me cook? Or watch the twins? It would really help.'

'Cook?' Nicola gave a sharp laugh. 'Think of your guests – are you sure you want me to?'

'Just to help out. Remember, Mum will be there too. And I'll email you the list of presents. Ben wants a Chelsea away kit, so I've put your name down for that. He's going to be seventeen in February. Can you believe it?'

'Seventeen?' Nicola hadn't realised, but she could believe it. To say that she had no relationship with her half-brother was an overstatement. When he'd been a little kid, she'd been at school or at uni, and now that he was a teenager, almost an adult, he might as well be living on a different planet rather than with her mum and Teddy in Esher.

'Yeah.' Jules sighed. 'And he's still a little twat. But family's family – right? And anyway, it will be good to see you.'

'I'll let you know by Friday,' Nicola said. Right now, all she wanted to do was put Christmas – everything really – out of her mind. A hot bath, snuggling up in her pyjamas...

'Mum, Lottie kicked me!' a tiny voice yelled from somewhere down the phone line.

'I gotta go,' Jules said. 'But tell your mysterious Ollie that we all want to meet him. It will be such fun.'

The call cut off.

'Yeah,' Nicola said into the dead line, raising her glass in a toast. 'Such fun.'

Chapter Three

Dmitri took a sip of his orange juice and leaned against the bar. He watched Sophie as she moved among the others, saying her goodbyes. She went up to Carole-Ann, the church organist, and they spoke briefly. Sophie gave her a kiss on both cheeks and went out the door. Carole-Ann shot a worried look in Dmitri's direction, but he gave her a reassuring smile. He'd been expecting this.

'Here you go, mate,' the bartender said from behind him.

Dmitri held out his card as the man put three pints of beer and a glass of white wine on the bar.

'Thank you,' Dmitri said. He picked up two of the glasses and went to find the new recruits: three men and a woman. They'd joined in with the singing at the station and then decided to give up waiting for their delayed trains and join the choir down the pub. Dmitri had already spoken to each of them, welcoming them and buying them a drink. Two of them lived close enough that they might come to a few rehearsals, maybe do a few concerts or join in the 'Pop-up Carolling', as some of the people referred to it, at venues around the city – like tonight's event at Waterloo. Dmitri liked new people and they tended to get quite a few this time of year. A good thing, as Sophie hadn't been the first young woman to quit the choir.

Dmitri sighed. Sophie had joined the choir at the beginning of summer. She had a nice vibrato and a soft, mellow tone to her voice that he'd liked – not shrill and harsh like some of the older, lifetime church choir sopranos. She seemed like a nice girl, a PA at some law firm in the City. Late twenties, early thirties, maybe. For the last month or so she'd started being the last to leave the rehearsals, helping him tidy up the church and stack the music books. She'd brought him a Christmas cake that she'd made herself, and then tonight, she'd tried to take advantage of the mistletoe hanging above the bar. Dmitri had nudged her gently away so that the others wouldn't see; tried not to embarrass her. He'd talked to her, told her that she was a valued member of the choir and that he didn't want to see her go. But when he'd clarified that they could not ever be more than friends, she'd whispered in a low fraught voice that she was leaving and wouldn't be coming back.

He knew that some of the older women, like Carole-Ann, warned the younger ones about him. But the younger ones never seemed to listen. Like a tick on an old vinyl record, Dmitri was forced over and over to try and 'let them down easy'. The problem with Dmitri's reputation was not that he slept with the women of the choir, but the fact that he didn't. Ever.

He delivered the drinks to two of the newcomers and went back for the other two glasses. The two new people that he thought might stick: a middle-aged man called John who'd told Dmitri that he was recently divorced, and a fifty-ish woman called Lynn who worked in HR, were chatting amiably to some of the more seasoned members of the group. People joined the choir for different reasons, and at different stages of life. Most of them joined for the company, the friendships – some of which became romances. Sometimes people joined who had recently come back to religion after years away from the church. Very few, he'd found, joined for the music.

But whoever they were or whatever their reasons, Dmitri always welcomed them. The choir was his life, and Christmas was when the choir was most popular. He liked to get caught up in sharing and spreading the joy of the season. Surrounded by friends, and the lively, bright music, there was no room for the darkness. No room for the other memories that lurked in the shadows.

He returned to the bar and finished his orange juice. As he set down the empty glass, he noticed that the yarn on one of his fingerless gloves had come undone. His mother had knitted him these gloves, bright and festive for Christmas, a few years before her death. Hopefully he could find someone to mend them before they came apart completely. He pulled at the thread, watching the stitches unravel—

'...Can't believe it – so incredibly rude.'

Dmitri turned. Jenny, one of the sopranos, was talking to Carole-Ann and newcomer Lynn.

'Yes,' Carole-Ann agreed. 'She's definitely the first heckler we've ever had. Right, Dmitri?'

In his mind, he pictured the woman at the station. Arresting and beautiful with long red hair, her green eyes flashing with anger like a wounded animal. He'd been unable to look away. What he'd seen in her had brought the ghosts out of their hiding places. For all his attempts to spread good cheer and get swept up in the joy and magic of the season, the hidden part of him had acknowledged the truth of her words. Not everything was merry and bright at Christmas. Not everyone had something to celebrate, or someone to celebrate with. She'd made him feel like a fraud, and that had not been a lie.

'That's right,' he said, pushing her from his mind. He walked a few steps over to the others and smiled warmly. 'Please believe me, Lynn, when I say that Christmas carolling is not usually so dangerous.'

Lynn and Carole-Ann laughed. Jenny looked on him with soft blue eyes. She had a husband and three kids, but he knew that look. He moved back a few steps towards the bar and was relieved when John, the other newcomer, came up and stood next to Lynn. His pint was nearly drained and Lynn was near the bottom of her glass of white wine.

'So, it's Dmitri, is that right?' Lynn asked.

'Yes. Dmitri Orlov,' he said, smiling.

John signalled for the bartender's attention. 'What are you drinking, Dmitri?' he asked in a husky baritone.

'Just orange juice for me,' he said.

Lynn frowned for a second, as if at this time of year, people out at a pub with friends or colleagues had a duty to drink alcohol. John turned back to the bartender to place the order.

'Orlov – is that Russian?' Lynn said.

Dmitri looked closely at her face. Perhaps she was younger than he'd originally thought – mid-forties maybe. Kids – yes. A husband – maybe.

'Yes, that's right,' Dmitri said. 'I am from Novosibirsk in Siberia. But I have been here, in London, since I was nineteen.'

'Wow, Siberia must be very cold,' Lynn said.

'Yes.' For most English people, this was the impression. A vast frozen wasteland with herds of reindeer, gulags, railroad tracks and snow. And of course, it was cold – winters were long, summers were short. But there was much more, too. When he imagined his homeland, he thought of the vast pine forests, completely silent as the first snow fell. Ice skating on the frozen lakes, sledding, the colours of the shadows on the ice. Sometimes, he missed it almost unbearably.

'And are you married, Dmitri?' she asked.

He ran a hand absently through his hair. 'No,' he said. 'Though sometimes, it feels like I'm married to the choir.'

'Hmm,' John said, turning back to them with the glass of white wine and the orange juice, 'I guess that's one way to avoid complications.'

Dmitri thought of Sophie, and the others like her who had come and gone over the years. He forced a laugh. 'I am not so sure.'

Though they had all just met, John seemed to be eyeing up Lynn. Dmitri's cue to step back, let them talk to each other. 'I live with my sister Tanya,' he said. He pointed in the vague direction of the door where he could just glimpse her sleek, dark hair through the crowd. She was chatting to Charles, one of the tenors, and two older altos – probably gossiping about him. Or about 'The Heckler'.

'Tanya. Of course.'

'Yes. She works at a café and bakery off Clapham High Street. It's called "The Braided Loaf".'

'I know it,' Lynn said enthusiastically.

'They supply all our mince pies. Which, as you will discover, is a very important part of choir practice.'

Lynn laughed brightly. 'Then I'll definitely be signing up.'

Next to her, John patted his stomach. 'A mince pie would certainly hit the spot right about now. Haven't sung in years, but with all that carolling, I've worked up a bit of an appetite.' He turned to Lynn. 'Fancy a curry or something?'

Dmitri smiled to himself. Yes, people joined the choir for different reasons, but at least they came. And whether they stayed for a single night, or for years, somehow, their lives would be changed.

He turned to the side as if he'd spotted someone in the crowd that he had to talk to. 'Excuse me, please,' he said to John and Lynn. He left the two newcomers to get to know each other and make their plans, edging towards the door. Although it had been a good night – that is, until the woman at the station, and then the business with Sophie – Dmitri was ready to leave. He could feel an attack of the holiday blues coming on. Because as much as he enjoyed the idea of Christmas, spreading joy and making other people happy, his life would stay exactly the same.

He went over to Tanya. Carole-Ann had brought her a drink, and the two of them were talking and laughing with Charles and the altos. He signalled to her that he was leaving, but she just nodded and returned to her conversation. The dark mood began to close in. He pulled the loose piece of yarn on his glove again and watched the stitches fall away, then shoved his hand into his pocket.

After saying his goodbyes, he made his way out the door into the freezing night. His breath came out in great white puffs that curled skywards, like spirits of winter. As he walked to the Tube, he considered his options. Go home to the flat in Clapham, a nice upper-floor two-bed in a red-brick Victorian conversion, or go and seek some company. Go to a different bar, find a woman, buy her a drink, let things take their course. No names, no questions, no exchange of phone numbers.

Inside the Tube station, Dmitri pinged his Oyster card on the reader. He went down the escalator. The platform on the left led south to home, the one on the right to the north – to central London and all that the night might have to offer. As he reached the bottom, he still had no idea which one he was going to choose.

Chapter Four

4th December

'I think that's the final point,' Nicola said. 'Shall we leave it to the lawyers now to redraft?'

The man on the other side of the conference room table nodded. Carl Anderson was a director of a Danish consortium that was looking to acquire a controlling interest in 'Timeless', a French luxury watch manufacturer, in order to take the brand global.

'Thank you,' he said, standing up and offering her his hand. 'You've done a brilliant job, Nicola. If we sign by Christmas, then I shall personally make sure that your whole team has Timeless watches under the tree.'

'I'll look forward to that.' Nicola kept her smile just the right side of professional as they shook hands. Carl had already asked her out for a drink twice in the last two months. She'd turned him down, of course, but in a way that had left the door open – in his mind at least. In her experience, until the deal was signed and the ink dry on the page, it was best to keep all possibilities alive.

She gathered up her papers and led her team: two analysts, a senior associate and two lawyers, out of the room. This was what she lived for – the buzz of adrenalin after a negotiation. Knowing that in this aspect of her life, at least, *she* was in control.

Outside in the corridor, she thanked her team and made sure everyone was clear on who was doing what to get the deal over the line. Then she went back to her office and closed the door. It was nearly six o'clock. Time to catch up on the day's emails over an early-evening Americano. She was even feeling good enough that she might have a look online about ordering that Chelsea away kit for Ben—

'Ollie's office – five minutes!' Despite the fact that the door was firmly shut, Nicola heard the summons. Ollie's PA was doing the rounds with gusto, summoning everyone to action.

The adrenalin ebbed away. Nicola had already deleted this morning's email with 'This Week's Advent Calendar – Christmas Jumper Day!' in the subject line, hoping that by doing so, it would just go away. She opened up her diary, but even that had conspired against her. For the first time all day, it was clear. Nicola skimmed her emails frantically – there must be something needing her immediate attention or an emergency conference call—

A knock on the door and Chrissie, her PA, poked her head into the office. 'Come on, Nicola, it's time.' Chrissie's voice was gratingly cheerful. She was wearing a light blue jumper with a fuzzy white penguin on it, the eyes and scarf done in sequins. She also had a clip in her white hair with a sprig of sparkly holly on it. That hair clip reminded Nicola of the women in the choir at Waterloo Station, and then, by association, the choir director – with his bright festive gloves and amused dark eyes. Maybe he hadn't been laughing at her – who knows? Either way, she still felt ashamed and angry whenever she thought about the scene she'd made, three nights ago now. She'd been feeling low ever since, but that couldn't be blamed solely on what had happened at the station. That was down to the choices she'd made.

'I can't, Chrissie,' Nicola said. 'I've got things I need to finish up.'

Chrissie put her hands on her hips and scowled in a very unfestive manner. 'It's mandatory,' she said, 'CEO's orders. Now, come along and at least have a glass of mulled wine.'

Nicola got slowly to her feet and picked up her phone from the desk. Even though she towered over Chrissie in her Jimmy Choo stilettos, she still felt like a naughty child being sent before the headmistress. For all her bluster and froth, Chrissie had a tough streak that Nicola liked and admired. Chrissie had been working at Privé Capital for over twenty years. This place was her life, which was something Nicola could relate to. And at this moment, she could tell that Chrissie wasn't going to take no for an answer.

'One glass. Then *some* of us have work to do,' Nicola said pointedly. It was ridiculous the amount of time-wasting that went on around the office at this time of year. Deals needed to close by year-end, and it fell to people like her – people without other commitments – to get them done. Another tick against Christmas, in her mind, at least.

'Yes, Ms Scrooge. And if you go without a jumper, it'll cost you a pound. I've got an extra one at my desk if you want to borrow it.'

'Thanks, but no thanks,' Nicola said.

Chrissie gave an exasperated little sigh and tsk and walked out of Nicola's office. Her penguin jumper had a white pompom stuck on the back – the penguin's tail. Not that real penguins had tails like that. The jumper was probably made in some sweat shop in Bangladesh by women chained to sewing machines who'd never even seen a proper picture of a penguin, let alone a real one. She'd have to point that out to Chrissie.

As Nicola made her way down the hall, she felt more and

more tense and on edge. Around the corner, a bottle of champagne popped and there were cheers. Then, someone started an up-tempo round of 'Jingle Bells'. Her head began to ache. She went around the corner and saw a large gathering of people midway down the corridor. Just about everyone had on a tacky Christmas jumper: elf jumpers, Christmas tree jumpers, two other penguin jumpers identical to Chrissie's.

Ollie's door had been decorated with red and green tinsel garlands and a sprig of mistletoe was hanging in the centre. Just outside, a table had been set up with mulled wine, mince pies, a charity collection box and some homemade-looking biscuits in the shape of angels, stockings, snowmen and bells. That was how 'Advent Calendar' worked. In mid-November, a calendar went up in the kitchen at Privé Capital and people would sign up for each day of advent. Each person would have a little – or not so little – 'do' outside his or her office or cubicle. What might once have started out as an informal holiday bonding event had spiralled out of control. Now, the partners and executives tried to outdo each other with festive holiday tat. Last year, Brian, the CEO, had brought in an entire hunk of venison, had it begrudgingly cooked by catering, and carved it in front of his office. Icicle lights, smoke machines, full-sized trees, chocolate fountains, a visit from Father Christmas... nothing was too over-the-top.

Nicola never signed up. For one thing, she was too busy. For another, she despised the fact that because she was a woman, she was *expected* to want to participate in the proliferation of Christmas cheer.

Her phone vibrated with a text.

Meet me under the mistletoe? – O

Nicola didn't even feel a trickle of joy. Ever since Ollie had cancelled on her, they'd barely spoken or had any contact. In the past, such a thing would have set her on edge – worrying, fretting, feeling insecure. Now, though, she just felt numb.

The singing finally fizzled out. She joined the throng near the back. As soon as she'd seen Ollie's name up on that damn calendar, she should have made a plan to avoid this particular do. For the most part, she had no problem interacting with Ollie as a colleague around the office. But this was different. Nicola could almost sense the presence of Ollie's wife – no doubt she had done all the shopping for food and decorations – and his kids had decorated the biscuits.

She moved through the sea of PAs and analysts towards the wine station. Nearby, Ollie was chatting with another partner and two junior associates. Ollie's Christmas jumper was red, with a lopsided Christmas pudding on it that looked hand-knit. His wife again, no doubt. Nicola took a plastic cup of mulled wine and drank it down quickly – she could barely even sew on a button let alone knit a jumper. She grabbed a second cup of wine.

'Isla's really looking forward to the nativity play this year,' Ollie was saying, a mince pie in one hand and a cup of mulled wine in the other. 'She's going to be the Angel Gabriel. And Chloe's helping make the costumes. All the stuff behind the scenes is so important—'

Ollie noticed her standing there just as she'd heard enough and felt her drink go down the wrong way—

'Nicola! Good – you're here!'

She turned around to see Brian, the CEO, coming up to her. In his late fifties with thinning white hair combed over his scalp, he was wearing what was by far the tackiest jumper of all – Rudolph the red-nosed reindeer with a fat light-up nose.

'Hi Brian.' The jumper aside, at least he would want an update on work. 'Things went well today with "Timeless". I think Carl will be ready to sign before—'

'Where's your jumper, Nicola?' Brian interrupted. Unlike the looks she was used to getting from other men, his gaze downwards at her chest held no ulterior motive.

'Forgot it at home,' she said with a shrug. So much for talking shop.

'Too bad. But look at this.' Brian pressed a button somewhere, and Rudolph's antlers began to twinkle with fairy lights. 'Pretty cool, huh. Melissa made it herself.'

Brian's wife was an interior designer, and this just proved what Nicola had thought all along from the choice of ties she bought him – that she really had the most appalling taste.

'Look, she used battery-powered lights.' He held up the hem of his jumper and Nicola saw the strings of lights taped to the underside.

In spite of everything, Nicola had to laugh. The CEO of one of London's most exclusive private equity boutiques was wired up like a suicide bomber!

'Um, very tasteful,' Nicola said. 'I'm sure you'll win the prize for best jumper – what is it? – two years in a row.'

'Three,' Brian corrected. 'Speaking of which, Ollie's just reminded me that it's been a while since we had the pleasure of you doing an Advent Calendar, Nicola.' Brian's enthusiasm was bad enough, but the fact that Ollie had a hand in it annoyed her no end.

'All the places were taken before I could sign up.' Nicola wasn't quite sure why she was lying. Probably because Brian seemed so genuinely clueless – the holiday season seemed to do that to people.

'Well, you may be in luck,' Brian said. 'Charlie's mum is getting in just before Christmas to have her hip done. He was down for the twenty-second. You're the only partner who's not signed up. So we'll need you to work some holiday magic.'

'Brian, you know I'm not good at that kind of thing,' Nicola began, knowing it was futile. That day, of all days. Fuck. Well, she wouldn't do it.

Brian gave her a fatherly look. 'You know, Nicola, you are in such a unique position. To be a mentor and a role model. I mean, look around you.' He waved his hand. 'The campaign to recruit more women has really taken off. And when those junior analysts see you, they want to be you. Have it all, just like you do – or could, if you wanted to.'

Nicola gripped the empty plastic cup so hard that it popped. Brian knew damn well that she didn't have it all. Far from it. And one thing she'd never be was a role model. She did what she had to do in order to succeed and do her job. Despite the fact that Privé specialised in finance for fashion and luxury brands that might appeal to women, behind the scenes it was still a difficult, sexist environment. Just like the earlier exchange with Carl, for her it had become almost unconscious: dressing the part, keeping just the right side of the line between flirty and professional – occasionally crossing over when required. Hardly something to be encouraged at a brown bag lunch for female empowerment.

'Brian, I don't want to do an Advent Calendar.' She heard the pleading note in her own voice. 'I'm sorry, but it's not my thing. I'm sure you can find someone else who'd love to do it.' She indicated the Christmas jumper brigade, snapping selfies and getting increasingly rowdy with the mulled wine.

'Come on, Nicola. It's fun. And so good for morale. I'll tell Chrissie that we're all systems go, ready for take-off.' With a full-on grin, he pressed the button and Rudolph's lights twinkled again. To her relief, he turned to speak to someone else.

Nicola tossed the broken cup in the bin and began contemplating her exit. An arm brushed hers – Ollie's. He'd heard the whole conversation with Brian, she realised. All that rubbish about being a female role model. How he must be laughing.

'You OK, Nic?' He held out a new cup of wine.

'Not really,' Nicola said, taking the cup. 'Nice jumper, by the way. Did your wife knit it?'

He gave her that cocky grin she used to love, but at this moment, set her teeth on edge. 'Her mum, actually.'

'Great.' Nicola felt a helpless surge of rage. 'You must really love Advent Calendar, Ollie.' She lowered her voice. 'Bringing in all this tat, having the darling little angels decorate the biscuits. Why don't you take on the twenty-second too, since it's so much *fun*?'

'Well, it is, I mean, I love Christmas.' Ollie looked genuinely puzzled. 'Don't you?'

Her hand shook with the urge to tip the cup of sweet, sticky red wine straight into his face. Mustering as much dignity as she could, she turned and walked away.

Chapter Five

Dmitri poured boiling water over the black tea leaves in the pot, stirred in two teaspoons of strawberry jam and put the lid on for it to steep. He took out a glass from the cupboard and sat down at the table. The little tree made him smile – Tanya had bought it for the table and decorated it with iced gingerbread hearts and stars. It was a nice thing, especially since she was home so rarely. Most nights she stayed with Mark, her boyfriend, at his place. Mark owned the bakery and they'd been together for almost three years.

Dmitri now mostly saw his sister at choir rehearsals and at the pub afterwards. She'd been very bright and cheerful for the last several days – since the night of the carolling at the station, he thought.

For him, the opposite was true. As much as he tried to hide it from everyone, the holiday blues had set in like a thick, impenetrable fog.

In the end, he'd gone home that night after the pub. Gone home to the flat and sat downstairs, drank tea and thought about the woman at the station – 'The Heckler' – what she'd said and done, and why she'd unsettled him. Wondering why at this time of year, even when he was busy and so often surrounded by people, the dark hours seemed so long.

He looked up at the pictures on the wall above the table. Pictures of his mother: some on her own, some with her long-time partner, Phil. Photos of Dmitri dressed in his black tie and tailcoat, getting ready for a choir performance; Tanya and their mother standing on the risers, singing; Tanya, kneading bread, her face covered with flour as she made a funny face at the camera; the three of them eating ice cream in St James' Park. The most recent photo had been taken a few months before their mother's death, just over three years ago now. The oldest of the photos had been taken when Dmitri was about twenty, not long after they'd come to the UK. There were no photos of before, no photos of his father. It was like the time he'd spent in Russia – over half his life – had never been.

When they'd first come to England, his mother had exchanged the roubles she'd had left for exactly eighty-two pounds. He remembered their arrival in London, his first impressions as they got off the bus: the rain, the cloying greyness – so different from the vast skies and snowy expanses of home. Those early days had been hard, but they were luckier than many and had met people who had helped them. People like his friend Kolya at the mission. Now, seventeen years later, the difficult times were like a hazy nightmare only half-remembered. There was so much to be thankful for.

He took out his phone and went through his schedule for the upcoming week. Private singing lessons at the local sixth form, children's choir rehearsal at a prep school in Wimbledon and two other local schools. Music had been both his doom and his salvation, but now, he mostly saw it as the latter. In his early twenties, he'd worked two menial jobs, studying at night to get a degree in music education. From there, he'd never looked back. He loved working with the children – loved their energy and innocent enthusiasm – almost more than the adult choir. When she was annoyed with him, Tanya would say that he was still the same nineteen-year-old boy who had come here so many years ago. She was right... and wrong.

He scrolled on. Tonight, rehearsal began at seven o'clock. If he left now, he might have time to go for a run or the gym. The choir was rehearsing the *Messiah*, one of his favourite pieces of choral music. He'd been rehearsing the soloists for two months now, but the choruses still needed more work—

The key turned in the back door. Tanya came inside, a little out of breath, hefting two large carrier bags.

Smiling, he stood up and gave her a kiss on the cheek. 'Tanusha,' he said. 'I was not expecting you.' He spoke in English. Tanya had struggled to learn the language when they had first arrived, and it had long since become a habit. He took the bags from her and lifted them on to the worktop. 'What is this?' he said.

'Some mince pies for tonight,' Tanya said. 'And because I'm sure you have nothing in there.' She pointed to the fridge, walked over and opened it. Rounding back on him, she tsked and shook her head. 'Anyone would think you were still in Russia.'

He gave her the goofy smile that had made her laugh when they were kids. Shit, he'd been meaning to stop and get some food, but he'd been too busy. The jar of jam, half a loaf of bread and an unopened pack of cheese were unlikely to impress Tanya, who loved to cook and bake.

'I had a sandwich earlier,' he said. It might even have been true; he mostly ate on the run between lessons and rehearsals. But had he eaten today? He couldn't remember.

'You are going to have to do better than that,' she said. She took a tea glass from the cupboard, removed her woollen overcoat and put it over the back of the chair. She was wearing a black T-shirt with 'The Braided Loaf' written in intricate white lettering.

Dmitri poured her a glass of tea, and then one for himself.

'I can take care of myself,' he said.

'Good, brother, I'm glad to hear it. Very glad.' All of a sudden, she smiled, and it was like the sun breaking through clouds. Her dark eyes, so like his, seemed almost to glow. 'Look.' She thrust out her left hand. A small diamond set in white gold twinkled on her finger.

'Oh Tanusha! He asked you!' Dmitri stood up. In a second he was over to her. He lifted her up and twirled her around, laughing and kissing her cheek.

'Yes!' Tanya said, breathless as he set her down. 'Finally.'

'I am so happy for you!' He swallowed back a tear. His little sister. Tanya had lost and suffered so much – mostly because of him – but now, she had found love. She would be happy...

She would be leaving.

He pushed the thought from his mind. This moment was for her.

They sat back down and he raised his glass of tea. He made a toast in Russian to love and health, clinking his glass against hers.

'So when is the lucky day?' he asked.

She took a sip of tea. 'It's not set yet.'

'No? Why not?' The words came out sharply. A flash of pain nearly blindsided him. A face invaded his memory... *Irina*... the words she had spoken when she left... the ring cast aside... He almost choked on the sip of tea, but forced himself to speak. 'You should set a date – the sooner the better. You know I have some money saved up. I will pay for it all. Don't worry about that.'

Tanya's smile was replaced by a frown of concern. 'Are you really OK, Dimochka?'

'Yes, fine.' Her use of the nickname softened him. 'I am so happy for you. I am, as they say, over the moon.'

'We have not set a date because I wanted to speak to you first,' Tanya said. 'It's just...' She paused, as if struggling to find the words. 'I'm worried about you. Being here on your own.'

He laughed. Too loud, too bright. Tanya's eyes narrowed. Fuck – she could see right through him. 'I am fine, Tanusha. All these years, and finally I can be rid of you!'

Tanya laughed at his joking manner, but he could tell it was forced. She stood up from the table and began unloading the carrier bag and turned on the oven to preheat. Dmitri was aware of the ache growing inside him. An ache that seemed only to grow deeper as time went on.

He stood up too and began helping to put the food away. As Tanya was about to hand him a box of loose tea, she stopped. She was looking at the Christmas-pattern half gloves that he had cast off by the sink three nights ago.

Tanya picked up the gloves. 'Do you want me to mend these?' She turned to look at him. He refused to acknowledge the pity in her eyes.

'Can you?'

'I think so. I do not knit as well as Mama did, but I can try.'

'If you like.' Dmitri shrugged. In truth, he preferred the plain grey or brown half gloves he usually wore, and was wearing now, to the Christmas ones that might draw attention to his hands.

His hands. By force of habit, he was about to lower them out of sight, but Tanya reached out swiftly. She grabbed his right hand and squeezed it, so tightly that it almost hurt. She raised it to her lips and kissed his fingers.

'I love you,' she said. 'And you know what I am going to say.'

'No.' He shook his head and pulled his hand away. He went back to putting away the food.

'It's been so long. Isn't it time to try again?'

'I said – don't, Tanya. Please. Now, I must go upstairs and get ready for rehearsal.' Before she could say anything else, he gave her a kiss on the cheek and left the room.

Chapter Six

Nicola walked along the river. Lights shimmered on the water as she walked towards Canary Wharf Pier. She'd stormed out of the office, unable to stand another minute of the Advent Calendar and everything it represented. She needed to clear her head, but so far it hadn't worked.

An old man was fishing from the bank as she walked by. He looked up at her and grinned toothlessly, giving her a little wave. Right now, she envied him. He had a purpose, which was more than she could say.

Her phone vibrated with a text. Predictably, from Ollie.

Hey babe, why'd you leave? Got a few things to finish here but maybe we can meet up later. I told Chloe I'm working late!!! Ox

Bile rose in her throat as she pressed delete. How had it ever come to this?

She stared down at the dark waves lapping below the pier. The night was cloudy, the air so chilly that it almost hurt to breathe. Advent Calendar – what a stupid tradition. She'd never even heard of it before she'd joined Privé, though apparently it was growing in popularity among the bigger banks and law firms.

It had been a Friday night in early December, three years ago now, when it had begun. The partner doing that night's Advent Calendar had hired out the entire restaurant on the top floor for the occasion. All of the PAs, analysts and juniors had sloped off early to get ready, the women donning sparkly dresses and high-heeled shoes in the ladies' loos. Nicola hadn't bothered to change. She was wearing a designer suit in a deep cherry red colour and a cream silk blouse underneath. She knew she looked good – not that it mattered. She wasn't planning on staying long.

The party was already noisy and raucous by the time she arrived. She accepted a flute of champagne from a roving waiter and declined a mince pie. She'd stay at most an hour, and then make her escape. Work was keeping her busy, but this time of year always felt lonely. It had been a long time since she'd been with anyone. She would leave the party, get a taxi to the Mandarin Oriental or the Four Seasons, one of the hotels where the foreign businessmen congregated. Pick out someone at the bar, have a few drinks, pretend not to notice if a wedding ring was slipped into a pocket. Names would be irrelevant, and she'd make the last train home.

Just as she was about to leave, she'd heard Ollie's voice behind her, his hand on her back too low for collegiality. He had joined the firm as a lateral partner about six months earlier. Though she'd felt Ollie's eyes on her before, she'd always dismissed it as strictly an appraisal rather than a call to action. Yes, he could be funny and charming – once or twice she had actually laughed outright at something he'd said at a meeting or a client do. But he also talked about his family around the office.

He'd clearly had a few drinks already. That hand on her

back, his eyes looking down at her curves. 'Are you enjoying yourself?' she'd asked him pointedly and begun to edge away.

But then he got this funny-looking grin on his face. He pointed upwards at a large sprig of mistletoe hanging from one of the chandeliers. Leaning in, he'd whispered in her ear. 'I've been waiting for you.'

As he'd bent to kiss her under the mistletoe, she'd laughed in his face. His handsome, clean-cut features morphed into something ugly and surprised. She'd kept laughing as she walked away, turning for a brief moment to blow him a kiss.

Why had she stayed at the party? She couldn't remember now. One hour had turned into two, one drink into three or four. She'd done the rounds, eating canapés and making small talk. Nicola could feel Ollie's anger from across the room. She was up for a challenge, and obviously, the flirtation could lead nowhere. So she cast him a few glances, taunting him, fuelling the flame she'd lit inside him by her rejection. And, later on, when things had become pleasantly vague, she spotted him at a corner table, nursing a whisky. She'd walked past him towards the door, trailing her nails over his arm. Then she left the restaurant, taking the lift back down to the deserted tenth floor where her office was.

She'd waited exactly eleven and a half minutes (three more than she'd been expecting), when Ollie appeared at the door. She made a bargain with herself: if he said something stupid – if he said anything at all – she would send him away for good. And, in the end, when he said nothing, just walked across the large office to the desk, she wasn't sure how she felt that he had won her silent wager.

She had removed her jacket and let him do the rest. He stood behind her, his hands moving everywhere underneath her clothing and over her skin, his lips and tongue hungrily exploring her neck. She didn't move as she heard the snap of a condom, didn't respond or make a sound.

Afterwards, it had ended. Days later they'd discussed what had happened; they'd both agreed it had been a Christmas party cliché. A one-off, a mistake.

And the time after that.

Now, three years had gone by. Three years of her life that she wouldn't be getting back again. The excitement of those illicit liaisons was long gone. The empty promises had fuelled the spark for a while, and then things had continued because it was easier than breaking them off.

Before the ill-fated night at Waterloo Station, it had been two months since they'd last been together. He'd made a few attempts to rekindle things, and the damn texts never stopped, but she'd made excuses. Then, when holiday loneliness had set in, she'd booked their favourite hotel on Charlotte Street and he'd let her down—

Come on, Nic, you know I'm sorry. I really want to see you. Tonight.

Nicola sighed, her finger hovering over the delete button. But she'd taken the coward's way out for long enough.

No.

Texting back the single word, she turned off her phone and put it in her bag. She walked back the way she had come. In her rush to leave the office, she hadn't brought her flat shoes with her. Her left shoe was already rubbing a blister on her heel.

She had to be strong. Over meant over. No more moments of weakness. She'd go home, regroup, call Jules back like she'd promised. Lie down on the sofa, put on some music. In the new year she'd start looking for another job. There were plenty of other private equity firms that would love to have her. She'd choose a new industry to specialise in – maybe energy or infrastructure. Raising finance to power villages in Africa must feel more worthwhile than taking another fashion brand or cosmetic company global. It would be a clean break from

Ollie, and generally, a new start all around. A new start... Yes, that was exactly what she needed.

Canada Square was buzzing with people. Office workers out for dinner or drinks, and tourists come to see the lights and decorations. The plaza had been transformed into a winter garden. Icicle-shaped lights hung from the trees and giant mythical birds made of wire and lights glowed overhead, swooping down towards globes shaped like golden apples. Part of the square was taken up by an ice rink, with strobes of coloured lights reflecting off the mirror-like surface. Had she come here as a child, she would have been transfixed. And even the way things were now, a part of her appreciated the effort it had taken to transform a city of concrete and glass into something so magical.

She walked towards the giant tree at the centre of the square, made entirely out of strings of white lights on wire formed into thousands of leaf shapes. All of a sudden, voices rang out above the background noise—

Good tidings we bring
To you and your kin,
We wish you a merry Christmas
And a Happy New Year
Oh, bring us some figgy pudding
Oh, bring us some figgy pudding
Oh, bring us some figgy pudding
And a cup of good cheer.

Nicola felt a strange lightness as the words floated through the air. Christmas carollers. There were lots of groups carolling at the Wharf this time of year. There was no reason to think that it might be the group she'd heard at Waterloo Station. Still, she walked as quickly as she could towards the din.

The conductor... she'd only seen him for the minute it had taken her to vent her frustrations. And yet, in that time, she'd felt something. It probably would make no difference, but she really did owe him an apology for what she'd done. Make a donation, start making amends. That way, she could put it behind her.

Could it possibly be the same group of carollers? What had they been called? The Choir of Saint something – St Anne's, maybe? Yes, that was the name.

In front of the Christmas tree, a stage had been erected, framed by large white light snowflakes. There was a choir on the stage, but it was a school choir made up of children, aged probably ten and eleven. The conductor was a round, matronly woman. A sign in old-fashioned lettering at the front read: 'West Ham Invitational Children's Choir'.

Fighting back an irrational surge of disappointment, Nicola sat down on a bench and took out her phone. Her inbox showed that there were twenty-seven new emails and two new texts from Ollie that she deleted immediately. Instead of checking her emails, she opened up a web browser and typed in: St Anne's Church London. There were quite a few listings in and around London and the immediate suburbs, all of which seemed to have choirs.

The first listing she opened was a church in Westminster. The choir was headed by one Stephen Richardson-Ward, Director of Music, with a load of degrees and initials after his name. The next had a Music Director listed as Catherine Evans-Jones. The fifth link, an Anglican church near Clapham Junction, had a broken web link in the choir section. Could that be the one? Maybe.

She stood up – her feet were killing her now – and limped in the direction of the taxi rank. It was complete and utter folly, that much she knew. But then again, she really had nothing better to do.

Chapter Seven

'Thank you. That's all for tonight.' Dmitri set down his baton on the music stand. 'Give yourselves a round of applause.'

Books were closed and clapping commenced. He made a few notes on the score in front of him as the choir members began chatting and coming down from the risers. It had been a good rehearsal – a reasonable turnout for a Friday night – and everyone had seemed full of energy. Quite possibly it was down to Tanya, who, before the rehearsal, had spread the news of her engagement and shown around her ring. Everyone had been delighted for her, giving her hugs and good wishes.

Mark, her fiancé, had come to the rehearsal directly from the bakery. Dmitri had taken him aside for a quiet word of congratulations. He liked Mark – he was what the English termed 'no-nonsense'. He would make Tanya a good husband and that was the thing that mattered. Not for the first time, though, Dmitri wondered how much Mark knew. Had Tanya told him about the things that they themselves did not speak of?

Now, as he gathered up his music, Carole-Ann stood up

from the piano and came over to him. 'Well done,' she said. 'It's coming along.'

'The sopranos were a little thin,' he said.

'Maybe.' She shrugged. They both knew the reason why – Sophie's leaving. But there was nothing to be done about that. 'Are you coming to the pub?' she asked.

'No. Not tonight,' he replied.

'Oh – is everything OK, Dmitri?' She gave him a worried, motherly look that, frankly, annoyed him. But he pushed that aside and gave her a warm smile. Carole-Ann had been widowed for over ten years. She had no other family nearby and was no doubt lonely this time of year. The choir was everything to her, just as it was to him. She had been friendly with his mother, Marina, who had been of a similar age. When she had died, everyone in the choir had pitched in to help him and Tanya through their time of grief. They'd endured endless visitors and cups of weak English tea, bottomless casseroles and many shepherd's pies. Carole-Ann had spearheaded all of it, and he was grateful – really. But sometimes, she went a little overboard.

'Yes. I'm fine. It's just that I want to stay for a while,' he said. 'I want to...' he hesitated – if he said it aloud, he might not go through with it – '...do some practising.'

Just for a second, her blue eyes widened in surprise. 'That's good, Dmitri.'

'Yes,' he said non-committally.

In truth, he had been planning on going to the pub after the rehearsal. Or at least, that was what he usually did, and he hadn't given it much thought. But at the break, when the choir members were drinking teas and coffees and eating Tanya's mince pies, two things had happened.

First, he heard one of the altos mention a new CD she had bought as a Christmas gift for a friend – a recording of Rachmaninov's piano concertos. As the woman spoke, his fingers had started to feel tingly and strange. It had been building for weeks now, this urge. Tonight, the music had flooded through his head, an impossible counterpoint to Handel's *Messiah*. He'd tried to silence it, but it was stuck there.

Second, as the choir was reassembling on the risers, Charles, one of the tenors, had mentioned that he'd seen 'The Heckler' – the woman from Waterloo Station – getting off a train at Richmond. A vision of her had instantly popped into Dmitri's mind. Alluring, beautiful – a face a Victorian painter might try to capture, but with sharper edges to it. Those sharp edges...

'And umm, Dmitri...' Carole-Ann was speaking but he hadn't been listening. He'd been thinking of *her* again – the woman from the station – which was pointless and stupid. She was like the Firebird in one of his favourite fairy tales. Stealing golden apples, captivating young Ivan by leaving behind a single glowing feather. But unlike the hero in the story, he would not be going to the ends of the earth to find her. He would never see her again, and that was for the best. 'Have you filled out the form yet? You know the application's due by the twenty-first?'

The application. Dmitri cringed inwardly. Carole-Ann had heard through a musician friend about an Oxford College that was looking for an assistant choir director. There was a bursary that went with it, and he'd have a chance to study for a doctorate in choral music. 'A very exciting opportunity', she'd called it – a perfect way for him to advance his career. And he'd agreed with her. Yes, it sounded wonderful, perfect. He'd promised her that he would fill out the form, get the letters of reference. It shouldn't be difficult. And yet, some part of him was holding back.

But now that Tanya would be moving out for good, he definitely needed to do it. He and Tanya 'owned' the flat they shared, but by rights it belonged to Phil, his mother's long-time partner. When she'd first got sick, she'd asked Phil to sign it over to Dmitri and Tanya, which he'd done, perfectly willingly. Phil owned lots of properties, had tons of money and connections. One flat more or less had made no difference to him. As a music teacher, Dmitri made very little money – he and Tanya would never have been able to afford to buy a flat on their own. Phil had always seen himself as a stepfather figure to Dmitri, even if the feeling was not always mutual. Now, the time was right to move on, do something else. A doctorate in choral music? Why not? He really did need to get his act together.

'I *will* fill out the application.' He said it forcefully, as much to convince himself as her. 'It's just really busy this time of year.'

'I know.' She smiled. 'And if there's anything I can do—'

'You have done so much for me already,' Dmitri said. 'And I appreciate it. I really do.'

'Yes, well…' Carole-Ann blushed, and still she was there, hovering. 'Take care of yourself, Dmitri.'

'I will see you on Sunday for the soloist rehearsal,' he reminded her. 'Now, go down to the pub and enjoy yourself.' He took out his wallet and peeled off a twenty-pound note. 'Here's a contribution.'

'No, really, it's not necessary.'

He waved his hand. 'Please take it.' *And go.*

Carole-Ann patted his arm in a motherly way. 'Thanks.'

She went out the door – at last.

Alone in the silence of the great church, Dmitri felt unsettled. He went through the pews, checking to make sure that none of the choir members had left anything behind, ensuring that the hymn books were in their place. He paced up and down the aisle: thinking; trying not to think. Feeling; trying not to feel. Trying to get the music out of his head, but at the same time, longing for it to stay.

All he had to do was climb those steps. Up to the choir loft and the grand piano. Very simple, one foot in front of the other.

Occasionally over the years, he'd tried to play again – something other than the usual bread-and-butter work of choral songs, hymns and vocal music for his students. His technique was a little rusty, which was to be expected. Concert pianists practised six to eight hours a day throughout their entire careers. That road had ended a long time ago. But when he did get inspired, he felt that his playing had a depth to it that it hadn't had back then. Experience, pain, life – those things meant more than just notes on a page, fingers on keys. And now, the music in his head, put there by an offhanded comment about a CD – the *need* to play – was battling against the fear of failure. This time, the music won out.

Steeling himself, Dmitri climbed the narrow wooden stairs. Before him, the golden pipes of the great organ rose up as high as the round, oriole window. The piano had been rolled to the far side of the loft. He took the cover off, opened the lid and propped it up. He sat down on the bench and adjusted it.

Taking a breath, he rested his fingers on the cool, smooth surface of the keys. Began by playing a few notes, then some slow scales and arpeggios to warm up. He'd played earlier in the day for music lessons at a school, but whenever he sat up here at the grand piano, alone with the music in his head and the pain tightening across his chest, it always seemed momentous and difficult.

Dmitri stopped playing and looked down at his hands. Hands that he had once trusted more than anything. His father had called them magic hands – able to call forth the spirits from the ether and tame them into something extraordinary and beautiful. So many hours spent in his youth practising; he couldn't remember a time when he didn't play.

His father sitting listening, his eyes closed, smoking a cigarette. Off in a world of his own that Dmitri hadn't understood the importance of. It had been a bond between them, he realised now. As much as the other good times: eating ice cream in the park in summer, skating and sledding in the winter, chopping wood, telling stories, picking wild strawberries...

Magic hands. He winced as he stretched his fingers beyond the point where the pain began. Had his father ever actually said that?

Dmitri picked out a few bars of the piece that had come into his mind earlier. A piece he had played hundreds of times in his youth. It reminded him of that day when the letter came, saying that he'd had been granted a place at the Moscow Tchaikovsky Conservatory, the most prestigious music school in Russia. The time when excitement had bubbled forth from his fingers and anything was possible.

He crashed a chord on the piano and stood up and paced again, wishing he could tear the notes out of his brain. This was madness. He had no business being here; doing this. The right thing to do would be to go home and start filling out the form. Get a doctorate in choral music and be fucking grateful for it.

Dmitri sat back down on the bench and breathed in deeply. He rubbed the tension from his neck. Then he took off the grey knit half-gloves and threw them to the side. He massaged the tight, mottled skin underneath.

The moon rising above the trees, sparkling on new fallen snow... eyes that glittered in the light of the fire...

He breathed in deeply, cleared his mind and began to play.

Chapter Eight

When Nicola entered the church, the sound nearly flattened her. The sheer force of that power, so low and deep; the melody echoing off wood and stone, almost to the edge of discord, sent her mind into freefall. To a dark, haunted place that she had glimpsed only in nightmares. And memories. The door shut behind her. All of a sudden, a starburst of fast, light notes flew above the dark bass. Uplifting and free, like a flock of birds taking flight. She felt quite literally like the sound might tear her in two.

She hadn't been sure this was the right place, or what she had hoped to find. Now, on some deep, unfathomable level, she knew.

The vestibule was heated and she took off her coat, folding it over her arm. The church was empty, the apse lit only by dim side lights near the altar. The only other light came from the choir loft above.

The music continued on, relentless. She couldn't hear her heels on the tile floor. There was a small wooden staircase off to one side near the back of the church. She began to climb. The sound drew her onwards, each step taking her closer to the source. The black bass notes, the sparkling treble, the giant pipes of the organ rising above her head. And finally, when she reached the top, she saw him.

His back was to her, his body moving trance-like, as his fingers danced over the keys of the grand piano. He was tall, that much she had remembered, and was wearing a grey jumper and dark trousers. As he played, his shoulders rose and fell in exertion, like David wrestling Goliath.

She took another step forward, tentative and unsure.

He stopped abruptly, the echoes of the sound still crashing against the walls. Then, he turned around. His eyes were black and wild, and at first, she wasn't sure if he'd even seen her. As reality dawned, his mouth fell open and then shut again.

'Don't stop,' she blurted out.

But he just stared at her, his eyes narrow and hawk-like. She couldn't read the expression in them.

'I'm... sorry I disturbed you,' Nicola stammered, unable to stand the silence as the last echoes died away. 'That was the most incredible... I mean, I've never heard anything like it. What was it?'

Her voice seemed to bring him back to his senses. 'It is a Prelude by Rachmaninov,' he said, his voice a rich, accented baritone. 'It is known as *The Bells of Moscow*. He raked back his dark hair and wiped the sweat from his brow. 'To be honest, I haven't played it in years. But tonight, it just came to me.'

His frown still hadn't wavered, but she could feel his eyes moving away from her face. Appraising all of her. She already felt stripped and raw from the music, and she was sure he could see right through her to the core of ugliness at her centre.

He turned back to the piano and put on a pair of fingerless gloves that had been tossed to one side. This time they weren't festive Christmas knit, but plain grey wool. He flexed his fingers and winced. It was as if the music had stolen something from him and he hadn't quite regained his equilibrium.

When he finally turned back to her, he didn't speak, and the silence seemed to pulse between them.

'I'm Nicola Taylor,' she said to break the tension. 'You may not remember me but—'

'I remember you,' he said. The rest was unspoken but sent a jolt of electricity down her body.

'I...' Nicola suddenly felt at a loss for words. 'I came to apologise for the way I acted the other night. It's just, well... I was annoyed with the cancelled trains. It had been a really bad day – you know how it is...' She laughed awkwardly.

He stood up from the piano and took a few steps towards her.

'I mean, I'm sure that lots of people love Christmas and carolling.' As he came closer, she felt unnerved and started to ramble again. 'You probably made a lot of people happy that night at the station.' She shrugged. 'I guess Christmas isn't really my thing. But I shouldn't have spoiled it. I'm sorry.'

Her heart accelerated as he came up to her and, for a second, his arm brushed lightly against hers. But whether he noticed or not, intended it or not, she wasn't sure. He went past her and sat down in the pew nearest the edge of the gallery, leaning his elbows forward on to the railing.

'And why, Nicola, is Christmas "not your thing"?'

Direct to the heart of the matter – and none of his goddamn business. The walls she'd built up around herself had been battened down by the music, but instantly, they sprang up again.

'I don't see why everyone has to act like they're so happy,' she said, frowning. 'I mean, don't you think it's all just commercialism? Get people to spend money – buy presents and food and alcohol? Overindulge and then spend the whole of January regretting it?'

He shrugged his shoulders, not broad, but lean and muscular. 'I suppose that's true – in a way. But isn't it also about getting through a dark time of year? Taking time to focus on family, and friends, the things that matter. In this world of ours, is this such a bad thing?'

'Maybe not, but why do we need all the trappings of Christmas for that?'

He didn't answer for a long moment. Here she was, arguing with him, when, really, she had come to apologise. Her *issues*, such as they were, hadn't given her licence to be rude.

'Yes,' he said finally. 'I can see your point.' He turned slowly to face her, his dark hair falling softly over his eyes. 'You're probably right. But what do you think is the answer? For the choir not to sing? For the people who want to meet other people – enjoy themselves – not to do so?'

She didn't have an answer for that. Most of the men she interacted with on a daily basis would just have accepted her apology and then moved on to make small talk or flirt a little. Yet this conversation with this man seemed much more difficult – more intimate – than she ever would have expected.

'I don't know,' she said. 'Obviously you have a right to sing where you want. Spread joy, good cheer – whatever you want to call it.'

'But you think you should have the right to walk away, is that it? Not listen if you don't want to. What was the word you used? "Trapped"?'

She looked at him in surprise. He'd obviously remembered the details of the whole unfortunate encounter.

'Actually,' he added, 'to me, that sounds reasonable.'

'I don't know,' she countered. 'Maybe if it had been another night, another place...' She shook her head. 'But, as it was, all I wanted to do was get on that train and go home for a few hours. Pretend I didn't have to get up for work the next morning and do it all over again.'

He looked at her quizzically. 'If that's how you feel, then why do you do it?'

'I don't know!' His calm poise was making her angry, just like it had the other night. 'Why does anyone do what they do? I mean, not all of us can play – what was it again? – Rachmaninov?'

'No, that's true.'

Nicola paced back and forth a few steps by the edge of the gallery. She hadn't come here to have a discussion with this man about the meaning of life and the joys of Christmas. She'd come here to apologise, and she'd done that. So why was she still here?

'Anyway, for the record, I wanted to say I'm sorry,' she said. 'I came here to tell you that. I thought I could make a donation. For... mince pies or something.'

He laughed, and that irritated her. Standing up, he came back over to her. Once again she felt that growing sense of tension as he stood in front of her, close enough that she could smell his scent: wool, sweat, an undernote of musky aftershave. He must be about her age, she thought – mid to late thirties. But the mischievous twinkle in his dark eyes reminded her more of a boy.

'For mince pies?' he asked.

'Or something...'

That look in his eye. This ridiculous situation. Actually, she had to keep herself from laughing too. Mince pies – God, had she actually said that?

'I'll tell you a secret,' he said, lowering his voice. 'I don't actually like mince pies.'

'No?'

'But the choir loves them.'

'Well then...' she shrugged.

'And Nicola,' he continued, drawing out the syllables of her name, 'I appreciate your coming to find me.'

Her pulse sped up and she felt a tightening in her abdomen as he leaned in closer to her, his face near enough that she could feel his breath on her skin. And just like in that one previous encounter she'd had with him, she was unsure whether his next action would be to slap her across the face or… reach for her and kiss her. She felt even more disconcerted when he did neither, instead turning away and walking a few steps, staring out at the expanse of the church below.

'You say that you are sorry for what you did. Then you argue your right to reject Christmas – which I accept, by the way. It can be… difficult.' Just for a second he turned back to her and she saw a shadow cross his face. But then, he smiled again, warily. 'You say you wish to make a donation – for mince pies.' He raised an eyebrow. 'Do your penance, make yourself feel better. Is that correct?'

'Yes…' Nicola said through her teeth. 'So where can I make the donation?'

'Take an envelope from the collection box. On your way out.' The words slammed into her. He wasn't smiling now.

'OK.' The instructions were clear enough. And yet, she didn't move.

Once again he moved past her and went back to the piano. He picked up some music that was stacked on the side and shoved it into his shoulder bag. Nicola noted that there was no music on the stand. He'd been playing *The Bells of Moscow*, or whatever it was, from memory.

For the hundredth time, she willed herself to go. And yet, she just stood there watching him. Aware of him. And he was aware of her too. Yes, as soon as the thought came into her head, she knew she was right. He was aware of her, and now, he was playing with her. A shiver wracked her body.

'But if you really wish to atone, Nicola – to me,' he turned and looked at her, giving her the full benefit of his dark eyes and sharp classical features, 'then tell me – what are you doing tomorrow?'

Dmitri watched Nicola Taylor walk down the steps of the church, her high heels clicking on the stone as she reached the street without looking back. She got into the taxi that was waiting for her. And then, she was gone.

What the *fuck* was he doing? He closed the heavy wooden door and collapsed against it. Why had she come here? Shattering his fragile equilibrium. Making him feel something; want something.

He thought of Tanya, so well-meaning, so loved up and happy herself, telling him that it was time to 'try again'. When she knew perfectly well why that wasn't going to happen. He felt angry with her. Angry at himself.

He'd deliberately not taken Nicola's phone number, or given out his. The stupid part of him even wanted to go ahead with this crazy idea that had formed in his mind.

Dmitri took out his phone. It was time to call in a few favours. He dialled the first number as he went back up to the choir loft to collect his things. Right now the only consolation was that, almost certainly, Nicola wouldn't turn up. He would never see her again, and all would be well.

- ii -

'Ivan rode through the dark forest, as the howling pack of wolves drew nearer. This was madness. She was a creature of flight; how would he ever find her? Suddenly, in the blackness before him, two great yellow eyes appeared. Ivan was thrown to the icy ground. The horse bolted and ran away. Before he could rise, the wolf stepped out.

"You are foolish to venture here, young Ivan," the wolf said, licking its jaws.

"Maybe so. But I seek the Firebird."

"The Firebird!" The wolf laughed. "You will never find her. For she is under a spell of enchantment. Trapped in a golden cage. And it is far from here."

"I will find her," Ivan said. "At the ends of the earth, if I must."

"You may be foolish, but you are brave too," the wolf acknowledged. It lowered itself down on to its giant paws. "Come," he said. "Climb on to my back. I will take you to see things that you cannot imagine."'

– 'The Firebird', *The Anthology of Russian Tales*

Chapter Nine

5th December

This was a bad idea. How could it be anything else? It was Saturday, and she never went into London on a Saturday, if she could help it. And yet, here she was on the train. She'd agreed to meet Dmitri at Waterloo Station.

Dmitri. She'd been startled by the whole encounter, and by his 'invitation', if it could be called that. It was only as she was half out the door into the freezing night that she realised she hadn't even asked his name.

'Dmitri Orlov,' he'd said as the question had formed on her lips. Almost by rote, he had rattled off the answers to some of the others. 'I am thirty-six years old. Originally from Russia. I live in Clapham and I have been here for seventeen years. You will meet me at Waterloo Station. Dress warm and wear comfortable shoes. I will need your entire day. Do you understand?'

No, she hadn't, and she didn't. But when he'd given her that enigmatic smile, shook her hand and said, 'see you tomorrow', Nicola had been intrigued. He would dole out her penance, that was what he had promised.

Now, as her mind raced with second thoughts, she

wondered what she was in for. Why had she gone to the church last night? And why the hell would she let some madcap Russian choir director commandeer her Saturday? If he even turned up.

And as crazy as it seemed – as crazy as it was to be on this train – she hoped he would.

The train sped past Barnes and stopped briefly at Putney. The other passengers looked like they were out for a day of fun and shopping in London. There were families: children, sticky with sweets and crisps, wrapped up like sausages in down coats and woolly hats; elderly couples, mums with prams. It was a totally different crowd to the Monday to Friday commuters. Everyone looked so excited and animated. Nicola felt out of place.

The train stopped at Clapham Junction. She should get off, cross over the platform and go home. She stayed in her seat.

Eventually, the train arrived at London Waterloo. She didn't have Dmitri's phone number. He didn't have hers. Would she even find him?

Nicola got off the train and walked to the barrier. And there, just on the other side, he was waiting for her. He was dressed casually, wearing a brown leather bomber jacket over a green jumper and jeans. His hair had fallen into his eyes and he raked it back, staring up at the boards as she had done that evening when she had first encountered him.

As soon as he spotted her, his face bloomed into a wide grin. Nicola, in spite of all her misgivings, felt relieved – and something else too that she didn't want to acknowledge. She found herself smiling back.

She pinged her Oyster card on the barrier and went up to him. He was wearing leather gloves, and reached out to take her arm, leaning in to give her a kiss on the cheek. A current of electricity glittered down her spine.

'You came,' he said.

'I can't quite believe it either.' In fact, her being here at all seemed almost unreal.

Drawing back, he appraised her openly. Her cheeks grew warm. She was wearing a long Burberry down coat in dark green. Underneath she had on jeans, suede boots and a tight long-sleeved black top that accentuated her small waist and large breasts. And underneath that... well, it was unlikely to matter.

'And you are ready to do your penance?' He gave her a dark, teasing look that she wasn't quite sure how to interpret. If Ollie was making her repent for something, she knew exactly what it would entail; that sort of thing she could understand. But if Dmitri's goal was simply to sleep with her, then why meet at a train station on a Saturday morning? She was getting ahead of herself, she realised, a little embarrassed. It was a strange feeling not knowing what he had planned, not being entirely in control. But if he made her feel uncomfortable even for a second, she would bolt and be done with it.

'Yes, I guess so,' she said.

He opened up the black messenger bag he was carrying and pulled something out: a floppy package wrapped in green tissue paper. He held it out to her. 'For you,' he said.

'Is this part of the penance?' She took it warily.

'Well, Nicola,' he lowered his voice, making her feel that frisson again, 'you tell me.'

She tore open the paper, then looked up at him, her face alight with horror. 'You expect me to wear...'

'I expect you to do as I say,' he said, with a mixture of authority and amusement. He took the... thing... from her, straightened it out and put it on her head. Amusement won out. He started to laugh. 'You look... perfect.'

'Oh for God's sake,' she bristled, wanting to rip the awful red Santa hat off her head. But she was even more taken aback when he reached out and took her hand. He led her into the crowd that was heading towards the doors to the South Bank. 'Come this way,' he said.

'Where are we going?' she said loudly, over the crowd.

'You'll see.'

A thousand emotions swamped her as she followed Dmitri out of the station, heading in the direction of the South Bank. On a normal Saturday, she would spend most of the day working from home, plus going for a run, or shopping, maybe seeing her sister. All of a sudden, in the wake of the supernova of energy that was Dmitri, that life seemed bland and devoid of colour, and a million miles away. For now, she gave in to the novelty of spending the day with a man who made her wear a Santa hat, took her hand in public, and was still pulling her steadily onwards.

They went down the steps and crossed the street, heading towards the Royal Festival Hall, and ultimately, the South Bank. As they drew near, she realised where they were going.

The South Bank Christmas Market.

'A Christmas market?' She gave Dmitri a sideways glance. 'You are trying to torture me, aren't you?'

Nicola could smell roasting chestnuts and strong coffee as they approached the banks of the River Thames. Along the embankment, a line of German-style huts had been erected, with fake icicle trim and little white fairy lights along the roof-lines.

'I knew you'd see it that way,' he said, laughing.

Even this early, shoppers and passers-by were flocked around the little huts, some browsing, others eating or drinking cups of steaming coffee or hot chocolate. It was a cold day, with the forecast calling for partly sunny skies and the chance of snow showers later on. Nicola's breath came out in white puffs. A fragile sun, still low on the horizon, was just beginning to light up the banks of the river.

They walked past the huts where people were selling crafts, souvenirs, artwork, and an array of different foods. Some of the vendors stood outside, handing out free samples of cheese and cold meats. There was a similar market at Canary Wharf, but she had never stopped to have a look. Now, though, she took it in with all her senses: the different smells and flavours, the bright colours, the people browsing despite the chill in the air.

'Are you hungry?' Dmitri said, slowing down as they passed an artisan bread stall giving out samples of pastry laced with cinnamon.

'Not right now,' Nicola said. Until she knew what he had planned, she couldn't even think of food.

'OK.' He smiled at her and continued to lead her on. 'This way.'

They went underneath the rail bridge, where more stalls were set up. The Santa hat drew a few looks, and an off-handed 'nice hat' from a roasted nut vendor. Dmitri kept her walking, directly towards the carousel.

'No!' she protested as he took her up to it. The carousel had fancy carvings painted gold, and brightly coloured scenes of happy children and animals. The lights were flashing and the music was garish and bright.

Dmitri let go of her hand and went over to have a word with the carousel operator. Nicola couldn't hear what he said, but they seemed to know each other. She considered doing a runner – back to the station, home, an afternoon of work, a takeaway, a glass of wine...

Dmitri came back grinning, a bit smugly, she thought. She knew then that he'd been half expecting her to bolt too, and the fact that she hadn't, well...

'This is ridiculous,' she said as he led her on to the carousel. He helped her on to a white horse with a golden saddle and hand-painted garlands of ribbons and flowers.

'Maybe,' he said, with a wry smile. He mounted the horse next to her: a black charger with a silver mane and tail. The crass, joyful music was loud in her ears as the carousel began to move and it was too late to get off.

Maybe it was the motion of the horse, or maybe it was the fact that she'd eaten only a piece of toast in the morning before getting the train, but as they bobbed up and down, faster and faster in vague time to the music, she felt light-headed and dizzy.

The carousel stopped and a few children and adults climbed on to the horses. Then it started up and went round again. Nicola stayed on her horse. It was like a bizarre fugue moment, an out-of-body experience, where she seemed to be staring at the world through the eyes of a completely different person. A child, almost like she might have been once, but too long ago to remember. It made her feel off balance and disoriented.

They went on the carousel three times in all. When Dmitri finally helped her down from the horse, and she found her feet again, she had to make a conscious effort *not* to smile.

She tossed the white pom-pom tail of the Santa hat over her shoulder like a stroppy teenager. 'Is this the best you can do?' she challenged.

He took her hand in his once again. Riding the carousel had warmed her and she'd unzipped her coat and taken off her gloves, but now her hands were cold. Dmitri had taken off his leather gloves but was still wearing a pair of grey wool half-gloves that he must have had on underneath. His fingers were long and slender – pianist's fingers. She supposed that he needed to keep them warm. He lifted her hand to his mouth and blew warm air on it. The gesture was intimate and a little alarming.

'Don't worry,' he said, his eyes bright and mocking. 'We're just getting started. Would you like something to eat now?'

He let go of her hand and for second, she felt unsteady on her feet.

'Maybe a coffee?' she said. Unfortunately it was much too early to suggest something stronger.

'Yes, good.'

They went over to a stall selling mulled wine, coffee and hot chocolate. There were also hearts and stars made of iced gingerbread hanging down from the window and an array of muffins, mince pies, croissants and buns.

'What would you like?' he asked her, taking out his wallet.

'Just a coffee, please,' she said. 'Milk, no sugar.'

'No mince pie?' He cocked his head.

'Actually,' she said, 'I don't like them either.'

He laughed. 'Good to know. What about gingerbread? I love gingerbread.'

'I... don't know.' Her natural urge was to refuse. But the hearts and stars did look good, and she suddenly felt hungry.

He was still looking at her, judging her reaction. 'OK, let's see.'

He ordered her coffee and a hot chocolate for himself. He also bought a large gingerbread star decorated with icing swirls and snowflakes. After he paid, and the drinks were ready, he went over to the railing overlooking the river and broke the gingerbread star in half. It smelled so good, and hell, the day was already so bizarre that she decided to indulge.

The gingerbread was warm as she bit into it, the flavours exploding in her mouth in a mixture of sweet and spice. Sweet and spice, just like the man standing next to her. Sunlight sparkled on the water, and on the other side of the river, Big Ben, Westminster Palace and the House of Lords glowed in the golden light. A thousand questions came to mind as she ate the gingerbread and sipped her coffee.

Dmitri turned to look at her, and she found herself drawn in by his dark eyes, still sparked with amusement.

'Are you OK?' he asked her.

'Can I take off the hat?' she said.

He raised his hand and lifted the hat off her head, putting it on his own. 'Is that better?'

She laughed at the wicked grin on his face. 'Much,' she said. She reached up and adjusted it on his head, pulling it down further over the dark hair that framed his forehead. For a second, he seemed to draw back a little bit at the touch, or maybe she was just imagining it.

He took a sip of hot chocolate, and then bit into the gingerbread star. 'Hmm,' he said. 'This is good.' He licked the crumbs off his lips. 'Though my sister, Tanya, makes it better.'

'Your sister?' Nicola said. All of a sudden, something clicked. 'Was she at the concert at the station?'

'Yes,' Dmitri said. 'She was passing out song sheets.' He raised his eyebrows. 'I believe you two have met.'

Nicola felt instantly embarrassed. The beautiful dark-haired girl who had borne the initial brunt of her anger. The one with the song sheet basket that she had kicked over. She could see the resemblance between them now: the high cheekbones, the shape of the dark, long-lashed eyes.

'I'm sorry,' she said. 'Maybe you can tell her that.'

'I will if you like,' Dmitri said. 'Though, to be honest, I barely see her these days. She recently got engaged.' He let out a small sigh. 'For many years, she and I have shared a flat. Now, she will be moving out. Everything changes.'

'I guess it does.' Nicola ate another bite of the biscuit. 'So, do you have any other family here?' She was probing, but subtly, she hoped. When she'd thought of him after the 'incident', she'd assumed that he was just another smug married man, rubbing his contented holiday bliss in the noses of the people like her who were alone. But meeting him one-on-one at the church had given her an entirely different impression.

'No,' he said. 'My mother died a few years ago. Cancer. It

was quite sudden, but maybe it is better that way, I don't know.' For a second, he frowned. 'Her partner, Phil, has, over the years, tried to be like a father to me. I haven't always been very receptive.'

'I can understand that,' she said. 'My mum has a second family. I've never really felt a part of it. Back when she left, I lived with my dad. But he's dead now.'

He looked at her gently. 'That sounds difficult,' he said. 'Especially this time of year.'

'Oh, it's fine, really,' Nicola said, remembering their conversation in the church. 'I'll spend Christmas with them. My sister, Jules, is having everyone over. She's married with kids. That's what it's really about, isn't it? Like you said – family, friends.'

'Yes, I suppose.' He sounded less convinced this time.

'So, what are you doing for Christmas?' she asked. 'Since you love it so much.' It was probably obvious now that she was fishing for information. But she had to know. If he was married or with someone, like she'd first imagined – if this were all just some kind of a game – then it needed to end right now. Nicola had never set out to be 'the other woman'. Things with Ollie had evolved that way, but she was finished with all that now.

'I will mostly be working,' he said. 'As you have seen, the choir is very popular this time of year. We have many rehearsals and concerts.'

'I can imagine.'

'As for the rest, I will spend it with my sister, and also our friends. You are right, I do love Christmas.' He tugged playfully on the pom-pom of the Santa hat.

He looked so goofy that she did laugh. At moments he seemed like an overgrown child. But he was easy to be with – charming, funny. So far.

'I liked it when I was a kid,' she said. 'I have good memories of... before. Baking, going to church – even singing Christmas carols.' She raised an eyebrow. 'I bet you liked it back then too.'

'Ah, but there you'd be wrong.' The teasing look was back. 'In the Soviet Union, we were not officially allowed to celebrate Christmas. Not until 1991, when I was nine.'

'Really?' She frowned. 'I guess that makes sense. I hadn't really thought about it.'

'We did have a big celebration at New Year's,' he said. 'On New Year's Eve, we would wait for a visit from "Old Man Frost" – *Ded Moroz* – who was like the Russian Father Christmas. He came in a *troika* – that's a kind of sleigh – with *Snegurochka*, the Snow Maiden. They would leave presents and sweets.' His eyes were shiny with the memories. 'And when finally, we could celebrate Christmas, it was on January 7th under the Orthodox Calendar. I think that nowadays in Russia, some people celebrate two Christmases: in December and January, with New Year's in between, and Epiphany afterwards.' He turned to her and grinned. 'You'd hate it.'

'Yes, probably.' She gave him a pained look.

'But for people like my mother, it was a joy to be able to celebrate Christmas. On Christmas Eve, she and my sister would spend all day cooking. We would go to the church, and there would be carolling. The old women would tell fortunes. And always, there was snow. It was quite magical.'

'It sounds like it,' Nicola said. 'I guess I've always just taken it for granted. My mistake. I'm sorry.'

'It's OK.' He glanced at her kindly. 'I barely even remember that time – when we could not do this and not do that. When we were not, as you would say, free.'

'So why did your family leave Russia?'

Though he was standing a few feet away from her, leaning against the railing, she was aware of his sharp intake of breath.

'Sorry,' she said, quickly. 'It's none of my business.'

'No, of course, it's an obvious question,' he said, not quite meeting her eyes. 'I suppose the answer is that my mother, and many others like her, saw the west as the promised land. My father did not agree. He was, as you say, very "old school". When the Soviet Union broke up, he found all the changes very difficult. He died when I was eighteen. After that, we came here.'

'God. I'm—' She broke off. She hated that word 'sorry'. And yet what else was there to say?

'Yes,' he said, as if he understood. He finished his hot chocolate and crumpled up the wrapper, putting it inside the cup. 'Shall we go on? It's a bit of a walk.'

'Yes,' Nicola said, feeling unexpectedly glad that there was a 'next thing'. 'Lead on, Lucifer.'

He gave her a fitting look in return. The shadow seemed to have passed.

They threw their cups in a bin and walked up the stairs to the Golden Jubilee footbridge that went across the river to the Victoria Embankment. On their way across, they passed several buskers: a saxophone player, a wheelchair-bound accordion player and a spray-painted silver mime doing a mechanical dance routine for a group of children. Dmitri had a coin for all of the performers and also stopped briefly and spoke to two homeless beggars bundled up in sleeping bags and cardboard on the bridge. Nicola stayed out of earshot, but she felt herself getting a little annoyed. Yes, it was a kind thing to do, but was he trying to prove something?

Dmitri glanced at her. He stopped along the bridge, leaning against the railing. The sun had disappeared behind a cloud. She stood beside him looking out at the skyline towards the east, a jagged line of buildings, cranes and bridges. From the wicked sharp point of the Shard at London Bridge to the elegant dome of St Paul's Cathedral across the river. A steady stream of cars and buses crossed Waterloo Bridge.

'When we first came here from Russia,' he said, 'we had almost no money.' Nicola could barely hear his voice over the wind and traffic noise. 'We didn't know anyone or have any place to go. We had to sleep rough – near Victoria bus station.'

'Really?' she said, a little shocked, and ashamed of her earlier reaction.

'Yes,' he said. 'For us, it was a very different world and we were not in any way prepared.'

'What did you do?'

He shrugged. 'My mother was determined to make a life for us. She found work as a cleaner, and I worked also. Two jobs – at a restaurant in the day and at a club at night. My sister was looked after at the shelter. And then, when my mother met Phil, things got better still. We got visas and a nice place to live. We were very lucky, but not everyone is.'

Nicola looked beyond him to the homeless people on the bridge. Huddled up against the chill, against the thieves and predators who might exploit them. Watching people pass – tourists snapping selfies, hardened Londoners like herself, working, or just wanting to get from point A to point B. Whereas Dmitri saw what she didn't – or didn't want to see. The idea of *him* suffering felt raw, and sobering. She gave in to her natural inclination – to get angry.

'Are you trying to make me feel guilty?' she challenged.

'No, of course not.' He looked at her, and once again the intense look in his eye gave way to humour. 'Well, maybe just a little.'

'It won't work,' she said, softening a little.

'No?' He laughed then. 'That's good. But now it's your turn,' he said. 'Tell me more about you.'

'What do you want to know?' Nicola said.

'Everything,' he answered. 'But tell me as we walk.' He took out his phone and checked the time on the screen. 'Your next penance awaits.'

Chapter Ten

Control. That was the key – the thing that was going to get him through this. Control of his feelings, of what he said and didn't say. Keep things friendly and light; stay detached. Keep her as far out of her comfort zone as possible.

It shouldn't be difficult. Everything would go to plan. They'd spend the day together. Have a good memory. Part as friends.

It was difficult.

The moment she'd walked into the church, with her flaming hair, guarded eyes and dangerous body, he'd felt something significant. It wasn't her looks or her sex appeal – not just that, anyway. Maybe it was the darkness he sensed inside her, hidden away beneath that beautiful exterior. A loneliness that resonated with his. Or maybe he was only imagining it – projecting himself on to her. He didn't know for sure, but either way, he had to be careful.

They walked side by side to the end of the bridge and down the steps to the embankment. Villiers Street was bustling with shops, restaurants, and people, as they walked up to the top and turned right on to the Strand.

'Where are we going?' Nicola said.

'It's my turn to ask questions now,' he teased. 'But I'll make it easy for you. Tell me about the things that are important to you – like your work.'

'That's not—'

He laughed, enjoying her look of outrage.

'OK, then.' She parried by launching into an overview of the finance firm where she worked, layering on the corporate speak. Her job sounded high-powered and glamourous, and it was obvious that she was hoping to confuse him. It worked. He did, however, manage to ask a few questions and hoped he didn't look like a complete idiot.

'Anyway,' she finished, 'it's a job. It suits me.'

'Smart and dedicated,' he summed up, steering clear of more descriptive words. 'I like that.'

'Well, yes.' She blushed.

'And you live in Richmond-upon-Thames?' he asked.

'Yes, I mean... wait – how did you know that?' Her eyes narrowed like a cat's.

'Someone in the choir spotted you on the train,' he said. 'I'm afraid they call you "The Heckler".'

'What? Who called me that?' She looked at him with such shock that he couldn't help but laugh. 'That's awful,' she said. 'Why are you laughing?'

'I'm just saying that you made an impression.'

Her eyes brushed his and he felt a delicious electric charge. If only things had been different... But they weren't. He had to remember that.

They continued to walk, crossing the busy intersection at Aldwych. A little further on, Dmitri took her arm and manoeuvred her towards a giant archway. She stopped, and he sensed her tensing up. They were standing on the pavement just outside the entrance to Somerset House. Beyond the arch was the ornate white façade of the building that now housed the Courtauld Gallery. The giant courtyard in front had been transformed into an outdoor ice skating rink.

'No, Dmitri, really, I can't.' Nicola gasped.

'You have never skated before?' he said, a little concerned.

'Not since I was a girl.'

'Yes, Nicola. If I were to make a guess, I would say that for you, many things fall in that category.'

She rolled her eyes. 'How do you know?'

'I think you just told me.'

With a look of sheer indignation, she crossed her arms. 'OK, where do we go?'

'This way.' He steered her directly to the front of the long queue and spoke to the person on duty. That person went to get the manager – the man that Dmitri had phoned from the church to make the arrangements. They had a brief chat, and Dmitri thanked him for helping out at such short notice. They were issued with their tickets.

'Now, we must get some skates,' he said. 'What size do you wear?'

'Six,' Nicola croaked.

Dmitri took her over to the bench and gestured for her to sit down. He crouched down and unzipped her boots, taking them from her feet. Touching her, he felt that spark again that made his mouth go dry. But the look of shock on her face was worth it. He got up quickly and took off his own boots. Then he went to the counter and exchanged their boots for two pairs of ice skates. While he was there, he took off the Santa hat and put it in his bag (enough was enough) and put his bag in a locker.

He came back and handed her the pair of heavy blue skates. Her lips were pursed as she shoved her feet in and did up the metal toggles.

Dmitri tightened his own skates, and then stood up, offering her his hand. She rejected it, instead popping up herself and finding her balance on the rubbery mat surface. 'Just a minute,' she said. She waddled like a penguin over to another window just past the skate hire. At the café window, they were selling coffee, tea and mulled wine.

When he came up beside her, she had ordered two 'winter warmers' – mulled wine in a cup with a cinnamon stick. Dmitri changed his to an espresso.

'Too early for you?' she said, colouring a little.

'I don't drink alcohol,' he said. 'But you go ahead.'

He handed her the warm paper cup of wine, watching her breathe in the smell of the spirits rising to her nose. He downed the espresso in one gulp and left the empty cup on the counter.

'Thank you for the coffee,' he said. 'Now, are you ready to skate?'

'Let's get it over with.' She looked bemused, but up for it. Her cheeks glowed with the cold and he wanted – way too much – to touch her. He put his hands in his pockets.

The rink was already crowded as they made their way out on to the ice. She was still holding the paper cup of mulled wine. As soon as she stepped out on to the ice, her whole body tipped and wavered. His instinct was to reach out to her, but he kept it in check, letting her find her balance. She clung to the side of the railing, as children, families, beginners and expert skaters whizzed, careered and fell all around her. She finished the wine and left the empty cup at the side. Her eyes were bright and he was pleased when she grabbed on to his arm tightly, taking small, awkward steps along the ice.

'Yes, you're doing it,' he said, loud enough to be heard over the voices and eighties music. As she began to relax into it and get a rhythm going, he began to enjoy it too.

On the ice, Dmitri felt solid and in his element. He'd loved skating as a boy – the freedom, the speed of it. He and his friends had all tried to outdo each other with jumps and spins, often landing flat on their bottoms, but it had been fun nonetheless.

'Don't go too fast,' she said. 'Please.'

Dmitri slowed down, feeling instantly protective of her.

They made it once around the ice. For a second or two, she let go of his arm, but then she hit a bump in the ice and quickly grabbed back on. A few steps later, she hit another bump and he put his hand on hers to steady her. He glanced at her face. She wasn't smiling, but her green eyes were soft when they met his. He felt pleasantly warm and very aroused.

All of a sudden, a few feet in front of them, a small boy holding on to his parents' hands lost his footing and pulled both parents to the ground. Dmitri tried to stop, but a freight train of skaters from behind pushed into them like falling dominos. Nicola shrieked as she took the impact. Dmitri tried to pull her to him, but her legs were gone from beneath her and they both went crashing down. The ice came up cold and hard underneath his bottom. He landed with his legs in a V-shape and her between them, his arms wrapped around her waist. She leaned against him and he didn't let go immediately. Having her in his arms, the smell of her hair on his face, the feel of her soft, delicious body...

She burst out laughing. Instantly, he let go of her. 'OK, big shot,' she said, putting her hand on his knee. 'Now what? I don't think I can get up.'

'Here, let me.' Dmitri tried to pick himself up, but at the last second, she pulled him off balance back down on to the ice. He looked at her in surprise, and then started laughing too.

She took out her phone and while they were both still down on the ice, held it out in front of them and snapped a photo. Dmitri caught a glimpse of it before it went off the screen. He had a silly look on his face, and her face was only half in view, her cheeks flushed, hair everywhere. She was about to take another photo when a group of teenagers ploughed into them and ended up in a heap on top of them. Dmitri managed to clear them to the side and get up. He helped her to her feet, and she shoved her phone back into her pocket.

They skated around some more; she kept a firm grip on his hand. When she said she wanted a rest, he left her at the side of the rink and went to the centre of the ice, making a schoolboyish show of trying to impress her with spins and little jumps. She was smiling, so maybe it worked. Not that it mattered.

This is not a date, he reminded himself sternly. It felt like one, though.

An announcement came over the loudspeaker that the session was ended. Dmitri left the ice a little reluctantly. He helped Nicola off the rink until she steadied herself on the rubber matting. They changed out of their skates and Dmitri got their boots and his bag.

'You're a really good skater,' she said as she took off her skates and put her boots back on.

'I did a lot of skating when I was a boy,' Dmitri said, happy that she'd noticed. 'And then, later on, in Moscow. The river used to freeze over. You could just walk across.'

'It sounds like you miss it,' she said.

'Does it?'

'*Do* you miss it?' she pressed.

He considered this as they went out. 'Sometimes,' he said. 'I suppose, after all these years, I think mostly of the good things. There are things I remember that seem so beautiful now, though I didn't appreciate them at the time. I miss the friends I had, and I miss my father.' His voice caught as he reflected. 'My sister says that I am too sentimental. She remembers the bad things: the noise and stink of the block of flats, the clouds of mosquitoes in summer, the freezing showers in the winter – when there was any water at all.'

'Ugh. I think I'm with her on that one.'

'Yes.' He laughed. 'You women like your creature comforts.'

'That's for sure.'

They exited the courtyard through the archway. He was relieved when she didn't ask anything further. They walked on, going east towards the Square Mile. There was a part of him that wanted to tell her everything, end this charade right now. This pretence that it could lead somewhere, that getting to know each other was anything more than a prelude to goodbye. Now, he knew he'd made the wrong decision when she'd come to the church. That was the moment when he should have been stronger. He should have invited her out, then and there. Bought her a few drinks, taken her to bed, let things come to a brief and final conclusion. It would have been so much simpler. But he'd chosen the second option – get to know her, risk letting her get under his skin.

'So now what?' she said, breaking the silence. 'What's next on your Christmas Torture Trail, Dmitri? Selfridges? Hamleys? Oxford Street?'

'No,' Dmitri said. 'I had planned for us to go to lunch. But not in a place like that.' The tight nervousness in his chest eased a little, which allowed in the inevitable sadness. This day would never survive the next stop.

'No?' she said. 'Then where? There's not much around here, is there?' They walked past the church of St Mary le Strand and Kings College, towards the Royal Courts of Justice. Here, there were no crowds of Christmas shoppers, skaters or family theatre-goers. Just a few people waiting at a bus stop.

'No.' He stopped and turned to her. 'There is not much here. And the next stop... well, it's less pleasant than the others.' He forced himself to smile. 'So, if you want to leave, Nicola, I'll release you.' He prayed that she would go; hoped, more than anything, that she would stay. Christ, what a mess.

She gave him a guarded look, and for a second, he thought he could glimpse the workings of her mind, thinking exactly the same as he was.

'Oh, go on then,' Nicola grumbled. 'Where is it?'

'This way.' He pointed to a road that lead down towards the river, and took her hand again. 'It is not far.'

Chapter Eleven

Nicola followed Dmitri down the road towards Temple and the river. What was the mysterious *next stop* that he had planned? If it did involve lunch, her stomach was much too turbid to contemplate food. The skating – her worst nightmare – had turned out to be fun, even if she'd had to cling to Dmitri's arm the entire time. He'd liked that, she thought. And then when they fell together and she landed between his legs, she *knew*. The whole experience had made her feel strangely giddy.

And all that might have been fine. The problem was, that as the day went on, she found herself liking him more and more. He'd clearly had a fascinating life, even if, she suspected, there was a lot he was holding back. When she'd accepted his invitation, she'd been intrigued and in the mood to take a risk. But she didn't want him to leave any impression on her. If it wasn't already too late.

Further down the road, Nicola could smell food and hear the clatter of plates and cutlery, but there was no sign of any restaurant. Then she noticed the abandoned trolleys, piles of cardboard and dirty blankets. Her senses reeled from the smells: sweat, filth, unwashed clothing.

Dmitri stopped in front of an unmarked doorway. 'Here we are.'

'Wait a minute, where are we?' Nicola said.

'Central Connection.'

'What's that?' She frowned.

'A homeless shelter,' he answered matter-of-factly.

'A homeless shelter? You brought me to lunch at a homeless shelter?'

'Yes,' he said. The mischievous smile from earlier was back. 'It is their Christmas lunch. And I've said that you will help with the serving. Of course, if you are hungry, we can eat, also. The food is actually quite good.'

'I'm supposed to *serve lunch*?' She glared at him.

'Penance, Nicola.' He gestured for her to go inside. She stood there for a moment on the threshold. After what he'd told her on the bridge, it really was too late to back out now.

The doorway led to a lower-ground-floor hall. At one end of the room was a small stage with a knackered-looking upright piano in front of it. People were sitting at the long tables – mostly men, but also a few women, and even some children. They were eating from heaping plates of steaming stew with Yorkshire puddings and Brussel sprouts. Above the tables, someone had hung a few strands of foil snowflakes that were engulfed by the giant room.

Nicola felt her stomach roiling from the smell of the food and the churning mixture of pity and distaste she experienced whenever she saw a homeless person even from afar, let alone this close up. It all brought back memories of her dad, his breakdown, and how sick she had felt watching the change in him. If it hadn't been for her – dealing with the bill collectors, begging his boss to give him another chance, pouring bottles of whisky down the sink – he might well have ended up someplace just like this.

Nicola had almost made up her mind to turn around and go out again. But just then, a huge bear of a man with a thick black beard peppered with grey came up to Dmitri.

'Dima!' he bellowed, giving him a hard clap on the back. 'You came.'

'Of course,' Dmitri said. 'You knew I would.'

'And please will you introduce me to your lovely guest?' The big man's smile was open and friendly and his accent was similar to Dmitri's. He was about six-foot six and was wearing a denim shirt, corduroy trousers and Doc Martens. Next to him, Nicola felt very small.

'Nicola, this is Nicolai Sergeivich. An old friend.'

'Oh please,' the man frowned at Dmitri, then smiled back at her, 'call me Kolya. We're all friends here.'

'Hello,' Nicola said. She was a little confused by the names. She'd worked with Russian clients before and vaguely recalled that they had a lot of nicknames and formal patronymic names. If she opened her mouth, she'd probably get it completely wrong.

Dmitri switched to Russian, and the two men spoke with animated gesticulations for almost a minute. Her itch to leave grew stronger.

Dmitri finally stopped talking and Kolya turned to her, returning to English. 'Sorry about that,' he said. 'We were just catching up. May I call you Nicola?'

She nodded and shook the large hand he held out to her.

'It's very nice of you to give your time to us today,' Kolya said. 'As you can see…' he gestured around him, 'we're very busy this time of year.'

'Yes, I see that.'

'Now, if you'll come with me, I'll show you around. Normally, I'd need you to fill out a form before volunteering.

But since you're a friend of Dmitri's...' He turned and began to walk towards the serving window and the kitchen.

Nicola shot Dmitri a glare. 'Are you coming too?' she hissed.

'I'm volunteering in a different way.' He grinned wickedly. 'One that you'll really hate.'

Shaking her head, she stalked off after the giant of a man. He went through a door next to the serving window. Inside, there were two other men in aprons and hairnets, who were cooking and plating up food.

As soon as they were inside the kitchen, Kolya turned to her again.

'How do you know Dmitri?' he said.

It might have been her imagination, but he seemed less friendly now. Maybe he was being protective of his friend, or maybe he didn't like the fact that she was so obviously not happy to be here. Either way, she knew there was no point in trying to bullshit him.

'I made a scene at his carolling concert,' she said, meeting Kolya's gaze unflinchingly. 'I'm "The Heckler".'

For a long second he peered at her, then began to roar with laughter.

'Are you?' he said, when finally he stopped. 'Yes, I can see why you have made an impression on Dmitri.'

'Look, what do you want me to do?' she said, getting annoyed.

Kolya pointed to a rack on the wall. 'There's an apron over there. Put it on and start washing dishes.'

'Fuck,' she growled under her breath. Her eyes locked with his. There was still laughter in them, and he rubbed his beard absently, considering her.

With a sigh, Nicola took off her coat and hung it up. She wished she was wearing a cardigan. Her top really was low-cut and tight. In her peripheral vision, she noticed the other two men eying her. Kolya said a sharp word to them and they went back to serving the food. She put the apron on over her head.

'And are you enjoying your day?' Kolya asked.

'It's been interesting,' she said, not knowing how else to answer. 'Dmitri is…' She didn't have the words to describe the whirlpool of feelings he evoked in her. Or why that was. 'I don't know,' she repeated.

Kolya turned on the taps. The industrial-sized sink filled with water. Nicola winced at the pile of filthy dishes next to it.

'Dmitri is unlike anyone else,' Kolya said. 'He is, as they say, a "one-off".'

Nicola nodded. She took the first dish and put it into the soapy water, scrubbing it with a scouring pad. Now that she was here, she might as well get stuck in.

'Did he come here for help?' she asked. 'Is that how you met?'

'When he came here with his mother and sister, many years ago now, they were very naïve. This is not uncommon, I'm afraid.'

'He seems to have done OK. Is that thanks to you?'

Kolya shrugged. 'It is mostly down to the person he is. Hardworking, focused and passionate. And he has a genuine love for people. That always helps.' He picked up a towel and began to dry the clean dishes.

Nicola ignored this last remark as she scrubbed at a grease-caked pan. 'So do you run this place?' she said, changing the subject. 'How is it funded?'

'It is funded by the council, but there are also private donations, especially this time of year. I am a psychologist and a counsellor. I work here, and at the teen centre, and also at a woman's shelter for domestic violence.'

'God,' Nicola said. She was genuinely impressed by this man and his commitment, if still a little repulsed by the place, and guilty for feeling that way. 'That sounds depressing.'

Kolya gave her a fatherly smile. 'Everyone has a story, Nicola. Sometimes it is a sad one. People come here for a hot meal, a cup of tea, a shower, a chat. Sometimes, just to get away from real life for an hour or two. I do what I can, but often, it is not very much.'

Nicola nodded uneasily. She remembered how hard she'd tried to chivvy her dad to get on with his life, turn things around. Get help, whatever it took. But once he had given up, there was nothing she could do. She'd felt powerless, and if there was one thing she hated, it was that feeling.

'And Dmitri? He helps out here?'

'Saint Dmitri, the patron saint of waifs and strays.' Kolya chuckled. 'Dmitri makes a lot of friends, all around the city. To him, everyone is a human being – someone who deserves a chance. Sometimes, I think I need a separate line item in my budget for the people he finds who end up here.'

Nicola frowned. The water was cooling down and getting slimy. 'So he's, you know, a good person?'

Kolya raised a bushy black eyebrow. 'Dmitri is as decent a person as you will ever meet. Though you are not his normal kind of waif or stray.' He frowned. 'Tell me again how you came to be here?'

'I went to the church. To apologise. Dmitri was playing the piano – Rachmaninov. We got to talking.'

'You heard Dmitri play piano?' Kolya said. He looked at her more closely now, his eyes narrow. 'When was this?'

'Last night. Why—?'

Her train of thought was interrupted. From the other side of the serving window, she heard a smattering of applause and then Dmitri's voice. 'Thank you for allowing me to join you at your Christmas lunch. Now, please can the children make their way forward to the stage? And for the adults, if you would like to join in, please feel free.'

There was a clamber of feet.

'We shall start with song number one. Page one of your books.'

A moment later there was a flourish on the piano. Then, the sound of children's voices:

Jingle bells, jingle bells
Jingle all the way
Oh what fun it is to ride
In a one-horse open sleigh, hey!
Jingle bells, jingle bells
Jingle all the way
Oh what fun it is to ride
In a one-horse open sleigh.

Nicola cringed. Not at the sound – which was joyous and lively, underscored by Dmitri's rich baritone, and a few adult voices joining in – but at her own behaviour. Her behaviour that night at the station, at work, to the world in general. She didn't belong here in this place; she hadn't earned the right to be working alongside people who were helping others. Her heart had been locked up for years, the sign firmly turned to closed. Dmitri might be a decent person. But Nicola knew, deep down in her soul, that *she* was not.

She continued washing dishes, with Kolya drying. A silent wave of anger flooded through her: anger at herself, anger at the situation these people were in. When finally, the last dish was washed, he directed her to pass out plates of pudding and handed her a hairnet. She pursed her lips as the large man looked at her closely.

'Are you all right?' he said.

'Yes. Of course.' Nicola put on the hairnet, grabbed two plates of puddings and stalked off through the door. She banged them down on the table in front of the first two people.

Most of the adults had now joined in the singing. The children looked happy and excited. Dmitri directed the carolling from the piano, playing again without music. He was clearly in his element. Music... making people happy. Spreading joy and cheer. Well, good for him.

'Jingle Bells' ended. Dmitri launched the makeshift choir into more songs: 'Hark the Herald Angels Sing', 'Santa Claus is Coming to Town', 'Rudolph the Red-Nosed Reindeer'.

Nicola served the puddings table by table. A few times she saw Kolya watching her, concern evident on his face.

When all the plates had been served, Dmitri announced the last song. 'Silent Night'.

'We are very lucky that today, Francesca will be singing the first verse for us,' he said. He gestured to a woman sitting near the front to come up and join him. Her hair was dark and lank, and she had a pale, almost otherworldly face. She looked at Dmitri and smiled shyly, her eyes locked on his as if they were the only two people in the room...

Nicola felt suddenly light-headed. Dmitri smiled back at Francesca. Then he nodded his head to cue the beginning of the song and played the introduction on the piano. Francesca began to sing, her pure, sweet voice rising up like an angel's. She was singing the song in a foreign language – Italian or Spanish, Nicola thought. Jealousy oozed inside of her. This woman might be down-and-out, but she was young, beautiful and obviously brimming with talent. How she'd come to be here, Nicola could only guess. The crowd stood spellbound, Dmitri never took his eyes off the woman, and even Kolya, who, since she'd arrived, had barely paused in his work of managing the kitchen workers, stood still to listen.

When the verse was finished, Dmitri cued in the others. Everyone sang at the top of their lungs. The sound was deafening, and Nicola felt dizzy, like she might faint. In the back pocket of her jeans, her mobile buzzed with a text message. She'd kept it off for most of the day, which seemed the polite thing to do. Although she'd turned it on to take the photo at the ice rink, she hadn't checked her messages once today. Now, by force of habit, she fished it out. There were thirty-six new emails that she didn't read, and several new texts that she did:

At Snow White Panto today with the kids. You OK? Ox

The next one, sent twenty minutes later, read:

Thinking of all the ways I want to fuck you right now. Ox

Nicola's hand trembled as she turned off the phone. Staggering to the door, she went up the steps to street level. She took the phone and hurled it as hard as she could out into the street. It skittered across the pavement and under a car parked on the other side.

She collapsed against the cold stone building, shivering in the cold, and gasping for air.

How long she was there, she had no idea. Time and space seemed to be reeling around her. All those people – lost, tragic. So happy at the little glimmer of hope that had been added to their lives by this strange, infuriating man. In the end, it was she who felt dirty, disgusting. Her life, Ollie… everything such a goddamn mess—

'Nicola!' Dmitri's voice sounded frantic and out of breath as he bounded up the steps. 'Nicola?'

As he came up to her, she was aware of his warmth, the sweat on his forehead, and, though there was half a metre separating them, his beating heart. His face was a mixture of concern and relief, his eyes had a wild spark to them, as they had when he'd been playing piano at the church. She felt an electric charge as he reached a hand up to her face, but then realised that he was just removing the hairnet that she hadn't taken off.

'I thought you'd gone,' he said. 'You forgot your coat. Let's go inside. You'll freeze out here.'

'I'm sorry,' she said, fighting back a ridiculous onslaught of tears. 'It was all just a little much. Hearing Francesca singing and all. She seems a lovely woman. I'll get my things and go. I can look after myself.'

'Francesca?' He stared at her for a moment seeming genuinely puzzled. Nicola looked away.

'I am sorry,' he said finally. 'Sorry that I brought you here. But I'd promised to come for the lunch. The children love the carolling. I know that it is difficult to see these people—'

'No, that's not it.' Nicola cut him off. 'It was nice. Lovely. I just felt – I don't know.' Her eyes flooded with tears. 'I'm just... a really bad person, that's all.'

'Oh Nicola, please!' he reached up and cupped her chin in his hands with his long, elegant fingers. Her body reacted to his touch before her mind could. She closed her eyes. But as she did so, his hands fell away, as if they'd been repulsed by a magnet. 'I do not think you are a bad person,' he said in a low voice.

'But you don't know me, do you!' she practically spat. 'Kolya called you Saint Dmitri. He says you're the most decent person he's ever met. I'm not a decent person. All I do, day in and day out, is work, and...'

He tried to reach out to her, but she pulled away. She dashed across the road and knelt down, retrieving her phone from beneath the parked car. The glass screen protector had smashed, but otherwise, it was in perfect working order. She pulled up Ollie's latest message – hell, all of his recent messages, descriptive and filthy – were there on the screen.

She was aware of Dmitri coming silently up to her side. Nicola thrust the phone in his face. 'This is who I am. This is the woman you're wasting your day on. A day in your life that you'll never get back.'

Nicola forced herself to look at him as he read the screen. His face was her penance, she thought, waiting for the look of judgement, surprise, disgust that she expected – that she deserved – to see. But she couldn't read any of those things there.

Dmitri handed the phone back to her. 'You are in love with this man?' he asked. His calm control never wavered, but something flickered across his face. His eyes became guarded.

'No.' She shook her head. 'No, I never really loved him, that's what's so sad. He's married, has a family. That made it easier, somehow. Knowing that there was no future. But now, I just want him to go away, leave me alone. I despise him – what he's done, what I've done. All that wasted time.' She swallowed hard. 'That night at the station, he'd cancelled on me. That's the real reason why I was so upset. It was the last straw... and it hurt.'

He nodded, a wistful smile crossing his face. 'I thought it might be something like that. And I think I understand.'

'No – you don't.' She was getting angry again. 'I don't know what your deal is, but at least you have your music. You have... these people.' She gestured towards the door of the shelter.

'Yes, I do have all those things. And I am grateful for them.' Looking towards the river, he flexed and stretched the fingers on his right hand absently, as if they'd suddenly grown stiff. His hands... She frowned. He saw her looking down and shoved them in his pockets. 'But once, a long time ago, I was engaged to someone.' He sighed. 'It didn't work out – for many reasons – but I know those feelings. What it's like to be in love. What it feels like when it ends.'

'God.' She hung her head. 'And here I am dredging it up for you. First I turn up at the station and ruin your carolling, and now I'm moaning on about nothing, when really, it's you who've—' She broke off. The look he was giving her was so opposite to all her feelings, it was the devilishly goofy look. The one that made her want to—

He started laughing first, but she wasn't far behind. There

was nothing funny – nothing at all. And yet, once she started, she was breathless with it. Silly, out of control. But for a brief moment, all her problems seemed so insignificant, insubstantial – like a shower of snow falling from a tree branch. Her side ached. She finally caught her breath. He too recovered.

'Sorry,' she said. 'It's really not—' She fell into another fit of laughter.

He was looking at her, his eyes warm, but unreadable. Eventually, when she came back to her senses, she realised that she was shivering with the cold.

'Come back inside and warm up a little,' he said, directing her back towards the shelter. At the top of the steps, he turned back to her. 'I think this day has been... unexpected, for both of us,' he said. 'And life is complicated – who knows what it will bring? But right now, on this day that I will never get back again, I had one more thing planned.' He smiled reassuringly. 'I know I have annoyed you, angered you even. You have done your penance. But if you would like to accompany me, it will be fun, I think. And it's on the way back to the station.'

Chapter Twelve

One more thing. What was it? Of course, he wasn't saying. Nicola went back down into the shelter with Dmitri, planning to retrieve her coat and say goodbye to Kolya.

But when she returned to the large hall, most people had finished eating the puddings and there were dirty dishes everywhere. 'This won't do,' Nicola said, giving Dmitri a look. She went to the nearest table and picked up some of the dirty dishes, taking them to the serving window. Went back for more.

'You don't have to do that,' he said, giving her a bemused smile.

'Yes, I do,' she said breezily. 'I agreed to wash dishes.'

Dmitri set down his bag, took off his jacket, and began to help her. This was foolish, she realised, but now she felt like she definitely had something to prove. Besides, she was never one to leave a task unfinished.

Nicola left Dmitri to clear (he was slower than she was because he continually stopped to chat with people). She marched back into the kitchen where Kolya and the other two men were putting away the excess food and a big sink of soapy water had already been run.

'Sorry,' she said to the big man. He appraised her for a second, and then nodded. Kolya had definitely got the measure of her, she thought. Washing and scrubbing a million dishes would not change anything. Still, she got on with it.

In the end, there was so much to do that she lost track of time. Tidying up the hall and the kitchen, putting everything back in its place. Twice Dmitri asked her if she wanted to leave, but there was too much to do. Finally, though, she took off the apron and he helped her into her coat. They said their goodbyes to Kolya (she shook hands, her skin wrinkled and waterlogged; Dmitri had another long exchange with him in Russian). And then it was time to go.

When they went back up to street level, Nicola was surprised to see that it was almost dark. The sky was a deep twilit blue, and the temperature had dropped a few degrees. Working at the shelter, she'd been too busy to think: about what came before and about what happened next.

Now, though, her mind began to race. Those texts – why had she shown him those texts? Been so intent on pushing him away? Bursting out laughing when he'd opened up to her, trying to empathise with her pain. He was silent beside her as they walked back in the direction they'd come. She was struck by how, despite her best unconscious efforts to ruin it, this day had been anything but penance – for her, anyway. But what was it for him? For all the hours they had spent together, she still had no idea.

Dmitri turned to her. 'Thanks for—'

'What was her name?' she said, cutting him off.

'Her?' he looked puzzled.

'Your fiancée.'

For a moment, he paused, not looking at her. 'Irina,' he

said. He gave a heavy sigh. 'Like I said, it was a long time ago. We were both very young.'

'I'm sorry I laughed earlier,' she said. 'Sorry about everything really. I've been rude and out of line.'

'There is no need to be sorry,' he said gently. 'And sometimes, it is good to laugh. Maybe...' he hesitated, 'it is something that I should have done a long time ago.'

'Maybe.' Nicola considered this.

They had reached Waterloo Bridge. For the first time since leaving the shelter, he took her hand as they crossed the busy road, like a child that he wanted to see safely across. Cars and buses whizzed past them, but all Nicola was aware of was the warmth of his fingers curling against hers, and the rougher fabric of his grey gloves. In the middle of the bridge, he stopped walking.

'Look,' he said, indicating the view. 'It's so beautiful!'

'Yes,' she agreed.

The city had come to life in a riot of lights. The brutalist concrete architecture of the South Bank Centre was lit up in a changing cycle of red, blue, and green. The London Eye, the high-rise buildings, even the cranes towering in the distance were lit up with coloured lights. A bank of clouds was closing in from the south, but in the velvet blue sky over the Victoria Embankment and the Houses of Parliament, a huge full moon had risen. Nicola stared down at the gentle silver light reflected in the ever-changing water of the river. She was spellbound by the beauty of the night, and just for a moment, allowed herself to enjoy these strange new feelings evoked by the man standing beside her. So much of her life was spent grappling, wrestling; everything always seemed like such a struggle. But what if it didn't have to be that way?

'What if it didn't have to be that way?'

Nicola was only aware that she'd spoken aloud when he squeezed her hand, holding it almost tight enough that it hurt.

She was so aware of him, his strength, his vitality – his vulnerability. He glanced at her and she smiled. What if all the years of hating herself, punishing herself had finally been enough? If instead of being trapped, she opened herself up to the possibilities that life might have to offer. What if it really was that easy?

'Come,' he said, his voice low and throaty. 'We should be on our way.'

What if it didn't have to be that way?

Her words – he didn't know the context she meant, but nonetheless, he understood. And in that moment, standing next to her on the bridge, they had seemed more true than anything else in the world. In that instant, he'd begun to question everything – all the choices, the reasons. He'd looked at her, seen something shining in her eyes that was more than just a trick of the light. And then he'd felt such a powerful rush of desire... It brought him to his senses and he let go of her hand.

They walked along the South Bank in the direction they'd come. The trees were lit up with strings of blue and white lights, and across the river, all of Central London seemed to be alive, electric, with colour. They passed families, couples, teenagers on skateboards, the stallholders selling second-hand books in front of the BFI. The moon was a perfect disk of rock and shadows. It seemed to follow them, though the clouds were closing in quickly now from all directions. The same moon that had been in the sky *that night*... The thought pushed the last of the possibilities from his mind.

They reached the stalls of the Christmas Market again. The little huts were lit up along the edges of their peaked roofs, and seemed to be huddled against the darkness and deepening chill. 'Are you hungry?' Dmitri said, as they walked. 'I should have taken you for a proper meal.'

'It's fine,' Nicola said. For a second, she looked almost shy. 'Maybe we can get something after... wherever we're going?' she suggested.

'Maybe.' His mind flashed with the signs of danger. 'How about a coffee now?'

'OK.'

He stopped at one of the stalls and bought them each a coffee. But instead of lingering, as they'd done earlier, this time he made sure they drank it as they walked. They passed the carousel – Dmitri felt a sharp pang of regret, remembering every moment of this extraordinary day. The carousel had been the beginning. Now, though, they were reaching the end.

The stalls of the Christmas Market thinned out as they walked through Jubilee Gardens towards County Hall. Dmitri stopped walking at the entrance to the London Eye.

'Here we are,' he said. Like every stop they'd made, he felt nervous. Worrying that somehow, he would let her down. This day had been more about penance for him than her, he realised. At least, he hoped that was the case. 'Maybe you've been before,' he said. 'But I never have.'

'No,' Nicola said, glancing at the queue. 'I haven't.'

Nicola looked up at the vast Ferris wheel that had been built for the millennium and had since become an integral part of the London skyline. White steel girders criss-crossed over each other to form the rim of the wheel, which was supported by high-tension cables. The whole thing resembled a giant bicycle wheel. The glass-walled capsules moved around slowly. From a distance, they seemed hardly to move at all. But at the front of the queue, where the loading and unloading occurred, Nicola could see that the wheel was constantly in motion. Near the entrance, a board was carved with the Wordsworth poem 'Composed Upon Westminster Bridge' in which the poet wrote of the view: *Dull would he be of soul who could pass by a sight so touching in its majesty.*

Maybe that was true. In the past she'd always dismissed the London Eye as something kitschy for the tourists. But now, with Dmitri, everything seemed different – unexpected. Things she had seen so many times before were suddenly brand new. He'd said it might be fun, and maybe it would be. More than that, though, she didn't want this day to be over just yet.

She found a bin and threw away their empty coffee cups. As before, Dmitri found his way to the front of the queue and had a discussion with several of the operators. Nicola had no idea what he said or how he did it. But she wasn't surprised when, a few minutes later, she was ushered to the front of the queue. It did surprise her, though, when the operator indicated for her and Dmitri to go into an empty pod by themselves. The door shut automatically.

They were alone.

Without any warning whatsoever, the breath constricted in her chest. A suffocating sense of panic took over her. *A snowy night, footsteps... a hand on her arm... ice...*

She went to the edge of the pod. Her hands were clammy as she gripped the railing, looking up at the ceiling until she spotted the CCTV camera. It wouldn't protect her, but it would be evidence...

Evidence of what? She forced herself to exhale, feeling her lungs ease into their regular rhythm. This man and this day had thrown her off balance, no mistake. But everything was fine. Dmitri came to the railing. When he looked at her, she saw the concern on his face.

'Are you OK?' he said.

'Yes, fine. A bit claustrophobic – that's all.' She managed a little laugh. 'What are you, anyway, Dmitri?' she said, deflecting the conversation. 'Russian mafia? How did you manage all this at such short notice? Or at all?'

His cocky smile set her at ease. 'Maybe it is just the magic power of Christmas,' he said.

'Yeah, right.'

Nicola moved a few paces closer to where he was standing. The pod slowly rose into the sky, metre by metre. The floor to ceiling glass made it seem like they were floating in the air. It was a little disconcerting, but fascinating too – a perspective she hadn't seen before.

'In a way, though, that's what it is,' Dmitri said. 'The choir opens many doors. We have sung at the London Eye. We have sung at Somerset House. At the Christmas Market. Even at Hamleys and Oxford Street and Covent Garden – though I decided to spare you those places.'

'Thank you,' she said.

His smile faded. 'Was it so awful for you? Listening to the carolling, helping out at the shelter?'

'No,' she said, truthfully. 'I was just surprised, that's all. The place wasn't at all what I expected. It felt good to be busy doing something worthwhile for a change. And I enjoyed meeting your friend.'

'Kolya, yes.' He nodded. 'Kolya is a very good person.'

'Which is exactly what he said about you.'

'Hmm,' he said absently.

She glanced over at him. Dmitri seemed pensive now – had been for most of the walk here. Standing on Waterloo Bridge, he'd understood what she was feeling; the strong resonance between them was more than just her imagination. But he had broken the moment. Now, she had even less idea of what – if anything – this was leading up to. Especially now that they were alone.

The view was captivating as they rose higher. On the other side of the river, the Houses of Parliament, Big Ben, and Charing Cross Station were illuminated. Beyond, the lights of central London sparkled like stars. The moon, though, was no longer visible. Thick clouds had set in all around them, and the sky had turned a strange purplish brown colour.

'It's going to snow,' Dmitri said staring outwards. 'I recognise the colour of the sky.'

Almost as soon as he had predicted it, the snow began to fall. A few flakes at first, swirling in the air, cascading downward to the dark river below. The lights on the opposite bank grew hazy and distant. Snow. Nicola breathed deeply. Once, a long time ago, she'd loved the snow…

As more and more snowflakes began to billow around them in a flurry, Dmitri's face took on a wistful, otherworldly expression. His hands were resting on the railing, the grey woollen half-gloves now dirty after a day about the city. Those fingers had seduced her without ever having touched her. The moment she'd walked into the church and heard the music. Even from a distance, she could almost feel the wild energy inside of him, coursing, seeking an outlet. But now, as she looked at them, she frowned. One of the edges of the grey knit had curved upwards slightly as if a thread was loose and it was beginning to fray. He'd taken her hand today, in a casual, friendly manner. His hands were almost always moving, she realised. Now, though, they were still.

'Your hands,' she said, before she could change her mind, convince herself that it was rude to ask. She took a step closer to him. 'They're injured? That's why you wear those gloves?'

Instantly, he removed his hands from the railing and clenched one inside the other in what seemed like an automatic, evasive gesture.

'Yes,' he said, still staring out at the view. 'It happened a long time ago. Stupid, really. I was trying to cook and a pan caught fire.' He gave her a quick sideways glance. 'I have always been a terrible cook. I find that takeaway is much safer.' He laughed, but it was too quick, too bright.

She forced a smile, but her throat had constricted. For much of the day his manner had been playful and carefree. But the music she'd heard him playing in the church... so dark, such unfathomable depths of emotion. The music held the truth, she realised. Those long, slender fingers. A pianist with injured hands.

'But you can still play piano – obviously.'

'I can still play. As I say, the injury was silly, superficial. Here...' He unclenched his fist and pulled down the left glove. The skin was twisted and mottled by a burn scar that began at his knuckles and ran across the top of his thumb to the underside of his wrist. Her breath caught, but she tried not to react. He pulled the glove back in place. 'There,' he said. 'Now you know all my secrets.' The amused, mocking tone was back, but the light was gone from his eyes.

She laughed – she felt she had too. He was putting on an act for her benefit. She recognised that because she was so used to doing it herself. Projecting an image – confident, self-assured – and, above all, in control. She didn't feel in control now.

'When I heard you playing at the church,' she said, choosing her words, 'the music seemed so raw, so powerful. I mean, I'm not musical. I like music as much as the next person, but I don't know anything about it. But something about your playing... it affected me.'

'Is that why you came today?' he asked in a low voice. She half-expected him to take her hand, bridge the gap between them. But, if anything, he seemed more distant than ever.

'I don't know.'

He was silent for another long moment. 'You have spent a day with me, Nicola. A day in your life that you won't get back.' He shrugged. 'I'll tell you about the piano, if you really want to know.'

She nodded, suddenly not sure at all whether she did want to hear.

He left the railing and paced back and forth in the pod, as if debating where to begin. Finally, he spoke.

'I was nine when the Soviet Union collapsed,' he said. 'My father lost his job, and for us ordinary people, things became much more uncertain.' He looked at her and she nodded. 'But even before that I was the great white hope. I went to a special music school from the age of six. I can't remember a time when I didn't play the piano. In school we learned from a rigid syllabus, but I also listened to music on the state radio stations. Whatever piece I would hear, I would work out how to play. It was easy for me.' He glanced wistfully at his gloved hands. 'The notes just made sense to my fingers.'

Nicola watched him. He stopped again at the railing and stared out at the dense, swirling whiteness of the sky – it was like he was seeing a different landscape entirely.

'I began performing at age eight,' he continued. 'By eleven, I was doing recitals and concerts at the auditorium in the city.'

'You were a prodigy,' she said.

'Maybe.' He frowned. 'In those days, there was only one goal – to get a place at the Moscow Conservatory. And when the letter came saying that I'd been accepted, it was the proudest moment for my parents.'

'It sounds like an amazing achievement,' she said, with true admiration.

'Yes.' He didn't look at her. 'My father did everything he could so that I could go. I don't know how he raised the money – friends, favours. Somehow, he managed it. Everyone was so proud. I went to Moscow. I arrived there just after my seventeenth birthday. I had never been away from home before. It was such a different world, all so new.'

'It must have been a lot of pressure,' she said.

'I suppose,' he acknowledged. 'And it was extremely competitive. We all had to meet certain standards to keep our place. To take class and hear the others play was a very humbling experience. It was even competitive to get a practice room – a freezing room in the basement. At exam time there would be a queue from five or six in the morning. And, believe me, Nicola, I am not a morning person.' He gave a little laugh. 'There was pressure, but it was exciting too.'

She smiled guardedly as he continued on.

'My first year, I did quite well. Though they did not tell you these things, in order to keep down your ego, I knew that I had much potential.' She was aware of his hands, tightening their grip on the railing. 'Then I came back for my second year. By then I had become friends with some of the older students. Sasha was in his final year. He made me his "project", you could say. I was stupid, naïve, and arrogant, but most of all, I was poor. The city was so expensive, and there were days when some of us did not eat. But someone always had vodka and cigarettes.

'Sasha knew where to meet the American tourists. We showed them around, translated the signs, practised our English. We took them to see the sights and also out to the clubs. They paid for everything.'

He sighed. 'There were many late nights. I remember doing everything but practice the piano. Exams were approaching, but I was still doing OK. I thought I could – you know? – "wing it"? In the end, though, I missed the exam. I slept right through it.'

He shook his head. Nicola could almost feel the waves of anguish coming from him. Slowly, instinctively, she moved closer. She reached out and put her hand on top of his. His fingers twitched, but he didn't pull away.

'In early January, before Christmas, I went home to my

family,' he continued. 'I was desperate to keep what had happened from my father. That I had lost my place. There were no second chances, and I would not be going back. That all of his sacrifices – all his trust in me – had been for nothing. But, of course, he had to find out. He was already in a bad way, drinking too much... and only the thought of me—' He seemed to choke on the words.

Keeping silent, she squeezed his hand.

'My mother tried to come up with a plan. I would take some time out, and then apply to the local conservatory, which was also excellent. Start again. Everything would be fine. But it was not fine.' He shook his head. 'My father became... well – it was very frightening. My mother was caught in the middle.'

He removed his hand from hers and raked back his hair. Nicola felt bile rising up into her throat. She'd suspected at the onset that this story couldn't have a happy ending. But she hadn't been expecting this.

'My mother began to make arrangements for us to get away. She had a friend who had managed to come to the west. Knew a person who knew a person – that sort of thing. She applied for us to get tourist visas. But by the time they arrived, my father was dead. A hunting accident in the woods – that was the official verdict. My mother decided that we would leave anyway. By then there was nothing left.'

Nicola opened her mouth to speak, but no words came out.

'So, you see, Nicola, I am not worthy of the name my friend has given me. Saint Dmitri. I am just a man who threw away his life and ruined his family.'

His cheek glistened as a tear rolled down it. She felt desperate to say something – do something – to make it better. She lifted her hand, traced the line of the tear with her finger.

'I'm sorry,' she said. The words sounded so hollow and futile.

'Thank you.' He put his hand up briefly and brought hers back down to the railing and let it go. 'But really, there is no need to be sorry. That was all a long time ago.' He smiled, and she wondered what it cost him to do so. 'Now, I have a good life. I may be conducting a choir who sing Christmas carols in a station, but for that, I am very grateful.'

'You say that. But are you really?' The words came out sharper than she'd intended.

He looked surprised, then gave a little laugh. 'Well, OK – sometimes I do think about what might have been. But, for many years now, I have barely even played the piano, except for giving voice lessons.'

'But why?' Nicola felt a stab of anger at hearing this. 'I mean, I understand why you feel like you do. But how is your not playing making things better?'

Dmitri shrugged. 'I suppose I couldn't play piano because I needed to put everything behind me. What happened with my father, and the difficulties when we came here. The music was gone – I had left it behind. I no longer had the urge to play. I couldn't play.'

'But it's not gone,' she said, challenging him. 'Is it?'

'That is what I have been trying to find out. Lately, I've been trying – dabbling, playing scales, exercises, things like that. Late at night at the church, where no one can hear me.' He met her eyes, looking a little embarrassed. 'I have been trying to push past how difficult it is. Turning the key in the lock – is the music gone, or is it still somewhere inside? Like the Rachmaninov.'

'What else do you play?' she asked. Whatever this day had or hadn't been, she knew that on some level these last few minutes were the most important. That she had to keep him talking.

'Chopin, Beethoven, Liszt. And the Russians: Rachmaninov, Mussorgsky, and my namesake, Dmitri Shostakovich.' He smiled. 'Those were the composers I liked in my youth. Beautiful, complex... dark.' He turned to look at her then, his eyelids half lowered. She felt a tremor travel down her body, sensing that he was no longer talking about the music...

'It has been an interesting experiment,' he said, once again breaking the tension. 'But now, with my sister getting married, I too need to focus on what comes next.' His face hardened. 'I have a chance to apply for a job in Oxford. It's a bursary, and some teaching, and I would work towards my doctorate in choral music.'

'Choral Music? Is that what you really want?' Nicola felt a frown deepening in her forehead. 'Why don't you just play piano?'

His eyes met hers again, and in that brief second before he looked away, she saw the truth. The impossible sadness underneath the joy and good cheer he tried to spread through the choir and the Christmas music. Doing good works, trying to atone for some sin, real or imagined.

'It is nice that you believe it might be possible,' he said. 'But that's not the way it works. My dream of being a concert pianist ended long ago. I am very lucky that I can make a living, though a small one, by your standards, doing what I love. In Oxford – who knows? I might have some occasion to perform. I think I would like that.'

'Oxford,' she mused. The wind was gone from her sails. Undoubtedly, he knew much more than she did about such things. And he was the kind of person – intelligent, talented, a bit naïve – who would probably fit in well at a place like Oxford. Still, to her it seemed a waste.

'I still need to fill in the application,' he said. 'And get letters of reference. It is by no means a given.'

He fell silent, seeming very distant now. Nicola was sorry

that she'd upset him. Sorry that she'd let the whole thing get under her skin, which had never been her intent. He'd obviously suffered so much already, and here she was, making things worse.

'And what of you?' he said finally. She recognised his bright attempt to change the subject. 'Are you happy in your job? It all sounds very glamorous.'

'No.' The word came out even before she could decide if she wanted to lie. Compared with his story, hers seemed so grubby and entitled – so insignificant. 'I mean, yes and no. I do well under pressure, and I like the adrenalin rush. But financing luxury brands isn't exactly saving the world, is it? And then there was...' she trailed off.

'Ollie?' He finished the sentence for her.

Nicola let out a long sigh. She deserved this, she supposed, after grilling him. 'We work together. Then we were lovers.'

'And now?'

'Now?' She considered. 'It's over. It's been over for a long time – whatever "it" even was. But still, it's painful. Having to see him every day.' She shrugged. 'In the New Year I might have a look around for something else. Another fund or a bank, I don't know.'

'But is that what you really want?' he asked, a hint of the former laughter back in his eyes. 'You asked me, after all.'

'I don't know!' Nicola felt suddenly overwhelmed by the situation, the question, and the change in the course of the day. 'How pathetic does that sound?' She shook her head. Her dreams, whatever they'd been, had long ago been taken from her – just like his had. She knew the exact moment it had happened – when the course of her life had changed forever. And the decision she'd made that had turned her life into a lie even to this day. Dmitri had told her so much. Opened up to her, shared his secrets. That was the difference between them. He was turning the key in the lock, trying to see what was inside, whereas she never wanted to go near that door that she so carefully kept locked. She *knew* what was there. 'I just want to be happy,' Nicola said at last. 'But I find it difficult.'

'Yes,' he said.

There was so much unspoken in that single word. She felt the intensity of his dark eyes on her, so deep and full of turmoil. The pod continued its slow descent, the snow flurry dwindling. Her heart began to race. Now was the moment for him to move in. Bridge the distance between them. Her heart sped up as adrenalin warmed her body. For a second she closed her eyes, waiting. She heard the step, felt the world grind to a halt, then... nothing.

Nicola opened her eyes, feeling idiotic. Dmitri had moved away from her to the other side of the pod. She realised then that they'd reached the unloading area and the door had opened.

'Nicola?' he said softly. 'Time to go.'

'OK,' she said.

She stepped down out of the pod, feeling an overwhelming sense of loss. The pod moved on; the cocoon where only the two of them had existed. Her questions, his story... time had raced on. He'd told her that this was the last thing he'd had planned. Is this how the day was destined to end?

Outside the pod, Dmitri had another long conversation with the operator. Nicola managed to smile at the man, say 'thank you'. As she walked beside Dmitri back to Waterloo Station, neither of them spoke, and he made no move to take her hand. The snow was now mixed with rain, and the pavements were slick and shiny. They mounted the steps to the main station, crowded with people on their way for a night out in London. She had no idea what he was thinking. Was he regretting opening up to her? Feeling the same turmoil inside that she did? If she hadn't asked, or he hadn't obliged by telling her about his past, everything now would be so much easier.

At the entrance to the underground, Dmitri inclined his head, speaking in a low voice. 'Thank you for a most delightful day, Nicola.' He took her hand and held it to his lips. 'I wish...' he faltered, unable to meet her eyes.

'Dmitri,' she said, putting a finger to his lips. 'It's me who's grateful.' And before she could talk herself out of it, she laced her arms around his neck. She moved against him, feeling his strength and warmth. There was surprise in his eyes as her lips brushed his. Surprise and then, in an instant, his mouth came on hers with a raw, unstoppable force and need so deep that it almost frightened her. His fingers tangled in her hair, as she drank him in, long and deep, feeling heat glittering through her body, and into his. His tongue sought and twined with hers. It lasted a moment, or maybe longer. She lost track of all time or place. All she knew was that she didn't want it to end...

The pressure on her arms was a gentle push at first, and then firmer with intent. His mouth broke from hers.

'No,' he said, breathlessly stepping back. He held up his hands as a shield. 'No, Nicola. No.' He gave her a nervous half-smile and took another step back. 'Goodbye,' he said.

He turned and walked off, losing himself in the crowd that was making its way down the escalator to the Tube. She was left standing there alone.

- iii -

'After travelling for days, the grey wolf took Ivan to a small village. The moon was bright in the sky as Ivan climbed off the wolf's back and knocked on the door of a cottage. The door was answered by an old woman and an old man. They both looked very sad. They invited Ivan inside for food and refreshment. He warmed himself by the glowing hearth and listened to their story. Childless until their later years, they had been blessed with a beautiful daughter made of ice and snow. Her name was Snegurochka. They loved her more than the fruit of summer, the first snows of winter, the wild flowers of spring.

"Where is she?" Ivan asked.

"Gone," said the old woman. "For she fell in love with a shepherd boy who played to her on his pipe."

And what of it?" Ivan asked.

"Her heart was made of snow and ice. As it kindled with love, she melted into a puff of snow."

"Then I am sorry for you," Ivan said.

"Remember our Snegurochka," the old man said as Ivan thanked them for their kindness and climbed on to the wolf's back. "And if you can, choose a heart of fire over one made of ice."'

– 'The Firebird', *The Anthology of Russian Tales*

Chapter Thirteen

Shame burned a hole in Nicola's stomach as she watched Dmitri disappear into the crowd. She had got this spectacularly wrong. Swallowing back tears, she walked further into the station and looked up at the boards. This time, there was no choir, and no delays.

The train wasn't due for twenty minutes. She went into M&S Food and bought a bag of salad, a carton of tomatoes and two bottles of red wine. Trying to push the day – the magical, unreal day – from her mind and focus instead on the evening ahead. She'd have a bath, eat dinner, catch up on work. Then she'd do a few internet searches, maybe browse some dating sites. Try to figure out what the hell she was going to do with the rest of her weekend. The rest of her life.

The platform number came up, and Nicola went through the barrier. Though she wasn't cold, she couldn't stop shivering. It wasn't the rejection – OK, not *just* the rejection – and in hindsight, she might well have brought that upon herself. Showing him those texts, acting rude and ungrateful, laughing... God. Then, she'd really set in: bullying him over the piano, picking at the scab of what was obviously a deep and painful wound. And then there was the mysterious Irina, the woman who had once captured his heart. In her mind she pictured a tall, blonde, Russian ice queen. '*It didn't work out,*' he'd said. What did that mean exactly? Was he still in love with her?

She'd never know, and it didn't matter anyway. Nicola boarded the train, slumping down in an aisle seat. Saint Dmitri, a man who had suffered great tragedy and loss in his life. A man who still found it in him to spread warmth and joy to others. He'd had no ulterior motive, she realised that now. For all his wit and charm – and the occasional flash of desire in the abstract – she was just one more person that he collected on his travels. Another waif and stray. His goal had been to shine light into the life of a person who lived a dull, grey existence. *Her.* That was all it had ever been.

How wrong she had been to build it up in her mind as a beginning, rather than an ending. To believe in those feelings she'd had on the bridge, when everything had seemed so clear; her life shimmering with possibilities like moonlight on water. And now, she was paying the price. This was what came with breaking the cardinal rule – no confidences, no emotion, just sex.

Except, there was the kiss... A warm flush softened her body. She hadn't imagined that. The deep, unsatisfied hunger. He'd wanted her, with a desire so complete and focused that it was beyond her experience. And then, he'd walked away.

'Stop it,' Nicola murmured aloud. It didn't matter. Not in the slightest. She was going to forget all about Dmitri, forget about the time they'd spent together. What she had to do now was survive the holiday season and start focusing on the future, a 'new start'. Find a new job; maybe even quit finance entirely. Find something more worthwhile in her life.

But right now, she hadn't even the slightest idea where to look.

Dmitri lost himself in the crowd. He could still feel Nicola's eyes burning into his back: hurt, rejected. He wanted nothing more than to rush back, take her in his arms, and lose himself in her. Satisfy that deep need that had been exposed by the extraordinary feel of her lips on his, her body against his. But it could never be. Although he'd told her the truth – for the most part – he had omitted one crucial detail. The only thing that still mattered.

He hoped that she would have happy memories of the day they'd had together, the time they'd shared. Let her remember the electric sparks between them; the moment on the bridge when the night had seemed alive with possibilities. Let her remember that kiss.

He clenched his fist, looking down at his hands. The gloves he hated, the tight red skin underneath. A cooking fire. He had the story ready if people asked, though few actually did. Had she believed it?

The underground station was full of people out for a Saturday night. He made his way through the long corridors, but instead of getting on a train, he went back up and out another exit that led to the street. It was still raining and the snow on the ground had already turned to slush. He walked back to the South Bank, letting the rain wash over his face. The day was a beautiful memory, and even the invocation of Irina's name hadn't spoiled it. He closed his eyes for a second, remembering the crystal flakes swirling and billowing around the pod on the London Eye. Nicola standing beside him, the warmth of her skin as he took her hand, the smell of her hair—No. He'd cherish every moment they had spent together, but ultimately, he'd been right to walk away.

Now, without her beside him, the city seemed drained of colour, the lights dim and hazy. He went back across the footbridge, through Charing Cross Station and on to Trafalgar Square. The square was crowded despite the weather and there was a carolling group in the centre near the giant tree. Out of professional courtesy, he stopped and listened. It was a teen youth choir, sixth-formers, most likely. The conductor was a white-haired man with a rounded back. Dmitri didn't recognise him. There were very few males in the choir, and to Dmitri, the balance sounded off. But what grated most was the music itself. Cheerful and bright, full of joy and hope. So opposite his mood. Now he knew what Nicola had felt like that night at Waterloo Station. Trapped. And so lonely.

Forcing himself to keep listening, he looked around at the crowd. There were families and theatre-goers and groups of students. The tourists and backpackers reminded him of Moscow. Playing tour guide to Americans, with their Levi jeans, their dog-eared copies of Dostoyevsky and Bulgakov, their perfect teeth, and their packs of Trojan condoms (back then no self-respecting Western tourist would ever trust Russian-made condoms). Stumbling out of a taxi in the early hours of the morning after a night of clubbing, trying to make it to class. Rarely succeeding.

Sasha was from Moscow, which had given him an edge. He'd been the golden boy at the Conservatory before Dmitri came on the scene. They had been rivals, and then friends. So he'd thought, anyway. For those few months in his second year, Sasha had orchestrated his entire life. From picking a girl for him to lose his virginity to, to teaching him English swear words, to introducing him to the club bouncers, to when he practised – or didn't practise – the piano.

When Dmitri had told Kolya about Sasha, the bastard had jumped to the conclusion that Sasha had deliberately sabotaged him. Dmitri had got angry. Because, of course, Kolya was right. He'd been too stupid and naïve to see it. Not to mention too drunk, or simply, too hungry.

Sasha had graduated from the Conservatory and gone on to have a career as a concert pianist, mostly in the Far East. Dmitri had followed his career from afar, even bought a few of his recordings. He hadn't listened to them, though. As much as he tried not to think about what might have been, the life he had thrown away was his crown of thorns. Sasha had burned out in his late twenties. Dmitri had lost track of him now. He was probably teaching music somewhere in Russia – perhaps their lives had not turned out too differently. Except in the ways that mattered.

He walked across the square past the group of backpackers, headed up St Martin's Lane, and over to Charing Cross Road. Today, he'd played tour guide again in very different circumstances. All he'd had to do was stay detached and in control. He'd failed. Nicola had bewitched him, with her intelligence and strength, and the vulnerability that lay underneath. He'd allowed himself to feel a powerful hope – that schoolboyish notion that the world was his to reach out and seize with both hands.

He'd been right to hide the truth, right to walk away. Squash that hope like a bug under his foot. He wasn't a boy any more. He never would be again.

Dmitri passed a few bookshops that were still open and kept walking until he found a convenience store. He went inside. The condoms were behind the counter. The bored clerk got the box down and put it in a paper bag. Dmitri paid in cash and stuck the bag in his pocket.

The night at the station when he'd first seen Nicola, he'd felt like this. That night, he'd gone down into the underground and made his way home. Tonight, though, he was going the other way.

Chapter Fourteen

Nicola got off the train at Richmond and went out of the station. She walked down the high street, past bustling restaurants and bars that were lit up and decorated for Christmas. She turned into a darker street that led to The Green. There were quite a few people out walking: couples, families, dog walkers. Some of the houses she passed were strung with lights and had shiny Christmas trees in the window. There was still a spattering of snow on the ground, but mostly it had gone wet and slushy. The clouds had begun to disperse, and for a few seconds, the moon was visible again. The same moon that she'd seen from Waterloo Bridge. She refused to look at it, glad when the clouds swallowed it up again.

The three mews houses – two of them lit up, and one dark – reminded her of the ghosts of Christmas past, present and future. Hers, as ever, the one that was cold and silent. Even the motion-sensitive security light above the door had burned out, she noted. Before opening the door, she checked around her to make sure she was alone. She was.

Inside, she took off her coat, and frowned down at the pile of post on the mat. Bills, circulars, and three heavy card envelopes that could only be Christmas cards. She picked them up and set them on the hall table along with her keys. Tomorrow she'd open the envelopes, read the cards, throw them in the bin.

She went up the stairs to the sitting room and over to the old piano. It was a Bechstein from the early 1900s made of dark, burred walnut. Opening the lid, she pressed middle C. The sound was a little bit tinny, and probably very out of tune – she couldn't tell. In the New Year, she'd get rid of it, along with the rest of the stuff in the attic that she'd kept after her dad died. Clear everything out. Start again.

Nicola closed the lid on the piano and went to the kitchen. She opened one of the bottles of wine she'd bought and poured herself a large glass. If Dmitri was here, she'd keep the piano – get it tuned. She drank the wine down quickly. Where had that stupid thought come from? She'd never invited a man here, never allowed anyone to invade her personal space. Some things were sacred.

Pouring herself a second glass of wine, she went upstairs. The master suite took up the entire top floor, and there was an en suite bathroom with a huge bathtub and walk-in tiled shower. She turned on the taps to run a bath. Being in the city and on public transport always made her feel grubby. But as the water began to rush into the tub, she turned it off again. Grubby or not, right now she didn't want to wash off what little remained of the day.

Nicola went back to her room and took off her outer clothing, putting it all in the laundry basket for the cleaner to wash. She stood in front of the full-length mirror studying herself. Her breasts were full in the black lace bra, her abs, arm and leg muscles toned and sculpted from lunchtimes spent at the gym. She thought of Ollie, and the other men over the years whose hands had been on her skin. As far as she knew, she had been Ollie's only woman – other than his wife, of course – though they didn't speak about it. She had had other men besides him. Not frequently, but whenever she felt hurt, angry, or lonely enough to bother meeting someone – usually at a hotel bar or on a business trip. No names, no stories. They were nothing to her.

Nicola took off the bra and pants. These she had bought herself, they weren't a gift from Ollie or anyone else. She threw them in the laundry basket and went to her top drawer in the walk-in wardrobe and opened it. Naked and shivering in the cold, she took out all the expensive, beautiful lingerie that she'd collected over the years.

There were carrier bags at the back of the wardrobe. Nicola filled one up with the armful of lingerie – anything that had been a gift or that she'd worn with a man. She put on a pair of old cotton pants that she wore at home when she had her period, slipped on a T-shirt and put on her favourite silk bathrobe. But the robe too had been a gift from Ollie. She took it off and put it in the bag with the rest of the lingerie. Though she'd been planning on throwing out the lot with the rubbish, there were hundreds of pounds' worth of clothing in the bag. There was an Oxfam on the way to the station, she could drop the lot off on her way to work Monday morning. She slipped on a pair of tracksuit bottoms, and an oversized jumper.

Nicola took the bag and the glass of wine back downstairs. She curled up on the sofa with her laptop and phone and checked her texts and emails. Though it was Saturday night, there were numerous work things she could be getting on with. But what was the point?

She opened up the stream of texts from Ollie, that she'd shown Dmitri. The whole thing made her feel sick, disgusted. If she hadn't shown him the texts, would things be any different now? One by one, she deleted the messages, then Ollie's number off her phone.

Dmitri didn't have her number, nor did she have his. He'd planned it that way deliberately– she realised that now. She looked at the photo she had taken of the two of them, fallen on the ice. His hair was half over his dark eyes, but he'd been smiling, laughing. As for herself, she didn't even recognise the woman in the photo. It was a moment of happiness, a ray of light shining down, making her glow inside. Now, though, that glow was well and truly extinguished.

She deleted the photo and turned off the phone, as fat, useless tears began to roll down her cheek.

Chapter Fifteen

The bar of the swish, five-star hotel was decorated for Christmas. There were tiny evergreen trees on each table trimmed with red bows and fairy lights and a fir and holly garland above the bar. Two of the bartenders were wearing Santa hats like the one Dmitri had in his bag – and at this moment felt like tossing in the bin.

He looked around at the people. There were a few couples sitting at tables, a group of businessmen and a few men on their own. He eyed up the women. He recognised two Ukrainian prostitutes who were sitting at the bar. They were speaking to each other, but one looked up and nodded to him. Standing near them was a third that he didn't recognise – a new girl. There was also a forty-something woman on her own sitting at a table near the bar with an empty glass, scrolling through messages on her phone. She looked up and he held her gaze for a long second, then took in the rest of her. On a business trip from out of town, he suspected. She'd be bored, feeling awkward being here on her own. She'd already have a room upstairs. He could buy her a drink. Start chatting. It would be so easy.

God, he suddenly felt sick.

He perched himself at the bar. The bartender came up to him. 'Orange juice?' the man said.

'No,' Dmitri said. 'Double vodka.'

The bartender raised an eyebrow but didn't question it. He poured the drink into a tumbler and set it on the bar. Dmitri scanned his card on the reader to pay. The man also made him an orange juice, setting it next to the tumbler of vodka. Dmitri nodded once, but didn't thank him.

He put his card back in his wallet, staring straight ahead at the shelves of colourful bottles and the mirror behind. Then he lifted the tumbler to his face and sniffed it. The smell made his stomach lurch. This clear liquid, so like water. Unthinking and unfeeling. And yet, so deadly potent. He knew the clichés about Russians and the curse of vodka. The irony was, that before the fall of the Soviet Union, he couldn't remember his father ever touching the stuff. His father had liked sweet tea, just like he did. And cigarettes. Dmitri had smoked from a young age; music could be a nerve-wracking business, and certainly most of the other music students at the Conservatory had smoked. But he hadn't had a cigarette near his lips since that night.

That night. Christmas Eve. The 6th of January. The envelope had arrived by post the day before. He'd intercepted it, kept it hidden. He knew what it contained. But his father didn't. There would be consequences. He'd have to move back home. Come back and suffer the shame, that he hadn't been able to hack it. His father had trusted him to be away from home for the first time, to be let off the leash. And he'd pissed away that trust. Nightclubs, alcohol, girls. He'd lost his place; his father was going to be so angry—

A tap on his arm brought him back to reality. The new girl had moved closer to him.

She flicked her long blonde hair back and smiled. Her front teeth were crooked.

He set the tumbler of vodka back on the bar and pushed it her way.

'Here,' he said. 'Take it.'

'Merry Christmas,' she said, picking up the glass. Her accent was Ukrainian or maybe Romanian. She switched to halting Russian. 'You looking for company?' She was right next to him now, her arm touching his.

He shrugged but didn't reply.

She lifted the glass to her mouth, licking the rim with her tongue. 'One on the house, maybe?'

He glanced at her. 'Why?'

'Because I like the look of you. And my friends – she gestured to the other girls – know you.'

He laughed. Time and time again he'd come to the same bars, come across the same women. Some of them wanted out; some wanted to keep their younger sister or cousin out of the game. And sometimes, he was able to help. Phil, his stepfather, owned a cleaning company. His mother had found work there when she needed it most. Phil knew people who knew people.

Unfortunately, many were beyond help. Drug addicts, or just with the cruellest pimps – it was often best to steer clear. Some of the women, though, over time, had become his friends. He'd buy them a drink, sometimes a meal. And when they'd offer more and he'd refuse, they'd laugh at him and tell him to grow up.

'No thanks,' he said, flatly.

Out of the corner of his eye, he saw the businesswoman at the table stand up to leave. She glanced in his direction, looking disgusted. He sighed. So much for that.

He turned back to the girl, leaning in closer. 'And here's a piece of advice.' He gestured in the direction of two men sitting at a table at the back of the bar. Not the worst, but still, dangerous. 'You can't be giving out freebies.'

She tipped back the vodka. 'Why the fuck not? I'll end up dead in a ditch somewhere anyway.'

'Maybe.' He passed the orange juice over to her. She drank it down greedily. He leaned his elbows against the bar, staring down at the dark, lacquered wood. His hair fell forward into this face. He let it stay there.

'So if you're not here to drink and you're not here to get laid, then why are you here?' The woman moved even closer to him. He felt a spark of desire and a wave of disgust as he looked sideways at her. She was young, early-twenties probably, and painfully thin underneath her tight black dress. Her hair was so light it was almost translucent, and her blue eyes reminded him of Irina. Bile rose in his throat.

He took her by the arm. She flinched as he pushed up the tight sleeve of her dress and looked down at her flesh. Pale and white, traversed by blue veins. No needle marks.

'You're new to this, *dorogusha*,' he said sharply. 'Or else you wouldn't still be here talking to me after I've said I'm not interested.' He squeezed her wrist. 'You've still got a chance.' He loosened his grip and let go of her. 'You should take it.' He dug in his pocket and removed the paper bag with the box of condoms. He opened the bag, took out one of Phil's cards from his wallet and put it inside. 'Call this number,' he said. 'It won't be much. Cleaning – that sort of thing. But this man knows people. I trust him.' He set the bag on the bar in front of her, got off the stool and turned to leave. 'And by the way,' he said, 'you're in London, not America. They say *Happy* Christmas here.'

He walked out of the bar swiftly, and without a backwards glance. He continued out of the hotel, and into the street.

Chapter Sixteen

6th December

At five a.m. Nicola sat upright in a cold sweat. She'd been dreaming of candyfloss and carousels, a long-ago day out at a funfair. A sparkly dress, laughter, the world spinning as the horse moved up and down. *And then he was there in front of her. Blue eyes, blonde hair... a hand on her arm... that smile. She was falling, her heels twisting beneath her. The ice was so cold against her back... that dreadful smile...*

A plane flew overhead. Nicola pulled the duvet over her head and willed herself to stop shaking, and go back to sleep. It didn't work. The worst thing was not the nightmare – she always had plenty of those this time of year – or the noise of the planes, or the cold darkness outside the window. It was the fact that it was five a.m., and a Sunday. So many hours to get through until the new week began and it was time to go to work.

Realising that sleep was futile, she sat up and turned on the light. She'd check her emails, do some work, go for a run. Maybe call Jules and see if she and the kids were up for a walk in Richmond Park. And then there was the bag of lingerie – she could drop it off at Oxfam today. What they'd make of it, or do with it, she had no idea. But even as the memories of the previous, magical day were becoming murky and indistinct, her resolve to make a new start was crystal clear.

Nicola got out of bed. After a few glasses of wine last night, she'd passed out and hadn't even brushed her teeth. Her head ached, but it was her own fault. Dmitri didn't drink alcohol. Maybe that was because of his father, who, from the sound of things, had been a violent drunk.

Dmitri. God, she wished she could just get him out of her mind.

She distracted herself by going downstairs to the kitchen and putting on the coffee maker. Sitting at the table, she ate some yoghurt and muesli and checked her emails on her phone. Her heroics yesterday had damaged the screen and she'd probably have to endure the hassle of getting a new one from IT. There were conference call invites to accept, documents to review, a few invitations to schmoozy client events in the new year. She thought of the homeless shelter – how surprisingly clean and cared for it had seemed. Not at all what she would have expected. People like Kolya obviously cared deeply for their work. It must be very difficult, but satisfying too.

She read over an email from a junior who'd been crunching some numbers for her on an Argentine company that made exquisite high-heeled shoes. They were looking for a buyer to take them into the European market. The numbers were a little marginal, but she had a few investors in mind. The prospects were strong enough that she could justify a trip there, spend a week in Buenos Aires, come back with a suntan and a suitcase or two full of shoes that would make Jules drool with envy. She should contact travel and start making the arrangements. *Shoes.* She scrolled down through her inbox. Other deals, other companies: specialising in jewellery, fashion, corporate away days. Her career had been built on these things, but right now, it all seemed so pointless, so lacking in humanity. That had never bothered her before. So why now?

Nicola continued to read and respond to emails until the sky eventually became light. Shutting down her laptop, she took her coffee mug and went outside on to the balcony that overlooked the river. The water was grey and murky but there was a bank of luminous pink clouds on the horizon. The temperature was still near freezing, and she blew out a white cloud of breath that mingled with the steam rising from her mug.

Nicola checked her watch. Eight a.m. Christ, maybe she should just go back to bed. Or read a book? She'd always loved books, and one entire wall of her front room had a built-in shelf that was full of them. But books evoked emotions, and that was something she wanted to avoid. *Feel nothing.* That was the goal right now.

Going back inside, she finished the coffee and put the cup in the dishwasher. It was early yet and the path along the river would probably be slippery with ice. But at least it wouldn't be crowded. Heading to her bedroom, she put on her running gear. Maybe the cold and the exertion would help to clear her head.

On her way out the door, she grabbed her phone and her Bluetooth headphones. She scrolled through her music playlists: Energise, Endurance, Stamina, Relaxation. All of it was gym music, most of it pumping and tuneless, or schmaltzy and tuneless. On a whim, she went to Spotify and typed in 'Rachmaninov piano'. There were hundreds of hits. She downloaded a popular playlist, realising that this was probably the last thing she should be doing. But it was done.

She put on 'Energise' and left her house. Having the piano playlist on her phone seemed daring and subversive enough. She'd save the listening to it for later.

Outside, it was even colder than she'd realised. In the

cobbled yard outside the mews houses, she did a warm-up, but still felt chilled. She made her way around the back of the houses to the path along the river.

Though it was still icy, Nicola ran as quickly as she dared. The sun had risen a little higher now, but the path was still mostly in shadow. She ran past the buildings along the river that made up Richmond town centre: bars, restaurants, boathouses. She continued on through Petersham Meadows and past Ham House and Eel Pie Island. She had to watch every step. Several times her foot hit a hidden patch of ice and she almost went over.

Nicola continued on as far as Teddington Lock. There, she stopped, leaning over, gasping out white clouds of breath. Her head was aching from the exertion, the wine and from the God-awful music. She switched it off.

There were a few boats lined up waiting for the lock. She watched the giant concrete space fill gradually with water. There was a bench nearby and she headed over to it to do some stretches, push-ups, and tricep dips. When she was finished, the lock had nearly filled. A child on one of the boats waved to her. She waved back. It was too quiet. Her own thoughts began to creep back into her head.

Nicola scrolled to the new 'Rachmaninov piano' playlist. She put it on, turned up the volume and started to run towards home.

Chapter Seventeen

'Where have you been?'

Tanya's voice had a frantic edge to it that he hadn't expected. In fact, he hadn't expected her to be here at all. It was Sunday morning and he'd been out walking for half the night. He'd walked all the way from the bar in Central London to the church, where he'd practised the piano into the early hours. Now, a hazy sun had risen above the horizon. It would be another short, cold day.

'I've been out,' Dmitri said. Absently, he walked over to the bookshelf and picked up the book of Russian fairy tales that his mother had found in a little second-hand bookshop on Charing Cross Road not long after they had come to London. The text was in both Russian and English, and the three of them had read the stories aloud, trying to improve their sense of written English. The book was illustrated with photos of Russian lacquer art: beautiful, whimsical images with bright, jewel-like colours against a black background. He opened the book and flipped through it, a sense of loss crashing over him like a wave. In his childhood, his father had liked making up his own versions of the classic tales. Dmitri had identified with the heroes: warriors like Ilya Muromets, Dobyrnya Nikitich, and Alyosha Popovich; the dashing and clever Ivan Tsarevich. Now though, he mostly identified with the host of other characters that were aptly named 'The Fool'.

Dmitri flipped through the book to the illustration of the Firebird, its tail a swirl of flaming orange and red as it swooped down from the sky to steal a golden apple.

The story in this book was a variation on the one he'd heard as a child. Not all of the versions were happy. In this tale, a beautiful maiden had been enchanted by a sorcerer and transformed into the fiery bird. Young Ivan, lying in wait, grabbed hold of one of her flaming feathers. He rode to the ends of the earth on the back of a grey wolf, performing heroic feats in order to release the Firebird from her golden cage and break the enchantment. Naturally, the beautiful maiden and Ivan fell in love, and they lived happily ever after.

Dmitri slammed the book shut and put his head in his hands.

Tanya came over and banged a tea glass down on the table in front of him. 'I will make your tea,' she said. 'And then you will tell me what the hell is up with you.'

'Yes,' he said, too exhausted to argue.

'I spoke to Phil yesterday,' she said, filling the kettle. 'He says you aren't returning his calls. And Carole-Ann came to the bakery.' She'd switched to Russian. He was definitely in for a telling-off. 'She told me about the Oxford thing. That she told you about *a month* ago.' Tanya turned around, her hands on her hips. 'She told me you could get money to study there and get a doctorate in choral music. And I was so happy for you.' She shook her head. 'And then she said she was worried. That you hadn't filled in the application or got the letters of reference yet.'

'I've been busy, you know that.' He got up and put the book back on the shelf. The idea of Carole-Ann bullying him through his sister was enough to make him want to throw the application in the bin. With all of its questions about his qualifications, his goals and aspirations, and his reasons for applying: 'How will a Doctorate in Choral Music advance your career plans?'

The kettle switched off. Tanya poured water into the ceramic teapot. He took the teapot from her and sat back down at the table.

'God, I want to shake you sometimes,' Tanya said. 'I wish *mamochka* was here. She wouldn't let you get away with this. I'm glad I'm leaving. So many times you've broken my heart, and now, you're doing it all over again.'

'Please, Tanusha.' His head felt like it might split open. 'I will apply for the job, if that will make you happy. You are right – I should have started by now. But I've still got time.'

'Do you promise that you will do it?' Tanya sat down at the table and took his hand in hers, tracing the line of his finger below his grey glove. 'Promise, on the soul of your mama?'

'I said I would do it.' He jerked his hand away. He was aware of her staring at him as he took a sip of tea. She'd made it too sweet.

'Fine,' she said. 'You'll do it.'

Tanya poured herself a glass of tea and took a sip, blanching at the taste.

'Too sweet,' she said. 'I'm sorry. I will make another pot.'

'No, it's fine.' He put his hand out to stop her. 'Do you remember how Papa used to take us to pick wild strawberries in the summer?' he said, more softly.

She set her tea glass down on the table. 'Yes,' she said, hesitating. 'I think so.'

'They were so delicious. The taste would just explode in your mouth, the juice would get everywhere. All over your hands, face and clothes.'

'Mama would get mad at the stains.'

'Yes.' He smiled wistfully at the memories and took another sip of the tea. 'Those were good times.'

'I'm sorry,' she said, the edge back in her voice. 'But I do not miss those days at all. What we have, right here, right now, is enough. More than we – well, I – ever could have dreamed of.'

'Yes, and I'm happy for you.' He was aware of the ache inside him getting stronger. Once Tanya was gone for good... He didn't want to think about it. 'You know how they say that someone must have done something terrible in a past life to deserve to suffer in this one? For me, I know what I have done – in this life. But it feels like a different life, if that makes sense.'

He could sense the anger coiling within her again from across the table. 'That's bullshit, and you know it,' Tanya said.

Dmitri sat back in the chair and stared hard at his sister. 'Because of me, our mother suffered and our father is dead. I made Irina, a perfectly innocent girl—'

He felt the sting of the slap even before the sound registered.

'Shut up,' Tanya said. She stood up from the table and turned away, facing the wall. 'I feel like I'm talking to a child, a stupid, self-absorbed little boy. A little boy who has skinned his knee and wants someone to kiss it better. But you're not a boy, Dima. Not for a very long time.' She turned back, her dark eyes that were a mirror of his, now shiny with tears. 'I have said it a hundred times, and I will say it one more time. But this is the last time.' She came back over to the table and sat down. 'Because I cannot bear to see you like this. Go to Oxford – go back to Russia – I don't care—'

'Tanya, please.'

'You were the victim, not the cause of what happened. Mama did what any mother would do for her beloved son.

And Irina…' her face twisted like the word was sour, 'Irina was a spoiled bitch.'

'No.' He sighed. 'I don't blame her for what she did.'

'But you should blame her.' Tanya's voice rose again. 'I do. She is not your precious *Snegurochka* from your precious fairy tales. Made of ice and snow, to melt at the first touch of a man. She was solid fucking ice.' Tanya shook her head. 'Do you think that if Mark was you, I would act as she acted? No. I would love him, care for him. Maybe even more than before.'

'Stop it, Tan'ka,' he said, his voice hardening. He didn't need to hear this, couldn't hear it. He was the one to blame, no matter what his sister said.

'How many years have you wasted? How many more are going to pass by? When you look back on your life, will you be proud of what you have done?' She picked up her glass and slammed it down on the table. 'Will you be proud of the time you have spent with your choir, your books, your one-night stands? Never allowing yourself to love or find the love you deserve.'

'Enough,' he said. 'You've made your point.'

'Have I?' She got up from the table and came over to him, kneeling down. 'I wish that were true,' she said more softly.

With a sigh, he put his arms gently around her and held her close, stroking her hair. There really was nothing more to say.

Finally, Tanya pulled away and stood up. 'I have to go, and you need a few hours' sleep.' She wrinkled her nose. 'And a shower. And then, you must get to rehearsal. Carole-Ann said she tried to phone you yesterday but you did not answer.'

'I was busy.' He felt the hollow gnaw of regret as he thought of the day he had spent with Nicola – 'The Heckler'. How Tanya would laugh if she knew. But he had already decided not to tell her. He did not want to laugh. He wanted to cry.

'Yes, you are busy.' Tanya shook her head. 'Too busy to continue with this self-pity. You must prepare the soloists for the concert. That is the important thing you must do today. I will tell Phil that that is where you will be if he still wants to speak to you.'

'Yes, OK,' he said, lacking the will to argue.

She kissed his cheek and stood up. 'And tonight you will start on the application.'

'Yes. I will.'

Chapter Eighteen

Nicola barely even realised that she was home. She'd been lost, utterly lost, in some strange world that she hadn't known existed. Dangerous and unfathomable, but also indescribably beautiful. Instead of going inside, she stood around the back of the mews staring down at the perpetual motion of the river, the complex shades of grey, white, black. The final movement of the piano concerto came to an end, the crystal notes dying away like the fleeting moments of a dream. She took off her headphones before the next piece could begin. It was too much to feel, too much to allow inside of her when, right now, the one thing she wanted to do was get back to normal. Accept that 'normal' was perfectly adequate. More than enough.

She went around to the cobbled yard and let herself into the house. The bag of knickers was by the door where she'd put it this morning on her way out. Taking it into town and dropping it at Oxfam would kill an hour or so. She could get lunch at the new place that did green protein smoothies, do a little shopping, call her sister – maybe even her mother. Surely, that's what she did every Sunday, though for some reason, she couldn't remember. Yesterday was a line drawn in the sand, with everything that came before being erased by the tide. Except, she was determined not to think about yesterday. Or listen to Rachmaninov. Ever again.

Nicola showered, plaited her wet hair, and got dressed in jeans and a cashmere jumper. As she was closing the door of the walk-in wardrobe, she noticed a few bits and pieces of clothing that she no longer wore, or that held too many memories. The dark red suit she'd worn the night she and Ollie had hooked up. A sparkly blue velvet wrap dress from Whistles that had been unwrapped so many times it made her feel like a package misdelivered in the post. She took them out and shoved them into another carrier bag. Then there were the shoes. Nicola loved her shoes and spent a fortune on them. Most of them she couldn't bear to part with, even if she could remember some occasions of wearing them – and nothing else – when she'd been with Ollie or others. It was worth clearing some space in the wardrobe, though, so she added a few pairs she hadn't worn in ages to the carrier bag, and went downstairs.

On her way out the front door she checked her phone, half hoping there would be something urgent from work that would occupy her for the rest of the day. There wasn't. There was, however, a text message from Ollie. Even though she'd deleted his contact details and the message came up as an unknown number, she recognised it immediately.

You OK, babe? Thinking of you.

Nicola deleted the message with a surge of anger. Ollie may be thinking of her – but Dmitri most certainly, was not. He was probably at church right now, conducting a choir, happy and uplifted in the music. He had that and she had... her life. She forced him out of her mind. He and his choir could go to hell – along with his sad story, his wasted talent and his music.

Nicola put on her coat and shoved her phone into the pocket. She grabbed the bags of clothing and lingerie and went out the door.

It was only a few minutes' walk to the high street. As she made her way along an alleyway lined with expensive shops and restaurants, she looked in some of the windows. If – and in her mind it was still a *big* IF – she did go over to Jules' house for a 'family Christmas', then she'd need to buy a few gifts. Soaps, candles, bath salts, knitted hats and scarves, wine. It didn't really matter what it was, as long as it was wrapped up and under the bloody tree. She could get Jules a nice handbag from a client that had recently acquired a designer leather goods company. And a 'Timeless' watch would be perfect for Teddy or Jules' husband, or both. At least her job made it easy to source Christmas presents.

Nicola kept walking past the nice shops and turned on to the high street, going towards the station. The street was busy with shoppers, families with expensive prams and well-dressed couples. Richmond was one of the most well-heeled boroughs of London. Yet, as she walked, she was aware of the occasional dark shape huddled in a doorway. Even here, there were homeless people. Like Dmitri and his family had been once. Like the people at the shelter yesterday, so transformed by the simple gift of song. She didn't look at them as she passed, or give them money. There seemed to be a lot more of them than she'd ever noticed before.

Finally, Nicola turned on to the Quadrant. Ahead of her was the Oxfam shop. An old man was rummaging through a pile of plastic bags piled in front of the door. The shop was closed. The sign next to the door said it opened at noon. She checked her watch. It was only half eleven.

The old man looked up at her and grinned. He didn't have a single tooth in his mouth that she could see, and even from a metre away she could smell his sour, unwashed skin and clothing. She gave him a deep frown. There was no way she was going to leave a bag with her unmentionables in it while he was here poking around.

Nicola walked past the shop and crossed the street. Wasn't there another charity shop just up the road towards the A307? She didn't know the name, but she went down the side street where she thought she'd seen it. She passed a second-hand bookshop and a nail salon.

At the end of the street, just before Paradise Road and the lanes that led up to the Vineyard and Richmond Hill, she spotted the shop, painted red, with a white sign that read 'Care – Charity Shop'. *Care*. She didn't know the charity, but the door to the shop was open. Someone must be inside; she could be rid of her bags and be gone. She walked up to the window. The display had a frightening-looking female mannequin with a painted face and a blonde wig. It was wearing a hideous ethnic-print summer maxi dress and a necklace of chunky beads. Totally off-putting, and totally wrong for the Christmas season. Behind the mannequin, the shop was cluttered and in disarray.

Hefting her bags, Nicola went inside. Just inside the door, she almost collided with a girl, who looked to be in her early twenties, with long black hair, dark eye-makeup, and a pierced lip.

'I'm sorry,' the girl said, 'I've got to close the shop for a few minutes. The manager had to pop out. I'm not allowed to have anyone in here when it's just me.'

Nicola frowned. 'I'm here to donate some clothing.'

'Yeah, OK,' the girl said. 'It's just, can you come back when—'

'No,' Nicola said. 'I'm here now.'

'But I really need to close up.'

'Are you a volunteer here?' Nicola asked frostily.

'Yes, I'm getting some work experience.'

'And what exactly does this charity – *Care* – do?'

'Well,' the girl hesitated for a moment like she was trying to recall something memorised by rote, 'they provide temporary care to people who are homeless, or refugees waiting to be rehoused, or who need a—'

'*We*,' Nicola cut off the spiel. 'You're a volunteer here, so it's *we* provide. Not *they*. If you're working here, you need to be a part of it. Own it.'

The girl gave her a look like she had two heads. 'OK…' she drawled. 'But I need you to go. I'm supposed to lock up.'

'The hours posted on the door say that you're open on Sunday from eleven a.m. to five. It's now eleven-forty. So you're open.'

'But Charles said we need two people here at all times.'

Nicola could tell the girl was a little thick and a lot clueless. On the other hand, at least this shop had better hours than Oxfam. 'OK,' she said, 'I get it. So why don't we say that I'm volunteering for your charity, for the next ten minutes while I'm in your shop.'

'Umm… I don't know… You're supposed to fill out a form.'

'I'm not going to bother with that,' Nicola bristled. Kolya, at the shelter, had said the same thing. It sounded ludicrous when *she* was the one giving up her time. 'Now, you take these bags up to the counter, and I'll do you a favour – help you price them. Some of the clothing is quite expensive.'

'Yeah?' The girl perked up a little.

'And by the way,' Nicola said, growing increasingly annoyed, 'that dress in the window is hideous. You need something that is going to attract holiday shoppers. Where are your charity cards and gift wrap? Where's your Christmas lights and tree?'

The girl looked blank. 'I don't know. Do we need those things?'

'If you want to make money for your charity, then yes, you do. Here...' Nicola rummaged through the bag and found the blue velvet wrap dress. 'Put this on the mannequin. And, for God's sake, give her some bling. Don't you have any jewellery or glittery handbags – that sort of thing?'

'I don't know. Maybe.' The girl seemed completely bewildered as she went to change the dress on the window mannequin.

'Why don't I have a look around and see what I can find?' Nicola said in a low hiss. 'This place needs a complete overhaul. It's pathetic. You're already off the beaten track. You need to be better than the rest. A destination. Not a complete tip.'

'Yeah, whatever.' The girl didn't even have the courtesy to sound offended. 'Be my guest.'

Nicola poked around the shop while the girl wrestled with the mannequin. She found a couple of decent handbags shoved on a tiny rack in the corner. The glass case underneath the till had some jewellery that would be passable, and on one of the overstuffed racks of clothing, she found a white faux-fur wrap that looked practically new. The majority of what was in the shop, however, needed to find its way to the nearest bin. She looked at a few tags that were on the nicer things. Nothing in the shop seemed to be priced at more than a fiver.

'Put this on her.' Nicola thrust the wrap and the jewellery in the direction of the girl. She took a pair of nude, high-heeled court shoes out of the bag she'd brought. 'And put these in the window as well. They're L.K. Bennett.'

The girl finished dressing the mannequin. The rest of the shop still left everything to be desired, but at least it was a start.

While she'd been looking for the jewellery, Nicola had spotted several unopened boxes behind the till. One of them was labelled 'Xmas lights and decorations – shop.' She opened the box.

'Put up some lights around the window,' Nicola directed the girl. 'You need to make the place look a lot more Christmassy. Here...' She tossed the girl a string of lights.

'*We*,' the girl said suddenly.

'What?'

The girl grinned. 'You're here now, volunteering. So you need to *own it*.'

'One nil to you.' Nicola smiled back grudgingly. Maybe the girl was not completely thick, just inexperienced.

Nicola helped her untangle the cord of lights. Luckily, there were some nails already in place around the window, so it wasn't difficult to drape the string of lights around the frame. But there was no plug. Nicola sent the girl out the back of the shop to look for an extension lead.

Not even a second after the girl was gone, the bell on the door tinkled and a woman came in, pushing a pram. She was wearing a baggy blue tracksuit with spit-up on the shoulder. Her curly blonde hair needed a wash and her eyes had dark bags under them. Nicola supposed that having a baby did that to you.

'Hello,' the woman said. 'Do you have any charity cards? The other shops are mostly sold out.'

'Of course,' Nicola said pleasantly. 'We still have a great selection – let me get them for you.' She walked quickly to the door to the back room. 'Charity cards – now!' she said in a sharp whisper.

'Um, in the box by the till,' the girl whispered back.

Nicola went back out to the main shop and found a box shoved under the counter marked 'charity cards'.

'I'm sorry for the inconvenience,' she said to the customer. 'If you want to have a quick browse around, I'll just get them out.'

'OK,' the woman said hesitantly. She pushed the pram up nearer the till where there was an open space. Nicola caught a glimpse of the baby, bundled up in a fluffy pink suit and hat. Its blue eyes were open, and it – she, probably – was sucking on a pink plastic dummy. Nicola looked away, feeling a little pang somewhere inside her.

Lifting the box on to the counter, she tore it open. There were packs of cards in twelve different designs. She took out one of each and put them on the empty card rack next to the CDs.

'Here you go,' she said. 'We've got a really nice selection this year.' She held one out with a picture of a robin in a Santa Claus hat. 'This one is cute.'

But she wasn't sure the woman even heard. She was staring at the blue velvet wrap dress on the mannequin. 'How much is that dress?' the woman asked. 'The one in the window.'

'It's beautiful, isn't it?' Nicola said. 'And so flattering on. It's from Whistles – completely sold out last season. It's hardly been worn at all. And that deep blue colour would really suit you.'

The woman blushed. 'Well, I don't know.'

'I happen to know that it cost over a hundred and fifty pounds new. You can have it for – say – thirty-five.'

'Well...'

Another first – at this moment, Nicola actually felt grateful for her PA Chrissie's annoying habit of buying and selling things on eBay during worktime and bragging about what she'd paid for this dress or that pair of shoes, and how much she'd got at auction for this handbag or that jumper. Nicola had never bought or sold anything on eBay but she wasn't about to let the Whistles dress go for a fiver.

'Really, you must try it on. Let me get it off the mannequin for you.'

'I don't want you to go to any trouble...'

'It's no trouble. That's what we're here for. And all the money goes to a great cause. Helping to rehouse homeless people and refugees. It's very difficult this time of year for people on the streets. So dark, and cold...' Nicola went to the newly dressed mannequin and stripped it bare. The girl had come back out from the back, and was staring dumbly at Nicola, watching the whole proceeding. Nicola gestured to the girl to plug in the Christmas lights.

Nicola had just got the dress and wrap off the mannequin when the baby started to grizzle. A second later, the dummy clattered to the floor. The baby started to cry.

'Oh dear,' the woman said. 'I suppose I should go. She needs a feed.'

'You're welcome to feed her in the back if you like,' Nicola said. 'Then you can try the dress on when you're done. Really, there's no rush.' She gestured to the girl. 'Take that dummy and wash it off. And make sure there's a chair and whatever else the lady needs for the baby.'

The girl's mouth dropped open. But she did as Nicola directed.

'Thank you, you're so kind,' the woman said. 'It's so hard to find a place to feed her in town.'

'I understand. Here's the dress,' she held it out to the woman. 'And try the wrap too. It's from Debenhams, and it's "as new". Ten pounds. Of course, we can give you a small discount if you buy multiple items.'

'What about those shoes in the window?' the woman said hopefully. 'The L.K. Bennett ones. What size are they?'

'Size 6,' Nicola said. 'Would you like to try them too?'

'Yes please.' The woman looked flustered but excited as Nicola brought everything to the back of the shop for her. Of course, the back of the shop looked like a cyclone had gone through it, but that couldn't be helped.

The girl brought the dummy back to the woman, holding it with two fingers like it was a dirty tissue. The woman took it gratefully.

'OK, I'll leave you to it, then,' Nicola said to the woman. 'You,' she gestured to the girl, lowering her voice, 'come give me a hand. We need all the Christmas stuff out now.' She closed the door on the woman and the baby. 'And by the way, what's your name?'

'Shelley,' the girl said, her mouth turned down like an open umbrella.

'OK, Shelley, I'm Nicola. Nice to meet you. But there's an awful lot of work to be done before this place is even remotely ready for the holiday season. Which, in case you didn't realise, is half over. You should have had this stuff out in early November. Late October even.'

'Charles said to go through the CDs.'

'Is Charles the boss?'

'Yeah.'

'Where is he, anyway?'

'He had to take some stuff to the shelter. I guess he's having a coffee there or something.'

'Fine, well, why don't we give him a nice surprise when he gets here? Get the shop looking more festive. Do you like Christmas, Shelley?'

'I dunno. I guess I did when I was a kid.'

'I think everyone feels that way a little bit,' Nicola said. For her it was certainly true. 'But the point is, at Christmastime, people are more likely to give to charity and *care* about homeless people and refugees. You got it?'

'I guess so.'

'So everyone that comes into this shop must buy something. The more, the better. So get those cards out and start clearing away some of the clutter so you can unpack these boxes.' Nicola pointed to two more boxes behind the till marked 'gift wrap' and 'ornaments'.

'Fine but—' the girl broke off. 'Who left this stuff?' She pointed to the carrier bags on the counter.

'I did. I said I had clothing to donate. Like that dress she's trying on.' Nicola gestured with her head towards the back room.

The girl stood up a little straighter, suddenly more *knowing*. 'We can't take this stuff. I mean, the bras, yeah, they're fine.' She picked up a black bra and ran her finger over the soft satin. 'But we don't take knickers. You'll need to throw those in the bin.'

'Throw them in the bin?' Nicola stared at her. 'Do you know how much those cost? There are sets there from Agent Provocateur, Boux Avenue, Intimissimi. It's all washed and in perfect condition.'

'Like I said, we can take the bras, but not the knickers.' Shelley crossed her arms.

'Well that makes no sense.' Nicola's voice rose. 'I mean, you can sell whatever you like in your shop, but don't homeless women need knickers too? Or refugees?'

'It's policy—'

Just then, the door opened and a man came in. He looked like he was in his late-twenties, early-thirties. He had thinning ginger hair and a bit of stubble on his face that Nicola thought might be an attempt at a beard. Above the stubble, his cheeks were pitted with acne scars. He was wearing a checked flannel shirt and a pair of baggy jeans.

'Charles.' The girl threw down the black bra she was holding. 'Thank God you're here. This woman, like, wants us to sell her old knickers!'

'Oh, for Christ's sake.' Nicola began packing everything back into the bag. Her face felt like it was on fire. But when she looked up again at the man, she could see that policy or no, he was far from horrified at the prospect of her donation. He gave her the kind of smile that she recognised well. The kind that made her want to get the hell out of there.

Too late. He was already up at the counter. Though he

didn't reach into the bag, he did take a good look. 'Designer, is that right?'

'High street,' she said, not looking at him. 'But expensive, and...' she lowered her voice, 'for heaven's sake, it's all been *washed*.'

'I understand,' Charles said. 'And we definitely appreciate all donations.' His eyes brushed hers and she could guess the extent of his appreciation.

'Well, it doesn't sound like it from the way *she* talks.' Cringing with embarrassment, Nicola pointed at Shelley.

'It's true,' Charles said. 'It's a big challenge for us to get enough clean clothing to supply to the people we're trying to help. But there are other issues besides hygiene. It's... I'm not quite sure how to put this... whether or not the clothing we distribute sends the right message. We've got a number of churches involved in funding the Care charity.'

'The right message?' Nicola wasn't sure if she felt more like laughing in his face or whacking him. 'So you're saying that you don't want your homeless women and refugees to have something nice – sexy. You're afraid they're going to look like sluts, is that it?'

'No, of course that's not—'

'That IS it.' And she did laugh then. At him, at herself, at the ludicrous situation. 'Will it help send the "right message" if I take away the gifts from my married lover?' she said, deciding to confront him head on. 'And things I've worn on one-night stands with God knows who?'

Charles' face turned an unflattering shade of pink. Shelley's cheeks were puffed out and she looked like she might burst – into giggles, Nicola assumed.

'Let's see...' Nicola rummaged in the bag and held up a green satin and lace bra, 'last time this one was on the front lines, it was an oil exec from Houston. He said his name was Colin, but I'm sure that was fake.' She narrowed her eyes. 'And then there's this one...' she pulled out a see-through black thong. Charles' eyes looked like they were going to pop. 'Ollie gave this to me after standing me up around Valentine's Day. It was his wife's mother's eightieth birthday or something. He has a lot of relatives, and they always seem to be having birthdays—'

The door at the back of the shop opened up. All three of them turned as the woman with the baby came out. She was wearing the midnight blue wrap dress, the L.K. Bennett shoes and the faux fur wrap. The baby was slung over her shoulder. She patted it on the back and it gave out a loud belch.

'How do I look?' the woman said.

Nicola stepped forward, gave the neckline of the dress a little tug, then stood back. The woman was rounder and plumper on the bottom than Nicola, and the dress hugged her figure. No longer did she look like the tired, overwrought mum who had walked into the shop earlier. Now, she looked happy and radiant. 'I think it's fabulous on you,' Nicola said, beaming her encouragement.

The woman eyed Nicola closely. 'This was yours, right? You donated it?'

'Yes.' Nicola felt the skin on her neck begin to crawl.

'And has it seen, umm... as much "front-line action" as the other stuff?' She had a twinkle in her eye now.

Shelley gave out a little snort.

Nicola gave the woman a knowing smile. 'As I said earlier, it's barely been worn at all.'

'I'll take it,' the woman said. 'And the wrap and the shoes.'

'May they serve you well,' Nicola said.

The woman returned to the back room to change into her normal clothes.

As soon as the door closed, Nicola turned to Charles and Shelley. 'She should get a discount for multiple items. Let's say – ten per cent. And really, Charles,' she lowered her eyelids, reached out and put a hand on his arm, feeling him jolt, 'this shop is a disgrace.' She removed her hand, sharpening her voice. 'You need to clear out all the rubbish and get the Christmas displays up. Today.'

'She told me to get the Christmas ornaments out,' Shelley moaned. 'I told her you said to do the CDs.'

'No, she's right,' Charles said, looking completely flustered now. 'We need to get the shop looking better for Christmas. This is our busiest time of year.'

Nicola shoved the last of the underwear back into the bag. 'You should start by redoing the window display,' she said. 'There are some more shoes in that bag, and a suit you can use.' Nicola pointed to the second bag she'd brought. 'The suit is from Jaeger. Don't sell it for less than forty-five pounds.'

'Forty-five pounds,' Charles repeated, sounding a little flabbergasted.

'Now, tell me where that homeless shelter is, and I'll go there now, and take the "unwanted items" with me.'

'Gosh, um... yes,' Charles stammered. 'I mean, it's up towards Sheen...'

'I know where it is.' The woman with the baby came out of the back. The baby was asleep in the pram and the woman put her purchases on the counter by the till. She took a pack of charity cards off the rack and added them to the pile. 'I'm walking that way – I can drop it for you.'

Nicola nodded. 'Yes, thanks. It'll save me the bother.' She wondered if the lingerie in the bag would actually find its way to the shelter. If not, fine – she didn't care. Let it go to a new home where it would be *appreciated*.

'Ring up the sale and give her ten per cent off,' she directed Charles. He didn't even open his mouth to question the order.

It seemed to take forever as he typed the numbers into the computer.

'That's...' he looked at the figures on the till screen a second time, like he didn't quite believe what he was seeing.

'Sixty-one pounds twenty-five.' Nicola did the maths quickly in her head.

'A bag costs five p,' Shelley said, unhelpfully.

Both Nicola and, to his credit, Charles, glared at her. 'Never mind about that,' he said.

The woman took out her card, put it in the machine and typed in her pin. 'Are you going to be donating any more lovely clothes to this shop?' she asked Nicola. 'I might come round again next weekend.'

'Maybe,' Nicola mused. 'So far, doing a clear-out has been quite... liberating.'

'I'm sure.' The woman smiled.

With a pout on her face, Shelley started to shove the woman's purchases in the bag. Nicola stopped her and made her fold the dress and the wrap properly. The woman took the bag of lingerie and shoved it underneath the pram.

'Thank you for stopping by,' Nicola said to the woman. She went to the door and held it open for her.

'Oh, you're welcome. Thank *you*. And Happy Christmas.'

'Happy Christmas,' Nicola returned, without hesitation.

As soon as the woman was gone, she went back to Charles and Shelley at the till to retrieve her coat.

'I'm off then,' she said. 'Good luck – I think you're going to need it.'

Shelley rolled her eyes, but Charles came forward from behind the till. 'Thanks,' he said. 'That sale was more than we make most days.'

'Well, that needs fixing,' Nicola said. 'You've got to put in more effort.'

'Do um... you want to come back?' he said. 'Help out with some volunteering?'

'I'm not going to commit to anything,' Nicola said. 'But I will come back sometime soon and drop off more stuff.'

'OK,' Charles said. 'Thanks for that.' He suddenly peered at Nicola in a way that made her quite uncomfortable. 'You know,' he said, 'you look familiar. Do I know you?'

She laughed. 'I may not remember names, but I can absolutely assure you that we have *never* met.'

'No, I don't mean that.' He met her eyes boldly. 'It's just I *have seen* you before. At Waterloo Station. And then again on the Richmond train.'

It was Nicola's turn to be mortified. It was all too terrible to contemplate. 'Are you saying that...?'

'I'm in the choir. At St Anne's. Yes – your hair is different, but I'm sure it was you.'

'You definitely have me mistaken for someone else,' Nicola said, moving swiftly to the door. 'Goodbye.'

Chapter Nineteen

Dmitri awoke with his pulse thundering in his head. He was lying on his bed, fully clothed, drenched in sweat. He'd been dreaming of *her*. Nicola. It was all so vivid. He'd been lying on a huge white bed. She'd been there, on her knees over him. Her long red hair fell into his face like waves of flame, possessing, enchanting him. Her lips brushed his, and she lowered her hips on to him, promising to take him to heaven. In the dream he'd closed his eyes, but the kiss hadn't come. When he'd opened them again, the face was Irina's. She'd cried out in horror and he'd seen the disgust in her eyes, and worse, the pity. She melted away, ice turning to freezing water, slipping through his fingers...

He rolled to the side, curling into a ball. His head ached and his eyes hurt from the light. The light.

He glanced at the alarm clock beside the bed. It was two-thirty. In the afternoon? What day was it? Sunday? Fuck.

He swung out of bed, panicking. The rehearsal started at three o'clock. He had no business being out all night and then sleeping all day. People were counting on him. The choir needed him.

There was no time to shower, but he put on clean clothes, shaved quickly and rushed off to catch the bus to the church.

In the end he was ten minutes late. As he walked into the church, he was relieved to hear that Carole-Ann had things in hand and had started the soloists on their vocal warm-ups. When she caught sight of him, he could tell from her face that he must look like an old shoe that had been chewed by a dog and spat out again. Which was better than he felt.

As the warm-ups continued, Dmitri took out the score, filled with his pencil marks, notes, and coloured tabs. He tried to get his mind on Handel and his great oratorio, the *Messiah*. For this concert, they were doing the Christmas section, consisting of solos for soprano, contralto, tenor and bass, plus a dozen choruses that would tax a professional choir, let alone what he had to work with. They were also doing the famous 'Hallelujah Chorus'.

His eyes skimmed over the sections to be rehearsed today. The bass aria in particular, and the chorus that followed:

But who may abide the day of His coming,
And who shall stand when He appeareth?
For He is like a refiner's fire.
And he shall purify...

The words gave him chills. Though Dmitri was technically an atheist, when the heard the words sung to Handel's divine music, he wished more than anything that he could believe. But he had seen too much – life had taken too much – for that. Fire did not always purify—

'Dmitri?' He looked up, realising that Carole-Ann was trying to get his attention. Warm-ups were over, and the soloists were sitting in the pews.

'Yes? Are we ready to get started?'

She nodded.

He didn't apologise or give an excuse for his lateness. Instead he went to the piano and called the tenor soloist, Jonathan. He'd sung the part twice before in previous years, though he'd missed last year because his wife had just given birth to their first baby. Dmitri talked him through the part: where to breathe, where to crescendo, reminding him to focus on the final consonant sounds of the words to ensure that the diction was clear. Jonathan was keen, and, for the most part, his voice was up to the job. He had a few problems with sustaining the long notes, and the notes near his break were weak. But then most people had the same issues.

When Jonathan had rehearsed his section, Dmitri called up Linda, the alto, to sing her aria 'Oh thou that tellest good tidings to Zion,' which was one of his favourites. Linda also knew the part well. Today, though, she sounded a little out of breath.

The next few solos went reasonably well, though Jenny, the soprano, was on the edge of a cold. He prescribed lots of hot water and lemon. This time of year, colds were always an issue, and Jenny had three school-aged children and a husband who worked in the City. None of that stopped her, however, from standing closer and putting her hand on his arm quite a bit more than was strictly necessary. He ignored it, but didn't move away either. He'd walked this thin line with other women in the choir before. As she was relatively new, he didn't want her to do a runner with the concert coming up.

All in all, he was glad when the last solo had been rehearsed. The singers stayed to chat for a few minutes, then left to go to the pub. Carole-Ann, though, stayed behind. Dmitri steeled himself for the grilling he knew he was due. About the fact that he looked tired and scruffy and hadn't done anything on the Oxford application yet.

But just as he was gathering his excuses, the door of the church opened and Phil walked in. For a second, Dmitri cursed his sister. She had made good on her threat.

'Phil,' he said, going up to him. There was a slightly

awkward moment when he wondered if he should hold out his hand for the older man to shake. Instead, he decided it was best to give him a brief hug. 'It's been a while. Sorry I haven't called.'

'Yes, well, you're busy, and so am I,' Phil said. 'But I'm still hoping I'll be able to drop in some evening, do some carolling.' His smile took in Carole-Ann too. 'Just like old times.'

'Yes,' Dmitri said, feeling wistful. His mother had loved singing carols, and everything else about Christmas. Phil had made sure that Marina had the best of everything. They always had a lovely tree, and a giant turkey with all the trimmings. Tanya and their mother would spend hours cooking and baking up a feast of Russian and English dishes. Some years, Phil's kids came, or Kolya and Nigel, Carole-Ann, other people from the church. With Phil at Christmas, there had always been a lot of laughter, joy, good food and company. Dmitri had even, at times, tried to convince himself that what had happened – their coming here – had been for the best. He'd never quite managed it, though. 'You should come along, Phil,' he suggested. 'We've got lots of concerts and carolling scheduled. You'd be very welcome.'

'We've missed you, Phil,' Carole-Ann added. 'It hasn't been the same without—' She broke off, looking embarrassed. Dmitri hadn't realised until that moment that it had been three years since Phil came regularly to the choir. Since Marina died. '...you,' Carole-Ann finished quickly.

'Ah, that's sweet of you to say.' He went over and gave her a kiss on the cheek. 'Time flies, doesn't it?'

'That's for sure,' Carole-Ann said, blushing a little.

Dmitri wished he could just slip out, leaving the two of them chatting together. But of course, that wasn't going to happen. Phil was a busy man. The fact that he was here...

well... Though the last thing Dmitri wanted was a 'friendly chat', there really was no avoiding it.

'Do you have time for a pint?' Carole-Ann asked him. 'It would be lovely to catch up.'

'I'm afraid I can't tonight,' Phil said, looking genuinely sorry. 'But I'm free a few nights this week, if you're doing any carolling.'

Dmitri nodded to Carole-Ann, happy to let her go through the schedule with Phil. They were doing Covent Garden and an old people's home in Barnes. Then there was a Christmas light switch-on somewhere in south London – he couldn't recall exactly where. In his present mood, the idea of Christmas carolling held no joy.

As Carole-Ann and Phil went through the details, Dmitri flipped absently through the score to the *Messiah*. He liked Phil, loved him, even. But being around him always made him feel like a boy of twenty, the age he'd been when Phil had first come into their lives. Saint Phil, ready to save fallen women from a life worse than death. In this case, it had been Dmitri's mother, Marina. When they'd arrived with nothing, they'd been lucky enough to meet Kolya early on at the mission. He'd helped them find a temporary place in a hostel while Marina tried to find work. But even that had been too expensive. Marina, who had been an accountant back in Russia, had got a job as a cleaner during the day. But even at the time, Dmitri suspected that when she sometimes went out on her own to work a so-called 'second-job' at night, it was something shameful, that he didn't want to think about. He worked all hours so they could stay off the streets, but London was such an expensive city, and even with Kolya's help, it had been a struggle to keep their heads above water.

But everything changed almost overnight when Marina met 'the boss' in person. Normally, Phil had managers who took the cleaning crew from place to place in a van, and

Marina had heard his name but never met him. That day, however, the manager hadn't turned up, and Phil had driven them to their jobs himself. Marina was a kind, beautiful woman, who had also worked very hard to learn English. Unwittingly, she had managed to charm her employer. Though they had never officially married, Phil and Marina were together for thirteen years.

Dmitri felt sincere gratitude towards this man and all he had done for them. It was thanks to Phil that they had a place to live; thanks to Phil that they were able to get visas; thanks to Phil that they had all had their teeth fixed; thanks to Phil that Marina could work as an accountant again for his business, and Dmitri had been able to do a degree in music education.

And it was thanks to Phil that Dmitri had met Irina.

'OK, Tuesday night then,' Phil was saying to Carole-Ann. 'We'll have a few pints afterwards and you can tell me all the gossip.'

'Great,' she replied, her eyes bright and shining. Dmitri wondered if Carole-Ann might fancy Phil. As far as he knew, Phil had been alone for the three years since Marina's death. Maybe he should take it upon himself to play matchmaker. But that could wait for another day. His head hadn't stopped aching since waking up earlier in the afternoon. All he wanted to do was play piano for a while, then go home and have a cup of tea and a shower. He'd make a start on the damn application – he'd promised Tanya that much. And then, sleep. Praying that this time, he didn't dream.

Eventually, Carole-Ann left the church, carrying her large handbag and 'Keep Calm and Join a Choir' canvas tote bag. When the door closed behind her, Dmitri took a long breath. Phil walked a little way down the main aisle of the church, rubbing his hands along the smooth, varnished wood of the pews.

'So Phil, is everything OK?' Dmitri decided it was probably best just to get this over with.

'Tanya's worried about you,' Phil said, straight to the point. 'She's worried about what happens to you when she leaves. So am I.'

Dmitri raised an eyebrow. 'I suppose I should find a new flat. We've imposed on your hospitality long enough.' He sat down in one of the pews, facing the front of the church, away from Phil.

'The flat is yours, so you can do what you like,' Phil said. 'Keep it or sell it. That's not what this is about.'

'Then what is this about?' Dmitri turned. He felt himself reverting to the role of ungrateful stepson, that sullen, damaged boy who didn't appreciate the fact that his mother had taken up with another man, even if it had been for the good of everyone involved – and even though Dmitri had been responsible for all their troubles in the first place.

'Aren't I allowed to come and see how you're doing? Since you never return my calls?'

'I'm sorry,' Dmitri said. 'I should have called you.'

'It's OK,' Phil said, a little too easily. 'I just wanted you to know that if you need anything...' he paused, 'like money. You know you only have to ask.'

Dmitri felt the shame creeping over him. He ought to be acting a lot more grateful to this man who had done so much. And who, even after his mother's death, was still offering to help out.

'Thanks Phil,' he said, putting aside his pride. 'I appreciate that. But I don't need money. You know I don't spend much. I'm fine.'

'Good.'

They both fell silent. There seemed to be so much to say, but Dmitri didn't even know where to begin. Didn't know how to bridge the gap.

Phil continued to pace. He opened his mouth, then closed it again. Finally, he spoke, bowing his head. 'I don't know whether or not you believe me, Dmitri, but Marina was the love of my life,' he said. 'And not a day goes by when I don't miss her.' His blue eyes grew cloudy. 'I would have given anything for a few more years.'

Dmitri felt his own throat tightening. He wished Phil would just stop talking.

'I did my best to make her happy,' Phil said. 'But there was one thing I couldn't give her. The thing she wanted more than anything else.'

'What's that?' Dmitri barely managed the words.

'She wanted *you* to be happy. And after Irina, when you closed yourself off, it broke her heart.'

He welcomed the anger that surged up inside him. 'I know what you're trying to do, Phil, but it won't work.' His tone was sharp. 'My mother is gone. You know perfectly well why things are like they are. And why Irina did what she did. Do you think that bringing it all up again is going to help?'

'I could find you ten girls tomorrow who would accept you as you are, Dmitri.'

'What?' he seethed, his voice low. 'Ten women who could come to the flat, clean my toilet and then stay a while, show their gratitude? Is that your idea of love, Phil?'

Phil clenched his fists. 'If you're implying – anything,' he said, his voice low, 'then you'd better shut the fuck up.'

'Look, sorry,' he said, forcing himself to look up and meet Phil's angry blue eyes. 'I know how much my mother loved you. You gave her a life she never could even have imagined. A great life. I'm glad you had the time you had. And I miss her too.'

Phil said nothing. His nostrils were still flared, his face red.

'And I'm grateful for you letting us stay on in the flat. Believe me.' Dmitri tried to smile but fell short.

'I don't want your fucking gratitude,' Phil growled. 'I never have.'

'I know that,' Dmitri said. 'Still, you have it.'

Phil shrugged. It seemed like a grudging acceptance of the unspoken apology.

'And speaking of business,' Dmitri drew in a long breath, 'how is Alexei Maximovich?' He gripped the edge of the pew. This was sheer stupidity.

Phil came up beside him. He stood over Dmitri and crossed his arms.

'You mean, have I had any news of Irina?'

Dmitri stared straight ahead – at the altar, the crucifix, the large, dark windows of the church. People came here for comfort, for hope. How did they do it? How did they make themselves believe?

'Yes,' he said. In truth, he didn't want to know, but he felt he had to ask. Alexei Maximovich, Irina's father, was a business associate of Phil's. He'd come to England in the early nineties and made a lot of money in real estate. Irina had gone to the best schools, been petted and fawned over all her life. Dmitri had met her one summer when she'd returned from studying at Amherst College in America. She had been twenty-two, he twenty-four.

'I know that she's still in America with her husband,' Phil said after a long pause. 'Boston, I think. They've got a second child now. A girl. Irina's a stay-at-home mum.'

'That's good.' Dmitri couldn't say any more. In actual fact, it was a relief trying to picture Irina in her life that he would never have any part of. Anything other than relive that awful time. He didn't love her any more. He was sure of that. But the sting of Irina was like alcohol being poured on to an open wound.

Phil let out a long sigh. 'Don't ask me again, OK? Humour an old man. It's been – what? – ten years? Ten fucking years, Dmitri. I need to know that it no longer matters.'

'*She* no longer matters. I can tell you that.'

'Well, that's something.'

'Yes.' For the sake of argument, he agreed.

'Hey, look,' Phil came over to him and put a hand on his shoulder. 'The last thing I want is a row. I just wish…' he hesitated, 'well, you know. But I also know that you don't want or need anyone's help. You're a grown man. You make your own choices and you live with them.'

'Yes.' For a second, Dmitri rested his head against Phil's arm. He *did* appreciate the love that this man had shown him over the years, whether deserved or not. And, in fact, he was burning to confide in someone. 'I did meet someone, Phil.' There it was said. 'Someone amazing.' The vision of Nicola standing on Westminster Bridge, with the moonlight shining gently on her face, awakened desire in every cell of his body.

'And?' Phil said, his face so hopeful, so round and shiny with love. Dmitri knew then he should have kept his mouth shut. Sometimes it seemed that in this lifetime, his destiny was only to hurt those who loved him.

He sighed. 'And, I lied to her, and then I walked away.'

Phil rubbed the bridge of his nose, shaking his head slowly. 'And?' he said finally.

'There is no "and", Phil. There never can be.'

The older man nodded. He shoved his hands in his pocket and, without another word, turned and walked out of the church.

Chapter Twenty

If he hadn't been three thousand miles away, Nicola could have kissed the banker in New York who sent her a two-hundred-page info memo about an investment opportunity at a Paris fashion house and wanted a conference call at eleven p.m. that evening. Anything to get her out of her own head.

Admittedly, helping get the charity shop ready for Christmas had been a bit of a lark – until the debacle with the knickers. If Chrissie had been there to see Nicola stringing lights and setting out charity cards, how she would have laughed.

When she'd returned to her house, Nicola did a few internet searches. Sure enough, most charity shops didn't take knickers (though many purported to want bras) and any donated knickers usually ended up being recycled into rags or else sent to landfill. Apparently donated swimwear did not suffer the same fate, which seemed a bit odd. Odder still, was the outing her ex-unmentionables might be getting now. Had the lady with the pram given any of them to the shelter? Nicola almost laughed. Yes, it would have been much better if she'd put them straight in the bin.

She also searched the web for more about the Care charity and pulled up their latest statutory accounts from Companies House. The charity seemed to be in difficult financial straits. How many homeless people and refugees this Christmas were going to be on the streets when Care had to start closing its shelters? It wasn't something she wanted to think about. Yet from what she'd seen of the management at the Richmond shop, it was hardly surprising.

The manager. Oh God. Dmitri had mentioned the fact that she, 'The Heckler', had been spotted by someone in the choir, but why, of all the flaming people in the borough of Richmond, did she have to have run into that particular man? Would he share this new 'funny story' down the pub after the next bout of carolling? Would Dmitri laugh, or show no interest at all? She'd already been dubbed 'The Heckler'. What would it be now: the 'Knicker Queen' or 'Santa's Little Helper'? Fuck.

To prepare for the call, she poured herself a glass of wine, printed and read through the info memo. The words on the page, the columns of numbers, the facts and figures, calmed her a little. She finished reading the document just before eleven. Two hours later, when the call ended, her head was drooping from exhaustion, but at least it had been a much-needed, if temporary, distraction. She made herself a cup of lapsang souchong tea and took it to her bedroom, breathing in the steam and almost burning her throat on the hot, smoky-tasting liquid. She lay down in bed but sleep wouldn't come. Instead, she got up and plugged her phone into the adaptor of her surround-sound music system. Turning off the light, she lay in the dark, floating in a sea... of Rachmaninov, Chopin, Beethoven... until the early hours of the morning.

He'd broken his promise to fill in the application, but what did it matter? It was four o'clock in the morning before Dmitri finally left the church, and the piano. It was freezing and he'd had to wait twenty minutes for the night bus. His hands ached, his neck ached. But still, it had been worth it.

He'd been in a bad mood after the conversation with Phil – ashamed of his own behaviour at alienating a man who'd done so much for him. And hearing about Irina...

It had taken all his willpower to go up to the choir loft and open the lid of the grand piano. He sat down and adjusted the bench, took off his gloves and began to play. As his fingers took on a life of their own, his muscles striving to remember what had once been second nature, his mind grew quieter too. He didn't play Rachmaninov, but tackled Chopin, another of his one-time favourites. As he launched into the *Fantaisie Impromptu*, he felt his hands stretching closer to their old twelve-note reach. He lost himself in the tension between the slow beauty of the middle section, and the almost infernal complexity of the allegro section.

Moving on, he tried *Pictures at an Exhibition*, a virtuoso piece for solo piano that Mussorgsky composed as a tribute to an artist friend. There was a recurring promenade theme representing a person walking around a gallery in St Petersburg. Each 'painting': from chicks in a barnyard, to an old castle, to Baba Yaga's hut on chicken's legs, to the Bogatyr Gate of Kiev, was a brilliantly coloured musical motif.

Playing through it took an almost athletic endurance, and by the time he reached the end, he was sweaty and exhausted. But as the last chords died away, he felt radioactive with adrenalin. He'd done it! It hadn't been perfect – not by a long way. Nonetheless, he couldn't remember the last time he'd had such a sense of achievement. If Nicola had heard him playing like this, she would be proud of him... Nicola. The thought of her turned his fingers to ice. She would never hear him playing like this. Not now, or ever.

Dmitri had got his things together and left the church. If Nicola had walked through the door, as she had on that one, impossible night, he would have told her to go away.

The night bus dropped him at his stop and he walked slowly home. There were a few stars out, and the moon was bright in the sky. All the houses in the terrace were dark. He let himself inside the empty flat, went to the kitchen and put the kettle on. He hadn't eaten since—? He couldn't remember. The flat was freezing. The heating, on a timer, had long since gone off. There would be no hot water either, but that didn't matter. He really needed a shower.

When the kettle boiled, he poured the water over the tea leaves to steep. Then he went to the bathroom, turned on the shower and discarded his clothes. The water was icy and felt like a million pinpricks to his skin. By the time he stepped out of the shower, he was shivering. He'd grown so soft since he'd come to this country. In his youth, hot water had been a rare luxury, and even in the dead of winter, cold or tepid baths were normal.

He dried off, wrapped the towel around his waist, and got out his razor. Squirting some shaving lotion on his hand, he rubbed it on to his face. He paused, looking at his hand in the mirror. Nicola had believed the story he'd told her – so he thought, anyway. Believed that it had been a silly, unfortunate accident, and that, really, everything was fine.

But everything was not fine.

As he picked up the razor, his eyes were drawn, as they always were, to what else he saw in the mirror. His own body, but even after all these years, the sight still horrified him.

Skin melted and twisted into a desolate landscape of scars. Covering his chest, his forearms, his wrists, his hands – everywhere that the flames had touched as he'd crossed his arms, doubled over in agony. His torso was criss-crossed by a patchwork of scars from those months in the burns unit, when overzealous doctors had diligently – but unsuccessfully – attempted skin grafts. Even now, so many years later, the skin sometimes felt painfully tight and hot, as if his own body was consuming him from inside.

He forced his eyes back up to his face, the part of him that the world saw, the part that made people question his 'choice' to be alone.

They didn't know what lay beneath.

You look like a monster.

Irina had spoken the truth that night when everything fell apart.

He began to shave. Sometimes he wondered if it wouldn't have been better if his entire body had been consumed. If his face and manhood had gone, would he still feel this desperate, unfulfilled need for love? Or would he have been purified, like Handel wrote of the refiner's fire?

Of course, in hindsight, it should have been blindingly obvious that no woman, certainly not one like Irina, would want to bind herself to a freak. Everyone: his mother, Phil – even Tanya, had warned him that the relationship was doomed from the start. They'd said it in different ways: Irina was from a different world, Irina was young and naïve, or, in the words of Tanya, Irina was an ice queen and a pig. But he'd been so crazy, stupid in love. In his mind, he'd built her up as the perfect woman – one who, like his mother and sister, would love him despite his disfigurement. But she was his fiancée, not his mother or sister. She needed – expected – different things.

It never should have got as far as it did. In the normal course of things, he would have taken Irina out a few times; they would have gone to bed – or not. Either way they would have got the measure of each other much sooner. As it was, he did take her out. They had a good time. All the people who had warned him about her didn't realise that underneath that ice-queen exterior, she could be warm and funny, accepting of the fact that their circumstances were very different. They'd been like any other young couple, he thought. In love with the idea of the other. They'd fooled around, of course, but Irina was a devout Catholic and wanted to stay a virgin until marriage. He'd obliged her by asking, giving her a ring that had belonged to his grandmother, one of the few things of value that they'd brought with them from Russia. Putting that ring on her finger... it was by far the best moment of his life. She'd kissed him goodbye and left to go back to uni. They'd kept in touch every day by email, and she'd agreed to set a date when she graduated. And then, she would be his.

That day had never come.

She'd seemed different that final year when she came home for Christmas break. He remembered feeling worried but didn't want to admit it. For one thing, she was busy with family and friends, and he'd barely seen her. When he did see her, she wasn't wearing the ring. To keep it safe, she'd said. Then, one night just before New Year's, she came to see him. She'd been out drinking with friends and had acted like her old self. And she was wearing the ring. He'd been so happy; he'd showered her with words of love and she'd rewarded him. She'd seemed up for anything that night, and it was she who had suggested they lie naked next to each other in his bed. It was she who had taken off his shirt in the circle of light given off by the bedside lamp.

In hindsight, he didn't blame her. The look of horror on her face. She'd known that he had burns on his chest – back then, he hadn't kept that a secret. But he had never shown her. That sound that caught in her throat... She'd thrown herself off him and put her top back on with frantic haste. And then her parting words: 'You look like a monster.' The ring left on the bedside table...

Afterwards, she'd sent an email of apology, tried to smooth things over. They had grown apart; there were things he should have told her about sooner. Her feelings had changed. She really was very sorry; it was nobody's fault—

But it was someone's fault. His fault. In the aftermath, Dmitri had spiralled downwards to the darkest place he'd ever been. Irina had changed him. He'd seen himself through her eyes. And was disgusted by what he saw.

He frowned so deeply that his face twitched and he nicked himself with the razor. A small cut on his cheek began to drip blood. He let it drip, watched as the tiny droplet rolled down his face and plopped into the sink.

Irina had got married to Andrew, an American friend from uni, not even six months later. Her parents threw the happy couple a big Catholic wedding at a cathedral in North London. As family friends, Phil and Marina had been obliged to attend. Dmitri had been sent to stay with Kolya, who'd been charged with making sure he didn't do something stupid. Though he'd barely touched alcohol since leaving Russia, he'd found solace in vodka, longing to escape the pain through oblivion. Kolya had poured bottle after bottle down the sink, even locked him in a room like a prisoner. But by then Dmitri had become resigned to the course of his life. He would never love again, never allow anyone close enough to hurt him again.

He finished shaving, put the razor away and stuck a piece of toilet roll over the cut. It was always a relief to get dressed. Even in the height of summer he always wore long sleeves, and he had never let a woman see or touch him without his shirt. He put on a T-shirt and a long-sleeved pullover. Now the man reflected back looked completely normal. He left the bathroom to get a few hours of sleep before it was time to start another day.

- iv -

'The wolf took Ivan to the ends of the earth, to the enchanted realm of the sorcerer. In the dead of night he entered the forbidden palace. His eyes were blinded by the sight of the bird in all her fiery glory, imprisoned in a golden cage. She wept molten tears and sang a mournful song, bewitching him.

"I will free you!" Ivan whispered.

But just then, the sorcerer came upon them.

"You will never free her," the sorcerer said, his eyes dark and dead like burned-out coals. "Because only the greatest act of love will free her. Are you so brave and so foolish, young Ivan, that you are willing to take her place?"

"No," cried the bird, imploring him. "Do not do this!"

But young Ivan, so brave and foolish, did not listen. He remembered the old man and the old woman and their daughter Snegurochka. He threw himself against the bars of the golden cage, where he was consumed by tongues of flame, and the Firebird's blazing heart.'

– 'The Firebird', *The Anthology of Russian Tales*

Chapter Twenty-One

7th December

'Chrissie, do you have a minute?'

Nicola ignored a familiar tug of annoyance as Chrissie looked up, startled. Not from doing any work, but from the conversation she was having with the two other PAs.

'Yes, of course. I'll be there in a second.'

'Fine.'

Nicola went into her office and shut the door. She took a sip of coffee, so hot it burned her throat, but she'd been up most of the night, and right now she needed a jolt of energy. It was Monday morning, and the week was going to be busy closing the 'Timeless' deal. Thankfully, Ollie was in Frankfurt for the early part of the week. There was bound to be a break in the barrage of texts, and she could put off the conversation that needed to be had.

In fact, she had no idea how Ollie would react when she told him things were over. Their 'relationship', such as it was, had gone on for a long time. She hoped that the ending would be quick and easy; a little death.

The door opened and Chrissie came in carrying her notebook. She was wearing a black pencil skirt, sensible M&S court shoes and a blue chenille jumper with gold, purple and green stars embroidered on it. Chrissie really did have the largest collection of Christmas jumpers that Nicola had ever seen. This was by far one of the more tasteful ones.

'Shut the door, please,' Nicola said, taking another sip of coffee.

The older woman did so and sat down in the visitor chair opposite the desk. 'You OK, Nicola?' she said. 'You look a little tired.'

'I had a late-night call with New York. But, guess what, Chrissie,' Nicola gave her a sly smile, 'I've got a special project for you.'

'A project?' Chrissie looked wary.

'A *special* project.' Nicola leaned forward. 'One that I think you'll like.' Lowering her voice conspiratorially, she explained what she needed Chrissie to do.

'OK...' Her PA's eyes got rounder and wider as she listened. 'So you're saying that you want me to go on eBay – during work time – and see if this charity called Care has any listings?'

'Yes. You've told me that sometimes charity shops list things, right? So see if this one does.'

'Some of the charities are also signed up to get a percentage of private listings.'

'What?' Nicola frowned.

'You can list things, and give, for example, ten per cent of the proceeds to charity. I can check if Care is one of the ones listed. Amazon has a programme too, I think.'

'Yes, do that. And I want a full set of their accounts printed off. And if there's a set for the Richmond shop, I want that too. Give the head office a call if necessary. Finally, I want to know what this stuff is worth – roughly.' She handed Chrissie the list she'd made in the middle of the night. A list of most of the clothing that she owned, including quite a few pairs of her beloved shoes.

Chrissie frowned down at the list. 'Am I allowed to ask what this is about?'

Nicola turned in her chair, looking sideways out the window. The sky was hazy and grey. From this high up, the rest of London looked far away. With a long sigh – she knew this was bound to be a mistake – Nicola recounted to Chrissie the overview of her weekend adventure at the charity shop. Minus the part about the knickers and the Christmas decorations.

By the time she turned back, Chrissie was trying hard, she could see, not to laugh. 'So, let me get this straight. *You* went to a charity shop, took over, made a sale and helped them get the shop tidied up for the holidays.'

'I *directed* them to tidy it up.' Nicola lowered her voice to a whisper. 'And you'd better not breathe a word about it to anyone.'

'Mum's the word.' Chrissie put a finger to her lips.

Yeah right, Nicola thought, ruing the bad decision she'd made to tell Chrissie the ins and outs.

'But what about the clothes? You want me to list this stuff for you? You'll need to take photos.'

'Right now, I'm not sure what I'm doing. The charity seems to be haemorrhaging money. I just want to see the full set of accounts. I don't know what I'm looking for, but I'm hoping I'll know it when I see it. In the meantime, if I do drop anything off at the shop, I want to know what the price ought to be, because Shelley and Charles certainly don't.'

'Got it,' Chrissie said, raising a bemused eyebrow.

'And while you're at it, get me a rundown on Privé's charity donations. It's all good and well making a few quid from Christmas jumpers, but I want the complete picture of the corporate contributions. Are we giving enough, taking advantage of all the tax breaks – that sort of thing. Ask Brian's PA.'

Chrissie made another note on her list. 'And can I ask what has prompted this sudden new interest, Nicola?' she said.

Fragments of the Saturday, which she'd omitted entirely from her account to Chrissie, flashed into her mind. The music of the carousel, the view from the bridge, the smell of the soup kitchen, Kolya, the voice of an angel, moonlight on water, snow swirling behind glass. *His* lips on hers, energy flowing through her body like a lightning rod. She swallowed hard and swept them away into a corner of her mind. Yes, those things made a difference, she supposed. But this *project* – if it could be called that, and if she was really going to take it on – was not because of any of those things.

'It's the right thing do to,' Nicola said.

'OK.' Chrissie gave her a maddening little wink. 'Is there anything else for now?'

'No.'

Chrissie stood up to leave.

'Wait,' Nicola said.

Chrissie paused at the door.

'How's your family doing?'

'My family?' Chrissie looked utterly surprised at the question. Nicola tried to remember the last time she'd asked Chrissie – anything, really. She couldn't do so. It was probably too late to make up for lost time, but right now, she felt determined to try.

'Yes. Is everyone all ready for Christmas? Are you having it at your house?'

'Well…' She hesitated. 'Yes. My daughters are coming down from Sheffield. One of them is bringing a boyfriend.'

Nicola smiled at Chrissie's clear motherly concern.

'And Mum's not too well, but...' she broke off. 'Why are you asking me this?'

'Just curious. If you need some time off to be with your mum, let me know.

'Time off?' The older woman looked shocked and horrified. No wonder the two of them rubbed along together despite their differences. Nicola was grateful to have Chrissie, even if the woman sometimes annoyed her no end.

'If you do, just ask, OK?' Nicola said. 'I know that Christmas is important to you. And... that I'm not the easiest person to work with.' There, she'd said it. Probably should have been said years ago, but there you go. Nicola wasn't quite sure about this new version of herself. Chrissie looked shaken too.

'No, you're not,' Chrissie said hesitantly. 'But we do OK, don't we?'

'Yes,' Nicola said. 'We do.'

Her PA turned and left the office, leaving the door wide open. Nicola sighed, got up and closed it. As she sat back down, an alarm beeped on her phone for a conference call. She silenced it. The junior associate could handle the call. She kicked off her high-heeled shoes and curled her legs underneath her.

Popping in her earbuds, she turned her chair back around towards the window. She lay her head against the soft leather of the headrest and closed her eyes. Only moments later, she was lost. In the one gift he'd given her – freely and unknowingly. The gift of music.

Chapter Twenty-Two

8th December

King of Kings and Lord of Lords,
King of Kings and Lord of Lords,
And he shall reign forever and ever.
Hallelujah!

As the last 'Hallelujah!' faded away, the crowd in the gallery above began to whistle and cheer. Dmitri turned and bowed and acknowledged the small orchestra that had accompanied them on the *Messiah* choruses and the other carols. It had been a good performance. The choir was energised, the acoustics of the Apple Market were good, and the trumpet player had, for once, hit all the notes in the 'King of Kings' section. Dmitri ought to be feeling on top of the world right now. Covent Garden was a worthy stage, and they had taken in quite a lot of money for charity from just this one concert.

As the crowd dispersed, the choir members began to step down from the risers. Phil had joined them tonight, and Dmitri saw him walk over to Tanya and Mark who had also been singing. Despite the triumphant performance, he wished he could just slip away into the crowd, avoid the chit-chat, the invite to the pub, the worried looks from Tanya and Carole-Ann. But after this event, he'd be expected to join in the festivities.

A few people came up, and they exchanged 'well done's and 'that was brilliant's. Dmitri felt like a ventriloquist's dummy, with a painted-on smile and words that were not his. Jenny, the soprano soloist, was chatting with a few of the other sopranos and looking in his direction. She gave him an inviting smile, her eyes bold and blue. Sighing inwardly, he gathered up the music and score and put it in his bag. As soon as they all got to the pub – there was already a place booked with an area reserved – he'd have to walk the familiar line of flirtation and detachment. Right now, he just felt so tired.

He'd barely slept over the last few days – just a few hours snatched in the early hours of the morning. Living on tea, water, the sweets brought by Tanya for the choir, and not much else. It was stupid. He needed to pull himself together—

'...Saw *her* again. You'll never believe it.'

He looked over to where Charles, one of the young tenors, was standing talking to Mark and Tanya. Charles worked in Richmond. It was he who had spotted Nicola on the train. Perhaps they were talking about someone else. He didn't want to join in the conversation or overhear it. He didn't want to think about Nicola. She'd unwittingly done enough damage – made him want things he could never have. Still, he couldn't help but tune in to what was being said.

'I'm not sure I should say it in front of a lady.' Charles grinned at Tanya. He leaned in and lowered his voice. Dmitri couldn't hear what was said, but all of a sudden, Tanya snorted with laughter.

'No!' she gasped.

'Yes! I'm serious.'

Dmitri was annoyed with himself for it, but he went up to them. Waves of anger were rising in his chest. They might be talking about someone else entirely. But if they weren't…

'You have to hear this, Dima,' Tanya said. 'Charles saw her again. The Heckler. And you'll never guess what she did.'

He took a breath, forcing himself to remain calm and detached. 'What did she do, Charles?' he asked.

Charles' face turned pink. 'She brought in a bag of fancy knickers to donate to the shop. She said she wanted to get rid of them. Clear them all out. Then she got mad when I said we couldn't take them. Seriously, she started giving us the history of every pair of —'

'Charles…' Dmitri's voice came out low and menacing. 'Do not say any more.'

Charles closed his mouth immediately, but Tanya took over.

'She was saying things like: "this one was from my married lover and this one was from a man from—"

'Tatiana,' he said, '*zatknis*.' Shut up.

Tanya glared. 'It's funny. What's up with you?'

He should walk away. Leave them to it. What did it matter if they wanted to laugh and joke? But he couldn't leave it. He pulled her a little way to the side, away from Charles, at least.

'It is not right to joke about this. Do you understand?'

Tanya cocked her head. 'You've seen her.'

'Just leave it, Tan'ka,' he said through his teeth.

'No – you have. When?'

He glared down at her like a dark thundercloud.

'She came to the church to apologise. To me – and to you – for what she did.'

'She came looking for you?' Tanya laughed heartily. 'When was this?'

He shrugged. 'I don't want to talk about it.'

'You slept with her, didn't you? Oh God.' Half laughing, she smacked herself lightly on the forehead. 'Yes, I can see that she would be just your type. Beautiful, cold. Unconnected. Sleeping around with whoever.'

'Do not speak to me like this,' he seethed. 'I am your brother.'

'*Did* you sleep with her?'

'No.'

'I don't believe you.' She gave him a sly look, and seriously, he almost lost it.

'I'm not going to stand here and listen to this.' He turned away from her, only to see that quite a few people were watching them argue. Fuck, what language had they been speaking? This was just the last goddamn straw.

Charles took a hesitant step towards him. 'Sorry, Dmitri, I didn't mean to cause a problem.'

'No worries, Charles,' he made a monumental effort to smile. 'There is no harm done. It's just, I did not find that it was something very nice to laugh at. I'm sure she...' he took a breath, '– The Heckler – has very good reasons for doing what she did. It is Christmastime. Are we not supposed to look upon people with kindness and charity?'

'Well, actually, that's what she did.' Charles gave a sheepish laugh. 'She kind of took charge. Got us to decorate the shop, clean it up. And the dresses and shoes she brought in made a lot of money for the charity. So I'm not complaining.'

'She did those things? Helped with the shop?'

'Yeah. I think we needed a kick up the backside.'

Dmitri couldn't help himself – he had to laugh. 'I'm sure she delivered that quite well.'

Charles laughed too and the others continued dispersing in groups to go to the pub.

Dmitri finished putting his music away. From across the

room, he was aware of Tanya glaring at him, and he was sorry he'd argued with her. He hoped he'd got through to Charles, and there wouldn't be any more talk of Nicola, her ability to transform a shop, or her underwear. He wanted her firmly locked away in his mind, which was the only place she could ever have in his life. And he wanted her there, all to himself.

Chapter Twenty-Three

10th December

Her vanity really was unforgivable. He didn't want anything to do with her – it was blindingly obvious. He hadn't taken her number, hadn't given her his. That 'goodbye' was as final as any she'd ever heard – or delivered herself. And yet, over the last few days, Nicola had been expecting to hear something. Been unable to believe that when he'd given her the brush-off and walked away, that it was final, irrevocable. She'd been wrong. Almost a whole week had gone by—

'...Thought we had already agreed two years?'

'What?' Nicola snapped back to her senses. She was aware of all the people in the room looking at her. The 'Timeless' deal was supposed to have closed today, but at the last minute, management at the target company had come up with a few final demands that were holding everything up. She looked down at her notebook, flipped through the thick binder with the accounts, the due diligence summary and the term sheet. Her mind had been elsewhere; she'd lost track of the discussion, couldn't find what had already been agreed. Worse, Ollie was there. He knew someone at the target and had 'popped in to say hello'.

'Yes,' she snapped, conceding (she assumed) the point as if she were talking to a particularly irritating bug. 'Fine. Now, can we just move on?'

Ollie raised an eyebrow. Nicola looked away. She was totally off her game – had been for most of the week. And the fact that Ollie was here to see it made her want to scream. As did the fact that he kept sending her texts, and she kept deleting them. He'd been in Frankfurt for most of the week, which had been a relief. But now, she was going to have to confront him in person.

'I think that's the last point for now,' the investment banker was saying to her. 'Thank you for that. Shall we have a break now and reconvene in, say, forty-five minutes.'

'Yes, fine,' she said. Thank God the meeting was ending and she could get her head together.

'Perfect.' The man she'd been negotiating with stood up and poured himself another glass of sparkling water. Nicola stood up too. The man's eyes roamed over her. The skirt on her beige suit fell several inches above her knee, the jacket was tightly fitted at the waist. She gave him a practised smile, more for Ollie's benefit, than his.

Nicola walked the length of the room carrying her notebook. Her high heels made no sound on the plush carpet. She went out the glass door of the conference room and down the hall to the executive washroom. Inside, the countertop was splattered with water, but she threw her notebook on to it anyway and locked herself in one of the black marble cubicles. She sat down on the lid of the toilet, her head in her hands.

It was gone – that 'fresh from the fight' rush of adrenalin that she used to have after a negotiation. She no longer had that feeling deep in her core that she was on top, in control and that nothing else mattered other than getting a result. In this game, desire was all-important. Desire to win, to achieve results, make money. Somewhere along the way she'd lost it and had barely even noticed.

Not until last Saturday, that is. For a brief moment, her life had been shaken up like a snow globe and filled with magic. Now, the flakes had settled, and inside, she saw something dead and plastic. Something worthless. The place where the desire had once been was hollow and cold, like a burnt-out star.

The door to the washrooms opened. Nicola waited until the door to the next cubicle banged shut, then went to leave. The good thing about men outnumbering women by four to one was that she normally had this loo to herself. She unlocked the door, flung it open. Only then did she realise that the bang of the door was a ruse.

Ollie was standing in front of her, his tie loosened around his neck.

'You're a hard woman to pin down, Nic.' He raked his fingers through his hair, mussing it up, and gave her that grin that once used to excite her. Part of her had wondered whether when she saw him again, she'd fall back into the old pattern. Take the path of least resistance. Now, though, as he licked his lips and his hands circled her waist, she felt a desperate, clawing sensation in her chest.

'Leave me alone, Ollie,' she said. 'It's over.'

Laughing, he lifted her up like she weighed nothing. He swung her around, on to the wet countertop. 'Is this a new game, Nic?' he said. 'Because I think I'm going to like it.'

Ice-cold panic flooded her as he pushed her skirt up, parted her knees and stood between them. She tried to push him away but he was much bigger and stronger. He started to undo his trousers.

'No, Ollie,' she gasped, barely able to breathe. It had come to this – again. She was powerless. Everything she had tried to build up in her life was nothing in the face of this one, inescapable truth. 'I don't want to.'

To her surprise, he stood back a fraction. She could tell that he was angry, trying not to show it.

'Come on, babe,' he said. 'Stop acting this way. I'm sorry I cancelled on us. I didn't want to, believe me.'

'I know, Ollie. But I can't do this any more.' She managed to wriggle off the counter on to her feet. Her knees were quivering so hard that she could barely stand.

'What's up with you?' He stood all the way back now, his face clouded with anger. But there was confusion there too. She felt weak with relief as she pulled her skirt back into place.

'Nothing,' she said. She grabbed her notebook and held it tightly to her chest. She tried to go past him, but he blocked her path again.

'Hey come on, Nicola.' The hard lines on his face softened. He looked genuinely surprised at the state she was in. 'It's me. I've missed you, that's all. Christ, I think about you all the time. I know I've been a bastard – I'm sorry.'

She nodded, unable to speak.

'Can't I at least have a hug?' He gave her his trademark lopsided smile that he'd used so many times to convince her of their glorious 'future' together – one she hadn't really wanted anyway. Being with Ollie had once been exciting, but now it was simply habit. Those promises he had made had kept her on the back foot, made her hurt. She felt like a caged animal that had only just become aware of its own captivity.

She allowed him to put his arms around her, pull her head to his chest. She had wanted this once, this tenderness from him. But now, as she felt his erection stir against her, she just wanted to escape.

'Let me go, Ollie.' She pulled away from him and made a lunge past him to the door. Fumbling to open it, she went out into the hall, gasping for breath.

'What the fuck?' she heard him say as the door closed.

Holding on to the wall to steady herself, she walked as fast as she could to her office. She grabbed her handbag, shoved some papers and her laptop into her satchel and made her way over to the PA desks.

Chrissie looked up from her conversation with one of the other PAs with concern. 'Nicola? What's happened?'

'I'm... not feeling well,' she said. 'Can you reschedule my meeting? I'm sorry...' Her mouth was suddenly flooded with saliva. She turned and ran off towards the lifts.

Chapter Twenty-Four

She was fine. There was nothing wrong. Nothing could be wrong; there was too much to do. Yes, she'd been stressed lately, working very hard. And the 'incident' with Ollie earlier had been difficult. He'd expected everything to be as normal between them, and the fact that she had changed… Well, he'd backed off. Sort of.

And seeing him had been a good thing. Her physical aversion had proved that she was over him. Yes, this new reality would take some getting used to. But most of the people she worked with were men. An ex-lover, more or less – she could handle that.

After running out of the office, Nicola had gone home. She was tired, her immune system was run-down from stress, it was all perfectly understandable. The journey had taken twice as long as usual. An 'incident involving a passenger at Surbiton' had delayed things at Waterloo. But it was *fine*. There was no choir to annoy her, no plans to disrupt or be spoiled, nothing at all waiting for her when she got home. Perfect.

As she poured herself a glass of wine, deleted the Rachmaninov and other piano music from her phone and ran a bath, she focused on how clear things had become. She needed some time off, and she'd take it, just as soon as the 'Timeless' deal closed. A month off, go somewhere warm. It didn't matter where, as long as it was far away from here. Clear her head, put some distance between her and Ollie, forget about Dmitri... she was well on her way to doing that already. Maybe she'd meet someone while on holiday and have a nice, uncomplicated love affair, the way other people did. And maybe, when she came back, she'd sell her house. Start over in a different part of London. Greenwich, maybe? That was nice, and close to work. Close to other firms too if she went through with her plans for a new start and quit Privé.

She needed a plan; she had a plan. Everything was more than fine – it was good. This evening she'd go through the detailed accounts of Care that Chrissie had printed out for her, along with the price list of items she'd noted down. There was plenty to do other than working and dwelling on the men who were not in her life—

Nicola's phone rang and she jumped. God, she was skittish today. The name that came up was her sister Jules'. Great – she'd been meaning to call her anyway.

'Hello?'

'Nicola.' In that single word, Nicola could hear the strain in her sister's voice. 'You said you would call me last Friday, but anyway I—'

'Sorry Jules,' Nicola said. 'I am coming – on Christmas Day. But it will just be me.' She gave a long exhale. Finally, she was on the way to telling the truth.

'No,' Jules said. 'Don't bother. I'm not doing Christmas this year. That's why I'm calling.'

'What? Why?'

'Oh Nicola!'

Nicola heard a loud, desperate sob. Hearing her little sister break down in tears made her feel like a hole had ripped open inside of her.

'Jules! What's the matter? You have to tell me.'

'Nothing. It's stupid, it's just...'

'It's not stupid – whatever it is.' Nicola stood up. 'Do you want to come over here? Or I can come to yours—'

'No – wait. Just a minute.'

Nicola waited, anxiety clawing at her chest. In the background she heard shouting and the sound of a child crying. She'd been so happy when Jules had married Stuart, had kids, bought a house in Putney within walking distance of a good school. It had made her feel like some of those years spent protecting her had had an effect. What could be going so wrong as to make Jules cancel Christmas?

'Stuart's home – finally.' Nicola heard the anger in her sister's voice. 'I told him I'm going out. I'll be at yours in half an hour.'

'Yes, great. And Jules – we'll sort it. OK?'

Her sister ended the call.

By the time there was a knock on the door forty-five minutes later, Nicola was frantic with worry. She'd tried to distract herself by going through the accounts, noting down a page of questions and points that needed clarification. But she couldn't keep her mind on the facts and figures. Why was Jules cancelling Christmas?

Nicola rushed downstairs and opened the door. Before her sister could even speak, she threw her arms around her and gave her a hug. She breathed in the warm floral scent of her hair that hadn't changed since childhood. They lived so close – why didn't they see each other more often?

Finally, she let go. She held her sister at arm's length. Jules gave her a strange look.

'What's that for? Are *you* OK, Nic?'

'Yes,' she said. 'Sorry, it's just good to see you. Now, come upstairs and tell me what this is all about. I have wine.'

'OK,' Jules said, like the single word was an effort. It had been about two months since she'd last seen her sister and Nicola noted the change in her. Jules had always been shorter, plumper, more bubbly and happy. Now, she looked tired, gaunt, and diminished. The light was gone from her blue eyes.

Nicola took Jules' coat and hung it up. She led the way upstairs to the sitting room, where she'd already poured her sister a large globe of red wine.

'Thanks.' Jules picked up the glass and started to bring it to her mouth. Then, with a sigh, she set it down again. Leaving the glass on the table, she went over to the doors that led out on to the balcony, opened them and walked outside.

Nicola came up beside her. It was dark and cold, but there were lights along the river, making oblong sections of the water sparkle. A few houseboats moored on the other side were outlined with Christmas lights.

'I hate this time of year,' Jules announced.

'No!' Nicola said, completely taken aback. 'No you don't, honey. You're upset, that's all. You're going to get through this. You have a lovely family, and you're young and—'

'I'm pregnant.'

'What?' Nicola stared at her, stunned. 'But that's wonderful!' She went again to hug her sister, but Jules pushed her away firmly.

'Wonderful? Is that what you think? You?' There was no mistaking the venom in Jules' voice. A cold wind blew down the river. Her sister started to shiver.

'Of course!' Nicola said. She had never seen Jules act like this before. 'Now come inside and get warm. I can drink your wine for you.' She said it lightly, as a joke, but Jules only sighed.

They went back inside and Nicola locked the doors. Jules went to the sofa and sat down.

'Do you want something else?' Nicola said. 'Water? Or coffee? Tea...?' She was embarrassed that she had so little to offer.

'Nothing,' Jules said. 'If I have anything, I'll just be sick.' She gave Nicola a recriminating look. 'How does everyone expect me to cook all that shit for Christmas when I can't even keep down water?'

'Of course you don't have to cook.' Nicola sat down next to her sister. As much as she really wanted a glass of wine, it probably wouldn't improve Jules' mood. 'I'm sorry that the burden always falls on you.'

'Are you?' Jules snapped. 'Because you sure as hell have never said.'

'Sorry.' Nicola shook her head, feeling ashamed. 'I thought you liked doing Christmas. And as you can see...' she gestured around them at the room that was devoid of anything bright or festive, 'I don't.'

'Yeah. I've never got why you hate Christmas so much. I mean, when we were kids – even up to the time you were at uni – you used to like it.'

The time at uni. Nicola felt her mind slide downwards towards the black hole of memories. Towards the thing she'd never told Jules. Would never tell her.

'Oh, I don't know,' Nicola said with forced brightness. 'I think it's just more fun for people like you who have a family. Kids.' *A perfect life*, she didn't add.

'Kids,' Jules snorted.

Nicola frowned. This was all so unlike Jules – it was starting to scare her. 'Why are you acting like this?'

'Look, I'm sorry. It's just that...' Her eyes suddenly filled with tears.

Nicola wanted to comfort her, but Jules shook her head.

'I've got three kids,' she said. 'And I love them, don't get me wrong. It's just that Stuart works all the time. He's never around because he's always got something *important* to do. I spend my time doing the shopping and having coffee mornings and doing yoga. And I know that people look at me and think I've got the perfect life.'

Nicola nodded reflexively. There was no point trying to pretend otherwise.

Jules eyed her. 'Yeah, I know you think I'm mad. But *you* have no idea. I'm so sick of it. So bored. Tired of wiping bottoms and tidying up. Watching Iggle-sodding-Piggle on C-sodding-Beebies. Reading *Aliens love underpants* for the fifty millionth time.' She sighed. 'And do you know, I had started to make plans. The twins can go to nursery full-time starting in March. I had this idea – this crazy idea – that I was going to get a job. Get a life – do something worthwhile. I mean, I'm not qualified to do anything, but I thought maybe I could go back to university. Finish my degree.' She wiped away another tear. 'I know it was a stupid idea, but now, it's impossible. I'll have a new baby. Four kids!' She grimaced. 'All I'm ever going to be is... a mum!'

As the tears rolled down her sister's face, Nicola took her hand. This time Jules didn't pull away. Between sobs, she continued.

'All I want, Nic, is to be like you. Have the things that you have. A clean house and an exciting, glamourous job. And someone like Ollie – God, to be able to jet off to somewhere exotic and warm. Lounge around on a beach all day and have hot sex all night. That's my idea of the perfect life.' She swallowed. 'Your life—'

'No.' Before Jules could continue, Nicola cut her off. The

time had come to end the lies. She never should have started them in the first place. Over the years, she'd told herself they were to protect Jules, shield her from the ugly truth. But that was a lie too. She'd told those lies to protect herself. 'That's not my life,' Nicola said. 'My life is miserable and empty. And there is no Ollie, either. Not any more.'

'What?' Jules looked shocked. 'You broke up? Why?'

Nicola recognised that look of shock and disappointment on her sister's face – the same one as when she looked out the window all those Christmas mornings and didn't see a pony grazing on the lawn or a puppy frolicking in the snow. In those days, Nicola had comforted her by saying that Father Christmas had got the wrong house; Jules would surely get what she'd asked for on her birthday instead. And later on, telling her sister that Dad was fine – no, there was no need for her to come round...

'Because Ollie's not free to go jetting off somewhere exotic.' Nicola said the words, bracing herself. 'In fact, right now, I suspect he's home with his wife and kids.'

Jules jerked her hand away. 'What the fuck are you saying?'

'I lied to you,' Nicola said. 'Ollie and I are not some glamourous, loved-up couple. We're just two colleagues who have sex when it's convenient, and then he strings me a line about this life we're going to have together someday. The life he already has. And the rest of the time, I just work.'

Nicola had barely even finished speaking when the slap came, hard and stinging across her cheek.

'You bitch,' Jules yelled. 'You're a tart, just like Mum.'

'Yes,' Nicola said. Her lower lip trembled as she put her hand to her cheek.

'I'm leaving. I never want to speak to you again.'

'No, Jules, please. Will you just hear me out?' The words came out sounding futile and hollow. Jules' reaction was no less than she deserved.

'Hear you out? What more can you possibly say? All these years, I've fucking worshiped you. I tell everyone – my sister is perfect. She has it all. I wish I was her. I've always wanted to be you, Nic, you know that. And now...' She slumped back on to the sofa, as if the fight had gone out of her.

Nicola sat where she was, unable to move. This was all just too awful for words. What possible gain had there been to tell Jules the truth?

'I'm sorry,' Nicola said. 'I'm sorry for what I've done, and that I lied about it. But I can't change the past.' It dawned on her then what Jules had said about their mum. 'Any more than Mum can, I guess. But I thought you were fine with what she did.'

'Fine!' Jules snorted. 'How could I be fine? She tore our family apart – tore you and I apart. But what else could I do? Where else did I have to go? You took sides, so I did too. But do you think I liked it when Ben was born? That stuck-up, entitled little brat. You don't see it – you're too busy "working" or having sex with married men – whatever it is you do. Dad's been dead for a long time. But you've left *them* all to me. "Jules doesn't work – she can do Christmas; pick Ben up from football; hang out with Mum's *family*".'

Nicola nodded slowly. She'd been so busy going through the motions of existing rather than living, and trying to avoid her own pain, that she hadn't even realised how selfish she'd been. It hadn't been enough to 'protect' Jules – not that that was even possible. She should have been doing more, putting herself out there on the front lines the way her sister did. 'Yes,' she acknowledged, 'that isn't fair. I should do more. I should talk to Mum, go see her. Take some of the burden off you.'

Jules shrugged. 'I don't even care any more. What does it matter?'

'It matters,' Nicola said. 'Family – even Ben.' She gave a

sad laugh. 'Do you know,' she continued, 'I think I understand why Mum did what she did. Life is short. She had a chance at happiness, and she took it. I don't blame her for that.'

'Could have fooled me.'

'OK, well, maybe I'm finally getting closer to forgiving her.'

'Yes, I guess *you* would.' Jules got up from the sofa. Once again, Nicola felt a rush of pain that her sister was leaving, walking out of her life. But instead, Jules went to the kitchen and took a tiny sip of the wine in the glass. For a second, her face looked like heaven. 'So how does it feel? Being with *Ollie*?' Her nose twitched as she said the name. 'Being with someone else's husband?'

'It felt safe – because it wasn't going to go further.'

'Safe – that's bullshit.'

Nicola sighed. 'OK, at first it felt exciting. Daring, I guess. But, as time went on, it felt painful. And then, it just became a habit. Habits are hard to break.'

'I just can't believe you.' Jules put down the glass and pushed it away. 'I mean, why would a woman like *you*, need to do *that*? You're gorgeous, smart, thin – you could have any man you want. Why?'

'Not any man,' Nicola said, half to herself. Those texts... the day she'd ruined... That damn music that she couldn't get out of her head. Pushing all of it aside, she turned to her sister. 'Look, what do you want me to say, Jules? That I'm sorry? That I'm a husband-stealing bitch? Fine. Guilty.' She held up her hands. 'Is that going to make things better for you? Or do you want my advice? From the *dark side*?'

'I don't know...'

'Well, I'll give it to you anyway.' Nicola took a breath. 'Love this new baby. And being pregnant. The sickness will pass. Go ahead and make your plans for the future but start enjoying *now*. Get your hair cut, go to a spa, buy some nice knickers – whatever it takes.'

Jules came back over to the sofa and sat down. 'God,' she said, finally, 'I must sound so ungrateful.'

'No,' Nicola lied. 'It's just that you already have so many things that count. A family, people who love you. Don't sell them short.' She took a breath. 'That's what Ollie did.'

Jules looked at her. 'So what are you going to do now?' she said. 'About *him*.'

'It's over. I told him so today. That's why I'm home early.'

'And how did he take it?'

Nicola sighed. Why was it so tempting to lie? Tell Jules that it was fine, like she'd told herself earlier. That Ollie was relieved; she was relieved. No one had got hurt and everything was going to be all right. But she'd been truthful for the first time. She didn't want to spoil that. 'He didn't believe it,' she said.

'So why end it now?' Jules asked.

'Because I'm tired of hating myself!' Nicola replied, the words bursting out. 'I'm tired of being complicit. Of doing the wrong thing and knowing, deep down, that I don't deserve anything better.'

'Why on earth would *you* feel that way?'

Nicola shook her head. Enough had been revealed for now. She wasn't going to lie, but she was still Jules' big sister. There were things that she didn't need to know. On the other hand, holding it inside for all these years had done nothing but cause a deep, gangrenous rot that infected her whole life. She *would* tell Jules, she decided. Just not—

A bright, happy, tune began to play. 'Let it Snow'. Of course, it was just like Jules to have her ringtone set to a Christmas carol. Dmitri would appreciate it, even if she didn't. *Dmitri* Taking a breath, she banished the thought of him from her mind.

Jules frowned at the screen and answered the phone. A man's voice spoke on the other end. 'Thirty-nine?' Jules replied. 'That is high. Did you give him Calpol?' Another pause and she spoke again. 'Yes, I think it's 50ml, but check the box. OK? I'll...' she trailed off, looking at Nicola. 'I'll be home in about thirty minutes.'

Nicola stood up with a sigh. She got her phone and called a taxi, wishing her sister could stay a little longer.

'I've got to go,' Jules said, getting up. 'Danny has a fever. He's asking for me. I'll wait for the taxi downstairs so I don't disturb your work.' She glanced over at the charity accounts, strewn out on the dining table. 'Another big acquisition?'

'No,' Nicola said. 'I tried to donate my knickers to a charity shop. They didn't want them, but I stayed and helped out a little. They're practically insolvent.'

For the first time all evening, Jules laughed. 'Your fancy knickers? God, I can just imagine.'

Nicola laughed too. As unfunny as the whole charity shop incident had been, if it had happened to someone other than her, well—

Jules came to her and gave her a hug. Nicola felt tears welling up in her eyes as she pulled her sister close and stroked her hair. 'We're going to be OK, aren't we?' Jules said.

Nicola saw her life flash before her eyes. Her sister's face when she finally got that puppy; her father's hunched-over form as he worked at the deli counter; a Christmas party, a snowy night, footsteps on an icy path. Like the needle on an old vinyl record player, she forced her mind to skip forward. To her office at work, Ollie's face in the executive loo, a phone thrown underneath a car. And finally, her memory came to rest on a man seated at a piano, his back to her, his long fingers igniting a spark unlike any she'd ever felt before. The aching sense of loss as he disappeared into the underground.

'I hope so,' Nicola said.

A horn beeped outside. Her sister pulled away.

'Call me,' Jules said. They both went downstairs and Jules put on her coat. 'We still need to figure something out for Christmas.'

'Yes,' Nicola said, smiling at her sister. 'We do.'

Chapter Twenty-Five

The church was freezing, but he barely noticed. Night after night he'd been here at this time – coming up to 4 a.m. Earlier in the week, he'd copied some sheet music from the library and playing from it, rather than from memory, had at first dampened his enthusiasm. So many years had been lost; this was ludicrous. But Nicola's comment, thrown out with such assurance: *'Why don't you just play piano?'* – had widened the seismic rift inside of him. At the end of the day, though, her arguments fell flat because she knew nothing about it. It was not possible to start again – it just wasn't. At thirty-six, he no longer had the potential that he'd had at eighteen. And, in any case, that was not why he was here now.

He played through the scales, arpeggios and exercises, again and again. Strengthening his fingers, lengthening his reach. Trying hard, not so much to get the notes flowing, as the words. The words to the essay he was supposed to write for the Oxford application – on why he wanted a doctorate in choral music.

The cold reminded him of his short-lived days in Moscow. He had taken masterclasses from some of the greatest pianists of the late- and post-Soviet era. He remembered that wellspring of terror bubbling up as his turn to play in front of the others approached. That certainty that when he sat down at the piano his fingers would be limp and useless. The knowledge that he was sure to fail and that the other students in the room were hoping he did just that. And then, the breathing exercises would kick in, the muscle memory. The years of training and the hours spent rehearsing. The music had a life of its own; his only role was that of a medium, channelling the spirit into tangible form. His hands were magic, the music was perfect, and at that moment, he would be perfect too. It didn't matter that it wasn't possible to please the tutors. Their role was to tear you down so you could be built up again. But if you did well, you *knew*, and so did the others. If you did well, then it was infinitely worth it.

Dmitri sighed and played the scales again, this time in lightning fast semiquavers that leapt from his fingers like showering sparks.

Had he kept to his career path as a pianist, he would potentially be at his peak now. His days would be spent rehearsing for concerts, making recordings, teaching the best and brightest students, and, of course, spending many hours alone in a small room practising. And each time he stepped out on stage, as he'd done so many times in his mind, it would all be worth it. What a joy it would be, performing in packed concert halls, sharing his love of music with a knowledgeable and appreciative audience...

His fingers stumbled and he crashed a series of chords, hoping to drive these stupid, pointless thoughts from his head.

I want to achieve my doctorate in choral music, because I love working with young singers to help them reach their vocal potential. He picked up the notebook and wrote the words down in Russian. He'd translate it later, then get Phil or Carole-Ann to check it, but it was important to get the sense of it right. *I believe it is the role of a choral conductor to both inspire and to be open to inspiration from the musicians in his charge. It is through this interaction that the music comes to life, and the whole becomes greater than the sum of its parts.*

God, he wanted to cross out the whole thing, but he had to write something. For once in his life, could he please just stop letting people down? Write the essay, send it in. Finish something, for fuck's sake. Make his mother proud – though she would never see it. And, his father...

He lay his arms and head down on the keys.

Christmas Eve. His mother had spent the day cooking, but the fear in her eyes made him sick; he couldn't look at her face. His father had gone off – Dmitri didn't know where to. Tanya was two floors down at the flat of her friend who had a TV. Dmitri unpacked his suitcase, took out Sasha's leaving present to him. A bottle of vodka. And God, he drank it down, waiting for the slow burn in his throat to become the blessed relief of nothingness. He went outside, not even bothering with his coat, just a scarf around his neck, his shirt and woollen trousers. Fresh snow had fallen earlier, and a few stray flakes were whirling in the currents of the air. The moon was out, bright and full, hanging just above the dark line of the pine trees. Beyond the block of flats, a fire was lit in a large steel drum, near the edge of the forest. There was a man on the other side of the fire, his eyes glittering orange and gold. His father. He was sitting on a log, smoking a cigarette. Next to the log was a vodka bottle cooling in the snow. Dmitri hefted his own bottle and took another drink. Perhaps oblivion was the one thing they could still share.

In the end, he'd left the letter on the table the previous night. Gone to bed, spent all night worrying about what to say. But what on earth was there to say? And then, this morning, his mother had bustled around the flat, trying to talk of hope, looking on the bright side, and the future. It had seemed as though he were watching the scene through someone else's eyes as his father stood up from the table, wrenched her arms above her head and punched her in the face. Then he left the flat.

One of her teeth had gone and her nose was broken. She had tried so hard not to cry as Dmitri held a wet cloth to her face to try and stop the bleeding. He couldn't cry, he was too numb.

And before he'd got out the vodka, she had begged him to go to a friend's, even though it was Christmas Eve and all that food was already made. Begged him to stay away for now – a few days – until the shock had worn off. If only he had not lost his place, if only he had listened to his mother. But instead he went outside, walked over to the fire. What was he planning to do? Sit on the log? Try to say he was sorry? Try to say nothing? He barely even saw his father stand up and approach him. It was all so hazy. His eyes stung from the heat of the flames, the smoke, the dire chill of the air. And then the blow had come. Well, he supposed he had been expecting it. And he deserved it too. He'd ruined his prospects, pissed away the thing he'd been working towards his whole life. The one thing that meant something to his father, his family. His jaw stung and he fell back against the log and hit his head. Fuck, could he even move?

And then, his father had held the bottle over his chest and poured the freezing liquid over him. It smelled of something – not vodka. Lighter fluid. The cigarette dropped...

And he shall purify the sons of Levi. Dmitri mumbled the words inside his head. Trying to drown out the smell of burning flesh, the sound of his own screams. And the pain. In only a few seconds, the fire accelerant had done its work, ripping through the layers of flesh. But he'd been lucky, the doctors said. Lucky to be alive. Though he didn't remember it, though it was like moving through water, he had managed to roll over in the snow, they said. The burns to his face, and those below the waist would heal in time.

He remembered those weeks in the burn bed. Screaming for morphine. The hatred he felt towards those doctors and nurses. The hatred he felt towards his mother, who sat by his bedside and prattled on about leaving – going somewhere where they would be safe and happy. To the west, where they would have a new life. He'd wanted his father to come to see him, that much he remembered. More than anything in his whole life. And vodka. He'd wanted that too.

The burns on his chest had got infected, and eventually, he was too weak even to feel the hatred. He'd come very close to death. He'd sunk down to an unreachable place, where there was sunlight, and music, and he could relive that day long ago, when he had first boarded the train for Moscow. And he'd seen the pride on his father's face, and the love. He'd wanted to stay there, in that place of memories; to live there, give himself up. There was no pain there, no guilt or loss. There were no tears: not those of his mother when she came to tell him that his father had been found dead in the woods with a shotgun bullet through his head. He gladly would have traded his life, the music, the future – anything – to stay there. But in the end, he was powerless. Powerless against his body slowly healing. Powerless against the relentless will of his mother to make him survive. Powerless to get off the train on that endless journey to the west, still bound in compression bandages. And, ultimately, powerless to escape the shadow that followed him every day of his life. He had forgiven his father years ago for what he did, if he had ever blamed him at all. But he had never been able to forgive himself.

Dmitri lifted up his head. Tears fell on to the page as he picked up the pen and began to write.

Chapter Twenty-Six

11th December

When Nicola woke up on Friday morning, her head hurt. She blamed it in part on the wine she'd drunk after Jules left. But she knew it was more than that. Ollie had a wife and kids, just like her sister did. He was a husband and a father. Just because she'd managed somehow to compartmentalise what they'd been doing, and just because Ollie seemed to feel no guilt whatsoever, didn't change anything. Above all, it must not change the fact that it was over.

She'd have to speak to him again, unfortunately. Tell him to delete those texts and all trace of her from his phone. Whether he did so or not would be up to him, but at least she would have tried to do the right thing.

Nicola forced herself to get up and dress for work. Walking out yesterday at a crucial time was unprofessional and might be detrimental to closing the deal. Before leaving the house, she gathered up the Care accounts and shoved them in her satchel. There were definitely a few red flags, though not enough to lodge a complaint with a charity watchdog. The accounts had been signed off by a firm of independent auditors. Was it pure financial ineptitude, normal practice or sheer laziness?

There was one person she knew who might, or might not, have some insight.

When she arrived at work, she closed the door to her office and did a quick internet search as she drank her morning coffee. For the phone number of the Central Connection homeless shelter. Nicola dialled the number and spoke with the harried employee who answered. Yes, Nicolai, the man she knew as Kolya, would be in after lunch. Did she want to leave her name?

No.

Nicola spent the morning making up for the time she'd lost the day before. It was good to be busy – too busy to question what she was doing. At one point between calls, she made her way around to the other side of the floor, to Ollie's office. His door was open but he was on the phone. When he saw her, he made a 'five minute' gesture, but she didn't have time to wait that long. He looked a little off – like he'd pulled an all-nighter and hadn't had a chance to put on a clean shirt. Or maybe he'd been out late drinking and was in even more of a rough state than she was this morning. Either way, she didn't care. All she wanted to do was draw a line under things for good. They'd have to carry on working together – for now, anyway. But surely, they were both adults and that shouldn't be a problem.

At lunchtime, Nicola forwarded her phone to Chrissie's desk and made her way out of the building. She got the Tube to London Bridge, and then got a taxi across the river. By the time she reached the shelter, it was half one. There were a few people milling around outside, but as she walked down the steps and inside the door, the place seemed less busy than it had been on the Saturday of the Christmas Lunch. As before, her first reaction was the smell – hot food, disinfectant – but she had to acknowledge that most of the shelter refugees looked like they'd had a shower and clean clothes. Nonetheless, the place made her feel uncomfortable and nauseous – and above all, guilty for her own reactions.

A clean-shaven male worker came up to her. 'Can I help you?' he said.

'I'm here to see Nicolai,' she answered.

'I'll need you to sign in.' He handed her a clipboard and she scribbled her name. 'I'll see if he's available,' the man said. He looked down at the scribble. 'What name shall I give?'

'Nicola Taylor.'

'And you want to see him because?'

'Look, I'm a friend of Dmitri, OK?' she said. Getting into this place was almost more difficult than getting past her office reception.

'Of course.' The man reacted instantly. 'Come this way.'

She followed him across the main hall. At the food service window there were trays of stew and vegetables. Steam rose up from a vat of soup that actually smelled good. She scanned the room looking for Francesca. There was no sign of her. Two young children were playing in the hall; one of them opened the piano and plunked out a few notes.

They went through a door to a corridor with a shower room, TV lounge and a children's playroom. At the end of the corridor was a door marked 'office'. Inside were three cluttered desks staffed by two men and a woman. The man knocked on another door opposite the photocopier. 'Yes,' the deep voice rumbled from inside.

Nicola felt unexpectedly nervous. The accounts – yes, she had some questions about charities in general and the Care accounts. But Kolya was a counsellor, not an accountant and this homeless shelter had nothing to do with Care. No – as soon as he saw her, he'd know why she was here.

The man opened the door. 'There's a woman here to see you,' he said. 'Her name is —'

'Nicola,' Kolya said, his huge frame suddenly filling the doorway. 'Hello again.' If he was surprised to see her, he showed no sign.

'Hi,' she said, sounding hoarse. 'I'm sorry, I don't have an appointment.'

'Never mind,' Kolya said. He turned to the man who had brought her. 'Thanks, Tom. I'll take it from here. Would you like some tea, Nicola?'

'Yes, please.'

She went inside and Kolya went to get the tea. The room was clean and bland like a police interview room, though someone had made an effort to put a leafy plant in the corner of the room, and the chairs and sofa were padded, if very worn.

Nicola sat down on one of the chairs and put her satchel on her lap. Kolya returned with a pot of tea and two cups on a tray. He set it down on the coffee table.

'When you phoned earlier, I hoped you would come at a time when I could see you,' he said. 'And here you are – your timing is perfect.'

'I didn't leave my name earlier.'

He laughed. 'I know.'

He wasn't going to make this easy – that much she could tell. And now that she was here, Nicola had no idea where to begin. It was the room that was throwing her off. There was no desk to sit behind; she was out in the open. A room with no place to hide.

Kolya sat down in a chair facing her. He was wearing a blue jumper, jeans and brown leather boots. His black beard was neatly trimmed. Something about him made her feel... safe. He poured tea into both of the cups and she declined milk or sugar. He handed one cup to her and put three sugars in his. She was aware of him watching her as she took the papers out of her bag.

'Is that an application to volunteer with us?' he said. 'That is what we usually require, you know, before accepting a volunteer.'

'I can't believe you expect people who are giving up their time to fill out paperwork.'

'We work with very vulnerable people here, Nicola,' he said. 'Our volunteers receive safeguarding and other training. This is the modern way of charity work.'

'Really?'

He raised a black, bushy eyebrow. 'Yes, Nicola. We are talking about people's lives.'

'Yes, of course.' She acknowledged the rebuke. 'I don't want to take too much of your time.'

'Yes.'

'Anyway...' she continued, 'since volunteering last week at your shelter, I've taken an interest in another charity.' She explained briefly about the mismanaged charity shop and the anomalies she'd spotted in the accounts. He listened, peering intently, not at the papers she tried to show him, but at her. By the time she ended her spiel, she was breathless and felt like she was talking in circles. Once again, she had the sense that he could see right through her.

She fell silent, and Kolya nodded. 'Yes,' he said, 'I can see that I was right about you. You are a very intelligent woman, and, I must say, wasted washing dishes.' He gave a little laugh. 'And while I am not an accountant, perhaps I can put you in touch with someone who can answer your questions.'

'OK... thanks.'

'But really,' he said, 'you don't need me to discuss accounts.' He fiddled with a gold ring on his left hand. She hadn't noticed it before now. It was a gesture she'd seen many times. At hotel bars, before a man invited her up to his room. But, oddly, she didn't get that vibe from Kolya.

'You're married?' she said without thinking.

'I am married to Nigel.' He paused to let this sink in.

'Oh, so you're...'

'Gay. Yes.'

'Is that why you came here?'

He laughed. 'I'm afraid that in my time, Mother Russia – or perhaps it was Grandfather Lenin – did not like her queer sons. From the moment it became possible to leave, I did anything – sold everything – to get the money to come here and stay here. You understand?'

'Yes,' she said, not really wanting to imagine the obstacles that this man, like Dmitri, might have had to overcome. 'I think so. Is that why you became a counsellor?'

'I suppose. I was lucky to meet Nigel. He pulled me out of the gutter, literally. The rest is, as you say, "water under the bridge". Now we have two children. Orphans from Russia.'

'That's... good,' Nicola said.

'Yes.' He gave her a kindly smile. 'But now, Nicola, it's your turn. You didn't come here to talk about accounts or hear about my life. So I think you should tell me why you're here. Then, we can talk.'

For a long moment, she didn't speak. She stared down at her nails, neatly trimmed and polished with clear gloss. 'You know why I'm here.'

Kolya sat back, steepling his fingers. He was going to make her come out and say it.

'You've known Dmitri for a long time,' she began.

'Yes.'

'I'm sorry.' She shook her head, frustration and hopelessness bubbling to the surface. 'This is complete madness. I shouldn't have come. It's clear he doesn't want to see me or know me. And if that's the case, I can live with it. I mean, for all I know, he might spend every Saturday with a different woman, taking them to silly places around London. But for me, it was more than that – or, it could have been.' She sighed. 'I guess I'm just... trying to understand.'

Kolya nodded. 'You are an intelligent, beautiful woman, and much more besides. You want to know why Dmitri walked away.'

She swallowed hard. 'Yes.'

Kolya sat back and put his hand to his forehead, rubbing the lines there. 'You ask a lot. You ask me to break bonds formed over many years. Possibly lose my friend.'

'Then I'm wasting my time.' Nicola began shoving the papers back into her bag. This was pointless and embarrassing. She'd already said so much more than she'd intended. She closed the clasp on her satchel and made to stand up.

'Please,' he said. 'Stay. Drink your tea. You have taken a big risk coming here.'

'I don't want tea,' she said. 'I want answers. If you won't tell me outright, then at least will you answer my questions? You've told me that he's a decent person. So I'm assuming that he's not a rapist or a murderer. Please do correct me if I'm wrong.'

'He is not any of those things.'

'OK, great, we're getting somewhere.' She sat forward. 'So is he gay? In a relationship? Married?' She rattled off the various possibilities. 'Or is it something to do with the fiancée he mentioned? Or is he just a player and I happened not to be his type? Because I've already embarrassed myself enough, and I don't have time to play games. Say the word, and I'll walk away right now.'

Nicola was even more annoyed when Kolya barely seemed to react to her outburst. He sat there calmly, watching her, assessing her. Finally, he spoke again. 'I think that what I would propose is a trade.'

'A trade? Of what?'

'Information, of course.'

'What information?'

'Look at it from my perspective,' he said. 'You walk in off the street. I know little or nothing about you. You ask me for answers. I am asking you for answers in return.'

'Fine,' she said. 'Ask. What do you want to know?' She could feel herself getting worked up again, her voice rising in pitch. 'Do you want to know about my work? How hard it's been climbing that ladder, getting where I am now? Do you want to know about my affair with a married man – how ugly and awful it is? Do you want to know about my mum leaving my dad and starting a new family? About my dad withering away and finally walking in front of a car? Do you want to know if I'm too messed up to be with your friend, or not enough to understand him? Seriously, you can ask me anything.'

'Then I will ask you this – why are you so angry?' Kolya said, showing no emotion. 'Why would a woman like you, who so clearly needs to be in control, allow her life to proceed in this way? I want to know the one thing that you are keeping back. The one thing that makes you like you are.'

'There is no "one thing",' Nicola said emphatically. 'Nothing that I'm... keeping back.'

Kolya shook his head. 'Nicola, I see a lot of women in my professional capacity. You will never be free from things that you keep hidden away.'

'No, you're wrong!' She was practically shouting now. She stood up ready to go out the door. Professional capacity or no, this man knew nothing about her. It wasn't like she had the truth branded on her forehead.

'Sit down.' Though his voice was soft, it was a clear command.

She sat.

He fell silent again.

Her heart was racing, her palms clammy with sweat. This wasn't how she had envisioned this going – not at all.

'I'm sorry if I have upset you,' Kolya said. 'Some day, if you wish it, we can talk more about you. Or I can refer you to someone else.'

'I don't need to see a shrink,' she said, trying to regain her composure. 'I need you to tell me about Dmitri.'

Kolya nodded. 'Ever since you came here that first time, I have been thinking about this. What I would say if – *when* – you came back under just these circumstances. I could see immediately that you were different. That, somehow, you were special. But Dmitri is a very damaged person. I don't think you understand this.'

'Damaged? What does that mean?'

'It means that he has suffered a great deal in his life and I don't want me – or you – to make that worse for him.'

'Does this "damage" date from his time in Russia? He told me about losing his place at music school. And that his father was a drunk, and violent to his mother.'

'His father was violent, yes.'

'And that he threw away his career as a pianist.'

'Yes, that is also true.'

'So all of that is very tragic, and I'm sure he's a very sensitive, artistic person or whatever. But what am I not seeing here?'

'He has not told you his "one thing".'

'Oh, for fuck's sake.'

Koyla stood up and moved around to sit in the chair beside her. 'You have put me in a very bad position, Nicola,' he said. 'If I don't tell you what you want to know, you may well go to him. He walked away from you before, but it was not for lack of wanting you. I do not think he could walk away a second time.'

Nicola stared at him, turning this over in her mind.

'But if you did go to him,' Kolya continued, 'then you might discover that all is not what it seems. You would be, as you say, "within your rights" to walk away, like his fiancée, Irina, did. But if that happened again…' Kolya's eyes darkened almost to black, 'then it might destroy him.'

'I don't want to do that,' she whispered. She felt like she was standing on the edge of a razor blade. On one side lay happiness, on the other, infinite darkness. And moving either way would cut her to shreds.

'No. You don't,' Kolya acknowledged. 'You came here because you have much love to give, and receive, if only it wasn't all trapped inside.'

'I said, I don't want to talk about me,' she felt obliged to argue.

'That may be. But if, on the other hand, I betray the confidence and my friendship and tell you the truth, then I need you to promise me something. If what I have to say makes it impossible for your "complete madness" to continue, then you must walk away. Never see him again. Live your life, such as it is. Allow him to live his – such as it is. It will be your choice.'

'Fine, I agree. If I can't handle the truth, then I'll go away.'

Kolya nodded. His face looked like that of a man condemned to the gallows. With the negotiation over with, Nicola sat back and drank the now lukewarm tea.

Thirty minutes later, Nicola ran out of the mission. She vomited the bitter tea into the gutter at the side of the street.

Chapter Twenty-Seven

12th December

'Ouch! Fuck!' Dmitri's hand stung as his fist connected with Kolya's eye, leaving not even the slightest mark. Kolya caught his arm by the wrist. 'I can't believe you would betray me,' Dmitri said. 'After all this time – all these years.' When Kolya had asked him to stay on after teaching music to the children at the shelter, he'd assumed they were a person down and needed an extra hand. Never in a million years had he expected... this.

'I did it for your own good,' Kolya growled. 'I've got your back, just like always.' He let go of Dmitri's wrist.

'I *walked away* from her. She was nothing to me.'

Kolya laughed grimly. 'Too bad you never got to join the Young Pioneers. They would have loved you. You believe any bullshit, don't you? Even your own.'

'Shut up.'

'I saw the way you looked at her,' Kolya said. 'She was not "nothing" to you. She deserved an explanation. More than what you gave her.'

'She *deserved*? What about me?'

Kolya shook his head. 'What do you deserve, Dima? You make your own choices.'

Dmitri sat down in the chair and put his head in his hands, letting his hair fall across his face. When Kolya had told him that Nicola had come here, seeking him out, he'd felt, for an instant, such a desperate surge of joy that it had dispelled all rational thought; eclipsed all the reasons for what he had done. But only for an instant. Now, all that was left was the shame. That she knew the truth – the ugly, sickening truth – about him.

'Come on,' Kolya said, sitting down next to him. 'You know how it breaks my heart to see you like this. I meant what I said – I thought I was doing the right thing. Trying to spare you another Irina.'

'I know,' Dmitri said, not raising his head. *Another Irina*.

'Why don't I go make some tea?'

'What did she say?' Dmitri looked up. 'How did she react?'

Kolya leaned back in the chair, pursing his lips. 'I wouldn't say she took it all that well.'

'Oh God.' He closed his eyes. Irina's face ballooned in his mind. Her words twisting themselves through the fibres of his mind. *Monster...*

'She was shocked and horrified about what happened to you. At the cruelty of it. Just like anyone would be.'

'I never wanted her – or anyone else – to pity me.' His stomach felt like it might turn inside out. 'What else?'

'I explained to her about Irina. And the others.'

'You told her all that?' he practically choked.

'Yes, because I can put it in a way she understands. And because, in some ways, I think that you two are very similar. Though, I'm afraid she ran out before I got to the bottom of her reasons.'

'So for all your so-called explanations, this is how it ends.

She ran out.' Dmitri opened and closed his fist, watching the tendons stretch and strain. 'You know that when I get up from this chair, Nicolai, we will never speak again. You were the one person I thought I could count on. The one person I have truly looked up to all these years. But what you have done is unforgivable.'

Dmitri stood up, half-hoping Kolya would make a move to stop him. That this whole thing was a great big joke. But Kolya stayed put, his mouth set in a silent line. Dmitri knew he should walk out. Go home or go find Tanya at the bakery. Go to the church and play piano, like he'd been doing for hours on end every night. But somehow, his desire to play the piano had become tangled up with his desire for Nicola Taylor. Both, he knew, were something that could never be fulfilled. This must be what it was like to go mad.

'No, Dima, you're not mad.'

Dmitri didn't even realise that he'd spoken aloud – that he was pacing back and forth in the small room – until Kolya answered.

'You are who you are, and I am sorry if now I have made things worse. That is what I wanted to avoid. You can leave, of course, and think the worst of me. We will never speak again.' He let out a long sigh. 'But before you go, I must know that you will be safe.'

Dmitri laughed bitterly. 'If you know me so well, Nicolai, then you know your fears are unfounded. I'm too much of a coward.'

'The vodka bottle makes men brave.'

'I haven't had a drink since Irina got married.'

'Yes, and what a state you were in then. It is something that I never want to see again. Please do not leave. Let me make some tea.'

The years flashed before Dmitri's eyes. Of all the time he'd spent hating himself, this moment was among the worst. He owed it to himself to go. But he simply lacked the energy.

Kolya got up and left the room. Dmitri sat down, staring at the beige walls that felt like a prison cell. Time and time again he had refused referrals for therapy, convincing himself that it was weak to seek help; that he had his life under control. As Kolya had pointed out, he made his own choices. Usually, the wrong ones.

Kolya came back in with a tray of black tea and a pot of strawberry jam. Dmitri was grateful – he knew Kolya had developed a taste for the Earl Grey tea that Nigel drank, rather than plain Russian black tea. Right now, tea seemed the only thing that was still right with the world. He spooned jam into a cup in silence. The tea still needed to steep.

'So you have decided my fate,' Dmitri said, his voice hoarse. 'You have told this woman everything about me. I hope you have also planned out what the hell I am supposed to do now.'

'No,' Kolya said. 'I don't know what's in her head. I gave her the choice to walk away if the truth was too hard to bear.'

'It seems she made her choice.'

'You did too,' Kolya reminded him. 'You walked away from her. And yet, she was not shaken off so easily.' He shrugged.

'You like her.' Dmitri narrowed his eyes.

'Yes,' Kolya smiled sadly. 'I like her. When she walked in here – both times, actually – I thought to myself that my boy was finally growing up. I thought: what a dark horse, he is. All along, he's been waiting, biding his time until *she* came along. Ruining his precious Christmas carolling. Shaking him from his world of fairy tales and strawberry tea.' He smiled wistfully. 'But although I like her, I love you. I may have hurt you, Dima, but I would not have her do the same.'

Dmitri sighed. He poured the tea into his cup. 'Isn't that my choice?'

Kolya raised his bushy eyebrows. '*Is* that your choice?'

'I don't know.' Dmitri shook his head slowly. 'I can't stop thinking about her. It's like she's there in everything I do. I think about that day, and how it was to be with her, and...' he took a breath, 'how wrong it felt to walk away even though I knew I was doing the right thing.' He took a sip of tea, feeling the burn in his throat. 'And now, she came here.'

'Yes...' Kolya hesitated.

Dmitri sighed. It was not the reaction he'd hoped for. So often, Kolya and Tanya had harangued him to take a risk. That all women were not Irina. But, in this case, Kolya didn't sound convinced, and neither was he. Nicola hadn't so much walked away, as run for the hills. Why should a woman like her settle for a man like him – damaged, deformed, ugly? But Tanya had said that if something happened to Mark, she would love him even more. Surely, despite what he'd told himself over all these years, it was not impossible? But a woman like Nicola?

Either way, he knew that he'd never be able to face her or talk to her. But was there another way? How could he find out once and for all, if there really was no hope?

'You have made things very hard for me,' Dmitri said. 'And things were already hard enough. Tanya, I am sure has told you about this damn application.'

'Yes. I was going to ask you about it.' Kolya seemed relieved at the change in subject. 'She is very worried that you are not doing it.'

Dmitri turned and found his bag that had fallen on the floor aside the chair. He took the papers out and shoved them at Kolya.

Kolya took them and frowned. 'This is completely blank,' he said. 'When is it due?'

'Read the first question. In the essay section.'

Kolya flipped through the pages, squinting at the writing. 'How will achieving your Doctorate in Choral Music advance your career plans?' He frowned at Dmitri. 'That should be easy enough to answer.'

'Yes,' Dmitri said. 'The answer is, that it won't. I'm not filling in the application. I haven't told Tanya yet. Or Carole-Ann.'

Kolya moved forward in his chair. Despite his friend's professional demeanour, Dmitri sensed his anger and disappointment. He took out the page from his notebook that he had written that night in the church. Since putting the words down on the page, he had thought long and hard about this. It really was the only way.

He handed it to Kolya, who frowned at the Russian script on the page, then began to read aloud.

'*When I was eighteen, I lost my place at the Moscow Tchaikovsky Conservatory. I went home to my family in Novosibirsk, Siberia. My father poured lighter fluid on me and I sustained fourth-degree burns over forty per cent of my body, including my chest, torso, arms and hands. Due to my physical condition and immigration to the United Kingdom, I was unable to complete my studies to become a concert pianist in Russia. I am now thirty-six years old. I work as a school music teacher, conduct a choir and have a number of private students. For many years, I have been unable to play the piano other than in my capacity as a teacher. This is due to something called post-traumatic stress disorder. However, I have recently begun to make an effort to overcome this condition, and I have started to play the piano again. At present, my goal is to work towards resuming my studies of piano. Whether this is for the purpose of performing or teaching, I do not know at this time and would like to seek guidance.*'

Kolya stopped reading and put down the paper. 'Come here,' he commanded roughly, standing up.

Dmitri stood up. He had thought that he'd feel nervous or embarrassed hearing the words he'd written spoken aloud. Expected to feel disloyal – well, he did – but then again, what else could he do? If there was even a chance, a dim flicker of hope, then didn't he have an obligation to try? And as Kolya practically smothered him in his arms, and Dmitri laid his head on his friend's chest, for the first time in a very long while, he felt like he'd finally done something right.

Chapter Twenty-Eight

Fire burned inside her head. Flames so hot they turned from orange to blue in the darkness, illuminating the soft, fresh snow. The images screamed and clawed at her. The agony, the senseless cruelty of it. And the fact that had she not been told, she never would have guessed.

Kolya had given her the option of walking away. She hadn't walked – she'd run. Her heart ached for Dmitri and what he had suffered. But some people were too complex, some problems too deep. He needed something that she couldn't give. Now, at least, she knew why he'd lied to her and left her there at the station; understood the finality of the goodbye. And she didn't blame him – not any more. He had done the right thing.

After meeting with Kolya, Nicola had gone back to the office. Gone about her day. Attended her meetings and dialled in to her conference calls, the work a welcome distraction.

Before leaving for the night, she had put in a month-long holiday request for January. Whether she went away or stayed in London, she needed time and space away from work, away from her normal routine. Focus on her new start. January would be a good time to look for another job. She would use the time off to reconnect with her contacts, and get the process started.

Nicola spent Saturday working, tidying the house, and putting some more clothing in bags to take to the charity shop at some point – right now she couldn't face it. Keeping busy, keeping Kolya's words out of her mind: 'difficulty making attachments with women'; 'a deep hatred of his own body'; 'blames himself for what happened'. Keeping at bay the images in her mind, and the gnawing sense of regret. If she'd been a different person, had more to give... Well, some things couldn't be changed.

On Sunday, she went to see Jules. They took the kids: Lottie, and the twins Danny and James, out to lunch at a pub along the river. Jules seemed much brighter. She talked about how she hoped the baby would be a girl and showed Nicola paint swatches for redecorating the nursery. Thankfully, there was no mention of Ollie. There was a part of Nicola that was dying to talk to Jules about Dmitri, but each time she decided to bring it up, a lump formed in her throat.

After lunch, Nicola watched the children while Jules had her hair and nails done. She played Snakes and Ladders with the twins and spent some time with Lottie looking through a Disney princess fashion book. After a while, she put on a DVD for the kids and went to the kitchen to make herself a coffee. As she was standing there drinking it, looking at the family photos and kids' artwork on the fridge, Stuart came in.

'Hi Nicola,' he said. He took a mug from the cupboard and put a teabag into it. 'Thanks for helping out. I've got a closing on Monday and the junior's off at a wedding. Such a pain, especially this time of year.'

'Yeah, it is.' Seeing Stuart: handsome, clean-cut, and seemingly the perfect husband home for the weekend, reminded her of Ollie. Which wasn't fair. Not all men were cheating bastards. Only the ones she got involved with.

'So,' he said, eyeing her frostily, 'I hear you're coming on Christmas Day. On your own.'

Nicola stared at him. Had Jules told Stuart about her affair? Her cheeks grew flushed. 'I thought Jules said she wasn't doing Christmas this year.'

'Oh, she still wants to have everyone over. It's just the cooking. The smell makes her sick.'

'Right. Well I could—'

'Stuart? Nicola?'

'In here,' she called out to her sister. 'Just finishing my coffee.'

Jules came into the room. Her blonde hair had been tamed and straightened, and she was wearing make-up. Her cheeks were glowing from the cold. She looked good... Perfect.

'Wow!' Stuart said. 'You look fantastic.' He went to Jules and gave her a kiss on her glossy lips.

'Thanks,' Jules said, smoothing her hair unconsciously. She had eyes only for him. 'Are the kids OK?'

'They're just watching a DVD,' Nicola said. She felt like a third wheel. Though she was happy for her sister, and glad that Jules had come to terms with her 'situation', the loneliness she felt inside was almost overwhelming. 'I'm afraid I need to get home. I've got a call that I need to prepare for.'

'You two,' Jules said, taking in both Nicola and her husband. 'Always working. You put the rest of us mere mortals to shame.'

Nicola forced a smile. 'I think you're the one doing the real work, with kids and a family.' She admired her sister's ability to give and receive love no matter what, wishing it was a quality she shared. Nicola gave Jules a kiss on the cheek and gathered her coat and her phone to leave. 'Take care of yourself. And each other.'

'Oh, we will.' Jules went up to her husband and put her arm through his. At that moment, Nicola was sure that Jules had told Stuart everything. And here they were – a united front against the 'other women' of the world.

'OK, say goodbye to the kids for me. We'll talk soon.' The first tear began to roll down her cheek. She turned away and went out the door.

Chapter Twenty-Nine

13th December

Another rehearsal, another concert. Somehow, when he'd met with Kolya, told him about this crazy, impossible idea – to play piano again – he'd expected to feel differently. But as the last person from the choir left the church and he prepared to climb up to the choir loft, all he felt was scared. Scared of his own life – of being alone.

The idea of telling his story was bad enough; that soon, everyone would know the truth that he had hidden away for so long. But if he was going to achieve his dream, he would have to do it. He was less resigned, though, about what to do about Nicola. He'd been debating, turning it over in his mind ever since he'd learned that she'd come to the shelter. A plan growing and taking hold, like a haunting melody that refused to leave his head.

The door banged open and he looked up, startled. Tanya came into the church. 'I left my scarf here; did you find it?'

Dmitri nodded. He took the red wool scarf out of his bag and held it out to her. He remembered their mother knitting it for Tanya, years ago now. He'd found it in the pew where she had left her things for the rehearsal. How sad that a lost scarf was Tanya's only reason for coming back, for speaking to him at all. After the argument they'd had over the incident at the Richmond charity shop, Tanya had apologised. But it had been brief, and not, he thought, very sincere.

Tanya took the scarf from him. Then she dug in her handbag and pulled something out. 'Here, I brought you these,' she said. 'I mended them as best I could.'

He took the gloves with the Christmas pattern from her, feeling a rush of emotion. That despite everything, she still cared enough to fix them for him. The stitches were a bit uneven and the wool not quite the same colour, but that didn't matter. 'Thank you, Tanusha,' he said. 'I appreciate it.' To show he meant it, he took off the grey gloves he was wearing and put on the mended gloves. Even in that fleeting second of having his hands bare, he felt self-conscious. Was this another thing he was going to have to get used to once the truth was out? Right now, it all seemed too daunting.

Instead of leaving, Tanya walked a few paces towards the front of the church. She seemed pensive, like she had something to say but couldn't find the words. After a long moment, she turned around and faced him.

'Why do you not come to the pub any more, Dima?' she said. 'People are wondering if you are OK. I tell them yes, even though I know it is not true.'

'I'm fine.' Although a part of him longed to confide in her, the way he used to, the lie slipped so easily off his tongue.

Tanya sat down in the front pew, toying with the fringe on the scarf. 'I am tired of arguing with you, brother. Tired of worrying. I know you have not done the application, even though you gave me your word. But can you at least tell me why?'

He came and sat down beside her. Took her hand. Her warmth felt like a precious gift, a lifeline. He traced the veins of her fingers. 'You can ask, Tanusha. Of course. And I will tell you.' All of a sudden, he was bursting to do so. 'But you must keep it a secret for now.'

'A secret?' She turned and looked at him. He smiled and waited until she smiled back, warily.

'All these nights when I have not been at the pub, or filling out the application, I have been here.'

'Here?' She looked stunned. 'It's freezing.'

He shrugged. 'It is not so bad.'

'What are you doing? Have you finally lost your mind?'

'Yes,' he grinned. 'Probably.' He leaned in and whispered into her ear, 'I am playing piano.'

'What?' She turned all the way to face him.

'I am not going to apply for the doctorate in choral music; I am going to apply to study piano again.'

'Piano?' Her face was a mask of disbelief. 'You mean here, right? Not,' she paused, 'in Russia.'

'Yes here, of course. At the Royal College of Music. Or at Oxford. There are many good music schools. I don't know yet. But I would like to see if...' he took a breath, 'I might be able to perform.'

'To perform?' Tanya's dark eyes widened in surprise. 'But you have always said... you have always had a million excuses.'

'Yes,' he said. 'And all of them are real. Nonetheless, I want to try.'

'Please say this is not a joke.'

'It is not a joke. Come here.' He put his arms around her and held her tightly. He had put her through so much, so many years of worry, when he was the eldest – it had been his job to look after her. He could never atone, but he could draw a line in the sand. Start again. From the very beginning.

When they came apart, her eyes were shining. Looking at her face was like looking in a mirror – at his younger, unblemished self. He felt a rush of love for her, for her trust, her strength, her unwavering stability.

'Have you told Kolya, yet? Or Phil?' she said. 'They will be so proud.'

'Kolya knows. But I have not told Phil. Please, until it is more certain, say nothing. There are so many variables. I have to apply. I have to get accepted. I have to get funding. I will have to change my whole life.'

'We can sell the flat,' she said immediately. 'You will need your half of the money.'

'Let's not discuss that now,' he said. 'I just wanted you to know that this is what is in my mind. So that you are not so worried. So disappointed.'

'I am worried, but I have never been disappointed.' She stroked the hair back from his face. 'Only you have been disappointed, Dimochka.'

'Yes, well. There is good reason.'

'Shh.' She put a finger to his lips. 'Will you come to the pub? Just this once?'

He could feel the smile slipping away from his face. 'I promise I will,' he said. 'But not tonight. Next time.' He looked away.

'What is it? There is something else.'

The word 'no' formed automatically. But she cut him off.

'Is it she?' she said quietly.

'She? You mean "her"?'

'She, her! You know who I mean. The woman from the station. I do not want to call her something you do not like, so please, will you tell me her name?'

'Nicola.'

Even saying her name aloud seemed to invoke her presence, and a rush of the mad folly. Because really, that's what it was.

'Nicola,' Tanya repeated, stretching the syllables. 'And what is this "Nicola" to you?' She put up her hand as he opened his mouth. 'And do not say "nothing".'

He laughed. 'You know me so well. But in this case, you are wrong. It is true what I told you before. She came to the church to apologise. I took her out. We went all over London together. We went ice skating, and to the shelter, and we rode on the London Eye.' He recounted the day, leaving nothing out. Feeling, just for a moment, the same magic that had shimmered through his body around her.

'So she kissed you,' Tanya was saying, gripping his arm firmly. 'And then what?'

'I pushed her away.'

'Oh, Dima, I could smack you.' She furled her brow in annoyance.

'Yes. Well, ever since then, I have been here every night. Playing piano. In part it was to get her out of my mind. Or maybe, if I'm honest, it was to keep her in my mind.'

'Yes... and...? There is a "and" – isn't there?'

Dmitri sighed. When Phil had asked the same question, he'd been quick to say no. But now? What *was* the answer?

'She went to Kolya,' he said. 'He told her everything.'

'What?' Her eyes darkened to black.

'Everything. All my secrets.'

'No! I don't believe it.' She put a hand on his chest. He drew back reflexively, his lungs deflating.

'Yes,' Dmitri said. 'He told her about that. He said he did it for my own good. To spare me another Irina. I was very angry. But I have chosen to believe him. If I am going to do this thing – apply to study piano – then I need his help.'

'Yes, but there is more. There must be.'

He shrugged. 'I'm sorry to disappoint you. Unlike Irina, she did not walk away. She ran.'

'Then she is a bitch!' She spat out the word with venom.

'Shh.' He stroked her hair as she bowed her head. 'I wish for your sake that I could tell you something different. Give you some hope, but what can I say? She came to find me, and then, when she learned the truth, she made her choice. In a way, I am grateful to Kolya that it was done without my knowledge. That I did not have to see her face.'

'He had no right!'

'And yet, because it is done, I feel strangely free. Like I have finally gone so far down that none of it matters any longer.'

'Please tell me you're not drinking vodka.' Her face clouded with distress.

'No,' he said, trying to explain. 'Like I said, I am playing the piano. I am working very hard, for many hours. Playing my warm-ups, doing scales and exercises. Then I am practising something for the audition I will no doubt have to do. But also, I am having fun. Testing myself. Seeing what I remember. And the music, Tanusha. To have the music back...' he felt his eyes welling up, and swallowed hard.

'Yes. But... tell me it is not all for her. For this Nicola. Because if she ran away like you said—'

'It is not all for her. It is also for you. And for Mama.' He looked down at the Christmas patterned gloves, feeling a deep sense of loss, but also, of hope. 'And, it is for me.'

'That is the only way,' Tanya said. 'It must be for you. But I will try and support you if I can. In...' she hesitated for a moment, 'whatever you choose to do.'

He took her hand and looked up at the altar. Stared at the benevolent face of a pale Jesus Christ nailed to the cross. A man who died for the sins of the world, and then lived again.

He breathed in and closed his eyes, but only for a second. The time had come, the decision made. He really had run out of things to lose.

'There is something you can do for me, Tanusha.' He squeezed her hand. 'A small thing. Perhaps I will regret it, or more likely it will have no consequence whatsoever.'

'What is it?'

He explained, and she listened, finally nodding when he had finished.

'And when would you like it?' she said.

'There is no time to waste.' He raked back his hair, once again feeling intoxicated by the pure folly of it. 'Can you do it tomorrow?'

Chapter Thirty

14th December

'Nicola?'

The knock on the door frame startled her. Though her screen faced away from the door, she quickly shut down the internet search she'd been doing, on jobs for charity executives and trustees. It was early Monday afternoon and she'd just got back from a session at the gym. Trying to exhaust herself into oblivion. It hadn't worked.

'What is it, Chrissie?' She looked up.

'A man came by to see you. Earlier, when you were out.'

Nicola looked up and frowned. 'What?' she said. 'Who?'

'He didn't have an appointment, and there was no meeting in your diary,' Chrissie said. 'He said he just wanted to leave something for you.' She came over to Nicola's desk and held out a white bag taped shut with a red and gold Christmas bow on it.

Nicola took the bag and held it to her nose. She could smell cinnamon and spice. It reminded her...

She opened it and took out a square box about the size of a small plate. The box had a logo on it: 'The Braided Loaf'. There was a clear plastic window on top. Inside was a gingerbread heart, decorated with complex swirls of white icing. A Russian church with intricate onion domes, and a flurry of snowflakes falling all around it. Taped on top of the box was a memory stick.

Instantly, her stomach churned with emotions – fear, hurt – and above it, like a bird taking flight – precious, beautiful hope. He took shape in her mind's eye like a ghost materialising from the ether. His dark eyes, his tall, strong body. The scent of his skin, the taste of his mouth, his warmth, the joy in him... and the darkness. The scars, underneath where no one could see. Scars on his skin, and scars on his soul. He deserved to love and be loved. He deserved someone better than her. He had walked away; she had run. She couldn't give him what he needed. And yet, he had come to find her.

Nicola stood up instantly.

'Is he still here?' Her voice was breathless now.

'No.'

The word felt like a door slamming in her face.

'He didn't want to disturb you,' Chrissie said. 'I think he was a little relieved that you weren't in.'

'Relieved?'

'He said he wanted to leave the bag for you. That you would understand.'

Yes, she understood. He had made an opening gambit. Testing and challenging her in that way he had. And, in truth, she didn't know what, if any, move to make in response.

'Did he say anything else?'

Chrissie was grinning now. 'He asked me my name. How long I've been working here, and how long I've known you.'

'Yes, he would,' Nicola found herself saying.

'He was very friendly. Which was nice. And...' Chrissie leaned in, 'very handsome, and quite sexy. Though, I am a bit surprised. He didn't seem your type.'

'He's not my type,' Nicola snapped. 'He's nothing to me.'

'It's none of my business,' Chrissie said, 'but—'

'You're right, Chrissie, it isn't,' Nicola interjected.

Frowning, Chrissie put her hands on her hips. 'But I'm going to say something anyway. Whether you like it or not.'

Nicola leaned back in her chair and put her hand to her forehead, rubbing at the frown lines. 'Is it anything you haven't already said a thousand times?'

'Maybe not.' Chrissie pulled the door shut, leaning against it. She picked up the box in front of Nicola on the desk and looked at what was inside. 'But, damn it, I want you to listen.'

Nicola leaned forward. 'What is it, Chrissie? Do you want me to hold out my wrist so you can whack me with a ruler?'

'I know about you and Ollie,' Chrissie said, her voice low. 'You think you're being careful, but you forget about us members of the underclass. PAs, post room workers, security guards. We know a lot more than you think.'

Nicola kept very still, not speaking.

'I've known about it for a long time. I never said anything, though I think it's shameful.'

Nicola opened her mouth, then closed it again. They *had* always been careful – or she had, anyway. Infrequent liaisons that usually took place well away from the office. Or late at night after most people had left. But, of course, even if her colleagues were gone, there were people around. People that, as Chrissie rightly suspected, they'd paid no mind to.

'And the thing that gets me – the thing I really don't understand – is how stupid you're being if you think he's going to leave his wife for you.'

Nicola took a breath, trying to summon her usual anger. 'Whatever you think there might be between Ollie and me, you're probably wrong. And if – *if* – there was something, then it's over.' Nicola let out a long sigh. 'So, feel free to update your underground network of cleaners and post room workers.'

'Well, I hope it's true. Because there are other rumours going around about him.'

'Other rumours?'

Chrissie ignored the question and ploughed on. 'I swear, Nicola,' she said, 'what makes me so angry – just kills me, quite frankly – is how much time you've wasted. When you started here, I thought you were amazing. A strong, smart woman who could take on all the dickheads and come out on top. I was rooting for you. We all were.'

'I'm sorry to have disappointed you.'

'You damn well should be.' Chrissie's voice was sharp.

'So, let me get this straight,' Nicola said with forced calm. 'Are you saying that if I hadn't thrown away three years with Ollie – if instead I'd been out there on match.com or Tinder or scientific dating – whatever it is people do now – if I'd been out there looking for a nice man to settle down with; found him, taken some leave, had a big wedding, got pregnant and had a couple of kids – then you'd respect me now?'

'I do respect you.' Chrissie was sounding more and more upset. 'I just don't understand why you're settling for being so unhappy. Someday, I hope you'll tell me why.'

Nicola swallowed hard. Someday... maybe she would. She knew that Chrissie meant well, though, God knew, any love between them over the years had been of the tough sort.

'Are you finished now?' she managed to say.

'Does Ollie make you happy?' Chrissie pressed.

'No, of course not. It's never been about that. It's... well... I don't even know any more.'

'This man who gave you the gingerbread heart – does he make you happy?'

Nicola thought back to the day they had spent together. It had been fun and confusing; uplifting and frustrating. But somehow, in a single day, he had changed her.

'His name is Dmitri,' she said.

'Does this Dmitri make you happy?'

'I don't know.'

'You haven't given him the chance, have you?'

'It's complicated.'

Chrissie laughed. 'I wouldn't expect anything less from you.'

An alarm sounded on Nicola's phone. Time for the next call, the next meeting, the next, and the next...

Chrissie crossed her arms. 'That's all I wanted to say. Thanks for listening. Do you want me to ask for a transfer to someone else?'

'No.' Nicola silenced the alarm. 'What I want you to do, Chrissie, is start arranging the Advent Calendar for the twenty-second. I want you to order everything from this bakery.' She pointed to the name on the box. 'And book the large conference room. No – the auditorium. I want it to be big – the best. Because I'll have an announcement to make.'

'OK...' Chrissie's eyes lit up, probably at the mention of Christmas arrangements. 'I'll do my best.'

'And when you're done with that, I need a Chelsea away kit for a seventeen-year-old boy. Can you get that?'

Chrissie wrinkled her nose. 'My husband will kill me. He's a Spurs fan.'

Nicola smiled. 'Well, sorry about that. Now, I've got to go on a call. Thanks for the chat.'

'Really?'

Nicola gave her a wry sideways look. 'You'd better go now, before I change my mind.'

Chapter Thirty-One

As soon as Chrissie was gone, the door firmly shut behind her, Nicola untaped the memory stick from the top of the box and plugged it into her computer. It was an audio file. She put in her Bluetooth headphones and pressed play.

There was a second or two of background noise, and then, the music began. She didn't recognise the piece, just that it was dark and perfect, and it filled her with a sense of longing that she had never felt before. She picked up the box with the gingerbread heart and swivelled her chair to face the window. The music swelled and ebbed, the crystal notes soothing the rips and gashes in her soul like a balm. She lifted the box to her nose and breathed in the smell of ginger and cinnamon, wishing she could conjure up the scent of *him* instead. Just the thought of him made her feel light-headed and flushed, and full of uncertainty. An opening gambit. But was she ready to play this game, to step off the chessboard that had been her life for so long? This man needed something. Something she had never been able to give to another person. But now there were no obstacles, other than the wall she'd built out of her own shame and regrets. A few hours ago it had seemed insurmountable. But now? He'd been *here*, on her turf. He'd come for her. She turned the box over, laughing to herself that he still hadn't left his phone number. But she knew where to find him.

Nicola swivelled back around in her chair as someone knocked on the door. She turned off the music, feeling a sense of violation that the moment had been interrupted.

The door opened. Ollie's PA, Mary, was standing outside.

'You know you're supposed to be meeting with Jean Bertrand and Ollie, right?'

'What?' Nicola stared at her. 'It wasn't in my diary.'

'They're having drinks at Le Coq d'Or. Ollie left fifteen minutes ago. He said to meet him there.'

'Shit! Why wasn't it in my diary?' Jean Bertrand was Ollie's contact at a big French fashion investment house – one that would be perfect for the new opportunity that her New York contact had tipped to her. There had been vague noises made about him coming over but nothing specific. Talk about terrible timing.

'It was kind of a sudden thing,' Mary said, looking a little evasive.

'Fine. I'll go. Tell Chrissie, OK?'

'Sure.'

When Mary was gone, Nicola took the memory stick out of the computer and put it in the bag with the white box. Opening the top drawer of her desk, she put the bag inside and locked the drawer for safekeeping. She checked her make-up and put on her Louboutins from the bottom drawer. Jean Bertrand was an important client, and she ought to look like she was making an effort. Though Ollie, damn him, would think that any effort she made was for him.

Nicola went down the lifts and out of the building. The restaurant was a five-minute walk. She knew the bar well.

Dark, with booths and tables that were secluded, even during busy times. It was one of her and Ollie's 'places'. *Not any more*, she thought. Best to get on with trying to make things normal between them. Two colleagues, drinks with a client. Then, she could figure out her *other* plans.

Nicola wasn't sure what she registered first as being wrong. The fact that Ollie was waiting for her outside the bar, the fact that once again he looked tired and rumpled, or the fact that there was no sign of the client anywhere.

'Where's Jean Bertrand?' Nicola said as she walked up to him, feeling annoyed.

'Hi Nic, you look beautiful.' Ollie pulled her close and tried to give her a kiss. She turned her head at the last second and he got a mouthful of her hair.

'This meeting wasn't in my diary, Ollie. I've got a lot on, and so do you. He'd better turn up.'

'Yeah, he's on his way to meet us. Let's go and order a bottle.'

He steered her inside the door with his hand low on her back. The touch made her flinch. When was he going to get it through his head that he didn't own her – had never owned her?

All she wanted to think about right now was Dmitri, and listen to the music he had given her. Imagining his hands on the keys. Hands that were magical, and now, she knew that he wanted her. A flush filled her whole body as Ollie led her to a booth in the back. She caught him eyeing her. The flush turned to anger that she was here with him.

He sat opposite her and flagged down a waitress to order a bottle of wine. A bottle with two glasses.

'So where the fuck is Jean Bertrand?' she said accusingly. 'Is he coming, or is this all some stupid game?'

'It's not a game, Nic.' He gave her the smile that used to

turn her knees to jelly, but now just made her feel sick. 'I wanted to tell you that I've got some good news.'

'Good news?' She eyed him warily.

'Chloe and I – well, we've separated.'

'What?' Nicola stared at him, taking in the normally perfect hair that was now rumpled, the too loose tie, the wrinkled shirt, the five-o'clock shadow. Part of her wanted to laugh – the world certainly was a topsy-turvy sort of place. She waited for the other part to register her feelings: hope, relief, joy... instead, there was a dizzying feeling of vertigo, like she was in freefall. 'Please tell me she didn't find the texts,' she said, barely able to get the words out.

He shook his head. 'Hey, relax, won't you, Nic?' he said. 'I told you, it's all good.' The waitress brought over the bottle and glasses. 'Have a glass of wine.' Ollie poured wine into a glass and pushed it in her direction.

Nicola picked up the glass, gripping the stem so tightly that she thought it might break, but didn't take a drink.

'When did this happen?' she asked.

'At the weekend. Saturday night. I spent last night at my brother's house.' He poured wine into his own glass and downed half of it in one go.

'So what exactly happened?' she pressed, her stomach in knots.

Ollie put his head in his hands. 'Well, it's a little embarrassing.'

'Come on, Ollie,' she said in a low voice. She felt a chill spreading through her, just like when her own mum had come into the kitchen that day so many years ago and made her 'announcement'. So many lies, so many lives ruined. 'I need to know – did she find out about us?'

'No!' he said. He finished the wine in the glass. 'She's met someone else – can you believe it? Some single dad who works from home that she met at the school gates.'

'Chloe *met* someone?' Nicola gave a little laugh, then regretted it. This was just *unreal*.

'Yeah.' He laughed too – a little too loud. 'A few months ago, apparently. All this time when I've been here, working my arse off to put food on the table and pay for private school.'

'Yes, Ollie, you're a model husband.'

He frowned at her, like they were having two completely different conversations. Maybe they were.

'Hey, Nic, come on.' In a second, he was around the table, sitting next to her. 'I don't want to talk about her.' He took her hand, gripping it tightly as she tried to pull away. He stank of sweat and alcohol. Nicola felt repulsed by him. 'I want to talk about us. This is a good thing. It's the best thing that could have happened to us.' He half-stumbled down on to his knees beside her. 'We can finally be together. We'll do whatever you want – get married, or not get married. You want kids – we'll have kids. I want to start over. Have a life with you.'

'Why?' The question shoved itself in front of all the others. 'Why on earth would you want that?'

'What?' Ollie looked frustrated and confused. 'Because I love you. I mean, we've been good together from the start. We're so similar – partners in crime, two sides of the same bad penny.' He grinned at her. 'Not to mention, the sex.'

'Get up, Ollie,' Nicola hissed. 'People are looking.'

'Christ, why are you being so awkward?' He did get up, sitting half in the chair, his thigh pressed against hers. 'I thought you'd be as thrilled as I am.'

'In a way, I am,' Nicola said. 'You've made everything so clear.'

'I knew you'd see it like that, babe.' He reverted back to his bedroom smile. 'In fact, I thought maybe I could come back to yours tonight. You know, I've never been. To that lovely little house in Richmond-on-Thames?'

'Well, Ollie,' she sighed. 'I'd love to say yes. But I'm afraid it's not convenient tonight.' She hardened her voice. 'Or ever.'

'Nicola,' his voice held a warning note, 'what are you doing?'

'I've been trying to tell you, Ollie – we're over. If I were you, I'd get on the train, find Chloe and beg her to reconsider. Start over again, focus on your family. Let me go. If Chloe truly doesn't know about us, then you've got a chance at making things right.'

'Make things right? Is that what this is about?' Ollie raised his voice angrily. 'You want to throw away everything we have because you're feeling guilty?'

'Yes, Ollie. I do feel guilty. And the fact that you don't – well, it's only one of the reasons why it would never work.'

'Come on, honey.' She was surprised at the real distress on his face. 'I don't feel guilty because I know you're the one. What do you want me to say? Do you want me to beg?'

'Please don't, Ollie,' she said. 'I want to remember what we had with some degree of dignity, if that's possible.'

'But I'm telling you that I love you. That I want to be with you.'

'Yes, Ollie. But sadly, I don't love you, and I don't want to be with you.' It hurt to say the words. Three years of her life... that she wouldn't be getting back again.

For once, Ollie didn't speak. He sat back in the chair, stunned. 'You... you don't mean that. You're still angry with me. Because I cancelled last time. I haven't been there for you as much as you wanted. But all that's going to change now. I know this is a shock, that's all.'

'Yes, Ollie. It's a shock.'

'I'm going to leave you here to think about it, Nic,' he said, hanging his head in defeat. 'I'm at Charlotte Street if you want to find me later.'

The Charlotte Street Hotel. Their 'place'. Cosy five-star

rooms with huge, comfortable beds. Dinner at a little Thai place around the corner... Some of those nights they had felt like a couple, something other than two colleagues sleeping together. And now, Ollie had said the words she'd waited to hear for so long. Was she making the right decision?

Ollie flagged down the waitress and asked for the bill. He looked sad and broken; a part of her longed to comfort him. But that would be a mistake.

Ollie paid for the wine and stood up, his shoulders drooped. 'You know where I'll be. I'll be waiting for you.'

'Goodbye, Ollie, take care of yourself,' she said.

Without responding, he turned and left the bar.

This is surely what it felt like to be the stupidest man alive. Dmitri watched the man kiss her, and then steer her into the fancy restaurant like he owned her. He slipped behind the pillar of the huge office building, feeling like a stalker. From the moment he'd come here – to this world of steel and glass, money and power – carrying a little white bag with an iced gingerbread heart and a memory stick, he'd known that, this time, he'd finally lost his mind. The only saving grace had been the woman, Chrissie, who had been nice, and treated him like a human being. He'd wished he had the courage to ask her the thousand questions that he wanted answers to. Ask her the one question he *needed* an answer to. Was there any hope?

No.

He'd left the building and sat on a bench that ran around the edge of a giant planter with a light-covered tree in the centre. A part of him – that stupid part that seemed to be taking over – had told him to wait. Filled his rational mind with a ridiculous fantasy. That Chrissie would give Nicola his gift right away. She would open it, and overcome with – something – she would dash out of her office and try to catch up with him. He thought of the Russian fairy tale, 'The Scarlet Flower', where the beautiful Nastenka was imprisoned in a tower by a beast, in order to pay for her father's theft of the flower. Eventually, the heroine grew to love and accept the beast for what he was – disfigured and ugly – and her kiss broke the enchantment and transformed him into a handsome prince. There were similar tales in almost every language, he knew. And they would live happily ever after, end of story.

Rubbish.

He'd sat there for twenty minutes, half an hour. He had places to go: lessons, rehearsals, practice. People came and went, in and out of buildings, all with a purpose. He stayed there; texted an excuse to the school and cancelled the lesson he was going to be late for.

When finally she had come out of the building, she'd had a purpose too. And it hadn't been to find him. He followed her, trying to get up the courage to make himself known. Speak to her, look in her eyes and see the truth there, once and for all. But he hadn't found that courage.

She'd gone to an expensive restaurant nearby. Then he'd seen the man – handsome, self-assured – a man from her world. They'd argued briefly, in that way of people who are intimate with one another. Was this Ollie? A dagger of jealousy ripped through his stomach as the man kissed her. This was not the image of her that he wanted to fix in his mind.

A text came in from the school receptionist: did he want to cancel all the lessons for the day?

He texted back.

No – I will be there in 30 minutes.

He had promised Tanya that he would turn his life around, with or without Nicola Taylor in it. He was going to keep that promise.

Dmitri began walking back towards the underground.

The ache he felt for her was almost unendurable. But at least now, the moment of madness was over. He had been wrong – to trust again, even to consider opening his heart. He should have learnt from Irina, realised that she alone had been right. He wouldn't be making the same mistake again.

Near the entrance to the Tube there was a busy Tesco Metro. He detoured inside – he should get a sandwich, something to keep him going. A busy afternoon of lessons, and then his students' showcase in the evening. When that was finished, he'd practise the piano. His music was not tied to Nicola Taylor. No matter what, he would see that through on his own.

Dmitri got a sandwich from the rack and prepared to go back up to the till. He should go… he had promised… Tanya…

Instead of going to the front of the store, he went towards the back. He stared at the shelf, warring with himself. Nicola didn't matter. Nothing in his life was bound up in her. She would never look at him the way Irina had. Never look at him at all…

He grabbed the bottle of vodka from the shelf, went back up to the front of the shop, paid for his purchases and shoved them in his bag.

Chapter Thirty-Two

Nicola left the restaurant. She couldn't possibly sort through everything she was feeling, so she might as well go back to work. The confrontation with Ollie had been final, and she was glad of it. But it was painful too. As she walked along the quay, the tears came, rolling fast and warm down her cheeks. In a way, they felt cleansing, a sweet, blessed relief. It was over.

She stopped in Canada Square to dry her eyes. Standing in the winter garden beneath the lights and the swooping, glittery Christmas birds, a strange new gladness bloomed inside of her, like the green shoot of a snowdrop pushing through the frozen ground. A fragile new hope.

The office was buzzing when she returned, and a few voices hushed when she entered. Nicola had little doubt that the rumour mill was churning over the news that Ollie and his wife were on the rocks. She hoped that was all it was.

For the rest of the afternoon, she lost herself in a frenzy of meetings and conference calls with people around the world. The adrenalin felt good, it masked the turmoil of emotions just beneath the surface. She managed people, delegated work, had financial models and reports checked and rechecked. If people were busy, they didn't ask questions. If she was busy, she wouldn't question what she'd decided to do.

She glanced at the gingerbread heart, in its box on her desk. The memory stick was just a thing, but it's wires and silicon contained a promise. When she thought of the gift he had given her, she felt a strange shifting sensation inside of her. Could she do this? Really do this?

At half four, she left her desk and went down to the shopping mall. Spent half an hour making a few purchases. Utter madness – had she lost it completely?

When Chrissie came in at half five, she frowned at the box with the heart, then at Nicola.

'I'm going now to get the train,' she said. 'Have you eaten?'

Nicola looked up from the document she was reading, her mind a blank. 'Yes... No. I don't know.'

'Here.' Chrissie put a box of salad from Pret on her desk. 'Nicola, are you going to be OK? I thought you might have... well, everyone's heard about Ollie and his wife.'

'Has my name come up?' Nicola queried.

Chrissie raised an eyebrow. 'Not in a way I couldn't handle. But have you decided what you're going to do? I mean, are you and he—'

'We're over. Like I said before.'

Chrissie let out a long breath. 'What about Dmitri?'

Hearing his name, the music began to play in her head.

'I don't know,' she said.

Chrissie smiled. 'You're not going to stay too late, I hope.'

'You know me.'

The smile faded from Chrissie's face. 'See you tomorrow, Nicola.'

'Yeah. Thanks, Chrissie.'

Nicola went back to reading the document. She wouldn't

think about what happened next. She ate the salad, went down the hall to a meeting in the conference room.

Seven o'clock. Eight.

She was too busy to do anything. There was too much work to do. The plan – no, she wouldn't think about it. But at every moment it was there, just below the surface, gathering force.

Nine.

Ten.

Anticipation was swirling inside her as she returned to her office from the conference room. Opening her desk drawer, she took out the bag with the purchase she had made earlier at the shopping mall. Was she really going to do this? What was she expecting to happen?

She took the bag down the hall to the loo and locked herself inside. Getting undressed, she changed into the midnight blue satin and lace bra and panties she'd bought. It was ten o'clock in the evening. Most likely, she'd end up angry and frustrated, the car waiting in the street as she got out and banged on the door to the church. Feeling incredibly foolish. He had told her that he often went to the church after his rehearsals and concerts, staying late into the night. As she changed into the clothing that no man had touched, she couldn't keep the possibilities from her mind.

Remembering what Kolya had said, she heeded the warning. The thing that had happened to Dmitri in his past, the horrific crime that had shaped him – she was out of her depth to heal him. She put her clothes back on and looked at herself in the mirror. All she had to offer was right here in front of her.

As she walked back to her office, she texted the number of the executive car company, asking for an immediate pick-up. It was now almost ten-thirty. The odds were miniscule. And yet, she had to try. She thought for a minute of Ollie in the little hotel on Charlotte Street. Maybe he'd wait there all night for her, or maybe find another woman to keep him company. Or maybe he'd get bored and go home. Beg his wife to come back. She hoped so.

It took half an hour before the car arrived. By then she had built up the negatives like a high, insurmountable wall. There were so many reasons why she shouldn't be doing this. Too many. In the end, she told Patrick, the driver, to take her home to Richmond. She couldn't do it...

The car sped down the embankment towards the west. Past Somerset House, towards the London Eye across the Thames. Tonight the moon was a slender silver crescent, hanging low on the horizon. She relived the bubbling sense of joy she'd felt in those few brief hours that had changed her forever. Falling on the ice, the view from the bridge, snow swirling in the air, a kiss at a station. And the music... always, the music.

'Actually,' Nicola called out, 'I want to stop somewhere on the way. Turn off at Westminster Bridge and go towards Clapham.'

Dmitri loosened his bow tie and undid the top button of his shirt. Tonight's performance had been a triumph and a nightmare. It was the Christmas showcase at the sixth-form where he taught, and he'd had four students singing, in addition to the school choir. He'd dressed formally for the occasion and tried to look the part: smart, confident, a talented and inspirational teacher. He'd played the piano for his soloists, conducted the choir in their Christmas numbers. Yet, all the while he'd been thinking about *her* with *that man*; *that kiss*. About how stupid he'd been. And about the bottle of vodka in his bag.

After the concert, he'd been on his way home. It was one bottle. He had nothing on tomorrow until the evening's rehearsal. A few shots in private, no one ever need know. Drown her from his mind. Was she on her way to meet that man right now at some hotel, or were they together at her house? Before today, he'd had his precious vision of her to cling to, but now, all that was spoiled.

When he got to the Tube station, the line was suspended. Just what he fucking needed. He'd gone back out again to the bus stop. None of the buses went near the flat, but one went to the church. He'd promised Tanya that he was playing piano again. Why had he done that? Gone and opened his mouth? But in truth, he still did want to play. *She* didn't matter now, but the music did. Tonight he was going work on *Moonlight Sonata* by Beethoven, and then the Chopin *Nocturne* he'd recorded on the memory stick. Yes, they were pieces that reminded him of her – so beautiful, dark, and perfect – but he needed to get past that. Once he was inside the music, he would be out of reach of the pain. But the bottle sang out to him too. One shot. No one ever need know.

He'd got on the bus to the church, and now there he was. At the piano, the bottle still wrapped up in paper in his bag. He raked the hair back from his eyes and began his warm-up exercises. He'd play for a bit, just enough to ease his conscience, then go home. Focus on the anticipation... the cool, bitter liquid hitting his tongue, that slow, cold burn in his throat. And then the swimming feeling as the warmth took over, and for a few minutes, everything would seem right with the world. He'd go outside, talk to his father, smooth things over somehow. Glittering eyes at the edge of the fire. The snowflakes swirling in the air, the moon rising above the trees...

———

The door opened when Nicola pushed on it. Immediately, she felt a rushing sensation as her ears processed the sound. The smooth notes, moonlight rippling over dark water. She recognised the piece, or thought she did. Beethoven. There were depths of despair in those notes that frightened her, but also a profound beauty. The tension knotted in her abdomen as her heels clicked on the stone floor; she didn't try to hide the sound. This was it, it should be simple, and yet, each step was like walking through quicksand. She went up the stairs.

The playing stopped for a moment, broke off in mid-phrase. He'd heard her. He knew she was there. No going back now. The music began again, each note sparkling in the air before disappearing, blending seamlessly with the next.

It seemed a long time that she stood there, watching him. The rise and fall of his shoulders, the muscles of his back, his head moving as he played, his long, graceful fingers on the keys.

She walked forward and stood behind him. His tie was loose. Caressing his neck, she removed it. She began unbuttoning his shirt, ignoring his sharp intake of breath and the tightening of his muscles.

He stopped playing; swivelled towards her. Panic on his face.

'Shh,' she said, kneeling down between his knees. She undid more and more of the buttons.

'No, Nicola,' he whispered. His hand trembled as he put it over hers. She took his fingers to her lips and kissed them.

'Yes,' she said, opening his shirt.

Her breath caught as she saw the scars. A wasteland of twisted skin, tortured like ridges of cooled lava. And yet, with a beating heart, hard and alive. She began at his waist and slowly ran her tongue upward. Exploring, tasting his skin. His stomach muscles contracted and his hands reached down to tangle in her hair, and for a moment she thought he was going to push her away. She continued, kissing, teasing, running her fingers along the lines of the scars. Solid, real, and part of him. She was aware of his body shaking, the weighty drop of a tear. He was crying.

'You are beautiful,' she said, meaning it more than any words could express. She flicked her tongue where his nipple had been and he responded with a gasp. His hand cupped her chin and she let him raise her head. She looked into his dark eyes and saw everything imprinted there, every moment of his life, from the pain, to the joy inside of him, and finally, the decision – to give in to his own desire. Then he pulled her to him, kissing her with a powerful force and need, parting her mouth with his tongue. And she felt that same drowning joy as she had when they'd kissed at the station, as she drank him in, only half aware of him lifting her up so that she was straddling him and she felt his barely contained desire. Her skin was cold fire as he took off her jacket and her blouse. He ran his fingers over the midnight blue lace and freed her breasts, kissing them and sucking hard at her nipples. She arched her back, moaning with pleasure, as his hands and mouth possessed her.

'I've got a car waiting outside,' she said, gasping out the words. 'I'm taking you home with me.'

'I'm not sure I can wait that long.'

She laughed, pulling his mouth to hers and licking his lips. 'Maybe you wouldn't have had to wait if you hadn't walked away from me.'

His eyes sparkled, as he ran his hands down her back, pulling her tighter against him. 'You know why I did it.'

'Yes. Now get your things.'

———

Dmitri kissed her again, even deeper than before, and lifted her off him. Her green eyes were soft as she put on her coat and zipped it up, without bothering with the rest of her clothes. He felt drunk on her scent, on the molten feeling inside him. He let her go down the stairs before him, and she too seemed a bit unsteady on her feet.

At the bottom of the stairs, she raised her face so he could kiss her. Their lips met, and he ran his fingers along the back of her neck under her hair, so that she shivered from something beside the cold. He didn't want to spend a single second without some part of his body touching hers.

He closed the heavy wooden door of the church behind them and locked it. The car was waiting at the bottom of the steps. They went over and he helped her inside.

'Excuse me a second,' he said. He walked quickly over to the corner where there was a bin. He took the paper bag with the bottle out of his satchel, and threw it in. It seemed like another lifetime when he'd considered taking that dark road. Now, all of a sudden, every corner of his soul was illuminated.

'What was that?' she said as he climbed into the taxi next to her.

He turned to her, his hand brushing the porcelain skin of her cheek. 'I saw you earlier,' he said. 'I waited outside your work. To see if maybe you would come. I saw you outside a restaurant. With a man. Then, I don't know. I think I lost hope.'

'I'm sorry,' she said, tracing the scars on his bare hands. 'I... it was all a bloody mess. I had to sort it. Ollie – well, he's no longer with his wife.'

Dmitri instantly felt a sharp pang of concern, breaking through the trance-like state. 'So why did you come to me?' he said.

'Because I want *you*.' She reached over and touched him again, running her hands underneath his shirt. Where he was most vulnerable. 'It was wrong of me to go to Kolya, but I'm glad I did. It helped me to understand, and then, I had to decide.'

He gripped her hand before she could take away all power of rational thought. The words she said, her touch... but he had to *know*. 'You have seen me, Nicola,' he said in a low voice. 'What I am. How can someone as beautiful as you...' he hesitated, 'settle for that?'

She laughed then, the sound like a balm to his soul. 'For the first time in my entire life, I'm not settling.' Her hand continued to move, and her lips caressed the skin close to his ear. 'I know you've been hurt, you've endured so much. But I don't want you to think of that ever again.'

'I can't think at all,' he said, as he tilted her lips to his.

She unzipped her coat partway. Without caring about the driver's eyes in the rearview mirror, he leaned in and kissed her neck, the tops of her breasts. He could feel a wild tide of desire rising inside him once again. Was Richmond-on-Thames far away?

She laughed, and he realised that he'd spoken aloud. 'Quick as you can, Patrick,' she said.

They spent most of the journey touching, kissing. Not even in his most secret fantasies had he imagined a feeling of such joy, such a deep sense of rightness. He let the feelings flood him, drown out the worries that were still whispering in the background. Was this a one-off? Was she really choosing him?

As the taxi drew near to Richmond Town centre, she turned briefly to look out the window. Even at this hour, many of the shops and houses were lit up with millions of fairy lights for Christmas.

'I've never had a man back to my house before,' she said in a low voice.

'Never?'

She turned back to him then. The look on her face – he recognised it only from a single fleeting moment on the London Eye when the door had closed and she'd realised that they were alone. Fear. But why would she feel fear?

He immediately sat back, keeping hold only of her hand. The car turned on to a smaller road leading away from the high street. 'Are you OK with it?' he said, quietly, next to her ear. 'If you would prefer, we could go somewhere else.'

She laughed then, and the dark moment seemed to have passed. 'No,' she said, pulling him close again, 'it's taken me enough effort to track you down. I'm not letting you out of my sight. Especially since you've never given me your phone number.'

'Ah,' he said, teasing his tongue along her chin to her mouth. 'You know – one can never be too careful these days. But in this case, I might make an exception.'

– V –

'As the flames began to scorch Ivan's skin, the Firebird spread her wings, and the bars of the golden cage shuddered and broke apart. The bird lifted Ivan into the air and they flew back, through winter and spring, to the magic garden of the Tsar.

As the walls were in sight, the Firebird began to falter, as the heat became too much to bear. She crashed to the ground beneath the tree of golden apples.

"I have brought you home," she said. "But now, I am dying."

"No," said Ivan. Risking the heat of the flames, Ivan held her close. Three crystal tears fell on to her fiery head. And there, before his eyes, she was transformed. Into a beautiful princess with hair of flames and skin of snow, and eyes the clear blue of the summer sky. And he kissed her, and loved her, and together they lived...'

– 'The Firebird', *The Anthology of Russian Tales*

Chapter Thirty-Three

So this was what it felt like. Her mind tried to process all the different sensations, while her body made it impossible to think at all. The car pulled into the little alleyway that led to her house. She felt full to overflowing. His touch on her skin, his taste, his warmth. Every cell in her body was vibrating with life. This was right; this was good. Things that had been missing from every casual encounter or so-called relationship in the past. She had been right to take a risk, to follow the light that led upwards, from a dark place, into the sky.

'Thanks, Patrick,' she said to the driver. 'See you soon.'

'My pleasure,' the man said. He would never look at her the same way again, but what did she care? She was aware of being almost naked under her coat, every second delicious with anticipation.

She led Dmitri across the cobbled yard. On either side, the other houses still had their Christmas lights twinkling in the windows. Her house was dark.

'Let me guess which one is yours,' he joked.

'Very funny.' She smiled wryly.

The house was cold as they entered – the heating had gone

off hours ago. She flipped on the light and adjusted the thermostat. Other than the cleaner, and her sister, she never had visitors. It was her private, sacred space. In the car, she'd had a moment of worrying whether she could do this, trust herself not to ruin everything. Dmitri had picked up on it right away, and she'd felt the tension rise in him. And she'd been sorry for it. But now, he was here; just like she'd planned. Exactly as she wanted it to be.

As soon as the door was shut behind them, he took her in his arms. 'More than anything in the world,' he said, 'I want to take this coat off of you,' he played with the zipper at her chin. 'But I think you should warm up first.'

She laughed, breathing in the scent of him. He was so easy to be with 'Why don't I make us some coffee? Or do you prefer tea?'

'Tea, preferably with one spoonful of strawberry jam,' he said, with a bemused smile.

'No!'

'Yes.' He pulled her to him, the puffy fabric of her coat an excruciating barrier between them. 'But you'd better make it very quickly, or else I am not responsible for my actions.'

'OK then.' Laughing, she went up the stairs. She watched Dmitri as he came up to the top of the stairs behind her, looking to see his first impressions. His eyes lit up in his face.

'You have a piano!' he said, going over to the Bechstein in the corner. He opened the lid and plunked out a note. 'Ouch!' He winced. 'When did you last have this tuned?'

'Never,' she said. 'That is, I... thought about it. When I first met you.'

He gave her a secret smile. 'And now?'

'I've got the name of someone local. I'll get him out tomorrow.' Just thinking about it, she felt an almost unbearable surge of happiness. This was right, it was good. She could do this.

She went to the kitchen and put the kettle on. When she came back, he was setting down his bag next to the piano and taking off his coat. Underneath, he was still wearing the tuxedo shirt and trousers that gave him an air of both charm and authority. He sat down on the stool and played a flourish of notes. The sound sent a shimmer of desire down her spine as she watched him play. His thick dark hair curled just above his collar. His face just as she remembered – classically handsome, except when he erupted into one of his boyish grins. Just seeing him there, was intoxicating. She wanted so badly to touch him—

He broke off, abruptly.

'Sorry,' he said. 'I suppose it is late, and you have neighbours.'

'No, please,' she said. 'Play.'

Enjoying the anticipation, she sat down on the sofa. She had expected him to go back to something rich and dark, like Beethoven, or Rachmaninov. But instead, he launched into something completely different. Fast and jazzy, a tune from another era.

He turned and looked at her, smiling mischievously. 'This one's for you,' he said. After an opening glissando and swinging intro, he launched into a tune she recognised: 'Ain't Misbehavin''. She didn't know the words, but she clapped along, smiling and delighted. He moved into a lively improvisation of another old song: 'By the Light of the Silvery Moon'. She swayed in time with the rhythm; it almost made her feel like dancing. Finally, he slowed down the pace of the music, adding delicate, romantic riffs. In a deep, velvety voice, he began to sing:

Let me call you "Sweetheart" I'm in love with you.
Let me hear you whisper that you love me too.
Keep the love light glowing in your eyes so true.
Let me call you "Sweetheart" I'm in love with you.

The old time song – where she'd even heard it before, she had no idea – was moving and heartfelt. His voice vibrated deep inside of her, his touch on the old, out-of-tune piano was magic. She was very warm now, but she didn't take off her coat. He continued on with his complicated improvisation, his fingers flying up and down the keyboard in a crystalline cascade of notes. When the song reached its ending gliss, she rose to her feet. 'Yeah!' she said. 'That was so brilliant! Thank you.'

He stood up and took a mock bow, his hair falling into his eyes. 'My pleasure, madam.' His eyes locked with hers, dark and seductive. She recognised that look from the day when he'd been calling all the shots. In only a few strides he was over to her. Instead of undoing the zip, he lifted the bottom of her coat and brushed her with his finger, feather-light between her legs over the silk of her underwear.

'Are you warm now?' he said, pressing her against him.

'Yes,' she gasped.

'Good.'

He unzipped her coat and took it off of her. Then he lifted her and laid her on to the sofa, and sat on the edge.

She tried to lean forward to undo his shirt, but he removed her hands, pressing her back down.

'My turn now,' he said. Smiling, he took her hands up over her head...

Her vision blurred and darkened. All of her muscles went rigid. She tried to struggle; to curl up in a ball. Tried to breathe, but the air was crushed in her lungs. She opened her mouth to scream, but all that came out was a panicked gurgling sound. Frantically, she tried to free her hands, tried to roll and push him off of her. But he was too heavy, too strong. She was blinded by the darkness...

The ice was so hard against her back. So cold. Powerless. She opened her mouth... nothing came out. Nothing she could do...

'Nicola!'

Her eyes flew open. She realised that Dmitri was off her, off the sofa, kneeling beside her. She was in her own house, wearing her high-heeled shoes, her knickers and nothing else. Shivering and gasping, she struggled to her feet.

'I want to you to leave, now!' she shouted. She ran, shivering, to the kitchen.

What was she doing? Her coat, where was it? The rational part of her mind began to find its voice. She was here with Dmitri. She had gone to the church, seduced him. Brought him home with her. He had played piano, sang to her. She was happy, experiencing what was by far, the best night of her life...

Her whole body was shaking. Had she come here to grab a knife? That was ridiculous. She cowered behind the worktop as he got slowly to his feet.

'I will leave,' he said, quietly. His face was stricken, all the brightness and joy gone from his eyes. 'I am sorry if I hurt you.'

She leaned against the breakfast bar, trying to force herself to breathe out. Opening her mouth, she tried to speak, but still, no sound came out.

He went back over to the piano and picked up his coat and his bag. 'Are you going to be OK on your own?' he said.

'Don't... come near me.'

He held up his hands. 'Can I at least make you a cup of tea?' he said.

She sank down at the kitchen table, her head in her hands. She was aware of him pouring water from the boiled kettle into a cup and bringing it over to her. Then he brought a faux-fur throw blanket from the sofa. She flinched as he draped it around her shoulders.

'I'm sorry,' she said, the words hoarse and barely audible.

He didn't speak but sat down at the table opposite her. He

made no move to touch her.

She pulled the blanket tightly around her.

'Please, drink some tea,' he said.

The tea was too strong but she drank it down anyway. The bitter taste couldn't fight against the sting of bile in her throat. Her life trapped in a snow globe, shaken up, dropped and smashed to a million pieces. Her skin felt itchy, dirty. Dmitri was still there, sitting in silence.

She pushed the cup away. Gradually, the panic began to subside. But what could she do now? She had ruined the evening, and possibly a lot more than that. Dmitri was fragile and yet she had gone to him. Planned out in her mind exactly what would happen. Taken a risk to bring him here to her house. He had played her a love song, made her laugh...

Nicola tried again to find her voice. She was desperate for him to leave and desperate for him to stay. How could something that had happened so many years ago still affect her like this? It was ludicrous and it was wrong. It had festered so deeply inside of her that it had turned all of her ugly and rotten. And now, she had tried to lift up this man and had let him drop like a stone. He deserved better than this, even if she didn't. He had done nothing wrong. All she could offer him now was an explanation.

'Something happened to me,' she said, her voice a whisper. 'A long time ago. And it was nothing really – nothing like what you suffered.' She tried to laugh, but all that came out was a sickly rasp.

'It is not nothing,' he said quietly.

She put her head in her hands. Not wanting him to see her, not wanting to look at him.

'I lied when you asked me why I hated Christmas,' she said. 'I mean, it's true about my family – that was difficult. But everyone has issues like that. You must have thought me so spoiled and entitled.'

'No,' he said.

'It happened at uni. A stupid holiday party. It was the night before classes were ending for the break. Normally they held it at the university, but that year it was at a bar. Everyone was really excited because it had been snowing earlier in the day and our professor had let us out early from the last lecture. Like we were little kids, or something.' She lifted her head, staring at the cold beige wall. 'Back then, I loved the snow.'

'What happened?' he whispered.

'I had a friend called Ashley. She was American, from New York, doing her final year abroad. I was very serious about uni. It was my final year and I had lots of student loans. I needed a good job when I finished. I kept my head down, wasn't looking for a relationship, or even anything casual. But Ashley was a flirt – she'd slept with practically everyone in the department by the end of that term. Anyway, I had a bit of a crush on one of the guys in my seminar group. He was called Kevin. Kevin Galsworthy.' She bit her lip as his face ballooned into her mind's eye. Tall and blonde, good-looking in a sporty boy-next-door kind of way. Good looks that hid something else underneath. 'I knew he liked me. He was always staring at me, trying to draw me into the discussions.'

She sighed. 'I don't know why, but I let Ashley convince me that, just for once, I should have some fun. She brought some of her clothes over to my flat and we had a couple glasses of wine. I let her talk me into wearing a sparkly sequin dress that barely covered my arse. She did my hair and make-up. I remember us talking and laughing, and how excited I was for that night.' She shook her head. The half-remembered excitement turning liquid in her stomach.

'Things didn't go to plan,' she continued. 'Everyone was looking at me, and I felt cheap and out of place. People were making jokes about how the ice queen had finally melted. Ashley left me on my own, and then I saw her with Kevin on the dance floor. She was all over him.' Nicola pulled the blanket more tightly around her. 'I didn't know why she was doing it. She knew I liked him. I was so angry – at her, and at him.

'I had more to drink. I danced with other people, but I was pretty off my face. I was supposed to catch an early train the next morning to go to my mum's house for the holidays. I just wanted to get the hell out of there. So I left.' She drew her lips into a line.

Dmitri was sitting so still, his face grave. She wanted to stop talking. Stop hurting him. Make the past go away.

She took a breath. There was nothing to do now but continue.

'By the time I left, it had snowed again. I remember how beautiful it was: like everything was covered in sparkly white icing sugar. But the path was icy and my feet were hurting in Ashley's high heels. I walked slowly so I didn't slip. Then I heard footsteps behind me, and I turned. It was Kevin. He had a beer bottle in his hands, and he was smiling. I remember that smile most of all.' She shuddered. How often that face, that smile, had haunted her memories. Her nightmares.

'I shouted at him. Told him to go home with Ashley. To leave me alone. I felt so betrayed and ashamed. He threw down the bottle and started to laugh. He said he knew how much I wanted him, and that I was turning him on. He grabbed my arm. I tried to yell, but he covered my mouth with his hand. He threw me down on the icy ground and stuck his knee between my legs. He pinned my arms above my head. I tried to scream. But I don't think I did. In the end, I didn't even try to fight him off. I just lay there.'

Tears erupted from her eyes. The pressure of his body like a dead weight. The pain and terror as he held her down and thrust inside her over and over again. His tongue slithering inside her mouth. The ice hard against her back, the cold seeping through her skin, into her heart. Helpless. Out of control.

'And after it was over, he walked me home,' she said. 'Held on to my arm while I staggered back to my flat. I tried to slam the door in his face but he kept it open with his foot. He came *inside* my flat. I...' she paused, her teeth were chattering now, 'he – put me on the sofa, and I thought he was going to do it again. I don't even know if he did or not – I blacked out. When I came to, he was gone. I slid on to the floor and curled up into a ball. I stayed like that for the whole night, shivering and crying. Then, the next morning, I got on the train.'

She glanced up at Dmitri. His head was bowed, his eyes filled with tears. She put her hand over her face so she didn't have to look at him.

'I didn't tell anyone. I went to my mum's house and went through the motions of that awful Christmas. I tried to pretend it hadn't happened. Then, I tried to convince myself that I'd wanted it – that, otherwise, I would have tried harder to fight him off.'

She was half aware of Dmitri getting up, coming round the table to sit beside her. There, so close to her, but not reaching out to touch her. She was sad for that, but grateful too.

'When I got back, I decided that I was going to report it to the police. It was the hardest thing I've ever done, going into that police station. And, of course, by then, the evidence was long gone.'

'But didn't they question him?'

'Yes!' she cried. 'They did. But Ashley gave him an alibi. By then they were "together". There was no proof, no one saw anything – it was my word against his. He was well-liked, whereas I was the ice queen. All they had to do was say that I was jealous.'

Her body shuddered as the tears flowed freely now. Dmitri

moved closer, wrapping his arms around the blanket that engulfed her. She rested her head on his shoulder.

'My sweet girl,' he said, tracing her tears with his fingers. 'You did not deserve what happened to you.' He buried his face in her hair. 'It was not your fault.'

Sobbing, she pulled away. 'There's more,' she said.

He reached over and took her hand in his. Right now, his strength and his warmth were a lifeline. But she could see in his face how hard this was for him too.

'I still had to see Kevin every day in class. He avoided me, but I could feel him looking at me, and I felt such terror. I told him that I was going to bring him down whatever it took. That I was going to tell everyone, find people at the party to back me up. He just laughed and told me I wouldn't be saying anything.'

She shook her head and swallowed. 'That term, we were interviewing for jobs. I should have had my pick of high-flying investment-banking jobs. But the day of my first interview, a man turned up on my doorstep.'

'Who was it?' Dmitri asked softly.

'Kevin's dad. He was a bigwig in the City. He asked if he could come in, and I told him no. I remember that conversation on my doorstep. He was so "nice" and "polite" at first. Asked me about my interviews. I told him to go to hell. That his son was a rapist. He shook his head like I'd disappointed him and held out a brown envelope. He told me that if I signed a confidentiality agreement, he'd make sure I got the best job at the best bank. But if I didn't, well... unfortunately, no bank would want to hire a lying, hysterical girl who was a prick tease. Whether I had a future or not was all dependent on me signing my name on a dotted line.'

'You signed.'

She stared at him for a second, expecting to see judgement in his eyes. But all she saw was a reflection of her own pain, and his deep compassion. 'I felt so alone,' she said. 'I had no one to turn to. I'd worked so hard and I needed a job. I deserved a job. I thought I'd get my own back by being successful.' She shuddered as the shame bubbled up inside her like an underground spring. 'I don't know what I thought.'

'Anyway,' she continued, 'after graduation, Kevin and Ashley both went to New York to work. Kevin's dad kept his word – I got a good job. No one mentioned "the incident". I worked there for a few years. Eventually, I moved to Privé. I tried to convince myself that I deserved my job, that I would have done well anyway. But every day when I go into work, I think about how I climbed that ladder, and how all of it is a lie.'

'No, Nicola, it's not a lie.' His voice was soft, but in earnest.

'Isn't it?' She grabbed her hand away. 'You're a man – you see what you want to see. What *I* want you to see – on the surface. When only I know the truth. I've never had a real relationship. I've stuck to one-night stands and other people's husbands. Because they're safe – I don't have to feel anything. I call the shots. They use me, and I use them, and every time, it's like I'm being held down on the ice all over again.'

Nicola fell silent. She stood up and let the blanket fall to the ground.

The sheer beauty of her body took his breath away. But this was a crisis point, and the next few minutes were critical. Everything he did, every word from his mouth, would decide their fate. When at first he'd noticed her lack of response, his own agonising self-doubts had kicked in. She was horrified by him, regretted everything. This was all some kind of sick infinite loop of pleasure and rejection that he was doomed to live out over and over. But luckily, he'd realised in time to stop himself hurting her further – so he hoped, anyway. And then, her terrible story had emerged. All the way through, he had wanted to interrupt her, demand her to stop. Take her in his arms and try to convince her that it had never happened; that it didn't matter. But it *had* happened. It *did* matter.

He stood up too, not touching her. He was hard again, but he ignored his own needs, focusing entirely on her. Leaning in, he whispered against her hair, 'Please,' he said, 'let me take care of you.'

She hesitated for a moment, then allowed him to take her hand in his.

'Where is the bathroom?' he asked. She gestured with her head to a staircase going up to the floor above.

Without speaking, he led her up the stairs to a large master bedroom. The en suite bathroom was shiny and pristine with iridescent blue-green tiles above the bath. She was shivering as he turned the taps on. He checked the temperature of the water. She took off her underwear and he helped her into the bath. He knelt beside her as she put her head back, her hair turning to a sleek, dark mass. She closed her eyes as he rubbed apple-scented shampoo into her hair. The water pooled over the glistening curves of her body. He rinsed her hair, and sat her up, rubbing her back with shower gel. Then he sat back on his heels. His body felt like it might explode, but he forced himself to keep his distance. Eventually, she opened her eyes. She stared at him for a long time, and the world shrank to what he could see in those slanted green eyes. The pain, the regret – his own reflection in her dark pupils.

'Get in,' she said, sitting up to make room.

He looked at her without speaking and caressed her cheek, waiting until she took his hand and he was sure she meant it. Then he stripped off his wet shirt and the rest of his clothing. He eased himself into the hot water and drew her body back against his. It reminded him of their fall on the ice, when she had landed between his legs and stirred his desire. Now, there were no physical barriers between them. But he stayed still, letting her take the lead.

She unlaced his fingers and moved his hands over her breasts. Closing his eyes, he felt the weight and fullness of them, the delicate softness of her skin. Then she took his hand and guided it lower, between her legs, and he rode the crest of the wave of desire. He gently kissed her neck just behind her ear.

'You deserve to be loved,' he whispered.

Her body arched against his as he continued to caress her, living each of her heartbeats as if they were his own. He brought her to the edge, gasping and writhing against him, and he couldn't stand it another moment. Shifting her from him, he stood up, lifting her dripping wet from the tub. He dried her off with a fluffy white towel, and dried himself off with another towel, securing it around his waist.

'Please,' she said, 'make love to me.' She ran the soft tips of her fingers down his chest, making him weak with need for her.

He led her out of the bathroom to the bedroom, a large room painted pale blue with an iron scrolled bed, and sat her there on the edge of the bed. 'Is this OK?' he said.

She undid the towel around him and moved up to lay back, her hair soft against the pillow, eyes bright with desire. His hands were shaking as he put on the condom. She spread her legs and pulled him over her. He opened her with his fingers, and then pressed inside her, filling her up. She wrapped her legs around him, pulling him deeper, crying out his name as they moved together faster and harder. And when he couldn't stand it any longer, he drowned her mouth with a kiss. A shuddering sweetness filled his body as he gave into a lifetime of longing, and the world shattered to glittering stars.

Chapter Thirty-Four

Nicola woke up in the dark. For a second she felt disorientated and confused. She was in her bedroom, at home, but—

'Nicola?'

The whisper jolted her senses. The curtains were open and the soft glow of moonlight pooled into the room. She turned and saw that Dmitri was propped up on his elbow. He'd been watching her sleep. The realisation could have made her tense, but instead, her body felt alive.

'Can I hold you?' he said, his voice husky.

She moved to press herself along the length of him, breathing him in, feeling the warmth of flesh on flesh.

'Was I snoring?' she asked.

'No,' his soft laugh brushed her ear. 'But it was beautiful watching you sleep.'

She could feel his arousal, and his light caresses were awakening her fully. But then his hand stilled. He took a breath, hesitating.

'I wasn't sure if I should stay,' he said, finally. 'I wasn't sure if that's what you wanted.'

'I'm glad you're here,' she said, taking his hand and kissing his fingers; marvelling at how true it was. How telling him her secret had freed something inside of her, allowed her to open up and make room for him, and all that they could give each other.

'I wanted to tell you something,' he said. 'Remember that choral music doctorate I was applying for in Oxford?'

'Yes.' She stiffened momentarily. Was Dmitri going to up sticks and move to Oxford? It wasn't so far away. But right now, it seemed like the other side of the ocean.

'I am not doing it.'

'Why?' Nicola pulled away and turned towards him. In the moonlit darkness, his eyes shone almost silver.

'Because I do not want a doctorate in choral music. I want to be a pianist.'

She blinked as his face came into focus and a thousand emotions she had no right to feel flooded through her. Pride, happiness, and something else too – something stronger that was taking shape inside of her.

'That's wonderful.' She took his face between her hands and pulled him to her, kissing him hard on the lips, letting her hair fall over him.

'Yes,' he said, a little short of breath. 'But it will be difficult. There are many reasons why it might not work out. But I have written down what happened to me. Why I did not return to Moscow.'

'You're going to tell your story?' She looked at him in surprise, knowing what this was likely to cost him.

He rolled on to his back and sighed. 'I don't know. I need to talk to my sister. It affects her too. But I have done some research. I have found the name of a professor at the Royal College of Music. He is Russian, and also studied at the Moscow Conservatory, though well before my time. I thought I would try to see if he would meet with me. Ask him what I should do. If I should apply to study, or... I don't know.'

Nicola ran her hand along his chest. She felt him shrink away under her hand, but she didn't remove it.

'Do you feel angry?' she said. 'Even now, I mean. He was your father. How could...' she broke off, choked by emotion.

Dmitri put his hand on hers. 'When it happened, I was in shock for a long time. I was in so much pain, that was all I could think of. All the while, when I was in hospital, I wanted my father to come and see me. I have no idea what I would have said – or what I wanted him to say.' He sighed. 'But he never came. He was off somewhere, drinking himself into oblivion. Totally coming apart.'

'That's why you don't drink?' she said.

'It is people, not alcohol, that are to blame for things that happen,' he said. 'But it did play a part – in me losing my place and for what my father did. I didn't drink for a long time – until Irina left me. But earlier tonight, when I thought you were lost to me...' He shook his head. 'My father drank because of the pain of life. I don't want to be like him.'

'Why the hell wasn't he arrested for what he did?' she said sharply. 'Put in jail?'

'It was looked into, of course. But this is Russia we are talking about. The people we knew were, of course, surprised by what happened, and sorry. But they also knew what my success – or lack of it – meant to my father and mother. When people heard what I did, I don't think the weight of sympathy was on my side. That is one of the reasons my mother decided that we would leave.'

'Your mother sounds like a very special woman.'

'She was.' His voice caught. 'I miss her a lot. And also, as strange as it may seem, I miss my father. I have many good memories of him from my youth. Back in the days when he would laugh, and tell stories, buy us ice cream... Sometimes, when he would listen to me playing the piano, tears would run down his face.' He pursed his lips. 'The night it happened, I was going out to beg forgiveness. I wanted to make things right, like they had once been. But it all happened so quickly. And then, he was dead. I feel sometimes, that his death is on my conscience.'

'No,' she said emphatically. 'It's not.'

'Maybe not.' He shrugged. 'And maybe if he had not died, I would have been angry – once we were safe and the shock wore off. I don't know. But in any case, I have long forgiven him. I know what I did, and why he did what he did. He loved me and wanted the best for me. I was too young to understand that. Too stupid to make him proud.'

'God, that's fucked-up,' she said, getting angry. 'You've forgiven the man who poured lighter fluid on you and lit a match, but even after all these years, you still haven't forgiven yourself.'

He laughed softly. 'I've never had cause to do so. Do you think it's too late?'

'I think you are the most infuriating, fascinating man I have ever met.'

He pulled her on top of him, his eyelids half-closed, awash with desire. 'Prove it,' he said.

So she did.

Chapter Thirty-Five

15th December

Somehow, Nicola managed to leave the house and go to work. The same way as always, and yet, it was as if she was experiencing the world for the first time. The colours looked brighter; the people were people, not simply obstacles to be avoided on public transport.

When she arrived at her desk, Chrissie brought her a cup of coffee and started talking about the Advent Calendar preparations. Nicola felt a strange languid sensation in her body – maybe it was just exhaustion. After making love in the middle of the night, she'd gone back to sleep and awakened as the first rays of grey light were coming in through the window. She heard Dmitri downstairs in the kitchen and she could smell coffee. She'd lain back in bed, feeling more contented than she could remember. Yes, she had to go to work, and yes, she was still the same person with the same problems – the same scars inside. And yet, in one magical night, everything was different.

Dmitri had come back into the room carrying a mug of coffee. He smiled at her and she felt a surge of warmth knowing he was there. That he was real. 'Just milk, no sugar, right?'

'You remembered?' she'd said, taking the warm cup in her hands. 'From that day?'

'I remember every moment I have been with you.' He nuzzled her hair, but something seemed to be on his mind. 'Do you need to go to work today?' he'd asked.

'I'm afraid so.' Nicola had felt a sudden rush of panic. This wasn't the end— it couldn't be!

'Then you will need this.' He'd set a business card on the nightstand.

Nicola had picked it up and smiled. She melted back into the pillow. 'I suppose you'll be wanting my phone number too?'

'That might be nice,' he'd said, his eyes soft but mischievous. 'I'll call you sometime.'

Her face must have reflected the fact that it was *not* funny, because his smile faded. He pulled the blanket down and kissed her breasts.

'I was joking,' he'd added. 'But I have to be sure that this is what you want.'

Nicola had pushed him away none too gently. She needed to get this clear between them, and she needed to be fully in her senses for that.

'What do you want?' she'd said, staring into his melting dark eyes.

'You, of course. But there is one thing, Nicola...' His face turned more serious.

'One thing – that's never good, is it?'

'I do not want to share you. I... couldn't stand that. If we are to be together, then it must be only you, and only me.'

'Of course,' she'd said, feeling a little offended that he would think anything else. But then again, why wouldn't he?

'As you know, I do not have much experience of a relationship. Or any...' He'd shrugged, not meeting her eyes. 'I will not always know when to stay and when to go. When you need your space. When you do not want me to touch you.' He hesitated. 'These things worry me. I do not want to make a mistake.'

She'd put her hand on his and drew it to her lips, kissing his fingers. 'I don't know all of those things either,' she said. 'But I want this too. I *need* this.'

He'd leaned in and kissed her lazily. 'Now you need to get in the shower and go to work. Tonight, I have a concert and, afterwards, I need to practise the piano.'

Nicola had nodded, feeling a pang of anxiety. They both had separate lives, separate commitments. But what was he saying? When would she see him again?

She'd voiced the question aloud. She wasn't used to feeling this... dependent. 'I can get the piano tuned,' she'd said. 'Maybe get it moved to one of the spare bedrooms. Then you could practise here sometimes.' She'd smiled. 'I'd like that – I love hearing you play. Unless... the piano's not good enough?'

He'd kissed her again. 'It is good enough. Let's do that.'

'OK. And before I forget, there's one more thing.'

Nicola told him about the favour she needed from him. He left the room to retrieve his phone and check his calendar.

'I will need to juggle a few things around,' he'd said. 'And I don't know how many people I'll be able to get that early. But it should be OK.'

'So I can make arrangements?'

'You can,' he'd replied with a little smirk, 'though now I am not quite sure that I am with the woman I thought.'

Nicola had pulled him to her. 'And is this new woman better or worse?'

'I'll let you know in a few minutes.' He pulled up the bottom of the duvet and disappeared underneath. She'd gasped as he parted her legs and she lost the ability to think at all—

'Nicola? Have you heard a word I've said?'

Nicola wrested herself back to reality. 'Um no.'

Chrissie put her hands on her hips. Even the appliqué reindeer on her Christmas jumper seemed to look annoyed. 'I hope you're not mooning over you-know-who,' she said in a low voice.

'No,' Nicola said. 'It's like I said – I told Ollie where to go. Back to his family, to patch things up with his wife.'

'Well, let's hope he can,' Chrissie said, sounding like a stern schoolmistress. 'But now, about the Advent Calendar...'

As Chrissie went on and on about her ideas – and the cost – Nicola began to wonder if she could really be this new woman. It wasn't going to be easy. She'd have to take it one step at a time.

'Did you book the auditorium?' Nicola said, when Chrissie finally came up for air.

'Yes.'

'Good.' She explained to Chrissie how the Choir of St Anne's Church was going to be making a guest appearance. It was fun watching Chrissie's blue eyes half pop out of her head in surprise.

'Christmas carolling?' she said. 'You?'

'No, not me.' Nicola smiled. She handed Chrissie the business card, the details of which were already safely stored in her contacts. 'This is the director. You can contact him to finalise the details.'

Chrissie looked down at the card. Nicola thought for a second that Chrissie was going to faint.

'You're a dark horse, aren't you?' She smiled slyly.

'No,' Nicola said. 'Just a happy one.'

Dmitri could still taste her on his lips. They'd walked together to the station so that she could get her train in to work. He'd kissed her goodbye, watched her go through the barrier. Unlike that other kiss, in another station, when their lips parted, he no longer felt like he was split in two. He felt alive. It was unlike anything he'd experienced before.

He bought a coffee, walked around Richmond for a while. Nicola had given him the number of the piano tuner, and the man had agreed to come around midday. Dmitri didn't have any private lessons scheduled until the new term started in January, so he'd decided to stay around to oversee the tuning. The trust she'd shown – letting him into her house, her life, was a humbling responsibility. He was determined to do his best in every way for her.

Dmitri sat down on a bench on The Green. Pigeons flocked around his feet. It was strange, this feeling of anticipation – like his whole life was ahead of him. That all the things he had ever wanted were there within his reach.

He took out his phone and sent a few texts. To Tanya, to Carole-Ann, asking her to arrange the schedule change for the day of Nicola's Christmas do. As he sent the texts, he smiled to himself. Nicola and Christmas. Whatever it had once meant in the past, from now on he wanted her to associate it only with him.

When the texts were gone, he opened up the email he had drafted but not sent. To a man called Mikhail Aslanov at the conservatory in London. In the message, he had told his story – typed up what he had shown Kolya – and asked for a brief meeting. To see what the next steps might be. As he read through it again, the worries seeped back into his mind. Was this really possible? Could *he* do it?

His thumb hovered over the button. Once again he thought of Nicola, and everything she had overcome. This was something he needed to do for both of them, to become the best version of himself. With a deep breath, he pressed send. The message went off with a swoosh.

Whatever happened now – if anything at all – it was out of his hands.

Chapter Thirty-Six

18th December

On Friday afternoon, Nicola went to see her boss, Brian. She closeted herself in his office while he was just finishing up a call. Already she was feeling conflicted about what she'd decided to do, and the winking star emoji in a Santa hat on Brian's latest Christmas jumper didn't help. In the end, she kept the announcement short and sweet. In January, she would be taking a backlog of holiday. Afterwards, she wouldn't be coming back.

If Brian was surprised by the news, he didn't let on. 'Can I ask you the reason?' was all he said.

'Because I want a new start,' she replied. Though she had thought long and hard about her decision, now that she was here, it was more difficult than she'd expected it to be.

'What are you going to do instead?' he asked.

'I'm not quite sure yet.' Feeling she owed him an explanation, she told him briefly about Dmitri, and the fact that, for now, she wanted to step off the treadmill and think about her next steps. She also found herself outlining a new business idea that had been growing in her mind ever since her visit to the Richmond charity shop.

'Interesting,' Brian said, when she'd finished explaining.

They chatted through her idea for a few minutes and he gave her a few suggestions and things to think about. Then, she stood up to leave.

'Thanks for letting me know, Nicola,' Brian said. 'It will be a blow to lose you, but you have my support in whatever you choose to do. You need to find your own happiness and grab it with both hands.'

'Thanks, Brian.' A rogue tear bubbled up in the corner of her eye. 'That means a lot to me. You're one of the good ones. Except for your jumpers.'

He laughed. 'Glad to hear it. And, of course, the door is always open if you change your mind.'

'Thanks.'

It was only as she left Brian's office that Nicola realised she wasn't going to be changing her mind. She expected to feel sad, or at least nostalgic. Instead, she felt oddly calm. It was done. Whether it was the right decision or not... only time would tell.

At half-six, she left the office. Dmitri had his first performance of the *Messiah* that night. He'd asked her if she wanted to come, if he should leave a ticket for her at the door. Nicola said she'd try – but work was crazy, and besides, she'd see him afterwards. He'd hidden his disappointment well. But she knew how hard he'd been working and how much he wanted her to be there. She wanted that too, for him.

Nicola managed to arrive just before the concert, buy a ticket and slip in the back row of the church between two elderly couples. The lights were turned down and the church was lit by hundreds of candles. Dmitri came out to applause and took a bow. Nicola felt a stab of pride – he looked so handsome in his tailcoat and tie, his dark hair combed back from his face – and also of longing. They'd had two wonderful nights together, but the last two nights, rehearsals had gone on late and he'd stayed at his own flat. She also had the sneaking suspicion that he felt he needed to give her space. All she knew for sure was that she'd missed him.

He lifted the baton and the small orchestra began Handel's haunting overture.

Nicola had heard the *Messiah* before, but in the candlelit church, the experience was magical. The soloists weren't professionals, but they performed well, and the choir members were as full of energy and emotion as their leader. It was mesmerising watching Dmitri conduct. She felt a deep admiration for him. He had been through so much, and yet, he still managed to reach out and share himself with others. As the bass aria began – *for he is like a refiner's fire* – her heart seized up. *And he shall purify...*

Nicola didn't realise she was crying until the old lady sitting on her left handed her a tissue.

'I'm sorry,' she whispered.

'Not a problem, my dear. It's a very moving performance.'

'Yes,' Nicola agreed. 'It is.'

The music continued through the Christmas section. Finally, Dmitri turned to the crowd and gestured with his baton for the audience to stand. Then, he gave the downbeat for the opening bars of the 'Hallelujah Chorus'. Facing the audience, he began to conduct. His face was a picture of concentration and joy. The music swept through the church, and everyone sang with energy and enthusiasm. Nicola didn't sing – she was still finding it hard to keep her emotions in check – but at the end, as the final 'Hallelujah' died away and the orchestra took over the last bars, she stood up just a fraction longer than the other audience members. Dmitri's eyes caught hers and his face lit up, making her glow inside. For an instant he seemed to forget where he was. But then, he turned back to the orchestra and the choir and the concert continued.

The last chorus was the stirring 'Amen', and the concert reached its end.

The applause was thunderous as friends, family and members of the public showed their appreciation. Dmitri took a bow, then each of the soloists. He acknowledged the orchestra and then turned and clapped for the choir. Nicola was swept up in the energy of it, but as the applause started to diminish, a fountain of panic rose inside her. As much as she wanted to stay and support Dmitri, doing so would mean interacting with the choir members – many of whom might have seen her that night at Waterloo Station. She took out her phone and drafted him a quick text:

Loved the concert. Meet you at mine later?

She pressed send, ready to make a quick exit.

'Such a lovely concert, didn't you think, dear?'

Nicola turned. The woman who'd given her a tissue was speaking to her.

'Yes, wonderful.' There were two people in the pew between her, the aisle, and the door. They were chatting to a person two rows up, not in any hurry to move. She was trapped.

'And did you know someone in the choir?' the woman asked her.

'Um, no. Just...'

'Nicola!' She heard her name shouted out and footsteps running down the aisle.

How Dmitri managed to push through the crowd she didn't know, but all of a sudden he was there, breathless. All thoughts of sneaking out left her as he leaned over and kissed her. She threaded her arms around his neck and he lifted her over the back of the pew.

'Oh, my!' the elderly woman said.

Dmitri set her down but kept his hands firmly planted around her waist. 'You are not going to escape out the back,'

Dmitri said in a low, authoritative voice close to her ear. Waves of pleasure coursed down her spine. 'You came here tonight, and now I want you to meet everyone.'

'Everyone!'

'Penance, Nicola,' he whispered.

The words she remembered so well electrified her.

'Now, come with me.' Dmitri led her by the hand up towards the front of the church, weaving through the crowd.

The closer Nicola got to where the choir members were gathered, the more unsteady she felt on her feet. To them, she was 'The Heckler'. Or worse. She spotted Charles from the charity shop. Had he regaled the group with the knicker story? Dmitri hadn't mentioned it – but she hadn't asked.

'I can't do this,' she gasped, feeling like she might faint.

'Nonsense. It's perfect.' He stroked her hair possessively. 'They are all dying to meet you.'

'I'm going to die of embarrassment.'

'No, Nicola, really, it is fine. Please...'

She pulled him close and whispered into his ear. 'You seriously owe me,' she said.

'And I shall pay that price with pleasure,' he said, his voice low and seductive.

They were so wrapped up in each other that Nicola didn't notice the woman coming up behind Dmitri until she was at his shoulder and looked at her with dark eyes that were a mirror of his. Tanya – his sister. The woman who'd invited her to join in the carolling that night at the station and who'd baked and decorated the gingerbread heart. The one woman, who, right at this moment, scared her to death.

'Dima,' Tanya said, frowning at her brother, 'are you going to introduce us?'

'Yes! Sorry,' Dmitri replied. Nicola had never seen him blush before, but he was doing so now. 'Nicola, this is Tanya, my sister.'

'Hello Nicola.' Tanya's voice was low and melodious. She wasn't smiling but didn't look hostile either.

'Hi.' Nicola's cheeks flushed as she held out her hand to the woman. 'I'm sorry for what I did that night. I want you to know that.'

Narrowing her eyes, Tanya put her arm on Nicola's elbow and moved her a step away from Dmitri. 'Do you make my brother happy?' she said in a low whisper.

Nicola swallowed, taken aback at such a direct question. 'I think so – yes.'

'Then we are fine.' Instead of shaking her hand, Tanya hugged her, a tear pressed between their cheeks. 'More than fine,' she said.

'I'm glad, Tanya,' Nicola said.

As the embrace ended, a large sandy-haired man came up to them. Tanya introduced him as her fiancé, Mark. Nicola thanked them both for the gingerbread (pretending that she had eaten it rather than kept it to look at). They chatted about the bakery and the concert. Dmitri had moved away, speaking to the many people who wanted to congratulate him on the performance. With the ice broken by Tanya, a few other people came up to Nicola and said hello. A minute or two later, Dmitri brought over the woman that he had often spoken of – Carole-Ann, the organist – and introduced her.

'My dear,' the older woman said, 'it is so lovely to meet you.' Her pale cheeks coloured and she smiled slyly. 'In truth, we're all dying to meet Dmitri's girlfriend.'

Dmitri's eyes widened as he looked at Carole-Ann and then Nicola. 'I had better go before I get in trouble,' he said. He gravitated over to another group of people.

Nicola laughed, feeling oddly delighted. 'I guess that's me,' she said to Carole-Ann. 'It's nice to meet you.' They shook hands. 'And... I'm sorry for what happened – you know – before.'

'Never mind that,' Carole-Ann said. 'What did you think of the concert?'

'It was beautiful,' Nicola said truthfully. 'It's been a long time since I've heard the *Messiah*. Other than the bits Dmitri has played on the piano.'

'Yes, I understand that his playing again is in part thanks to you.'

'To me? No, I don't think so.' The idea was a little daunting.

'Either way, it is a good thing. And I'm glad he's found somewhere to play piano other than the draughty choir loft.' She gave Nicola a little wink. 'I'm sure you have good central heating.'

Nicola blushed. 'Um yes,' she said. 'I think he'll be warm enough.'

Other people came up to meet her, the names slipping from her mind as quickly as she heard them. It was like she had been parachuted from nowhere into a fully formed family, all of whom cared deeply about Dmitri.

One person who seemed to be avoiding her, however, was Charles. Nicola decided that they needed to speak, but as soon as she looked in his direction, he looked away. It was proof enough that he had recounted the 'knicker incident' in all its glory. The only thing for it was to confront it head-on.

Nicola walked boldly up to him while he was talking to the soprano soloist – Jani or Jenny. The woman gave Nicola a look of sheer hatred that Nicola chose to ignore. While most of the people had been very welcoming, she'd noticed a few similar looks from some of the female members of the choir. She glanced over at Dmitri. He was talking to an old man and woman, bowing his head attentively as they spoke. Nicola didn't blame the women for being jealous. Not only was he extraordinarily good-looking, but his energy was intoxicating. Also, despite his talents, he was not condescending or pompous. She was lucky, and it was going to be difficult to share him, even with his flock.

'Hi Charles,' she said, smiling both at him and the woman. 'Lovely concert.'

'Um, Nicola, isn't it?' Charles said. The soprano moved away, looking eager to be out of Charles' company.

'Yes, that's right. How are things at the shop?'

'Much better. I think you'd be impressed at what we've done. You haven't been by?'

'No – I've been busy. Restocking my knicker drawer and all that. As I'm sure you can imagine.'

Charles' face flushed pink. He tried to laugh but it came out more of a choking sound as Dmitri came up to them.

'Charles?' Dmitri said. The single word held a note of authority, and, Nicola thought, warning. 'You have met Nicola, I believe.' She felt a melting sensation as he put his hand very low on her back.

'Um yes,' Charles said. 'We were talking about... how much better the shop is doing.'

'The shop, yes,' Dmitri said. 'Nicola, would you like to go soon?'

'Yes,' she said, almost purring. 'I've called for a car for us. We could give Charles a lift.' She glanced slyly back at the other man who looked like he wanted to crawl into a hole.

'I am sure Charles will be going to the pub with the others and will be perfectly happy to get the Tube later,' Dmitri said. He ran a finger along her chin, his eyes never leaving hers. 'Isn't that right, Charles?'

'Um, yeah, pub,' were the only words Charles seemed capable of getting out.

'Good.'

Nicola laughed as Dmitri steered her off. 'So he did tell everyone about "the incident"?' she said.

Dmitri sniffed. 'I told him that men do not speak of a

woman in such a way. It is rude and it will not be tolerated. And besides,' he lowered his voice, 'there is only one man who need be concerned with your knickers, and it is not him.'

'That's for sure,' Nicola said.

'And I promise you...' he leaned in close to her ear, 'that as soon as we get in that car, I shall be very concerned.'

Chapter Thirty-Seven

19th December

They spent Saturday morning in bed. Nicola felt that, finally, they were making up for all the lost hours they'd been apart the rest of the week. After the concert when she'd told Dmitri how much she had missed him, he'd laughed and said that he missed her too; then spent all night showing her how much.

Nicola took another sip of the coffee on the bedside table. Dmitri liked bringing her coffee, taking care of her. She had to think back long and hard, to the days of her early childhood, before she could remember anyone wanting to do that. It was definitely something she could get used to.

'We should get up,' Dmitri said. He ran his hand along her thigh under the covers in a way that was absolutely no incentive to get out of bed.

'It's only ten o'clock,' she said. 'I thought they weren't coming until noon.' Kolya was coming down, along with his partner and his children. They had agreed to meet for lunch at a pub near the river.

Dmitri gave her a sly smile. 'Yes, that's why I thought we had better start getting ready now.'

Nicola laughed. It was true – on the days Dmitri had slept over, she had ended up hopelessly late for work. Not that she was complaining.

By the time they finally left the house and made it along the riverside path to the pub, they were fifteen minutes late.

Nicola spotted Kolya near the riverbank. He was chatting to another man: his partner, she assumed. Nearby, two children were feeding the ducks from a bag of crisps. Kolya waved when he saw them approach, hand in hand.

'Ah, the lovers,' he said, his smile radiating warmth.

Nicola hugged him – he was like a giant bear. 'Nice to see you too,' she replied.

Dmitri went off to find a table at the pub. Kolya introduced her to Nigel and the children, Alex and Katya. Nigel was a tall, but slight Englishman with wavy blonde hair and small, wire-framed glasses. The children were also blonde and elf-like.

Nigel shook her hand vigorously. 'I'm so pleased to meet you,' he said. 'I hope you're keeping Dmitri out of trouble.'

Nicola liked the twinkle in his blue eyes. 'I don't know,' she said. 'I've hardly seen him the last few days. He's got so many rehearsals, and then he's also practising the piano for hours on end.'

'Sounds like we'll have you to thank when we see him performing someday. Do you think that will happen?'

'I hope so,' Nicola said, smiling. 'If that's what he wants.'

The children had wandered off nearer the river. Nigel excused himself to go after them. Nicola and Kolya stood side by side. She was happy just watching the children, the birds and the play of light on water.

'It seems that things happen in their own time,' Kolya said, his voice deep and reflective. 'But it took a catalyst. A reason to change. I think you are that reason.'

'I'm sorry I put you in a bad position before,' Nicola said. 'Dmitri told me how angry he was at you.'

Kolya gave her a kindly smile. 'I'm sure you too understand that sometimes, the ends justify the means.'

Nicola laughed. 'Yes, you could say that.'

'And things are good?' Kolya said, quizzing her now.

'Yes... but...'

Kolya stayed silent but she knew he was listening. Though Nicola had only met this man twice, she could understand why Dmitri hero-worshiped him. He was intelligent, insightful and good.

'You were right,' Nicola said. 'That day at the shelter. I didn't tell you my "one thing". But now, I need your help. Things are good – very good. I don't want to mess it up.'

Nicola recounted to him a very brief version of what she had told Dmitri. Talking about it – reliving it in her mind – made her feel sick and out of control. And though she hadn't had the same physical response of fear and recoiling that she'd had that first night, all week long she'd found herself becoming panicky and tearful at odd moments. The walls were down, and there were a lot of things trying to get out.

Kolya shooed a duck away from a bench and gestured for her to sit down. She did so. He sat beside her and stared out at the water. 'You have lived with this inside you for a very long time,' he said. 'You took it upon yourself to handle everything alone. And you have borne the consequences of that decision. But now you have taken the first step. To finally live the life that you want, and that you deserve.'

She broke down then, the tears flowing freely from her eyes. She wrapped her arms around herself, and Kolya made no move to touch her, but she was aware of his presence and that was enough.

'What you have done for Dmitri, I do not think you can

even fathom,' Kolya said. 'An act of kindness, of love – that was inside you all along.'

She nodded, as the tears kept coming.

'But as I say, this is the beginning. There is a long way to go before you will be free of this thing. It will be very difficult for you. Probably for Dmitri too. But you *can* be free of it. I will help you find the proper support. But—'

'Are you coming inside or not? I've ordered drinks—' Nicola looked up and saw Dmitri approaching. The smile dropped from his face when he saw the state of her. He looked at Kolya, his eyes fierce. 'What have you done?'

'Nothing,' Kolya said calmly. 'We are talking.'

Dmitri sat down next to Nicola. He seemed unsure whether to comfort her or not.

'It's OK,' she said. Smiling through her tears, she took his hand, twining her fingers with his. 'I've told him the truth – what I told you. It may be difficult, but I'm going to get through it. For us.'

Nicola rested her head against Dmitri's chest and let him stroke her hair. Nigel and the kids came back and Kolya directed them to go inside the pub and order. Eventually, she sat up again, taking a deep breath. She could do this – she *could* heal.

'I know it is difficult to talk about.' Kolya said. 'But talking about it is what you must do – when you are ready, and in the right environment. And it would be helpful to have some more information. Do you know if this... individual has harmed anyone else?'

Nicola shuddered. If she'd acted sooner, gone straight to the police, would it have made a difference? Maybe, maybe not. Either way, the past couldn't be changed. 'Not that I know of,' she said. 'He lives in New York now. He has a wife, a family. They are innocent. I don't want to mess up their lives. I just want to rebuild mine.'

Kolya nodded. 'Yes. I asked because sometimes people are set on revenge or justice. They are disappointed to learn that, often, that is not the way of it. Many times, Nicola, there is no justice.' He sighed. 'I know this from personal experience.'

'You?' she stared at the big man. Beside her, Dmitri clasped her hand more tightly.

'Yes,' Kolya said. He stared out at the ever-changing water. 'As I said, we all have our "one thing". For me, it was when I was a boy. Doing so-called service for my country. Other boys can be very cruel when the adults choose to look the other way.'

Nicola swallowed hard. Dmitri looked like he was going to be sick.

'But as you see, I am happy now.' Kolya smiled. 'It *is* possible. To have a good life and a strong relationship. To no longer be a victim but a survivor.'

Nicola reached over and took his hand, clasping it together with Dmitri's. She felt such a strong sense of... love – for both of them. It was joyous and painful all at the same time. It was real.

'Now,' Kolya said, 'let us talk of something more pleasant. Like Christmas. I'm sure you have other invitations, but Nigel and I would love to have you both over during the holidays, and Tanya and Mark too. I have texted them.'

Nicola smiled as Dmitri gave her a goofy grin. 'Christmas, Nicola?'

'Sounds perfect,' she said.

Chapter Thirty-Eight

Dmitri spent most of the afternoon after the lunch practising piano in Nicola's spare room. He liked the Bechstein and the rich sound of the newly tuned strings inside old wood. Earlier in the week when then tuner had come round, it had taken the combined efforts of both of them, plus a jogger commandeered from the path, to move the piano downstairs to one of the bedrooms on the ground floor. He liked knowing Nicola was there, doing her work one floor above. In the late afternoon she brought him tea (a little too sweet) and a sandwich. He had another *Messiah* performance that night, so at half past six, he kissed her goodbye (the goodbye kiss had started almost an hour earlier and was much more than just a kiss) and then caught the train to Clapham Junction.

On the train, he closed his eyes and had almost fallen asleep. Life with Nicola did not involve much sleep – not that he was complaining. But there was one thing that was niggling below the surface of his shiny, new-found happiness. It had been several days, and he'd had no response to his email.

Opening his eyes, Dmitri checked his phone again, carefully scanning the junk email folder in case he'd missed something. Nothing. He sighed. It had been so difficult baring everything in the email to this man that he'd hoped could help him. Yes, Mikhail Aslanov had been a renowned pianist and now must be a sought-after teacher. And yes, they were complete strangers. But all Dmitri had asked for was ten minutes of his time. Was that so much, one musician to another?

When he got to the church, he was confronted with a disaster: Jenny was apparently sick and wouldn't be turning up. Dmitri had seen her face last night when Nicola had been there and word had swept through the choir like wildfire that she was his girlfriend. He suspected that in Jenny's case, 'sick' meant 'would not be returning'.

At literally the last minute, he asked Carole-Ann to step in. Her voice was thinner and reedier than some of the others, but she was the only one whom he could count on to know the part well enough to perform it. As soon as he asked her, Carole-Ann had given the expected 'oh no, I couldn't possibly', but her face was glowing with happiness. Part of it might have been because Phil had texted to say that he was coming to the performance. Dmitri had felt bad for not realising before how much Carole-Ann had wanted to be a soloist. It was something he'd have to look out for in the future – especially now that it was looking like he'd be a choir director for the rest of his life.

The performance went well, though without Nicola in the audience, Dmitri felt a little flat. They got a standing ovation, though, and that lifted his mood considerably.

After the concert, Phil came up to him, along with Tanya. Phil practically smothered Dmitri in a hug, and Dmitri was grateful for his support.

'I'm sorry for before,' Dmitri said, remembering how

childish and ungrateful he'd been on their last encounter. That now seemed like something from another lifetime.

'Hey, don't mention it,' Phil said. 'You know I was just worried when I hadn't seen or heard from you.'

'Don't expect to see more of him now, Phil,' Tanya interrupted. 'He's off with his sexy girlfriend.'

Dmitri shot her a black look. 'I'm sure you've told Phil *all* the details, haven't you?'

'Just that you couldn't keep your hands off each other last night.' Tanya giggled like a schoolgirl. 'No wonder Jenny quit.'

To Dmitri's relief, Mark came up and took Tanya away to meet someone. Last night he might not have minded her joking, but tonight, it grated.

'I'm so glad it's worked out for you,' Phil said. 'I can't wait to meet her. It's Nicola, is that right?'

'Yes,' Dmitri said, feeling better just for hearing her name. 'She's very special. I really can't believe it myself.'

'And you're happy?' Phil asked.

'Yes. With her, I am more than happy. But there is one thing.' He found himself telling Phil about the email he'd sent, and the lack of a response.

'I understand,' Phil said. 'But you can't let this set you back. There are other schools, other ways to go about it.'

'But is it because I'm too old, do you think? Is there really no hope at all?'

'That's the conclusion you jumped to about the other thing. And look at you now. You seem grown-up all of a sudden. Maybe I don't have a right to say this, but your mother would be very proud. And happy.'

'You have every right to say it, Phil.' Dmitri smiled. 'I think I finally understand that now. And one more thing...' He leaned in closer to Phil as Carole-Ann came towards them, her eyes still shiny from her triumph as a soloist. 'My mother would want you to be happy too.'

Phil glanced up at Dmitri, looking a little surprised. 'Thanks,' he said, 'I'll keep that in mind.' As Carole-Ann came up, Phil turned to her. 'My dear,' he said, 'what a stunning performance.'

'Yes, it was.' Dmitri kissed the older woman on the cheek and took her hand, which he placed firmly in Phil's. 'And now, please excuse me.'

Maybe it was the good karma of finally making peace with Phil, or maybe it was his mother looking down on him and smiling. Either way, as he sat on the train back to Richmond and read the new message – it had come in during the concert and gone to junk mail – he whispered, 'thank you,' to anyone up above that might be listening.

The hours they were apart seemed impossible and wrong. As soon as Dmitri had gone, Nicola knew she should have gone to the concert. Been there to support him, just be with him. But she had so much to do – so many things to wrap up at work in only a very short time. Second thoughts rattled through her head about leaving her job and stepping out into the unknown. She tried to silence the doubts and listen to the new voice in her head – the part of her that had changed – that said it was the right decision. It wasn't easy.

Nicola phoned her sister and had a very brief chat about Christmas. The lunch at Jules' house was back on. Jules sounded like her old self, going on about seating plans and menus. Their mum, it seemed, had agreed to come early to help out with the cooking. Nicola felt obliged to do the same.

'Come as early as you like,' Jules said. 'Seeing as it's just you.'

'Actually, it's me plus one,' Nicola said. Just saying the words, she suddenly felt much better about the whole thing.

'Oh? And who's that?' Jules' voice was guarded. Nicola thought there might be a 'Who's husband now?' unspoken at the end.

'His name is Dmitri.' She explained very briefly to Jules about who Dmitri was, leaving out – most things, really.

'A Russian pianist?' Jules said. 'You're serious?'

Nicola checked her watch. The concert would only just be starting now. She felt like something inside of her was torn and waiting to be stitched back together. It was painful, but on the other hand, the anticipation – knowing that he would return later – was delicious. It was a very strange and unsettling feeling, and one that she was almost certain she'd never had before this week.

'Yes,' she said. 'Absolutely.'

Dmitri came home around eleven. She was aching for him by that point. He came in, hungry for her too, but with a strange nervousness about him. He kissed her, pulled her on to his lap, took out his phone, showed her a message, distracted her so she could barely read it, then, sat back, not touching her, raking his fingers through his hair.

'This is brilliant,' she said, 'congratulations. It's what you wanted, right?'

'He said to come in on Monday. So soon! How can I be ready?'

'Hey,' she said, 'come on.' She slid off his lap and turned to him, caressing his face. 'You said yourself that this was just ten minutes – to get this man's thoughts on what you should do next. There's no pressure.'

He stopped her hands. 'No pressure! This man could be the key for me. I should have waited until after Christmas.' He shook his head. 'I don't know.'

Nicola hadn't seen him like this before – so full of anguished self-doubt – but there were probably many sides to him that she didn't know. It scared her a little. Of course relationships were hard work, but she had no experience. Then she remembered what he had done for her that first night, when she had almost thrown it all away.

She got up from the sofa, went to the kitchen and made him a pot of tea and a sandwich. Right now, it was her turn to take care of him. She opened the freezer and took out the ice cream. He'd told her that one of his favourite things as a child was eating ice cream in the park on Sundays with his family in the short Siberian summers. It wasn't summer, but she'd bought the ice cream anyway. She put some in a bowl for him. It looked so delicious and cold. Nicola almost never ate ice cream or sweets, but just this once, she decided that she was going to have some too. She put a tiny scoop in a bowl for herself and put everything on a tray.

Dmitri seemed to have recovered a little by the time she returned. 'I'm sorry,' he said, as she came into the room and set the tray on the coffee table.

'I want you to eat,' she said. 'You don't sleep, you barely eat. You need to keep your strength up.'

He looked at the tray, and his eyes lit up.

'Ice cream!' he said.

Ignoring the tea and the sandwich, he took the bowl of ice cream, just like a boy on a hot summer's day. Nicola laughed at his enthusiasm – of course, he was the just the type who would eat dessert first. But just as he was about to put the spoon to his lips, he stopped.

'Was I supposed to have the small bowl?' he asked.

'No! Of course not.'

'But it is not fair. You have practically none.'

'It's fine.'

'No, it is not fine. Here.' He fed her the first bite of ice cream with the spoon. Laughing, she kept her mouth closed until the last second and it got all over her mouth. He leaned in and licked it off. 'Much better than a spoon,' he said.

He made sure she had just the same amount as him, kissing her between bites. They laughed, and eventually abandoned the second bowl. When once again, the mischievous seductive look appeared on his face, she gave in fully, in a way she had never done before. This time, when he took charge, laid her down on the sofa and gently held her arms over her head, she didn't mind at all.

Chapter Thirty-Nine

21st December

'I'm... not sure I can do this,' Dmitri said.

As soon as they had come inside the building and been directed by the receptionist to this room, he'd felt his stomach liquefy. He was used to schools, teachers and students. Used to performances – choir performances, that is. But coming here, he felt so insignificant. And so damn old.

'You'll be fine,' Nicola said. Dmitri looked down at her soft white hand entwined with the twisted skin of his own, and felt worse, not better. But she had told him not to wear the gloves. She had convinced him that if he really wanted this, his past was the building block for his future. He believed her, and it had been he who had sent the email in the first place. He breathed in deeply and tried to clear his mind. Since Saturday night, he'd been practising almost non-stop in Nicola's spare room. This was what he was born to do, and he was ready. But he still felt nervous.

At first, when they reached the door, he thought there must have been a mistake. Inside, a pianist was playing a passage from *Rhapsody on a Theme by Paganini*, a virtuoso piece by Rachmaninov. The music was cut off abruptly.

Someone was speaking. The passage began again, slower this time.

'The woman said just to go in,' Nicola said. Even she looked a little flustered. She was wearing a dark blue suit, a white silk blouse and black patent high heels. He felt a surge of desire as he remembered the look on her face this morning as she'd had to get dressed in that suit twice before they'd finally walked out the door. She looked beautiful and sexy in whatever she wore, but he *did* like her in a suit. Him and probably every other bastard at her work... The thought did little to improve his mood as he opened the door and they went inside.

The room was set up like a small lecture theatre. At the bottom of the raked seats, instead of a podium, a grand piano stood in the centre. A young man, who looked Chinese or Japanese, was sitting at the piano with beads of sweat on his forehead. There were three other students: two men and a woman, in the seats near the front. All were much younger than he was. On the other side of the piano, a man strode back and forth, talking and beating out time with his hands. He was in his mid- to late-sixties with thinning dark hair combed back from a sharp, well-defined face. Though his website photo was probably taken ten years ago, Dmitri recognised him. Mikhail Aslanov. Dmitri had had professors like him and had attended masterclasses like this many times. Classes designed to tear you down. It was up to you to build yourself back up again... Or not.

Mikhail Aslanov frowned as they entered. The young pianist played the passage a final time and the others in the room clapped.

'That's enough for today,' Mikhail Aslanov said. 'But next time, Yoshi-san,' he looked down at the pianist, 'I will expect perfection.'

The man looked so relieved to be up and away from the piano. Dmitri felt for him, remembering the nerves, and how it felt knowing that the others in the room may not be wishing you entirely well. For him, it was as if all the years since he'd last taken class had melted away, exposing the rawness, the inadequacy. Could he really do this?

'Well done,' he whispered to Yoshi, as he and the others left the room. The young pianist smiled gratefully. Compliments could be few and far between in this game.

Dmitri forced himself to walk down the steps of the hall towards the man at the bottom. He was glad that he'd at least had the presence of mind to ask the woman at the desk Mr Aslanov's patronymic name so that he could address him formally. He was also aware that Nicola had stayed sitting in the top row. Dmitri knew that this was up to *him* now.

'Good morning, Mikhail Petrovich,' Dmitri said in English, 'I am Dmitri.' He held out his hand.

The older man looked wary and stern as he took it, frowning down at Dmitri's hand as he shook it.

'Thank you for responding to my email,' Dmitri said.

'Your email, yes.' Mikhail Petrovich rubbed his chin thoughtfully. 'Your story, is... well, it is not for me to say. There is only one important thing now.' He gestured to the piano.

'Yes,' Dmitri replied.

He set down his bag and went to the piano. He adjusted the stool, feeling the familiar boneless sensation in his fingers, like he had never played a piano before in his life. He took three deep breaths. Then he put his fingers on the keys to warm up. He cleared his mind, finding the place where nothing could reach him; the place inside where the music lived. He finished the warm-up. It was time to show this man what he could do.

With another deep breath, he launched into Chopin's *Fantaisie Impromptu.* It was lightning fast, impressive, the treble line flying through the air like restless spirits, battling the complex base notes that anchored the music to the earth. And then, as if reaching an uneasy peace, the music changed into the almost impossibly beautiful and rich melody of the middle section. He gave himself to the billowing chords, lost himself in the magic of each note coming alive and shimmering into the next.

Dmitri was barely aware of the last chord, the sound evaporating into the ether. The room coming back in focus. Nicola, sitting in the back row, Mikhail Petrovich in the front row. His heart was beating so hard, the adrenalin ripping through his body. Had he played well, or had it all been in his mind?

He looked at Mikhail Petrovich, tension tightening across his shoulders as he awaited the verdict. The man was staring down at his own fingers, long and lithe, like Dmitri's own. His performing days were most likely over. Was he remembering what it was like? Or thinking of a way to let Dmitri down easy? Or not easy at all?

'That was... interesting,' he said, finally. 'You have come here hoping to impress me. Hoping to convince me that the years do not matter.' He got up from the chair and began to pace back and forth thoughtfully. 'Chopin,' he mused.

Dmitri waited, unsure what to say. Had the Chopin been wrong? Going back over it in his mind, he'd played it flawlessly. More than that, he truly thought that he'd captured the essence of the piece. The dark and the light. The conflict, the romance. But this was why he needed more instruction. A coach. Someone who could tell him if his head was in the clouds, or just up his arse.

Mikhail Petrovich stopped pacing and turned back to Dmitri. 'Play something else,' he said. 'Something that will tell me about you.'

Dmitri thought for a moment. His fear was slowly beginning to vanish. This was why he was here – to tell his story. A story that, for him, words could not adequately express. Only the music could do that.

He put his fingers on the keys, then began to pick out the melody of a simple lullaby, the berceuse from Stravinsky's *Firebird*. It wasn't something he had been practising, and yet, it came to him now. The soundtrack in the back of his mind ran on that this was madness. This wasn't going to impress anyone, let alone this important man. But the haunting melody reminded him of playing as a boy, when everything had been so easy. The time before the darkness, his father listening to him, lost in the shared beauty of the music. Feeling that powerful hope, so full of possibilities, that only now had a chance of being reborn.

He finished playing, gradually returning to the present. Nicola... he looked up at her, drawing strength just from knowing she was there. Admiration shone in her eyes and he felt a warm flush of pride. He was aware of Mikhail Petrovich watching the two of them.

'Yes,' the man muttered under his breath. 'I think I begin to see who you are.'

Dmitri nodded, unsure of the subtext.

'I have some questions for you. Beginning with what you want, and why you are here?'

Dmitri took a breath, but before he could speak, the man cut him off.

'You are not young. You did not finish what you started.'

'No.' Dmitri said, his head bowed.

'Do you think that this is what you need? To come here and take class? To be torn down, built up? To what end?'

'I don't know.' Dmitri raised his head, finding his voice. 'I am here to get advice. Everything you say about me is true. But for many years, I have been torn down. Now, I believe the time is finally right to build myself up again. After all this time, I need to play again. I *will* play again.'

'You *need* to play,' the older man mused. He pointed back at the piano. 'What do you need to play – for her?' He had ignored Nicola the whole time, and now gave her a passing glance. 'Play something for her.'

Dmitri tuned out the room, the situation, everything. For him, he was back to that first night in the church, when everything had begun. The reason she was here now. Not something romantic – that had come later. No, what he had found that night was the darkness. And a way to release it. Whether it was the right piece or not, he didn't know. But somehow, it had been right for *them*, and the only reason he was here right now.

He closed his eyes and began to play again. Rachmaninov, *The Bells*. Moscow. That time was part of him. The past was part of him. Fire on snow. The darkness there. And the light.

'Stop. That is enough.'

He hadn't even been aware of playing. Of coming to the end of the piece. Or was he even at the end?

He opened his eyes. The light was almost blinding. The face of the man watching him came gradually into focus. Stricken with its own memories. He raised his hand to his face, and for a moment, Dmitri was sure that his eyes glistened with tears.

'I will help you,' Mikhail Petrovich said.

Nicola was used to difficult situations. Difficult negotiations, involving difficult people and millions of pounds. But how Dmitri could sit there at that piano, with that man Aslanov looking on, dissecting every note – every nuance – she had absolutely no idea. Several times, she'd almost got up from her seat. Clomped down the carpeted stairs. Told the old man where to go. Because that was easier than enduring the tension that was so thick she thought she might choke.

When Dmitri played the Rachmaninov, she almost lost it. It was so powerful, so raw. It catapulted her back to that night in the church when she'd first heard him playing; that first wrenching of the key that had unlocked everything inside of her. And yet, as he played it now, she heard a new beauty in it, a new depth. And when she saw the effect it had on Aslanov, she knew that whatever she heard with her untrained ear, she wasn't just imagining it.

'I will help you.'

As soon as the words were spoken, Dmitri seemed overcome. He opened his mouth to speak, but nothing came out. Nicola immediately stood up and went down the steps. If Aslanov thought that her presence here was purely decorative, then he could think again.

Aslanov looked at her as she came down to his level. 'And you are?' the old man said.

'Nicola Taylor,' she held out her hand and shook the old man's firmly and with purpose. 'I'm Dmitri's... manager.'

He raised a single grey eyebrow. 'I bet you are.'

'You know the situation,' she said. 'So we need to know what he needs to do next.' She looked at Dmitri. 'Right?'

'Yes.' The single word seemed to be a struggle.

Aslanov looked from one of them to the other. He finally settled his sharp gaze on Dmitri. 'You have come here out of nowhere. Walked in off the street, with your story, and your ability. But I have checked up on you. I verified that you were in Moscow the year you said. And as surprising as it seemed, they remembered you. As someone with great promise. Had you gone back, perhaps in a year or two when you were older, then they would have made you into something different. You would have lost that innocent, untrained quality that you have to your playing now. A quality that was not valued back then. But today...?' He shrugged. 'Maybe.'

Nicola kept a close eye on Dmitri, who was staring down at his scarred hands. He seemed to be able to do little else but nod in agreement at what Aslanov was saying. Nicola had the idea that the old man could probably go on all day like this. Lecturing, thinking aloud. Now that they were here, she felt angry with herself. She should have spent some time over the last few days doing her own research. Trying to figure out how to turn a man who 'walked in off the street' into a bloody concert pianist. At least known the right questions to ask.

Aslanov turned back to her. 'He will need an agent. Someone who can open the right doors. There is really no time to lose.' He turned back to Dmitri. 'There is no point sitting here in masterclass, working towards a degree. Right now, you need to get your name out there. Tell your story, make recordings, sell them. Then, and only then, will you be able to achieve your dream of performing.' The man barely paused for a breath. 'You will need to be ruthless in your focus. And have much courage. Do you understand?'

'I... think so—' Dmitri began.

'Yes,' Nicola interjected. 'Yes, we do. Now, do you have a name of an agent?'

'The one I have in mind is called Bill Campbell.'

Nicola typed the name into the notes section of her phone.

'He will know how to proceed,' Aslanov said.

'Good,' Nicola said. At the end of the day, Dmitri's career was a business like any other. Concert pianists were paid to perform. There had to be some reason for people to come and listen and pay for the privilege. Dmitri had told her that there was often an element of novelty to it, such as a very young or very old performer, or a competition winner. Or – a man with a past who had overcome serious obstacles. Either way, it was all going to have to be carefully managed. 'And you will speak to him first?'

'I will do it today.' Aslanov said.

'Fine.' Nicola handed Aslanov her card and one of Dmitri's. She respected his total no-nonsense and upfront manner – no platitudes, and no bullshit. She assumed the interview was over when he took the cards and put them in the breast pocket of his suit jacket. But Aslanov turned back to Dmitri.

'Play something else.' He pointed to the piano. Nicola almost laughed. The interview was over, and now, Aslanov simply wanted to enjoy the music.

Dmitri instantly sprang to life, his eyes glowing with a strange fire. Then he closed his eyes and played a piece that was perhaps her favourite of all that he'd been practising. The one he'd recorded for her on the memory stick. He'd had to tell her more than once what it was; Chopin seemed mostly to call his pieces by their number and key signature. *Nocturne No. 20 in C# Minor.* The opening trill, dazzling like the glitter of moonlight on ice.

Nicola smiled as she sat down in the front row and closed her eyes, letting the music carry her away. At this rate, she really was going to be ridiculously late for work. But she didn't mind. At all.

It was really happening. Everything he'd dreamed of – no, hadn't even allowed himself to dream about – was there, almost in front of him. It was as if he'd been wandering for his whole life underneath a stormy black sky, and now, the clouds were shifting, allowing him a first, and infinitely precious, glimpse of the stars.

Dmitri spent the whole afternoon with Mikhail Petrovich.

He played through more of his repertoire – feeling a profound joy even when performing for an audience of one, that took him by surprise. They had tea together, talked: about music, about Russia, about life in general. As a boy at the Conservatory, he would have been in awe and fear of a man like this. But now, even though they were not equals, Dmitri appreciated this opportunity to spend time with a master.

In the late afternoon when he finally left the Conservatory to go back to his flat and change before the night's carolling, he felt like another missing piece of him, dislodged and directionless, had been found and reinserted. Between Nicola, and his piano, he experienced something that he'd never expected to feel again.

He felt whole.

Chapter Forty

22nd December

Even though she wanted this, Nicola still felt a little overwhelmed and a lot queasy. The auditorium, usually reserved for training events, client seminars and presentations, had been transformed into an Advent Calendar wonderland. There were fairy lights strung everywhere, and a Christmas tree on the stage. There was eggnog, mulled wine, champagne and sushi ordered in from Nobu. Chrissie had outdone herself. Had it been any other occasion, Nicola would have put her foot down, told her PA to stop the ridiculous expenditure. But she allowed Chrissie to go all out. Because it would be the first time... and the last.

Dmitri was due to arrive around four o'clock, along with the choir members he'd been able to gather. He'd had to rearrange a previously scheduled carolling concert and call in favours as only he could do on such short notice. Some of the people who were coming along to the Christmas carolling weren't part of the main choir and Nicola suspected that they were mostly coming out of curiosity – to see Dmitri's new girl-friend, the 'The Heckler', up close and personal. Now that the day had finally arrived, Nicola was glad that she'd already met some of Dmitri's people, like Tanya and Carole-Ann. Having that hanging over her head today would have just been too much.

Yesterday, after going with Dmitri to meet Mikhail Aslanov, she'd gone into the office as the 'Timeless' deal was finally signing. Everything had gone smoothly, even telling Carl that she wouldn't be going out for a drink with him, because she was seeing someone. When she got home, late that night, Dmitri was practising in the spare room after his carolling concert, and as far as she could tell, hadn't had anything all day other than a cup of tea. All he could talk about was Aslanov – whom Dmitri insisted on referring to as Mikhail Petrovich, no matter how many times he used the man's name in a sentence. The two of them had ended up spending the entire afternoon together. Whatever did or didn't come of the whole thing, Dmitri, it seemed had made another convert. In the end, she'd only been able to shut him up by ordering him into the shower with her and proceeding to render him speechless.

After that, he'd gone back to practising late into the night and being, in Aslanov's words, *ruthlessly focused*. He'd come to bed only as she was getting up. But that was fine – whatever hours he chose to keep, she was determined to support him in building the life that he deserved. On her way into the office, she'd googled the agent, Bill Campbell. To her relief, the man seemed legit. He represented a number of big-name stars in classical music, a few of which even she had heard of. When she phoned his office, she discovered that Aslanov had been true to his word and already spoken to him. They had a brief conversation and organised a meeting for early January.

All of it had kept her busy; focusing on Dmitri had taken her mind off how nervous she felt about this afternoon's do. But even that was a ruse – an attempt to keep the memory, shrouded in the mists of time, out of her conscious mind. She hadn't succeeded. It had happened a long time ago, but it had happened today. The twenty-second of December. A day – and night – that she would never forget. A night that had begun with two girls laughing, giggling, putting on make-up, dressing for a party. And ended sprawled out on an icy pavement, unable to move, breathe, or scream…

Now, though, as she stood frowning over the table with the chocolate fountain and the small army of wine and champagne bottles, she forced her mind back to the here and now.

'Nicola?' She turned. Chrissie was holding two large white boxes. 'Can you help me put these out?'

Nicola obediently took one of the boxes and looked inside the clear plastic window on top. What she saw made her smile. Gingerbread hearts and stars, decorated and iced by hand. From 'The Braided Loaf'. As she set the gingerbread out on the platters that Chrissie had brought up from catering, a few people began filtering down the corridor, coming in to see the final preparations and to have a pre-party cup of eggnog.

She'd just set out the last gingerbread when a text came in on her phone from Dmitri:

Train delayed, be there soon.

She clenched her teeth. Not today of all days.

Before Nicola could reply to the message, Brian, came up to her. 'It's all looking good,' he said. 'So you're really going through with it?'

'I think so,' Nicola said, feeling not very sure at all.

'Well, you deserve a healthy dose of happiness,' Brian said. 'We will miss you though.'

Nicola felt a tear welling up in her eye. She didn't want to cry. Because once she started, she might not be able to stop. 'Yes,' she managed. 'Thanks.'

As Brian went back to his office to send the email around to come to the auditorium, Nicola was relieved to spot Carole-Ann, Tanya and some of the other choir members being ushered in by one of the PAs. They were wearing their festive outfits, just like the first time she'd seen them at Waterloo Station. The night her life had changed forever.

'Hi,' she said to Carole-Ann. 'Thanks so much for coming.'

'Oh, we wouldn't miss it,' Carole-Ann said with a little wink. 'All this posh food and wine.'

'Yes,' Tanya said, giving Nicola a quick hug. 'It looks wonderful.'

'Yes, well, it helps to know a fabulous bakery.' Nicola smiled at her. 'And Chrissie, my PA, did a great job.' She pointed to Chrissie, bustling around on the other side of the room, putting out even more food. 'The woman in the jumper.' Chrissie was unmissable. She was wearing a Christmas jumper with a smiley tree made from green pompoms. Taking inspiration from Brian's wife, she'd wired it up with flashing, battery-powered lights that surely wouldn't pass muster with health and safety.

'Lovely,' Carole-Ann said. Nicola thought she probably meant Chrissie's jumper, but she wasn't going to hold that against her. Nicola had opted not to wear anything festive – no surprise there. But she was wearing an elegant, curve-hugging Dior dress in dark green crepe with a matching jacket. Without the jacket, the dress was possibly a little too low-cut for the office, but she didn't expect any complaints.

Carole-Ann leaned in to her. 'And we heard you did a great job too – standing up to that frightening man at the music school.'

Nicola laughed. 'Mikhail Aslanov. Actually, he *was* pretty scary. Though, of course, Dmitri charmed him in the end.'

'And thanks to you, my brother may finally, after all these years, be a concert pianist!' Tanya said, smiling warmly.

'Well, it's early days,' Nicola said. The last thing she wanted to do was raise false hopes. 'But let's hope so—'

'Nicola! I am so sorry I'm late!' Dmitri came in, looking flustered and perfect in his formal black coat and tails. He reached for her and gave her a kiss on the lips, then pulled back. 'Sorry,' he said, 'this is your work.'

'No, it's fine.' She stood on her tiptoes and kissed him back. Just having him here – his warmth and his energy – chased away the shadows and made everything all right.

Dmitri sent Tanya and Carole-Ann off to get everything set up on stage for the choir. He stood there, looking at her, his eyes shiny. 'You look so beautiful,' he said. He ran a finger down the column of her neck—

'Ahem.'

Nicola looked around startled. Chrissie was there, giving her a very sly look. 'Do I get to say hello to your handsome stranger, Nicola?' she said.

Dmitri stepped forward and gave Chrissie a quick kiss on the cheek. 'Chrissie,' he said, as if they were old friends. 'It's so good to see you again. And what an amazing jumper.'

Nicola laughed and rolled her eyes. 'Thanks!' Chrissie said, blushing. 'Now, has anyone offered you any food or drink—?'

As Chrissie continued to chat to Dmitri, Nicola noticed another figure hovering by the door.

Ollie.

Looking absolutely murderous.

'I think we need to get started now,' Nicola said, interrupting the conversation between Chrissie and Dmitri. 'Can you get the choir singing in, like, five minutes?'

'Of course.' Dmitri took her hand in his. She was surprised to see that he wasn't wearing his gloves. He was still very self-conscious about his scars, and Nicola suspected that when she wasn't around, he still kept his hands mostly covered. But today he had not. She was proud of him for that.

'Thank you,' she whispered to him. He brought her hand to his lips and kissed it, then went off towards the stage.

People began coming in in droves. Chrissie went over to supervise the food and drink, and Nicola ushered in a few late choir members. Two men from IT were in the front by the stage, dealing with the sound system.

Nicola went to the drinks table. In the time she'd been with Dmitri – a very short time, granted – she hadn't had any alcohol. She hadn't missed it either, but right now, a glass to steady her nerves wouldn't go amiss. Taking a glass of champagne, she moved away from the table to the side of the stage near the large speaker. As she lifted the glass to her lips, a hand grabbed her arm and she almost spilled it.

She whirled around to find Ollie there. He was clearly on his second or third eggnog already, because his breath stank of rum.

'You seem very *friendly* with the choir director.' Ollie leaned in towards her. He still had hold of her arm.

Nicola removed his hand from her arm. Seeing him around the office was one thing, but having him and Dmitri here in the same place... She should have given more thought to damage control. But it was too late now, and she wasn't going to lie. Her eyes never leaving his, she took a sip from the glass. 'Yes,' she said. 'We're together.'

'For how long?' He raised his voice.

'Not long – obviously. Are things OK with Chloe?'

He ignored her question. Before she knew what was happening, he grabbed her one-handed by the waist, pulling him closer to him. 'So let me get this straight,' he said. 'While I was camped out in that bloody hotel waiting for you to come to me, you were off with that Russian?'

'That's none of your business.' She tried to move away but he kept hold of her.

'I'll take that as a yes.'

'Do what you like,' she hissed, 'but get your hands off me.'

'Nicola. We are ready.' She felt rather than saw Dmitri

approach, coming up beside her. He stood, facing Ollie. Dmitri was the taller of the two, though less broad-shouldered than Ollie. Ollie let go of her. She could almost smell the waves of hatred coming off the two men, like two wild dogs facing off. 'Is everything OK?' Dmitri said, leaning possessively close.

'Yes fine.' She turned and kissed him. 'Go ahead.'

Dmitri arched an eyebrow in Ollie's direction, then turned and walked on to the stage. Without fanfare or introduction, he launched the choir in to a rousing rendition of 'Ding Dong Merrily on High'.

Ollie grabbed another eggnog from a roving waitress. Nicola began to move nearer to the front of the stage, where a crowd was gathering to join in with the singing. Ollie drifted along beside her. She was uncomfortably aware that people were starting to look their way.

'I'm sorry, Ollie,' Nicola said. 'But you can't keep following me around. We've both made our choices. For you, your family is the most important thing right now.'

'Fuck you.'

'What did you say?' She'd seriously had enough. She rounded on him, raising her voice. 'Would you like me to go to HR and chat it through with them? I'm sure IT would have a field day going through your phone.'

'You wouldn't dare.'

'No? Are you sure about that?' Nicola set her still half-full glass of champagne on to a waitress's tray. She lowered her voice. 'If I were you, *I* wouldn't put it past me.'

'I can't fucking believe you,' Ollie said.

Nicola spotted Brian and Chrissie looking worriedly in her direction. She began to walk off again.

'So tell me—' Ollie said.

Damn it, the man really was making a scene. Thank God the choir was in full voice and Dmitri hadn't noticed.

'Yes?' she turned back, seething.

'Why him?' Ollie lowered his voice. 'What does he have that I don't?'

Nicola thought for a moment. About all the hours she and Ollie had spent together; all the emptiness, the lies, the disappointment. And, above all, the guilt. None of it had ever seemed to bother Ollie one bit. Nicola gave him a pained smile. 'He has a heart.'

'That's bullshit.'

Nicola shrugged. Chrissie and Brian both began walking over; clearly they had realised that she needed rescuing. Nicola turned back to Ollie and gave him a half-smile, her eyelids lowered. Just to be a little bit mean, she leaned in and whispered close to his ear, 'and an extra inch and a half.'

She left Ollie standing there, choking down the rest of his eggnog.

Nicola went over to stand with Brian and Chrissie, who were joining in with the carolling. A lot of people were standing around chatting, with the choir only as background music, but it didn't really matter. Everyone seemed to be enjoying themselves. It was the last Advent Calendar before Christmas, so that was as it should be. She began to relax a little and enjoy the festivities too, much more than she thought she would.

But, eventually, Chrissie nudged her. The choir had just finished an enthusiastic rendition of 'Santa Claus is Coming to Town.'

'You're up now,' Chrissie said.

'What?'

'Time for your speech.' Chrissie walked over to where Brian's PA was holding out a microphone. She took it and brought it back to Nicola.

Nicola had thought she was prepared for this moment, but now that it was here...

From up on the stage, Dmitri looked at her, his eyes warm chocolate. He'd been so focused on conducting that she'd thought he'd forgotten about her. But no. He reached a hand down to her and pulled her on to the stage.

Chrissie handed her the microphone.

'Thank you for coming today,' Nicola said through the microphone. She waited a second for the chat to die down. 'We have Chrissie to thank for all the food and decorations. So please give her a round of applause.'

The crowd obliged, and Chrissie raised her hand to wave. Her face was flushed a fresh-rose colour, and she looked as proud as Nicola had ever seen her.

When the clapping died down, Nicola continued, 'I'd also like to thank Dmitri, and the choir of St Anne's Church, for providing us with the entertainment.' She took a breath. 'I first encountered the choir at Waterloo Station while waiting for a delayed train. I was in a bad mood that night, and – though I'm sure none of you will believe it – I was actually quite rude.'

She waited until the laughter died down.

'But, luckily, Dmitri did not hold it against me. He agreed to bring the choir here for the Advent Calendar.' She smiled at him, feeling the familiar glow that she always did in his presence. 'Now, in case you're wondering why I suddenly wanted to go all out on this occasion, it's because it's my swansong. In January, I'll be leaving Privé.' Her throat tightened. 'For me, it will be a new direction. A new start. But I wanted to say, thank you – for putting up with me all these years.'

There were mutterings of surprise, and a few claps. She relinquished the microphone back to Brian's PA and was about to step down from the stage. But Dmitri stopped her and led her by the hand over to a piano that had been rolled out on the stage. Nicola looked at Dmitri in surprise. It hadn't been there before, so it must have been put there while she was speaking.

Dmitri sat her down on the bench, and then sat down next to her, his hip touching hers. He cued the choir from the piano and played a jazzy gliss of notes. Not a Christmas song, but one she recognised immediately – from when he'd played it for her in her house. The choir members were all smiling as they began to sing, and the audience began to sway and clap in rhythm:

Let me call you "Sweetheart" I'm in love with you.
Let me hear you whisper that you love me too.
Keep the love light glowing in your eyes so true.
Let me call you "Sweetheart" I'm in love with you.

Happy tears welled up in Nicola's eyes as Dmitri glanced in her direction and smiled. She watched his fingers fly across the keys, mesmerising and brilliant. It didn't matter that she'd known him such a short time; the past didn't matter – his or hers. The only thing that mattered was that he was in her life. Only him, and only her.

Joy bubbled up inside of her as she leaned in and spoke quietly in his ear. The words that she knew were just right. 'I love you,' she said.

Not pausing or faltering for a second, as the song continued on into the next verse, he leaned over and brushed her lips with his. 'I love you too,' he said.

Chapter Forty-One

24th December

On Christmas Eve, Dmitri took Nicola for dinner at Kolya's house in North London. All of his nearest and dearest were there: Tanya and Mark, Phil (who had brought Carole-Ann as his guest), Kolya and Nigel, and the two noisy and excited children rushing around, shouting and playing. The house was shiny with decorations and candles glowed on the table. The night was filled with laughter, warmth, the smell of Nicola's perfume and the feel of her (very distracting) hand on his thigh. It was as if she had been part of him – part of all of them – forever, not just a few weeks. After dinner, he played the piano for them. Christmas carols, jazz, and just for her, the Chopin *Nocturne*. Their time, their songs.

When they got home, he gave her her gift. In truth, he'd been a little worried about what to get her. But she'd ripped it open with enthusiasm, laughing when she saw the first gift – a box of lingerie.

'Is this for you or for me?'

He'd laughed too and kissed her. 'Well, seeing it's Christmas, I thought we could both benefit.'

It took a while before she got to unwrapping the other gift

he had for her: the small, leatherbound book of Russian fairy tales that had belonged to his mother.

'It's lovely,' she said, flipping through the pictures. 'But...' she looked concerned, 'it seems very special.'

'That is why you must have it,' he said, fingering a lock of her glorious red hair. He opened the book and read the opening of his favourite tale, 'The Firebird'. How young Ivan had waited in the magical garden for the Firebird. She had come down from the sky, stolen a golden apple and left behind a single flaming feather.

'The song sheets I scattered,' she said with a laugh. 'Was that the magic feather that I left behind?'

'Maybe,' he said. 'Or perhaps you are young Ivan. Was it not you who went to the ends of the earth to find me?'

She laughed, kissing him. 'A Christmas market? Skating? A freezing cold church? Yes, I see your point.'

She had a gift for him too – she'd booked them a long weekend away at New Year's. At a five-star hotel in the Cotswolds, which was somewhere he had never been.

'Don't worry,' she assured him, 'they have a piano, and they say you can play it as much as you like. We can't have you interrupting your practising for something so romantic as a holiday.'

Dmitri appreciated the fact that she understood. Whatever was coming next was going to be a long road, and he had to be 'ruthlessly focused'. 'Thank you,' he said, nuzzling her, 'but it may take some persuading for me to leave the room at all.'

They didn't get much sleep that night, and by the time Dmitri finally closed his eyes in the early hours of Christmas morning, it was nearly time to get up again. He left Nicola asleep in bed and went home to get changed. He was conducting the choir for the morning service, and then, later on, meeting Nicola at her sister's house in Putney.

By the time he left the church he was feeling nervous. He'd worn his grey gloves, even though she preferred him without them, and though, for all he knew, she might have already told her family everything. Besides which, once he went public and 'told his story', everyone would know. God, it was going to be difficult. He needed this to go well.

When he rang the bell, the door was answered by an attractive woman in her early sixties – Nicola's mother. She seemed friendly, if a little reserved, as she shook his hand and ushered him inside. Jules, a plumper, paler version of Nicola, and her husband Stuart were sitting on the sofa in the lounge, along with Nicola's stepfather, Teddy. There were several empty bottles of beer on the coffee table between them. In the family room off the kitchen, Ben, the half-brother, was playing a game on his phone, and Jules' three kids were squabbling in front of the TV.

Nicola came out of the kitchen wearing an apron. Her hands were covered in flour and she looked flustered, and out of sorts. She brightened when she saw him, and when he bent his head to kiss her on the cheek, she turned her head so that it landed on her mouth. Fine with him.

After introductions were made (and although Nicola had told Jules that he didn't drink alcohol), there was an awkward moment of him having to refuse a glass of wine. Dmitri volunteered to help out in the kitchen. But before he could do so, Jules asked him if he wouldn't mind looking after the children – see if any of them wanted to play a board game or something. Teddy and Stuart went out in the street to look at Stuart's present to himself: a brand new Porsche in mid-life crisis red. Dmitri made a valiant effort to pry the younger children away from their DVD or strike up a conversation with the older boy. When ultimately, he failed, he went to find Nicola.

The kitchen was a vast, enormous space with immaculate units and a huge table. Nicola was taking something out of the oven that smelled like burnt vegetables. Her mother and sister were there, doing not very much, and he worried that if he tried to help he'd only get in the way. But as soon as she saw him, she summoned him over to her. She took his hand, her eyes flicking for a moment to his gloves.

'Mum, Jules,' she said. 'There's something I need to tell you.'

Whatever he'd been expecting her to say – and in truth, he had no idea – he was surprised, even a little shocked, that she chose this moment to tell them the secret she'd been keeping for so many years. About the party, the rape, the job offer... nothing held back.

Her mother and sister stared at her, their faces expressing shock, and horror, and pity. He slipped his arm around her waist and stroked her hair as she began to cry. By the time she was finished, they were also crying.

'I'm sorry that I've had to hurt you like this,' Nicola said to her mother and Jules. 'But I needed to get it out in the open. And if I'm going to get through this, I need you on my side. All of you.'

'So what are you going to do now?' Jules asked, dabbing her eye with a rumpled tissue.

'Go to counselling,' Nicola said. 'Take some time out to think about what I want to do next. I'm leaving Privé. I'm going to do something more worthwhile. I have a few ideas.' She smiled up at Dmitri and he kissed her tenderly. He was so proud of her. But still, hearing the story again hurt him too.

Nicola's mother finished the wine in her glass and finally spoke up. 'I'm so sorry,' she said. 'Sorry that I wasn't a better mum to you. That you couldn't talk to me, or ask for help, because of what I did to your dad.'

Nicola seemed to hesitate for a long time before speaking. He knew that this was difficult enough for her already, and the mention of her dad probably made it even harder. 'You saw a chance to find happiness, and you took it, Mum,' she said. 'I think I finally understand that. And that's what I'm doing too.' She looked down at Dmitri's hands, then up at his face. He nodded gently and she removed his gloves, tracing the lines of his scars. 'Luckily, in this case, no one has to get hurt.'

Her mum came over then, and hugged both of them, with Jules joining in.

'I'll go with you to counselling,' Jules said. 'If it will help.'

'I don't know yet,' Nicola said. 'We'll see.'

Dmitri was surprised when Nicola's mum reached out for his hand, looking down at the scars. 'I see you have your own story. And I hope that I'll learn all about it. Welcome to the family.' She stood on tiptoe and kissed his cheek. 'I'm so glad you're here.'

Dmitri swallowed back a tear of his own. He missed his own mother, but more than that, he wished she – and his father – could see him now. See the person he was finally becoming, and be happy and proud. But then again... maybe they could.

'Thank you,' he said, smiling at Nicola's mum. 'It means a lot to hear that.'

What had come over her, Nicola didn't know. After a wonderful night at Kolya's house, she had known that today would be hard, and it was. All through lunch (her mum had taken over the cooking so it was mostly edible) she felt raw from her revelation and sorry for the pain she had caused her family. And yet, this was a step that she had to take. A new start, something to build on. The past was behind her. She was no longer 'The Heckler', no longer defined by the scars inside.

Dmitri somehow managed to work his magic even on her family. By the end of the afternoon, he had the kids playing card games. When the game switched to poker, Teddy, Stuart, and even a grudging Ben joined in. Later on, when gifts were exchanged, even though Nicola had put both their names on the tag for the wretched Chelsea away kit, somehow, it was Dmitri who had got all the thanks from her half-brother (and who knew that Dmitri could actually talk football and have a proper heated argument about the Premier League and Chelsea's Champion's League prospects?).

Despite the day turning out better than expected, Nicola was relieved when it was time to go. Before they could leave, Dmitri had to promise to take Ben to a football match and to teach Jules' kids to ice skate. Nicola had hugged her mother and sister and promised to be in touch. She meant it too, now that the truth was no longer an obstacle between them.

On the train home, Nicola laid her head against Dmitri's chest and closed her eyes as he stroked her hair.

'What you did was very brave,' he said.

'It was hard,' she said. 'But I felt I needed to do it. No more secrets.'

'I understand.' He sighed. 'All too well. It is going to be difficult for me to tell my story, too.'

She opened her eyes and took his hand. His skin was warm as she traced his fingers with hers. 'You don't have to do it.'

'We'll see.' He shifted underneath her. 'Look—'

Nicola raised her head as he pointed out the window of the train. A few large flakes of snow had begun to fall, dancing on the wind and settling to earth.

'Snow!' she said, excitedly. 'A white Christmas!'

The train pulled into the station and they got off. Dmitri

led her by the hand through the streets and across The Green. The snow was falling harder, thick and fast. As they neared the house, Nicola stopped.

'What the—?'

The doors on either side of her house were trimmed with their wreaths. But in the middle, her house was a riot of light. Tiny twinkling fairy lights around the door, icicle lights around the windows. A beautiful evergreen wreath with white lights and a red bow. And just above the door, a large sprig of mistletoe.

'You didn't!' she said.

He gave her that teasing look, his eyes glowing amber. 'Maybe it is the magic power of Christmas.' He shrugged. 'Or maybe I've just got to know your neighbours.'

'My neighbours!' Standing against the door, she grabbed him by the collar and pulled him to her. The snow settled on their hair and clothing, as he tangled his fingers in her hair and kissed her deeply.

'The snow reminds me of that night on the London Eye,' she said, breathlessly when they came apart.

'Yes.' His cheeks flushed in the cold. 'I wanted you so badly.'

'Did you?' she teased. 'Could have fooled me.'

'Oh yes,' he said, his warm breath close to her ear. 'You have no idea.'

She unlocked the door, and they went inside. 'And did you have any other Christmas treats in mind that I don't know about?' she said, brushing the snow from his jacket.

'I think this Christmas, it is all about making new memories.'

'Oh? Like what?'

His eyes turned dark and mischievous and he took something out of his bag, then leaned close and whispered in her ear.

And Nicola laughed as the Santa hat made a reappearance.

He put it on his head, swinging the tassel over his shoulder. 'Now, shall we see who's been naughty or nice?'

He lifted her into his arms and carried her up the stairs to the bedroom.

– vi –

'...Happily ever after.'

– 'The Firebird', *The Anthology of Russian Tales*

Chapter Forty-Two

1st July – 6 months later

Nicola was aware of the people in the room staring at her as she left the conference room. She smiled to herself and tucked the cheque into her portfolio. Her new business partner, Alan, gave her a sideways look.

'What's that they say about ice and Eskimos?' he said when they were out of the room. 'I've been trying for two years and never got a cent out of that lot.'

'Well, I guess it's all about presentation,' Nicola said. Yes, the well-produced video, with before and after stories of people aided by the charity, helped. But her well-fitting suit and high heels probably hadn't hurt either. Whether it was for shares in a company or a six-figure donation to a charity, if there was one thing Nicola felt confident of, it was her ability to walk into a room full of men and get them to shell out money. Some things never changed, but at least now it was for a good cause. 'Now,' she added, 'do you want to call Care and give them the good news, or should I?'

'You do the honours,' Alan said.

'OK,' she said. 'I've got some more calls to make anyway.'

They gave their temporary passes in at reception and

walked out of the office tower. As they entered Canada Square, Nicola felt a rush of nostalgia. The last time she'd been here, it had been decorated for Christmas, with an ice rink, Christmas tree and the great swooping birds and golden apples that were straight out of a fairy tale. Now, it was summer, the sky a deep blue above the grey concrete and glass. Office workers: men in shirtsleeves and women in business casual summer dresses, were basking in the sun on benches or sitting at outdoor tables. Had she ever been one of them? It seemed like a lifetime ago.

'Do you have time for a coffee?' Alan asked. Since setting up their business as independent charity consultants in April, they'd been too busy to look for office space. Kolya was the one who had introduced her to Alan Franklin, a semi-retired financial advisor in his mid-sixties. They'd met up early in the New Year, gone over her questions about the Care accounts, got to talking and one thing had led to another. Now, they already had five charities as clients, hiring them to advise on fundraising, presentation and financial management. It had been a steep learning curve, but so far so good.

'Actually,' Nicola said, 'I'm supposed to meet Chrissie, my former PA. Since we're here. We've been meaning to meet up, but this is the first time we've actually made it happen.'

'OK,' Alan said. 'In that case, I'll give you a call later on. And see you at the concert. If not before.'

'Thanks Alan.' They shook hands and Alan went off to get the Tube.

Nicola sent a quick text to Chrissie. She went to the café where they'd agreed to meet and found a table. While she waited, she checked her voicemails: one from Bill Campbell, Dmitri's agent, one from Tanya and one from Jules.

She listened to Jules' message first. At thirty-eight weeks pregnant, Nicola knew that Jules could go into labour at any time. Listening to the message, she breathed out a sigh of relief. Jules was only calling to finalise a date for the christening and double-check the guest list. So like her sister!

Bill Campbell's message was in a similar vein; he was calling to see how many tickets she needed for next week's concert. Dmitri was making his London debut at the summer proms, and she'd invited everyone she knew. Nicola liked Bill Campbell and had to admit that he was earning his (generous) cut of Dmitri's earnings. From their very first meeting, Campbell had begun to make things happen. The plan was simple. Get Dmitri into the studio to make some recordings, and then get his name and his story out there to sell them.

In truth, neither of them had been prepared for what was to come – that Dmitri would cause such a fervour in the classical music world. But as soon as the story was out – about a talented prodigy whose career was stolen from him by a cruel act of violence – social media went viral. At first, Dmitri had refused to name his father as the perpetrator. It was Tanya who had taken it upon herself to fill in the gaps. It had taken a lot of effort and 'ends justify the means' speeches by Kolya to smooth things over between brother and sister. Nicola had warmed to Tanya over the whole thing, and now considered her a friend.

Nicola remembered how overwhelming those early days had been. She'd spent hours hanging around studios making sure Dmitri ate and drank. She'd helped him prepare for interviews, attended meetings with concert promoters, conductors and sponsors, checked over all the financial details. She'd helped him get past the occasional black mood, when he questioned what he had done, and whether he was good enough (and she still wasn't sure if the long hours he spent with Mikhail Aslanov were a help or hindrance in that regard). And, of course, she'd attended all of his performances – sitting white-knuckled in the audience, praying that it all went well.

The first ones had been small, regional affairs. Just enough to make sure that Dmitri was the real thing and up to performing on a stage. He was. With his poise, good looks and piano playing that was described in the press as 'joyous, free and whimsical', he'd been an instant success. In late April, he'd had his big break: the chance to step in for a pianist (a much bigger star in Bill Campbell's stable) who had been taken ill, and perform the Grieg piano concerto with the Liverpool Philharmonic. The performance had been a triumph and paved the way for the concert next week.

Nicola left a message with Bill's PA about the tickets. While she was on the phone, a new message arrived from Charles at the charity shop, asking if she could cover a shift at the weekend. After Christmas, it had taken her a month before braving going back to the shop and filling out the form to volunteer.

On her first day, she'd come in with a roll of bin bags and a marking pen and gone through the entire shop, getting rid of unsaleable tat and repricing anything that was fit to sell. Charles let her unofficially take over on the days she was there. She'd even had him close down for a few days to repaint, get proper shelves and shop fittings put in and then restock. The shop had tripled its turnover since Christmas. But being in the trenches only made her think harder about the idea she'd chatted through with Brian. The shop revenues were a drop in the ocean compared to the resources needed by Care and other charities. From the moment she'd begun to dabble in the business of helping people in need, she'd tried to think of ways to do it in a more efficient and cost-effective manner. To find a way to apply the same financial strategies she used to catapult fashion brands into the stratosphere to the not-for-profit sector. Meeting Alan, who had the right contacts and practical knowledge, had been the final missing piece.

She sent a quick text to Charles, and one to Tanya, just as Chrissie arrived. Chrissie was dressed for summer in a sleeveless flowered top and white linen skirt. She'd had her hair coloured and her face had a touch of sun. Seeing her, Nicola had to swallow back a rogue tear. Chrissie had always done her best to support her and try to be a friend. It was only now that Nicola had left – that she had changed – that she was finally able to appreciate it.

'Hello!' Nicola said, giving her a kiss on the cheek.

'Hi, Nicola. It's so great to see you.'

'Thanks. You too.' Nicola grinned. 'You're looking well. Working for someone else definitely suits you.'

'Ah, now you know that's not true.' Chrissie laughed.

They ordered drinks, and Chrissie filled her in on the latest gossip – that Ollie was leaving the firm too to spend more time with his family.

'That's good,' Nicola said without missing a beat. 'I'm glad they patched things up.'

'Yes, it seems so. Best for the kids and all that.'

Nicola agreed. She rarely thought of those grey, lifeless days now, when all she had to look forward to was a stolen moment with someone else's husband. The time before she met Dmitri Orlov and became caught up in his gravitational pull. Their lives had collided like two dark stars; her world had exploded with light. His energy and kindness – his love – had made her into the different person she was today.

'But how are you, Nicola?' Chrissie asked as their drinks arrived. 'You look great – as always. Things are good with Dmitri?'

'Yes.' Chrissie's sly look made Nicola blush. 'Very good. I mean, we're both busy, as you can imagine.'

'I can imagine. Just think – performing at the proms! How exciting. Your man is a celebrity.'

'Yes, well, it is exciting. But it's all been pretty overwhelming too. I don't know how he does it – he's so focused and dedicated. He spends so many hours practising. But he loves to perform. He's in his element when he's up there on stage.'

'You're glowing – do you know that?'

'No. I...'

'It's wonderful to see you so happy.'

'Thanks,' Nicola said. 'I think I am. I mean then there's my new business. I've told you about that. And Jules is at thirty-eight weeks already – can you believe it? And Dmitri's sister Tanya's wedding is in a fortnight... In fact, maybe you can help me. I still need to buy gifts...'

Chrissie put on her best prim schoolmistress face. 'I see you still haven't paused to take a breath, have you?'

'I guess not.' Nicola smiled. Chrissie always could see right through her. It was easier to keep busy, just like she always had. Too busy to focus on the one thing that was still a blot on her new-found happiness, like a cloud threatening to swallow the moon.

The phone rang. She glanced quickly down at the screen and silenced the call, hiding a little grimace.

It was Elsie, the counsellor at the therapy group Kolya had bullied her into attending. Calling, no doubt, because Nicola had cancelled their last two sessions. Though Dmitri encouraged her to go, and had been there for her every time she came out, she had begun to worry that Kolya was wrong – that she would never be free of the past. The sessions brought out too many things. Not only about the rape, but also her anger at her mum, and her dad – for giving up the way he had. After nearly six months of working on her 'recovery', she still felt powerless. She hadn't come any closer to letting go of the anger she felt towards Kevin Galsworthy. Anger at what he'd done, and the fact that she'd let it shape her for so long. That day by the river, she'd told Kolya that she didn't expect justice. She wanted it, though.

'Are you OK, Nicola? Do you need to take that call?'

Nicola looked up. She'd been so busy ruminating that she'd almost forgotten Chrissie was there. Now though, the older woman was giving her the familiar look of concern from when they'd worked together.

'No, but…' She took a breath. 'Do you remember when you said you hoped that someday I'd tell you why things… were like they were?'

'Yes,' Chrissie said, sounding wary.

'Well, can I tell you something – get your advice?'

'Of course.'

'It's kind of a long story…'

Late that night, Nicola picked up the phone. After having coffee with Chrissie, she'd come home; tried to focus on the million things she had to do. But the conversation, which had left Chrissie in tears, weighed so heavily on her that she couldn't focus on anything else. They'd talked through the options. Agreed that it would probably come to nothing. Maybe even make things worse. And yet, Nicola felt that this was something she had to do.

Her hand trembled as she checked the number and prepared to dial it. She had a story ready – a lost cell phone in a taxi – in case a PA picked up. Or she could just put down the phone and stop this right now. Go to Dmitri who was practising on his fancy new Yamaha piano in the spare bedroom. Bring him a cup of tea, or a sandwich. Kiss him, touch him, tease him into coming to bed. Be happy – forget about this stupid plan.

She took a breath and punched in the numbers of the investment bank in New York. The ringing went on and on. It was after hours. Had she plucked up her courage for nothing—?

'Hello?' a voice answered. *That voice*. Kevin Galsworthy had picked up himself, just like she was expecting. Just like she would have done.

'Kevin,' she swallowed hard, 'it's Nicola Taylor.'

There was a long pause. Nicola stared at the face of the man on the bank's website. He'd aged – but then again, who hadn't? And the smile. A wave of bile rose in her throat. The smile was still the same.

'Nicola,' he said. Another pause. On the other side of the Atlantic, a door shut.

'You know it's been—' She broke off unable to continue. Whatever she had been planning on saying – whatever she had rehearsed in her mind – it was all gone as soon as he'd picked up the phone.

The silence was heavy and uncomfortable. For a second, she panicked. He would put the phone down, and she hadn't said... anything.

She heard him take a breath. Then, he began to speak. 'Why are you calling me, Nicola?'

'You... you know why.'

'I have nothing to say.'

'Nothing?' She choked out the word.

'There's nothing I can say.'

'But...' she swallowed, 'I have something that I want to say to you.'

He sighed. 'Go ahead.'

'You raped me, Kevin,' Nicola said, finding the words. 'You followed me, then held me down on an icy pavement and did... that. And I have to live with it every day of my life. For years I've let it eat away at me. It's affected my whole life.'

'Yes.'

'What did you say?'

'I said "yes", Nicola. Is that what you want? For me to admit it? Is that going to help somehow?'

'I don't know.'

'I don't know either. Because to be honest... well...'

Nicola waited, unable to speak.

'Here's how it is,' he said after a long pause. 'I've got a daughter. She's seven. And sometimes, when I look at her, I think about what I did. And how, if someone did that to her —' He broke off, a strangled sound coming from his throat.

Nicola bit her lip. She'd imagined him over the years: a wife and family, a big house in the suburbs. Skiing holidays, a summer house on Cape Cod, a mistress in the office. Congratulating himself on everything he'd achieved, and the fact that, many years earlier, his dad had bought off his youthful 'mistake'. But, over time, she'd changed. Was it possible that he had too?

'I'm sorry, Nicola,' he said finally. 'For what I did.'

She didn't answer. Now that she'd heard it – now that he'd finally confessed – apologised – what else did she want him to say? What could he say?

'I—' her pulse thundered in her head, 'need to know if you hurt anyone else, Kevin. If there are others out there. Or was I the only one?'

He answered without pause. 'I don't know if it makes it better or worse, but you were the only one. I was drunk – it happened. And afterwards, I felt awful for what I did. Well, maybe not immediately...'

'No, obviously not immediately.' The sarcasm sounded hollow and flat.

'I didn't know what to do when you went to the police. I got Ashley to give me an alibi. Got my father to make it go away.' He sighed. 'But it never has gone away, I guess.'

'No. It hasn't.'

In a single second, Nicola relived it all over again – the fear, the footsteps, the smile... the pain... Her eyes filled with tears. But this time, it was different somehow. Instead of the anger and the panic – the clawing sense of powerlessness – a strange sense of calm swept through her.

'So what happens now?' Kevin's voice was heavy and desperate. 'What are you going to do? Go to the police? Try to get justice after all these years? Do you want me to tell you everything I have to lose? My job. My family – my kids. Their names are Ella and Sam.'

'Do you swear that I was the only one?' Nicola said.

'Yes. I swear.'

She swallowed hard, her voice gaining strength. 'I want you to go home, Kevin. Go home to your daughter, and for fuck's sake, protect her. And I want to say—' A tear dripped from her eye. This was not in the script. Whatever she had planned to say – it was not this. '—That I forgive you.'

Nicola ended the call.

Her legs were so unsteady that she could barely walk. She managed to make her way downstairs to the room where Dmitri was practising and went inside. He stopped playing immediately, turning to her, a smile on his face. The look quickly turned to one of shock. 'Nicola, what has happened?!' he said.

She rushed over to him and collapsed, shaking, into his arms. It took a long time before she could speak – tell him what she had done. Once she started, the words gushed out of her, tearing her open all over again.

'And I said… I mean, I wasn't planning to…'

He stroked her hair, holding her close.

'…but now, I don't know. It seemed like the only way ever to let it go.'

I forgive you.

She buried her face in his neck, breathed him in, and kissed him.

'I'm proud of you,' he said a little breathless. 'And I think you're right – it was the only way.'

'I don't know. I just feel so...' It was impossible to describe what she was feeling. That after all these years, she'd finally done something. Taken action. Let go.

'I love you,' he whispered, as he'd done many times before. But this time, with the cracks wide open, his words and his touch filled up the void, and she finally began to believe it.

Smiling, she wiped away the tears on his cheek – his, hers – she didn't know. Then she began to laugh. Hard and breathless, like she might never stop. She kissed him, wanting to share this strange new sense of joy inside of her. Of something bright and magical, spreading its fiery wings and launching into a shaky, tentative flight.

Epilogue

7th July

His hands were ice, but in the heat of the lights, they felt like they were burning. The biggest surprise was that he could feel them at all. The rest of his body was completely numb. The applause fell silent as he sat down on the bench and adjusted the tails of his coat. The silence thundered in his ears. Had he ever played a piano before?

He took a breath, then another. He stared down at the row of black and white keys. In that moment, his entire life was there before him. All the people he loved, and who loved him. The people he had lost, the people whom he had hurt, and the people who had saved him, over and over again. And somewhere out in the sea of faces in the packed concert hall, *she* was there, probably just as nervous as he was. Because she loved him and knew how much this meant.

How it had all happened in such a short time, he had no idea. Sometimes, late at night, it all seemed like a dream that belonged to someone else. He waited for it to shatter into a million pieces like a sparkly bauble dropped on the floor by a careless child. But in the morning, everything would begin anew. The rehearsals, the interviews, the hours spent in recording studios and concert halls. He was neglecting his family and friends, the choir – that was inevitable for right now. Every hour in the day was spent making up for years of lost time. But everyone had been so supportive, shown so much love and understanding. And now, everyone he knew was here tonight.

The conductor made eye contact and he nodded. The baton was raised, the orchestra raised their instruments and came to life. And as the opening bars began, he pushed aside all thoughts, hopes and memories, all the lightness and the dark. He went deep down inside to that place where only the music lived and let it fill him, consume him.

Dmitri raised his hands and put his fingers to the keys.

How he did it, she had no idea. Nicola felt like she had lived a thousand years and died a thousand deaths – and that was before the concert had even started. And now, as Dmitri stood up and took a bow to a standing ovation, smiling and looking impossibly handsome, she was as happy as she had ever been in her life. On her left, Tanya was gripping Mark's hand and crying. On her right, Kolya took her arm, because she was so overcome with emotion that she could barely stand up.

Dmitri shook the hand of the conductor and the concert-master, went off stage and came back on for another bow. Kolya and the others in the row – Phil, Carole-Ann, half a dozen members of the choir, Mikhail Aslanov – all of them made room to let her pass. And at the end of the row, Chrissie handed her a large bouquet of flowers.

Walking up the steps to the great stage was like walking into the sun. Somehow, just as she thought she would never make it to the top, Dmitri was there. His eyes shining as they met hers, his hands, as always, there to steady her.

'Congratu—' she half got the word out before his mouth was on hers, in front of the entire crowd. The applause turned to a few whistles and shouts of 'bravo'.

Dmitri came to his senses long before she did. He took a single red rose out of the bouquet and handed it to her. Then, he took her hand and pulled her off the stage to the wings.

As they half ran down the corridor to his dressing room, Nicola could barely keep her sharp heels from catching on the thick red carpet.

Dmitri pulled her inside the room, closed the door and locked it. 'Was it OK?' he asked, panting for breath, his dark hair slick with sweat.

'Was it OK?' Nicola took a breath, drawing out the words. She walked very slowly and deliberately over to the make-up counter and mirror. Setting down the rose, she made a show of checking her lipstick and adjusting her dress. Dark blue and glittery, it hugged every curve of her body, was too low-cut to wear a bra and had a mile-high slit up the side. Dmitri had picked it out. Nicola had rolled her eyes at him when trying it on, but now, when he looked at her like he was doing now, she was proud to wear it.

'I think you were a little bit OK,' she said, giving him a seductive smile.

She sat down on the counter as he came over to her. In an instant, the straps were down on to her arms and his mouth was on her neck.

'I think you were quite a bit brilliant.' She gasped as he pushed her skirt all the way up and ran his hand up her thigh. 'And I think you are incredibly sexy.'

She arched her back, pulling him against her, untucking his neat formal shirt. But as she was about to undo his trousers, he stepped back.

'Hold that thought,' he said.

Dmitri rushed over and grabbed his bag, bringing it over

to her. She readjusted the straps on her dress, but as soon as he was back over, he pulled them down again.

Someone knocked on the door. 'Dmitri?' Bill Campbell's voice. 'I've got some people for you to meet.'

'I need ten minutes,' Dmitri growled.

'If you need to go—' Nicola said.

'They can wait.' Dmitri sounded more authoritative than she'd ever heard him before. 'First I have something for you.'

He took out an oblong box wrapped with a ribbon.

'Not more lingerie, Dmitri,' she said, laughing.

'This is special,' he said. 'Open it.'

She did so and was surprised by what she saw. 'White?' she said. She lifted out the lacy silk and found another smaller light blue box underneath. He took it out and opened the box. If she was surprised before, this time, she gasped.

'I wanted to do well tonight,' he said, 'because I wanted to see if you would accept this.' His hands – those hands she trusted; hands that could master the most difficult music with rock solid perfection – were shaking now as he took out the ring. The icy diamond solitaire flashed rainbows of fire. 'I love, you, Nicola,' he said. 'You are everything to me. I want you to be my wife. Please say yes.' His voice was so fraught with emotion that he could barely get out the words.

'You should have played badly,' she said, smiling even as a tear formed in her eye. 'That way you'd know that no matter what, the answer is still yes.'

The ring dazzled in the light as he put it on her finger. She brought his hands to her lips, kissing them, never wanting to let them go. He twined his fingers through her hair and lifted her face to his. She kissed him hard and deep, drinking in his warmth, savouring the healing power of the love between them.

Desire rushed through her body, arcing to his until finally, his hands were on her and he finished what he had started.

A Letter from Lauren

Thank you for reading *Moonlight on the Thames*. I hope you enjoyed reading it as much as I loved writing it. If you enjoyed this book, please can I ask that you leave a review. It really helps other readers find my books and might help someone discover their perfect next read. If you want to keep up-to-date on my new releases, or are interested in becoming a beta reader for my books, please sign up at the following link. Your email address will never be shared and you can unsubscribe at any time.

https://www.laurenwestwoodwriter.com

This book is a work of fiction and is not based on any real person or event (with apologies to the lovely choir at Waterloo Station who brightened up a tedious night of delayed trains!)

The issues, however, that are raised in this book are very real and affect the lives of millions of people all over the world. I am not a counsellor or an expert in these subjects, I am just a writer telling a story. Any mistakes that I have made in portraying these situations are purely my own. The book is intended as a romantic fairytale, and I know that in real life, things are much more complex and not wrapped up so easily in 'happily ever after'. If you or anyone you know are affected by any of the issues raised in this book, I would encourage you to seek help, even if taking the first step seems difficult or impossible. A good place to start is the Samaritans (www.samaritans.org) who can provide further advice. While justice may seem like a thing of fiction books or Hollywood films, it is only by people speaking out that we move closer to banishing these dark things.

The original edition of this book was published in 2018, long before the recent tragic events on the world political stage involving the Russian invasion of Ukraine. I don't intend this book to be a commentary on political or cultural issues. I believe that people are people no matter where in the world they hale from, and when there is injustice and cruelty in the world, we all suffer for it.

In this book, I have tried to portray my Russian characters in an honest and non-stereotypical way, but again, any mistakes are my own. I visited Russia going on twenty-five years ago, and I was captivated by the culture and its people. At that time Russia was undergoing a transition from its Soviet past to what seemed like a much better future. I very much regret the current world situation that has derailed this, but I remain hopeful that human ingenuity and love will help us move beyond another unfortunate entry in the history books. If only we can start learning from our mistakes, we can create a better world.

The tale of *The Firebird* in this book is my own amalgam of several classic Russian fairytales, and I have taken some liberties in the retelling. I believe, however, that the power of fairytales is that their archetypes apply far beyond whatever their original contexts may have been, and as such, they are often adapted in the retelling.

I would like to thank my dad, who raised me to love and appreciate classical music (and my mum who did the running around and paid for music lessons). It is a legacy that I feel strongly about passing on to my own children. We listen to a lot of Classic FM in the car, and I listen to a lot of piano and violin practice at home. I have a particular love of Russian composers and their music has always resonated with me. Many years ago, I studied music – oboe performance – at university. It took me only one year to determine that, unfortunately, I did not have what it took to be a professional musician. In addition to raw talent, it takes a ruthless focus, a lot of luck and a lot of hours in a tiny room practising, not the world's greatest music, but scales and exercises.

Looking back now, I've discovered that I do have that kind of passion, focus and drive – but as a writer, not a musician. Some days when I'm deep in the process of editing a book, I long for those 'simpler' days of my music studies. I've always wanted to write a book that explores the heights of ecstasy and the depths of despair that music can evoke. I don't know if I've achieved that here, but if you do feel inspired to listen to the music referred to in this book, I've put together a *Moonlight on the Thames* playlist on Spotify. My words may not be sufficient, but the music can speak for itself. The link is here:

https://www.laurenwestwoodwriter.com/playlist

I'd like to thank my family for their continued love and support. I'd also like to thank my readers and all the people who have championed this book, despite it being a somewhat dubious interpretation of a 'Christmas romance'. I hope to be able to continue writing books that are a little different to what else is out there and am reliant on readers to help spread the word. I am also happy to receive correspondence and feedback via my website.

Thank you for reading, and may your days be filled with love and music.

Best wishes,
Lauren Westwood

Loved Moonlight on the Thames?

Discover a emotional and intelligent new romance today...

If you save a crumbling mansion, will it mend a broken heart?

A month ago, Amy Wood had her perfect home, perfect boyfriend, and perfect job in London. Now she's broken-hearted, living in her parents' tiny bungalow, and working in a local estate agents in Bath.

But Amy gets a new lease on life when she undertakes to sell Rosemont hall, a crumbling Georgian mansion riddled with woodworm, dry rot – and secrets.

Amy searches for the perfect owner to restore the house to its former glory, but time is running out. As she clashes with unscrupulous property developers and the enigmatic heir to the house, Amy uncovers pieces of the past that some people would rather remain hidden.

Can Amy unlock the secrets of Rosemont Hall and find the keys to her own happy ending?

A sparkling and intelligent feel-good romance.

Will the secrets of the past be the keys to the future?

Alex Hart loves her job as manager of Mallow Court, a historic Elizabethan house. But the discovery of a precious jewelled locket changes everything, and things are not as they seem.

From an old diary, to a charismatic barrister, a mysterious clockmaker, and the darkest hours of the London Blitz, Alex must uncover the truth about the things she holds dearest. Her heart hangs in the balance, and someone is determined not to let sleeping dogs lie!

A brilliant feel-good romance with a satisfying old-house mystery.

An old house, a secret heartbreak, a second chance at love.

Lizzie Greene is about to lose everything. With no money and no job to pay her late husband's debts, she is resigned to selling her quirky old house, Tanglewild.

But a lifeline appears when Lizzy's house is chosen as a location for a film based on a best-selling romance novel. Her household is turned upside down by a cast of colourful characters: an enigmatic author, a handsome location scout, a brooding director, a heart-throb leading man – never mind her ex-mother-in-law camped out in her drive.

But behind the Hollywood magic, all is not as it seems. Someone has a hidden agenda in coming to Tanglewild and will stop at nothing to keep its secrets hidden. Will Lizzy's desire to save her house lead to new love or to mortal danger?

A delightful and heart-warming story of overcoming past heartbreaks and finding a new beginning.

Emotional Women's Fiction from Lauren Westwood

What readers are saying:

"It hit every emotion"
"Pulled hard on my heartstrings"
"Powerful and evocative"
"Moving and compelling"

Discover more at https://www.laurenwestwoodwriter.com

Printed in Great Britain
by Amazon

17489649R00205